GILBERT-AUGUSTIN THIERRY

STIGMA AND
THE POMPEIIAN FRESCO

TRANSLATED AND WITH AN INTRODUCTION BY
BRIAN STABLEFORD

ISBN: 978-1-64525-105-7

STIGMA AND
THE POMPEIIAN FRESCO

GILBERT-AUGUSTIN THIERRY (1843-1915), the son of the writer Amédée Thierry and the nephew of the historian Augustin Thierry, was a novelist, poet and journalist, who published extensively in the *Revue des Deux-Mondes*. In 1875 he debuted with the intensively-researched historical novel *L'Aventure d'une âme en peine*, followed in 1882 by *Le Capitaine Sans-Façon 1813: épisodes de la contre-révolution*. His subsequent works, which include *Marfa* (1887), *La tresse blonde* (1888), *La Savelli* (1890), *Le masque* (1894) and *Le stigmate* (1898), often dealt with the occult and the supernatural.

BRIAN STABLEFORD'S scholarly work includes *New Atlantis: A Narrative History of Scientific Romance* (Wildside Press, 2016), *The Plurality of Imaginary Worlds: The Evolution of French roman scientifique* (Black Coat Press, 2017) and *Tales of Enchantment and Disenchantment: A History of Faerie* (Black Coat Press, 2019). In support of the latter projects he has translated more than a hundred volumes of *roman scientifique* and more than twenty volumes of *contes de fées* into English. He has edited *Decadence and Symbolism: A Showcase Anthology* (Snuggly Books, 2018), and is busy translating more Symbolist and Decadent fiction.

His recent fiction, in the genre of metaphysical fantasy, includes a trilogy of novels set in West Wales, consisting of *Spirits of the Vasty Deep* (2018), *The Insubstantial Pageant* (2018) and *The Truths of Darkness* (2019), published by Snuggly Books, and a trilogy set in Paris and the south of France, consisting of *The Painter of Spirits*, *The Quiet Dead* and *Living with the Dead*, all published by Black Coat Press in 2019.

CONTENTS

INTRODUCTION

This is the third volume of fantastic fiction by Gilbert-Augustin Thierry to be published by Snuggly Books, following *Reincarnation and Redemption*, which contains translations of "La Rédemption de Larmor" (*Nouvelle Revue* April 1882; tr. as "Larmor's Redemption"), "Rediviva" (*Nouvelle Revue* November 1883; tr, as "Redivia") and "La Bien-Aimée" (*Revue des deux mondes* December 1891; tr. as "The Beloved"); and *The Blonde Tress and The Mask*, which contains translations of "La Tresse blonde" (*Revue des deux mondes* July 1888; book 1889; tr. as "The Blonde Tress") and "Le Masque" (*Revue des deux mondes* January-February 1894; book 1894 tr. as "The Mask"). The present volume contains the final two items in the series, "Le Stigmate" (*Revue des deux mondes* July-September 1897; book 1898; tr. as "Stigma") and "La Fresque de Pompéi" (*Revue des deux mondes* March 1912; tr. as "The Pompeiian Fresco").

The first two stories in the sequence were identified as the opening items of a series entitled "Histoires de Mort et de Vivants, récits étranges" [Accounts of the Dead and the Living: Strange Stories], but no further items in that series appeared in the *Nouvelle Revue*. Two further novellas that the author published in the *Revue des deux mondes* in the 1880s, "Le Palimpseste" (March 1887; reprinted in book form in the same year as *Marfa, ou Le Palimpseste*; tr. as *The Palimpsest*) and "La Tresse blonde" can be seen as continuations of the sequence, recapitulating and elaborating themes introduced in the two novelettes in the

Nouvelle Revue. The remaining three novellas also carry forward the theme of expiatory redemptions, but only "Le Masque" does so in the context of reincarnation; although the two stories in the present volume reproduce the basic theme and story-arc of "Le Masque," they alter the context in which that fundamental narrative is worked out quite considerably, transforming the tacit metaphysics of the events they depict. In doing so they complete a remarkable evolution in the series as a whole, which is only clearly visible and appreciable if all seven of the works continued in the present trio of volumes are read successively.

Gilbert-Augustin Thierry (1843-1915) was given his second forename after his uncle, the noted "Romantic historian" Augustin Thierry (1795-1856), who was more scrupulous in his consultation of documentary evidence than many historians of the era but who routinely adopted a colorful style of narrative reportage that affiliated him strongly to the French Romantic Movement. Augustin Thierry's enduring fame eventually encouraged his nephew to transplant the hyphen in his signature and begin to sign himself "Gilbert Augustin-Thierry"; both the novellas in the present volume bore that signature in all their French versions, but I have retained the baptismal version of the author's name in order to maintain continuity with the first volume in the present series of translations.

Gilbert's father, Amédée Thierry (1797-1873), was also a historian, and was also significantly associated with the Romantic Movement, but he obtained his principal reputation as a journalist—a profession that he was initially obliged to adopt because he was dismissed from the chair of history at the University of Besançon for being too liberal in his expressed opinions during the repressive reign of Charles X. His bold opposition to absolute monarchy guaranteed him favor after the July Revolution of 1830 issued in a new era of constitutional monarchy; he was appointed prefect of the Haut-Saône, and he held various other administrative posts before and after the 1848 Revolution, before becoming a Senator in 1860. In the meantime, he was a regular contributor to the *Revue des Deux-Mondes*, which began as a Radical Romantic publication but moved considerably to the right in response to changes in the political climate after Louis-Napoléon's 1851 *coup-d'état* launched the Second Empire and a new era of stern censorship. By the 1880s it was a staid and thoroughly respectable periodical.

Gilbert followed in his father's footsteps, publishing extensively in the *Revue des Deux-Mondes* and enjoying a successful career in journalism, but he was also heavily influenced by his uncle; he became an assiduous researcher and employer of documentary sources, and he followed the example of the Romantic writer of flamboyant historical fiction S. Henry Berthoud in labeling many of his works of fiction "historical studies" in order to emphasize their scholarly underpinnings. Gilbert's work might, however, also be held to illustrate that an assiduous interest in dubious documentary sources can easily tempt a historian, however scrupulous he might be, to fanciful conclusions. It is also arguable that his intellectual scrupulousness became somewhat questionable when he became very interested in, and temporarily involved with the French Occult Revival, which had begun as an offshoot of the Romantic Movement in the movement's decadent phase. A substantial fraction of his fiction was written under that influence, including his first novel, the intensively-researched *L'Aventure d'une âme en peine* [The Adventure of a Soul in Pain] (1875).

As a result of his occult research, the supernatural became much more explicit in Thierry's works in the 1880s, a trend that continued in the two novellas translated in the second volume of the present series of translations, but "La Blonde tresse" and "Le Masque" also exhibited a burgeoning interest in new interpretations of phenomena that had previously been considered purely in a religious context, offered by pioneers of the nascent science of psychology. Both of the novellas in that second volume introduced a measure of ambiguity into the interpretation and representation of the supernatural events that they feature,

9

in which the notion of "mental alienation" provides an alternative explanation for the experiences of the protagonist. In "La Blonde Tresse" the religious implications of the events of the story retain their hegemony, but in "Le Masque," in spite of a scathing hostility to alienists and to the treatment of patients interned in mental hospitals, the balance of interpretation is more even, and the suggestion is clear that if the phenomena of reincarnation are, in fact, to be construed literally, then the unlucky individuals subjected to them would, indeed, have to be reckoned quite mad as a result.

"Le Stigmate" is, to some extent, a break with the pattern developed in the previous works in the series. In the opening chapter of the novel the protagonist, a playwright at the beginning of his career, enjoying something of a *succès de scandale*, is congratulated by the Minister of Fine Arts on that success but strongly advised not to do it again, but to produce something more politically acceptable. It is not inconceivable that, after publishing "Le Masque," Thierry received similar advice. It might be significant that a new editor-in-chief, Ferdinand Brunetière, had taken control of the *Revue des deux mondes* in 1893, and although Brunetière had been a sub-editor of the periodical when the earlier stores were published, they might well have been bought by his predecessor as editor-in-chief, Charles Buloz. The previously freethinking Brunetière underwent a much-publicized conversion to Catholicism in 1895 after visiting the Vatican, and that might well have affected his attitude to Thierry's work. In the novel, the protagonist's intentions are rapidly sidetracked, and instead of putting Louis XIV on stage, as suggested by the minister, he begins to work on a very different project. As to whether something similar happened to Thierry we can only speculate, but it is noticeable that he did not publish any more fiction in the *Revue* while Brunetière remained at the helm, "La Fresque de Pompéi" appearing during the editorial reign of Francis Carmes, who replaced Brunetière after the latter's death in 1906.

In "Le Masque" the religious context of the expiatory reincarnation that shapes the plot is provided by the worship of Isis,
supposedly renewed in modern Paris by a charismatic mystic
who calls himself Hermes. Isis was a key figure in the Occult
Revival, celebrated by the theosophists, and also by Jules Bois,
one of the most significant literary mystics involved in fashionable occultism, who is referenced and quoted in the story. In
"Le Stigmate" that pagan apparatus, which echoes similar exotic
pagan materials employed in previous novelettes and novellas in
the series, is replaced by an entirely Catholic species of mysticism
drawn from the history of the Church: specifically, the extraordi-
nary sect of Convulsionnaires born in the burial-ground of the
Parisian church of Saint-Médard in 1731, which endured for
half a century thereafter, eccentrically transformed and driven
underground, before finally petering out.

The Convulsionnaire sect was itself a bizarre offshoot of a
heresy that had been subjected to active persecution in Paris for
many years and was endangered with extirpation: Jannsenism,
based on the posthumously-published work of the Dutch theologian Cornelius Jansen (1585-1638). Taking his inspiration
from Saint Augustine, Jansen's writings put a heavy emphasis
in the legacy of original sin, the consequent degradation of humankind, and the necessity of divine grace in the achievement of
salvation by the very few Elect predestined for paradise.

Although Jansen and his followers did not emphasize the
point heavily, the notion that the vast majority of human beings
are predestined for Hell is a logical corollary of the assertion
of God's omniscience. Although humans have free will, an
omniscient God must know in advance how they are going to
exercise it, and must know therefore, even before a person is
born, whether the person will succumb to temptation and damn
themselves eternally. Thus, in spite of free will, God already
knows which of his creations will be worthy of his grace, and
are thus destined for Paradise; obtaining that grace therefore becomes a matter of demonstrating in action that one already has

it. A similar attitude was adopted by some Protestant sects, and Jansenism therefore came to be suspected in the eyes of orthodox Catholics—especially the Jesuits—of Calvinist tendencies, and was therefore anathematized.

The novel fills in much of the background of the history of Jansensim in France and the strange genesis of the Convulsionnaire sect, and I have filled in further detail at the relevant points of the story by means of footnotes, so no further introduction is necessary here, except to say something about the way in which it affects the context of Thierry's characteristic themes and obsessions. Like "Le Masque" and "La Fresque de Pompéi," "Le Stigmate" is essentially a story about the power of Amour, and the ability of that force of Nature—potentially, at least—to overwhelm the power of religious faith. In the literary universe of Thierry's fiction, the quest for a spiritual Ideal, normally expressed in artistic and intellectual terms, is routinely undermined or deflected by erotic attraction. The essential purpose of reincarnation is the redemption of sins committed in past lives, and Thierry's works of fiction take it for granted that, as the principal motive for past sins was erotic, the principal threat to their present expiation is a similar eroticism, if not the same one repeated almost mechanically. The repetitive pattern can be defeated, but only with enormous difficulty.

The theology of Jansenism, unlike the hypothetical religion of Isis described in "Le Masque," does not include a notion of reincarnation, but that does not prevent Thierry from importing his own obsession into his story; he simply has to reintroduce it, as it were, by the back door. He is assisted in that by the history of which he was so fond. From the very beginning, writings concerned with the Convulsionnaires were sharply divided between believers who accepted that they really were divinely inspired, in ecstatic communion with God, and skeptics who took it for granted that they were insane, and who attempted to identify the pathology of their particular mental disease, producing pioneering exercises in attempted psychological analysis a hundred years before the science gathered any significant academic impetus. Although Thierry does not reference the pathological analyses (I have indicated the key examples in the footnotes) he must have read them, and his own story, in which a sect of Convulsionnaires is revived in contemporary Paris, offers both explanatory schemas in an opposition that is not only ingenious but melodramatic, exploring the bizarre features of Convulsonnaire conviction to fuel a horror story much starker than "Le Masque."

"La Fresque de Pompéi" reintroduces the antiquarian and pagan aspects of Thierry's earlier tales of reincarnate redemption, but it retains both the Catholic theological framework of "Le Stigmate" and the pathological interpretation established in opposition to it, so that the *femme fatale* at the center of the plot is amibiguous, a Siren of Greek mythology and a demon of Christian mythology, and her victim is also ambiguous, a Christian mystic whose quest for the Ideal is initially expressed in the composition of religious music and a pathological visionary whose delusions consume him and tear him apart. As in "Le Stigmate," the reincarnation of the central characters is figurative and pathological rather than crudely literal, but is no less important for that.

In his employment of *femme fatales*, and the awesome power that he credits to them, Thierry was following a particular thread of French Romantic thought most strikingly developed in the antiquarian fantasies of Théophile Gautier—two of which are credited in passing in "La Fresque de Pompéi"—and renewed in the *fin-de-siècle* not merely by Pierre Louÿs' best-selling and archetypal *Aphrodite* (1896) but, perhaps more significantly, by Anatole France's *Thaïs* (*Revue des deux mondes* 1889; book 1890). Anatole France was very upset by cuts made to the serial version of that novel—which he considered to be his masterpiece—by Ferdinand Brunetière, in his capacity as sub-editor, and Thierry must have been aware of that quarrel, and the reasons for it. Undoubtedly, Thierry would have sympathized with France, and it must have helped to make him apprehensive of Brunetière, an Academician and professor at the École Normale who had very firm views on the direction that French literature ought to be taking, to which Thierry's idiosyncratic brand of neo-Romanticism was ill-fitted. It might have been, in part, that very opposition, so close at hand, that impelled Thierry to become excessive in his defiant assertion of the awesome power of Amour, first in "Le Stigmate" and even more extravagantly in "La Fresque de Pompéi." However it came about, though, "La Fresque de Pompéi" is certainly one of the most dramatic examples of that curious subgenre of French fiction, and an entirely appropriate conclusion to a determinedly idiosyncratic literary career.

There is a world of difference in terms of ideology and narrative strategy between "Le Rédemption de Larmor" and "La Fresque de Pompéi," but that difference was the consequence of a logical process of development whose phases are mapped out in the stories assembled in the present series of translations. "Le Stigmate" is undoubtedly the masterpiece of the set, being the longest, the most complex and the most intense. It is a horror story on two levels, not merely in terms of the relentless suffering inflicted on the characters, but also in the subtler sense in which it gradually undermines the identification that the reader initially assumes, automatically, with the narrator—a sympathy that is gradually and clinically drained away to the extent that he too, like every other character in the story, is stigmatized as a victim of universal human corruption, an existential condition in which the "help" rendered by a quasi-Jansenist God is as horrifically ironic as that rendered by his deluded minions. A similar track is followed in "La Fresque de Pompéi" to a scathing coda—which, juxtaposed and coupled with the melodramatic climax—raises the question of how, in the hands of an honest writer, stories can and ought to end, once Amour and Faith have both been discounted as realistic possibilities of happiness.

The bulk of the two translations were made from the serial versions contained in copies of the *Revue des deux mondes* reproduced on the Bibliothèque National website *gallica*, but the volume containing the fourth part of "Le Stigmate" is missing from the BN collection, and the translation of that part was made from the copy of the relevant volume held on JSTOR, accessed via the London Library

—Brian Stableford.

STIGMA AND
THE POMPEIIAN FRESCO

STIGMA

I

. . . And the curtain fell, while the most flattering applause rose from the stalls. It rose again immediately and the actor Saint-Réal advanced to proclaim my name:

"Mesdames et Messieurs, the symbolist drama that we have just had the honor of performing for you, an adaptation of the play by Némo, is the work of Monsieur Germain Surville."

There were acclamations, the sound of canes and the stamping of feet: an entire delirium of enthusiasm. "Author! Author! Surville! Surville!" They wanted to oblige me to appear on stage. Two of my interpreters had already seized me by the arms, in order to constrain me to do so by means of amiable violence.

"Come on, dear Master, and defer to all wishes. Your *Nazaréen* is an affirmation of the new Art, the pure triumph of the Théâtre de l'Idée!"

Yes, certainly, and they were right; however, I resisted. Without being afflicted by an importunate modesty, I have always reproved the practices of certain litterateurs, the ridiculous exhibition of their person behind the footlights: my scorn for charlatanism and a sentiment of my dignity as a writer. A poet is a poet, entirely different from an actor, and quite recently, in my revue *La Minerve*, I had even protested again the love of hamming that is becoming the mania of my contemporaries . . .

Huddled behind the scenery, and surrounded by my protagonists, I nevertheless listened with delight to the tempest of voices pronouncing my name. The file of complimenters was already commencing:

"Superb, your *Nazaréen*, Surville!"

"A wing-beat, taking flight toward the Ideal!"

"What a radiant masterpiece!"

And, shaking me by the hand, each of those good comrades sang me his dithyramb with a taut smile or an envious gaze.

Well, yes, it was a frank success. The director of the theater, the tragedian impresario Saint-Réal, slapped me on the shoulder familiarly. He had taken off his tunic, beard and wig, all of his costume of a prophet of Israel, and, clean-shaven now, but still vermilion-tinted, he swelled majestically behind the gardenia in his jacket.

"A good evening," he said, "which surpassed my hopes. Confess nevertheless, O poet, that you owe us a fine candle! The play certainly isn't without value, and several tirades are encountered therein, fortunately wrought, but good God, what a subject! What a confused postulate! Illogical action and an absurd denouement! Many a time I saw Messieurs the Critics nudging one another and sniggering. The distant rhymes and the decadent prosody don't yet have the gift of charming those mamamouchis; one of them almost seemed to faint at the shock of a line with fourteen feet."

"Idiots," I replied, dryly. "In any case, the approval of the 'young ones' consoles me and is sufficient for me."

With a gesture I indicated the now-compact circle of my disciples, the "young ones," Symbolists or Decadents. Grouped around us, cravated in the manner of Royer-Collard, clad in Lamartinian frock-coats, my friends the "esthetes" recounted their impressions, the words exchanged during the entr'actes, the anger or alarm of the aged pontiffs of the old guard.

"They're furious, dear Master, and will take their revenge . . . you'll be castigated."

"It doesn't matter to me, Messieurs; I have fought the good fight."

It did matter to me, however, and a great deal. The slightest pleasantry in the newspapers is a sting more painful to me than a sword-thrust.

"Bah! Everything's going well," the sonorous Saint-Réal went on. "But what a fright, my lads. I was particularly apprehensive of your terrible scene—you know, the third of the four."

"Ah, yes; the one in which the Nazarene, reincarnated on earth, comes to beg at the bishop's door . . ."

"For a morsel of bread that is refused him. Jolly pathos—meaning no offense."

"Get away!" I riposted, angrily. "It's the nail of my play, a savantly scenic expression of our social claims. I was sure of the effect, and the effect was produced, thunderously."

"Of course! I launched my abuse so well!" cried the vainglorious player. "There there, don't get annoyed; we have an equal share in the victory . . . and now, enough talk. Come, the Minister is asking for us."

The Minister! He had arrived very late, the excellent Noirot, almost at the end of the third act, but his entrance had produced a sharp sensation. The director, the actors, the stage-managers and the secretary—the entire population of the wings—had swelled with pride. The Minister of Fine Arts in the Théâtre de l'Idée! Never yet had such an official honor come to a simple amateur stage. It is true that for two weeks all the newspapers had been entertaining their readers with nothing but *Le Nazaréen*: a big scandal in prospect.

And immediately, I had received the aureole of a martyr, censure had been up in arms against my audacity, and cantankerousness had uttered a cry of alarm. "A dangerous, not to say immoral, play, attacking respectable beliefs and capable of becoming a source of embarrassment for the government." Personally, I had laughed. We know your scrupulous modesties, my beauty, and we know how to offend them. I immediately set forth on campaign: note after note to the theater reporters, articles of high farce or vibrant indignation, letters, visits, admonitions by députés, my friends—nothing had been spared. Noirot, Octavien Noirot, an old comrade from college, a Solognot like me, like me a proud freethinker and a freemason too, a venerable of the Grand Orient; so, having been scolded roundly, Dame Anastasia had been obliged to curb her head, and *Le Nazaréen* had finally been performed.

Standing in his box and already putting on his overcoat, Monsieur le Ministre was about to leave. He was agitated and impatient; we had kept him waiting. Next to him stood two other people: an attaché of the ministry, a young fellow from my homeland, the son of an influential elector of Romarin, and a thin man, very stiff, bilious and unpleasant, Monsieur Ravine, the deputy head of the cabinet: a scribbler of novels, an ardent "naturalist" and my personal enemy, that one!

When I went in the Minister extended his hand to me.

"Good, very good, a triumph! Admirable, even! Continue."

I bowed gratefully

"Nevertheless, let's understand one another," he said. "When I say to you: *Continue*, I mean, henceforth, do something else. Certainly, I esteem very ardently your freethinking convictions, your hatred of obscurantism, and your superb disdain for outdated superstition. Clericalism is overflowing; we need to establish a dike! But between us, I ask you: what does your play signify?"

I started.

"Symbolist art!" murmured the young fellow from Romarin, my compatriot, sly and venomously.

"Symbolic," rectified the deputy head of the cabinet, "or rather, Ibsenian: an enlivened imitation of the bitter thinker Némo."

"Who is this Némo, then?" asked the Minister. "I don't even know the name."

"A writer of French Switzerland," I replied. "A Vaudois, I suppose."

"I would have believed him to be Norwegian," said Ravine, immediately.

I contented myself with shrugging my shoulders. "The pamphlet, Monsieur, has been printed in Lausanne: a booklet in French; I have it at your disposal."

"Lausanne is a universitarian city," opined the Minister. "Némo must be a professor there."

"No, I've made enquiries. His person is unknown there. According to all appearances, he's dead now."

"And also, his name is so mysterious. *Némo, neminis, O Némo!*"

"A mystification," growled Ravine, again. "You symbolists, you . . ."

"Symbolics or symbolists, they're on a bad road," Noirot interrupted. "Do you think, Messieurs the poets, that one can galvanize the masses with symbols? Personally, I say no. Let's fashion men! Oh, if I courted the Muse, like you, Surville. I'd like to nail to the pillory of the stage some of the despots, the shame of humankind: a Tiberius, a Napoléon or a Louis XIV."

He paused, "taking a moment" like an actor, and then, still magnificent: "Above all, a Louis XIV, in his monstrosity! A social drama, in the time of the Sun King, Monsieur Surville, that's what would be new, instructive and popular! So, to work, my poet, and we'll go to applaud you next time in the sanctuary of the great Corneille!"

With an Olympian gesture he put on his hat, opened the door of his box and went past Saint-Réal without even noticing him; escorted by all of us, he went to the exit.

The rumor had spread through the hall that the Minister had summoned the author of the play in order to congratulate him, and people were lying in wait for our passage. In the narrow corridors of the Théâtre de l'Idée there was nothing but curious faces and indiscreet gazes. The customary All-Paris of sensational premieres was under arms: critics of the column or the feuilleton, flanked by their reporters, star actors and actresses; clubmen with white carnations; and the ardent practitioners of young and old gallantry. Conversing in groups, approving or arguing, they cluttered the foyer, the perimeters of the galleries and overflowed on to the staircases. As we passed by, a moving hedge soon formed and I collected a few small smiles, little nods of the head and little plaudits of gloved fingers from the right and the left. An ovation!

Suddenly, I stopped. Among the illuminated faces and plumed coiffures, I had just perceived a bizarre accoutrement, and an even stranger face.

It was a young woman whose sad and poor costume cast a somber stain in the midst of all those fashionable frills. She was simply dressed in a narrow sheath of black wool, and the whiteness of a broad collaret descended over her shoulders. A formless and grotesque hat with a long crepe veil framed her face and made her resemble a deaconess. Ready to leave and already on the last steps of the staircase, she was stretching her head and observing me curiously; curiously, I looked at her: young, very young, eighteen at the most; and very beautiful: slim, tall, pale and blonde, with large dark eyes! In spite of the outfit of Sister Sainte-Agnès, her manner was elegant and coquettish, her face simultaneously candid and decided. Our gazes met, and a sudden emotion seemed to take possession of the unknown woman. A strange blush reddened her forehead; with an abrupt movement she pulled down her veil. At the same time she threw herself backwards and soon disappeared into the eddies of the crowd.

Meanwhile, the Minister had rejoined his vehicle; with his fingertips he addressed a protective adieu to me; then the carriage rolled away, carrying the great man toward the satisfied dreams of his bedroom. On the sidewalk of the Rue Boudreau, Saint-Réal watched him draw away, discomfited and furious.

"Not very affable, your Noirot of Romorantin," he growled. "I've known many ministers more illustrious than that parvenu, who weren't such poseurs."

"Oh, please, no politics," I put in. "The man is my friend; I can't permit . . ."

"Since he's your friend," retorted the peevish director, "you ought to make him understand that the Théâtre de l'Idée is an idea, Saint-Réal a champion of Art, and the violet ribbon a recompense."

The wretch had just opened up to me the dolorous coverts of his soul. For ten years that ambitious fellow had been soliciting "academic palms" without being able to obtain them.

"You'll have your violet ribbon, Saint-Réal; I'll make it my business."

"No, no humiliating steps!" he cried, very dignified. "I don't beg; I expect . . . and now, Surville, let's have super. I invite you. Anyway, I have to talk to you, about a very noble lady who wants to meet you. Go and wait for me in my box: I'll stop at the office and catch you up."

Supper? The prospect of a meal was not very alluring; I went upstairs unenthusiastically.

On the stage the curtain had just gone up for the final vaudeville: *Déjeuner de Pruches*, an inept farce by a colleague, a Montmartean furnisher of songs to the Souris Blanche cabaret. Not a comrade, that braggart! He had recently attacked me in the *Revue Lilus*, calling me a "quadragenarian ephebe" and a "collector of cigar-ends," stupid allusions to my age and Némo's pamphlet, which I had extracted from oblivion, put into verse, arranged and embellished.

Having reached the director's box I consulted myself. Was it necessary to go in? What was the point of warming bile listening to the platitudes being spouted at present: fossilized words worthy at the most of a fairground or a suburban dive. No, better to observe for myself the number and quality of my listeners. I had been loudly applauded up there under the eaves: a success not prepared in advance; I had not offered myself to the "knights of the chandelier." What if I were to visit those worthies? I retraced my steps, therefore, and climbed to the top floors.

In the third gallery the usherette welcomed me with a smile; the receipts of her cloakroom had been lucrative.

"A lot of people here, Madame?"

"Enough to make the floorboards creak."

"So much the better! Tell me, pray, did they applaud, your spectators?"

"With full hands, as at the Ambigu. Some even wept."

"Wept? Tell me about that. A few women, doubtless?"

"Yes, sensitive ones."

"Pretty, at least, your sensitive ones?"

The lady in the pink bonnet eyed me with a mocking expression. "They're all pretty in the Paradis, Monsieur—especially a little blonde who swooned at every tirade. A friend of Monsieur's, I suppose . . ."

A friend? In the vaults? No, I didn't know . . . when a sudden idea struck me that it might have been the nice face I had glimpsed a little while ago.

"I can guess: a young woman dressed in black, with the headgear of a deaconess?"

"You've got it—yes, a kind of nun, oddly dressed. Should I be indiscreet?"

"Why that question?"

"I understand! There's one that admires you! And curious! She's very well-informed about you, asked me for more. In love with you, I bet. Read your writings, and knows where you live: 24 Rue Chanoinesse in the Cité. I was amazed. Oh, yes, she's a fine specimen, your deaconess, but no millionaire. Refused the little bench and three sous for the usherette."

"That's too little; let's repair the omission, dear Madame. This is for your little 'profits.' She was greatly amused, then?"

"Amused? Sobbed like the Magdalen!"

"Is she still here?"

"No; she flew away during the entr'acte."

Well, well, my unknown! So you wept at the music of my rhymes! Intelligent and literate, without a doubt. And what eyes! Eyes full of flame, brilliant, so strange in the strangeness of that face! Came for my play and left afterwards—thank you, Mademoiselle.

I went back down to the lower floors and pursued my enquiry; evidence of a dazzling success everywhere. In the corridors, however, the echo of noisy gaiety reached me, provoked by the vulgar vaudeville; the insolent Montmartrean had a winner. Perfect; I'm not jealous . . . but what an indignity for Saint-Réal to kill the proud and pure effects of my *Nazaréen* so stupidly! All the same, these directors: envious and sly. Well, no, I wouldn't have supper with such a joker. He might have invited the coxcomb, my insulting enemy; in such company the Chablis or Sauterne would have an acidic taste, a splash of vinegar . . .

What, they were still laughing, the people in the hall, shaking their sides at those lewd jokes? Sad, sad . . . Then too, the discourteous words that the director had spoken to me returned to memory: *confused postulate, absurd denouement, jolly pathos* . . . treating me like that in front of my friends, my disciples! No, Monsieur Saint-Réal, I won't sit down at table with you. And as for the very noble lady you mentioned to me, I don't care to met her. An antique, I'm sure, a displeasing bluestocking with manuscript-sickness, giving birth to some indigestible vaudeville. In any case, I was exhausted by lassitude, utterly enervated. Bonsoir!

The miserable rhapsody was about to finish; it was necessary to hurry. In haste, I scribbled banal apologies on a visiting card and had it delivered by an aged actor.

II

In order to warm the success and produce a noisy publicity, the façade of the theater had been lit up brightly at seven o'clock. The veranda was still illuminated, and its crackling gas jets were projecting a ruddy glow a long distance. On the sidewalk of the Rue Boudreau there was a noisy crowd of people of every sort, idlers in search of adventures, street-traders, door-openers, newspaper criers: the scum of the Parisian pavement. I must already have been known to those parasites, for a kind of young lout detached himself from a group and called to me in a thick voice: "A carriage my author? To carry away all those laurels?"

No need! No carriage—the night was too beautiful; the author would go home on foot. I waved the joker away. Almost immediately, a tall man accosted the facetious youth, pointed a finger at me and interrogated him.

"Yes, that's Monsieur Surville, Germain Surville," replied the urchin.

"Germain Surville" named by all those people signaled, as I passed by, a present popularity. I swelled up with self-importance, and went on my way.

Scarcely midnight: a sky diamond-studded with stars; piquant autumnal freshness, and a walk of three-quarters of an hour or more to the Rue Chanoinesse: calming for my nerves. En route then! I traversed the boulevards and set forth along the Avenue de l'Opéra . . . Sill plenty of people in spite of the advanced hour: passers-by, idlers going up toward the Chaussée d'Antin, couples coming back from the Comédie-Française . . . the Comédie-Française! A delightful bliss spread through my heart. Before long, Monsieur the secretaries, you're going to proclaim my name there. I've received a promise—better still, a commission—for the Minister: a drama of the time of Louis XIV. Yes, but it was necessary to hurry; like the dead in the German ballad, Ministers go so quickly!

While plying my hamstrings I was already working. What subject should I adopt and which Louis XIV should I put on stage? The lover of Mademoiselle de La Vallière? Bah . . . romance! The organizer of the Dragonnades? Vulgar melodrama, too romantico-bourgeois. No, something new: a "creation." I sensed that the critics were lying in wait for me, keeping me under surveillance among my friends, on the edge of the woods and under the claws of the "Ibsenians."

Oof! What fatigue, and above all, what hunger. I had been fasting since morning. One scarcely thinks about dinner on the day of a battle, and my stomach was crying famine. At the corner of the Rue Petits-Champs a restaurant-brasserie was still open, and the figures in the windows seemed to be appealing to me: hairy kings raising their tankards of beer, Palatine knights sitting on barrels, Viviane fays or Bavarian Gretchens swilling large glasses. Always symbolism! I went in.

There were few customers that evening in the flamboyant tavern.

"Waiter! Waiter, I want supper: oysters and cold grouse."

"Beer, Monsieur? Brunette or blonde? Strasbourg? Munich? We have . . . why, what's this?"

He had not finished his patter, and had turned round. The door had just opened, letting a new arrival pass.

It was a man of tall stature, but very stooped, with the face of a negligently-shaved sacristan, with long unkempt gray hair. His pitiful thinness, the wrinkles that furrowed his face and his earthen pallor, denouncing suffering and hunger, might perhaps have attracted compassion had it not been for his dreary and burlesque appearance, which excited laughter. Sordid garments, almost rags, decked his skeletal frame. Clad in a long maroon coat holed at the elbows, a lustrine kerchief dissimulating the absence of linen, with trousers that were too short revealing blue cotton stockings; shod in flat, gaping shoes, worse than patched; coiffed by an old-fashioned hat, shiny and singed, the individual presented an aspect that was both disquieting and bizarre. Yes, what was this? Doubtless some vagabond rejected from a night shelter; one of those noctambulists who trail from one café to another before lying down on a bench to sleep under the stars.

"Monsieur, Monsieur, one can't beg here!" cried the waiter.

Indifferent to that insult, the man darted a glance around and came to sit down at my table, facing me.

"A glass of water," he requested.

At the same time, he took a fistful of coins out of his pocket and laid them on the marble.

The waiter hesitated.

"Serve!" enjoined the lady at the counter, dryly. And she added, in the manner of a soliloquy: "We're closing soon . . . not for you, Monsieur," she added, smiling, while a tablecloth, napkins and victuals were being prepared for me.

During those preparations the ragged man stared at me. He had been brought a glass, a carafe, and sugar. He paid and then, without touching the sugar, commenced drinking avidly. Truly sober, the poor devil, a gourmand of fresh water, who, in the land of gin, would not have spoiled a temperance society . . . and still his gleaming green-tinted eyes, plunged in the undergrowth of their eyebrows, remained turned to me . . . Oh, no, enough! He fatigued me at length, the old clown, with his indiscreet face of a mummer.

"Waiter, newspapers!"

An armful was brought: morning and evening papers, white, blue and pink, political or simply playful. They all entertained the public with my *Nazaréen*, advertising the play, amiable for the most part, not to say eulogistic. Here and there, nevertheless, there were little perfidies. Those journalists! What glib effrontery, what imperturbable assurance! Some talked audaciously about the late Némo, claiming to know that unknown: a Finn, an Icelander, a Norwegian, a Bavarian or a Magyar, to believe them. The most malign made him a Russian, a sort of mysterious Tolstoy. Some Russian, Messieurs!—perhaps a nihilist, who had taken refuge in Switzerland, and printed in Lausanne; I wasn't going to contradict you; I didn't know anything. What did it matter to me, anyway? I'd won the game.

At times I moved my newspaper aside and risked a glance at the water-drinker. He was still observing me persistently. Sometimes, a deep sigh was exhaled from his breast; then he muttered a few words, and a comical gesture brought his hands together. Another in despair, a lover of the great plunge into the river. Yes, sad, old man, lamentably sad, life!

Taking a cigar, I settled my bill and I left.

"After a good meal, a hygienic walk," the school of Salerno ought to have formulated. The fumes of a certain Château-Yquem, savored just now, were obscuring my brain somewhat; I resolved to dissipate them in the open air.

I was living at that time in an old house in the Cité, a veritable hermitage in which the life of olden times still seemed to dwell, the soul of counselors of the Grand Chambre or Présidens de la Tournelle. From my windows I could see the enormous bulk of the cathedral, its sniggering gargoyles, the delicate lacework of its rose-windows and the tapering plumes that surmounted its buttresses. On days of bell-ringing festivals, the vibrant drone, dispersing in the air the flats of its voice, collided in sonorous waves with the window-panes of my bedroom and made the building shake all the way to the foundations. A deafening neighborhood, which pleased me nevertheless—that corner of old Paris is so peaceful! I love the provincial silence of the back streets of my Lutèce, the solemn aspect of its manses, their scrolled windows and their coaching entrances surmounted by tritons with inflated cheeks. I also liked my shopkeepers, bourgeois smooth talkers standing together, as in farces by Molière, on the pavement of the great city, the placid faces of my petty rentiers who went to bed on a capon in order to get up at cock-crow, and the noble paunches of my canons when they came home after the offices, bare-headed, with their capes folded over their arms; all that quietude, all the charm of the reposed life that our forefathers loved. It was there that one could meditate mildly, prepare a book, sculpt verses; and it was there that I had finished my *Nazaréen* . . .

My *Nazaréen?* Was that possessive pronoun justified? No, certainly not, for the applauded play scarcely belonged to me. The history of the drama remained a nagging enigma for me. I had discovered it the previous year in Switzerland, in a second-hand bookshop in Vevey. A yellowing pamphlet with uncut pages, it had interested me at first glance. It was an essay in new theater, a kind of prose tragedy, musical and symbolist. The action, sometimes confused, flagged at times, but the first reading revealed a master thinker, and a breath of eloquent wrath, a plaint of religious despair, traversed the pages . . .

The author supposed that the Nazarene, the Son of Man, had wanted to put on human flesh for a second time, in order to observe the results of his doctrine and harvest the crop of good grain that he had sown in our hearts. For a long time he had traveled the world, going from one king to another and one priest to another. O stupor! The abomination of the earth had remained the same as in the days of his Passion. Pilate and his publicans continued to pressure peoples; Caesar pursued the course of his killings; Salome still danced before Herod; and the rich man still refused the starveling Lazarus the slightest crumbs from his table. Nothing had changed in the desolation of the Vale of Tears.

Nothing? Yes, though! Once, in Galilean villages, the wretched had got up in a crowd to make an escort for the mild preacher. In our cities, today, the wretched rejected him. In the course of his new mission, Jesus had climbed the steps of the workshop, and the workshop had abused his name. Jesus had descended into the depths of the mine, and cries of insult and malediction had risen up from the mine. Jesus had wanted to lift up the Magdalen again, but the Magdalen no longer knew how to weep . . .

Hatred everywhere, and everywhere its menaces; not even, as in the days of Tiberius, the Pax Romana and its vast repose! No, the entire world under arms; peoples rushing upon peoples; the strong exterminating the weak; warfare, war between races; and in its nascent atrocity, the implacable conflict, social revendication; the poor, as evil as the evil rich, jealous of fortune, coveting enjoyment, and the fury of heavy blasphemies, outraged the Evangelist, his law of charity, his precepts of resignation . . .

That was what the Nazarene had been able to see. In the darkness of the rising night he had perceived the Cross, the sign of his Redemption, fade away and disappear, like those temporary meters that are extinguished without tomorrow. And then, cursing the creation of his Father, he had begun to doubt himself. Alas, your life's work, O Christ, was derisory, then, and the blood of Calvary had flowed in vain!

Who was the author of that pamphlet? On the cover, a bizarre name, Némo, and a simple indication of a city: Lausanne. Very intrigued, I had interrogated the bookshops, consulted the erudition of our libraries: no information. But the work was very curious and imposed itself on attention. In these times of the renewal of the book and the theater, it merited being known. I had therefore cleared away the brushwood, smoothed out the rough edges, transformed the slightly old-fashioned prose into "modernist" verse; and *Le Nazaréen* had earned me tonight's resounding success. As for Némo, he . . .

Suddenly, I stopped. Who, then, was pursuing me stubbornly?

For a long quarter of an hour, someone had been walking behind me. Already, as I turned on to the Pont Neuf, I had noticed a man who seemed to be following me. He was keeping at a distance, hastening his pace when I increased mine, slowing and idling if I moderated my stride. Yes, a pursuit!

Now, he was advancing rapidly, lengthening his stride, gaining speed; he was trying to catch up with me . . .

At that moment, I had passed the parvis of Notre Dame and I had plunged into the shadow of the cathedral. A disquieting solitude: closed windows, sealed shutters; here and there, coaching entrances, tenebrous and suspect. The man was approaching very quickly . . .

With an abrupt movement, I turned round; at the same time, I brandished my cane. Well, if it was necessary to fight, we would fight.

The man doubtless divined my thought, for immediately, in a soft voice, he said: "Have no fear . . . I'm only an old man, and only want your soul."

He stopped in front of me. Surprise! The vagabond of the brasserie, the philosopher of the dolorous sighs.

"Go on your way!" I cried. "Or else . . ."

Without any emotion, however, he said: "You have just accomplished, Monsieur, the most abominable of infamies. A sacrilegious document was asleep in the dust, forgotten; you have extracted it from its oblivion to render it public; the unknown blasphemy has become a scandal. Well, look: by virtue of your action, a wretched sinner has outraged his God for a second time, has troubled Christian consciences, and, responsible for your crime, has perhaps merited the eternal Abyss. Be accursed, Monsieur; you have worked for Satan."

Bewildered by such a tirade, I examined the strange speaker. He had straightened his stature, and in the night his eyes were gleaming with indignation. My only response was a burst of laughter.

"Oh, don't laugh!" he cried. "Death, according to the word of the Scripture, falls upon us like a thief: if you were to die tonight, what would become of your soul?"

He paused briefly, and suddenly, lowering his voice, putting his hands together very humbly and elongating his fingers, he said: "A good deed, Monsieur! Look, I'm imploring you: destroy the ignominious diatribe, your play attacking God. By my voice, repentance adjures you. Pity for Némo, and pity for yourself!"

Némo? What name had he just pronounced? Stupefied, I drew nearer to the individual. His obstinate pursuit, that romantic setting, his mysterious and solemn objurgations excited my curiosity. Was I finally about to know?

"You know Némo?"

"I know him," he said, sadly. "I am his spiritual director."

"He exists, then?"

"He exists, alas . . . unfortunately for him and for us."

"Where does he live? What does he do?"

"He is expiating."

"A singular profession. I'd like to see him; I have to talk to him."

"He won't receive you."

"Can I at least know his name? Is he called Némo?"

"He no longer has a name among humans."

Impatience overtook me. A mystificator! The thought had occurred to me of some stupid joke; perhaps, too, I was dealing with a madman.

"Go on your way; I don't like this kind of joke. We're not at carnival yet."

He raised his head. "So you're one of those reproved individuals that my God abominates even before their birth . . . ! Oh, pardon me!" he said, interrupting himself. "I've just made a reckless judgment: I'm sinning, at this moment, against charity. The necessary and religious anger of which Nicole[1] spoke took possession of me, but the Son of Man forbids humans to lie down in anger. I repent: pardon me. Oh, Monsieur, the tide of our anxieties rises and rises before the Eternal. Once, the suppliants of Port-Royal might perhaps have been able to soften the justice of the Terrible Being, but we, less saintly than such saints, can no longer do anything to disarm the Hand that threatens us. Yes, the time is nigh, and the precursory signs of the redoubtable Day are already visible on the horizon. The Enemy is advancing, the priests and the guardians of the people have not uttered the cry of alarm, and the people will perish in their iniquity!"

While declaiming, he had taken a sealed envelope from his rags, and he presented it to me.

"Take it, my brother, and read it. You will then understand the motives for my bizarre action. Many years ago, the wretched Némo imposed a harsh martyrdom on himself, and we, his friends and family, are weeping for him in order to repair his crime. Will these penitent tears be futile, because of your impi-

---

1 The Jansenist Pierre Nicole (1625-1695), a teacher at the school attached to the Abbey of Port-Royal, who played an important role in the collation and translation of Blaise Pascal's works. With Antoine Arnauld (1612-1694) he wrote the "*Port-Royal Logic*," employed as a standard text-book for many years, and he fled to Belgium with Arnauld in 1679 when persecution of the Jansenists intensified, although he was allowed to return in 1683.

ety? You will have compassion and, suppressing the scandal, you will lighten the weight of the account that Némo will soon have to render . . .

"Yes, read it," he continued, forcefully . . . and this very night! It is always in mid-sin that God likes to seize the sinner, for the sin is often the work of his secret designs. Pascal burned in the fires of his concupiscence when he saw, in memorable ecstasy, the flame that alone ought to consume our hearts; and it is among the actors that the summoning Voice summoned the repentant Racine . . ."

Saluting me then with a horrible reverence, the extravagant preacher drew away slowly. For a few minutes, I followed him with my eyes; his meager spine was curbed again now, and he was walking painfully, like an old man. He went past the buttress of Notre-Dame, went on to the Pont Louis-Philippe, and finally disappeared into the obscure depths of the Île Saint-Louis.

III

The fantastic fellow! He had stunned me with his verbiage and I remained pensive for a few moments. Who could that wanderer of the night be, that spouter of inanities and enigmas? A wily actor, for sure, and a skillful scene-setter. Why, wanting to relate his laments, had he not approached me in the brasserie, and with what design had he chosen a solitary street under the shadow of Notre-Dame? Better to strike my imagination, and thus to produce an effect planned in advance? A ham, then!

As for Némo, thick darkness still remained around his person: the mystery enveloping that unknown man was becoming irritating. He is expiating . . . he no longer has a name among humans . . . destroy the work of his blasphemy and you will lessen the weight of his sin . . . In truth, so much the worse for that bold thinker if he had fallen into devotion today; personally, I had no cure for his penitence. In any case, I could not withdraw my drama; I had made an agreement with Saint-Réal for fifty performances, either in Paris or the provinces, and *Le Nazaréen* was about to commence a triumphant tour of France . . .

And yet, I was delighted with my encounter. Without intending to do so, that importunate fellow had just clarified my ideas; thanks to him, I had my new dramatic subject. Certain names and a few words pronounced just now had not fallen on deaf ears: Nicole, Pascal, Racine . . . Efficacious Grace . . . sin, the very work of God: the great men and the jargon of Jansenism. Well, what if I were to put the Jansenists on stage? Yes, yes. An original premise, an unexploited vein: an entire drama to write. I had found it!

I went home and went to my bedroom. Josias Gaulier, my young domestic—a singular forename and an even more singular forehead—was awaiting my return, yawning broadly. A curious little clown, that peasant from Maine, a great keeper of secrets, umbrageous and sly; I had procured him from an employment agency, freshly disembarked from his village—Mont-Saint-Jean near Sillé-le-Guillaume—and equipped with the most superb certificates: "exemplary conduct, unassailable probity, etc., etc." In brief, a white blackbird, a phoenix. In fact, a drunkard, a boor, a perfect good-for-nothing. In the more than six months that he had been in my employ I had tried in vain to devulgarize the bumpkin, but he had remained familiar and loquacious.

When I came in he got up, grumbling, his face sullen. "Monsieur is back very late! Is Monsieur satisfied?"

"Very satisfied . . . and you, my lad?"

The day before I had given him a theater ticket, a seat in the third gallery, recommending him to applaud and to encourage enthusiasm.

"Me, diverted, Monsieur? I left after the second act."

"So quickly? Why, then?"

"I don't like to hear the good God mocked."

A perfect imbecile, who had not understood anything!

"I didn't know that you were so devout, Josias. Good for you—but then, why your bad habits, the taverns and the women?"

"My word!" he replied. "It's one thing to drink for one's thirst and run after amours, but quite another to enliven oneself with ignominies. Oh, Monsieur, you're wrong; when you're older you'll have to make a formidable *mea culpa*."

"When you're older" was one of his customary amenities. It displeased me; I had reached forty, and my hair was already going gray at my temples.

"You talk like a breviary, my good man. That's perfect. Why do you never go to mass?"

"To your curés' masses? No, for sure! But out there, in Mont-Saint-Jean, I walked my four leagues every Sunday to listen to the Ancient, the Father, the true priest of the good God."

"What priest of the good God?"

He looked at me brazenly, and then announced, in his offensive voice: "I won't tell you anything about that."

"Keep your secrets, my lad, but I know them."

"If Monsieur knows them, why ask me?"

"You are, like certain of your laborers, a sectarian of the Little Church, in revolt against the Pope and the Roman Church."

"For that, yes; I don't like Babylon. As for the Pope, the Beast with ten horns and seven diadems . . ."

"Good, good, I know that story. Go to bed, then."

But the rustic did not retire; he remained planted in my bedroom affecting airs of familiarity. "This afternoon," he said, "Monsieur received a visit from a lady . . . a young lady."

"Some actress from my theater?"

"No. Not one of your hussies who trail behind the footlights but pure and simple youth. No frills and tinsel with flour on the face, but a black dress with the white collar of one of our true demoiselles: the innocence of the good God."

"Begging at the domicile. I don't know; forbid her my door."

The fellow began to laugh. "Monsieur doesn't know, but Monsieur is known. She was at the play this evening, listening open-mouthed and weeping."

She was weeping? I stood up, suddenly stirred. An image, already effaced from my memory, was designed there again, clear, luminous and utterly charming.

"You said a woolen dress and a long white collar, Josias? A very young woman? Very pale blonde, with beautiful dark eyes? It's really her . . . did she leave her name?"

"As for her name, hush—but she insisted greatly on seeing Monsieur, and Monsieur was absent. She's bound to come back. Will it be necessary to receive her?"

"Yes, yes, as soon as she presents herself."

The vivacity of my order amused the youth. "Understood," he said, winking. "Either I'm much mistaken or that turtle-dove must nest not far from here. I've often encountered that pretty little bird in the quarter. If Monsieur desires, one could seek information."

I made no reply and soon dismissed the devoted but libertine joker. The night was well advanced, it was necessary for me to decide to sleep.

Sleep! After such a fatiguing day, to be finally able to repose! Under the undulating drapery of its baldaquin, by the discreet glow of the night-light, my bed seemed to be inviting me, saying: "Come, then! You'll be content: I'll lavish ambitious dreams upon you, dreams of fortune and glory . . ."

But no; sprawled in an armchair, I didn't budge; fever was still burning me; I wasn't drowsy. With my eyelids partly closed and my arms dangling, I reviewed in their details the slightest episodes of my moving evening; I heard the bravos of the public resounding, the Minister's flattering compliments, his formal promise of . . .

Then: "You have just accomplished, Monsieur, the most abominable of infamies . . . By virtue of your action, a wretched sinner has outraged his God for a second time, troubled Christian consciences, and, responsible for your crime, perhaps merited the eternal Abyss." With what an indignant voice the man in rags had launched his invective at me! His vibrant speech was obsessing me now, like a refrain. I had taken from my pocket the paper that he had handed me, and, leaning over the envelope, gazed at it curiously . . .

"Take it and read it, this very night . . . !"

After all, why not?

The letter was sealed with a large black seal, and on the wax the imprint of a crucifix stood out. I examined it . . . what a tormented design and what a bizarre composition! The nailed arms of the God were not elongated on the cross but raised their desperate contortions vertically toward the sky. A Jansenist Christ? No, I must be mistaken. Jansenism disappeared from France a long time ago, and . . .

Yes, yes! Jansenist, without any possible contest. Bah! So the vagabond who had accosted me just now was a Jansenist! I should have suspected it; he employed words in the fashion of Quesnel,[1] and his attire had all the blessed dirtiness of a Deacon Pâris[2] . . . the ghost of Port-Royal, the specters of Saint-Médard were now walking abroad in the moonlight, then? They were in-

---

1 Pasquier Quesnel (1634-1719) was banished from Paris in 1681 during the Jansenist persecutions and spent the rest of his life in exile, in Brussels and Amsterdam. His commentary on the New Testament became the focal point of Jesuit attacks on Jansensism, and was a principal target of the papal bull *Unigenitus* (1713), intended to define the Jansenist heresy for the purpose of its extirpation.

2 François de Pâris (1690-1727) was the deacon of the oratory of Saint-Magloire; he attacked *Unigenitus*, gave his property to the poor and lived in extreme poverty until his death; he became far more famous thereafter when his grave in the grounds of the church of Saint-Médard became the focal point of alleged supernatural occurrences and the principal stage, in 1731, of the quasi-epileptic displays of "Convulsionnaires" supposedly possessed by the Holy Spirit, who became a much publicized minority sect, almost entirely composed of Jansenists but rejected by "mainstream" Jansenism; the crucifixions and tortures they imposed on one another in order to induce quasi-ecstatic states increased in violence throughout the 1730s. The sect still existed in the 1770s

doctrinating around Notre-Dame? I believed them, however, to be buried forever in the most unbreakable of tombs: indifferent forgetfulness!

I tore the envelope open and threw it behind me. Oh, what a sinister grimoire!

It was an entire notebook written by hand, the extract of a formal statement, but incomplete and truncated. On the heading was the convulsive image of the Jansenist Christ, and the following inscription in capital letters:

MISSIONARIES OF THE COMING OF ÉLIE—
BROTHERHOOD OF THE STAINLESS LAMB,
RECONSTITUTED IN ACCORDANCE WITH THE
REFORM OF THE BLESSED CLAUDINE-ARMANDE.[1]
ASSEMBLY OF THE HOLY REPARATION.
God of Abraham, God of Isaac, God of Jacob, not of the philosophers and scholars.

The last and devout epigraph was borrowed in its entirety from the celebrated invocation inscribed on Pascal's Amulet, the mysterious nonsense that the sublime visionary kept sewn into the lining of his doublet. But what did not recall in the least the author of the *Provinciales* and the *Pensées* was the demented story that came afterward. It related an event already ten years old, and the copy must have emerged from the archives of some religious community.

---

1 I have retained the name Élie as it is given in the original, although its normal English form is Elijah, because the relationship between the Convulsionnaires' Élie and the Biblical prophet cannot be taken literally, the name having been adopted as a pseudonym by the leader of the sect, Abbé Vaillant, who issued most of his apocalyptic prophecies from jail between 1728-31 and 1734-61, dying in the latter year. He prophesied that the fall of Élie from Heaven would be the prelude to the conversion of the Jews and the Millennial Day of Judgment. Claudine-Armande is fictitious.

The seventh ecstasy of the Reverend Mother Angélique-Marie des Cinq Plaies, the renovator of the Brotherhoods of the Stainless Lamb and the directrice of the Work of the Holy Reparation.

Today, the twenty-eighth of March in the year of the Incarnation 1883, the day of Holy Friday, before our assembled brothers and sisters, we, Matthias Silvat, doctor in medicine and doctor in law of the University of Leyden, have examined, checked, verified and certified the facts of which mention is made below.

For thirteen days—from the Sunday of the Passion to Holy Friday—our Mother Angélique-Marie has practiced the most rigorous abstinence and has refused to take the slightest nourishment, relating and applying such a fast to an intention.

On the thirteenth day, at the hour of prime, the holy reparatrice fell into a state of complete anesthesia and apsychia exactly similar to death: the face absolutely exsanguinated, the eyelids closed, the limbs inert and in cadaveric rigidity. The heart-beat was then interrogated in diastole; the heart was no longer functioning.

The state of the five stigmata was then examined, on the forehead, the palms of the hands and the tarsals of the feet. They were livid red, swollen and vesicular, similar to the blisters of burns, but were not bleeding.

Toward three o'clock in the afternoon, we noticed mysterious frissons on the apparent cadaver. The body resumed living, but traversing in reverse order all the throes of agony. It gasped, tried to draw breath, and then respired with anguish. Gradually, the very feeble movements became a spasmodic agitation. At three o'clock precisely—the hour when the *Consummatum est* was pronounced—the reviving individual went into convulsions. On her bed of ashes, Angélique-Marine raised herself up in spasms and—a marvelous phenomenon—remained suspended in mid-air for long moments. The suffering endured appeared to be atrocious; a sweat of effort trickled over the temples. We all watched, mute with amazement.

Suddenly, our Reverend Mother uttered a cry of fright: "Oh! Oh! Terror, agonies of terror! There he is!"

Then, approaching her, Cornelius Wagen, the deacon delegated by Monseigneur the Bishop of Deventer, and I, Matthias Silvat, appellant priest of the Holy Catholic and Apostolic Church of Utrecht, interrogated her.

"Mother, what do you see?"

"The Beast, the abominable Beast . . . the Demon."

"Where is it?"

"Here, crawling around this dwelling, prowling in order to devour . . ."

"Which of us is it threatening?"

"Him! Him again! My miserable brother. Oh, for pity's sake, the *helps*."

We immediately ordered that the *helps* be lavished. For several minutes, Sieur Eliacin struck the suppliant with blows of a heavy club; two of our messieurs, expert and zealous helpers, twisted her flesh with pincers. She did not appear to feel anything, and continued repeating, imploring us: "More! More! You're sparing my delights too much. I want the great, the *bruising helps*. Courage! Courage! I have so much to repair!"

In order to obey, we rendered the voluptuous tortures more intense. At each blow that bruised her head, Angélique howled and laughed.

But abruptly, she clamored, joyfully: "Enough! The Beast has disappeared; I can see Élie!"

At those words, we all fell to our knees; and the voice of our Mother rose up in the silence, very softly, saying:

"Finally! Finally! Here you are, then, O precursor of the divine Day! But is it truly you? How wretched your appearance seems to me! What, humble among the humble, scarcely covered in verminous rags, a lover of thirst and hunger? Yes, yes, it's you! The Jews who rejected Jesus have recognized Élie; they are prostrate, requesting baptism. Victory! Élie has cast his rags over the world and the world has immediately put them on. Henceforth, no more rich with miserly hearts; no more poor with envious gazes. I hear rising toward the Almighty the buzz of the human hive. Humans have put their fortunes in common; the labor of all forms a canticle to the Eternal. Alleluia! The thousand-year reign is commencing . . ."

"Alleluia!" we repeated, with the seeress.

"And immediately it has entered into a state of seraphic love, in rapture . . ."

I leaned over our saint then in order to observe the action of her heart and the sounds of her respiration. The heart was beating normally; her respiration had become even, and on the face a rosy tint had covered the mortal pallor.

The stigmata of the five wounds were bleeding abundantly.

A dozen signatures and attestations followed: Matthias Silvat, priest; Cornelius Wagen, deacon; Oscar Larfouillat, known as Eliacin, helpful brother; etc., etc.

Two further enclosures were added to that account. The first was a crude chromolithograph, a painterly image of an aged nun in a black veil and a white robe traversed by a scarlet cross. Repulsive ugliness, low forehead, snub nose, nutcracker chin and a wide mouth open in a blissful rictus. The whim of the portraitist had depicted the eyes entirely white, and beneath the figure a printed legend indicated her name: *Mère Angélique-Marie des Cinq Plaies, Expiatrice of the sins of France . . . the eyes of her flesh are closed forever; but celestial light illuminates her soul.*

The lady of the stigmata,

Finally, a sheet of letter paper had been pinned to the deformed print, and two lines were written thereon that were evidently addressed to me:

October 1893. You now know how, for a number of years, we have been praying and suffering. Have pity on Némo. Annihilate his blasphemy.

Who could the authors of those mystifying insanities and monstrous practices be? Where were the missionaries of the advent of Élie hiding their Brotherhood of the Stainless Lamb and their assemblies of the Holy Reparation? No indication was given to me on that subject. People who undoubtedly had to avoid the police and operate in protective darkness!

The ringing of the Angelus caused me to raise my head. Through the shutters and curtains, the first pallors of dawn spread around me. Six o'clock in the morning already! I shut the Reverend Mother Marie-Angélique and the narrative of her ecstasy in my writing desk; then, undressing in haste, I slid beneath the eiderdown and went to sleep peacefully.

Toward midday, the entrance of my domestic woke me up. Still oppressed by fatigue, half-dreaming in the semi-darkness of the bedroom, I glimpsed the silhouette of my peasant vaguely. He was walking on tiptoe, coming and going, putting a little order into the previous day's disorder. Qualities in that simpleton! On the carpet, in a streak of light, he perceived the envelope with the black seal—the one I had torn open and dropped behind me. He leaned over, picked it up and, indiscreetly, examined it. Suddenly, I saw him approach the window, part the curtain and gaze attentively. And just as suddenly, he bowed his head and gave a kind of amorous kiss to the convulsed Christ, detached the imprint and slipped it into his pocket.

I dozed for a while longer in the warmth of the bed, and then decided, finally, to quit the covers. Josias had set out the habitual collation in the dining room: eggs and green tea; the esthete's breakfast.

Under the fuming samovar was a whole wad of the Argus of the Press, the reports of my drama, already cut out and dispatched.

Good Gods! What a scandal, but what a triumph! Invectives from the Catholic papers, dithyrambs from the freethinking papers; all the chords, all the "tongues" of the lyre, as Ronsard would have said. Furthermore, some of my colleagues—dear friends, those—recounted my interview with the Minister and announced a future masterpiece. So be it! In the meantime, I had a fine subject for the play, and I had even found my title: *A Jansenist Family Under Louis XIV*. Yes, but it was necessary to hasten the execution and get to work as quickly as possible.

"Josias! I'll give you a break today. You don't understand? Leave, my lad. No need to wait for me this evening; I won't return before midnight.

An hour later, I was travelling in a train that was carrying me to Versailles. There, on the Place du Château, I stopped a carriage. I was going to visit Port-Royal.

IV

"We've arrived, bourgeois," announced the coachman, a fat and facetious Beauceron.

I got up in the vehicle and looked. In front of me, under the evening mists, an abrupt slope descended, a thicket of trees with tearful crowns, corroded by autumnal rust.

"Where are the ruins? I can't see anything."

With his whip he pointed to a sunken path, rugged and bumpy, buried under the foliage.

"Oh, it needs good eyes! There, down below in the vale. You follow that path. I'll wait for you here. Anyway, you were wrong to disturb yourself; it's too late."

"Too late to visit the abbey?"

"The rubble? Yes, Monsieur; it closes at dusk, and at half past four now."

I looked at my watch; it was well past five o'clock. What a disappointment!"

I had miscalculated my affair. Supposing Port-Royal to be much closer to Versailles, I had thought that I could accomplish my pilgrimage before nightfall. The Beauceron, in any case, had abused my ignorance unworthily.

"Where are we going, *patron*?"

"To Port-Royal; is it far?"

"Oh, not far . . . not far . . . a simple tail-ribbon."

"How long will it take us to get there?"

"A few quarters of an hour."

The simple "tail-ribbon" had been transformed into an interminable route and the few quarters of an hour had lasted an hour and a half.

Sitting in the carriage I was perplexed, and did not know what to do.

"Is there an inn around here in which to dine and spent the night?" I asked my coachman.

"Yes, bourgeois, Joseph Déchard's . . . Papa Virgil, they call him."

He indicated a kind of tavern before which haulers' wagons were stationed. Come on! I had fallen into a trap; my clown had dragged out the route in order to deliver me to this Déchard and receive his tip—a good old trick of the good old times. Anyway, the sight of that inn, built on the edge of a great wood, was not made to displease me. It resembled the stage-set of a melodrama; I was about to find myself in my element, and—who could tell?—perhaps receive the creative spark of which I had me in search.

"Go for Papa Virgil! Put me down there." A few seconds later, I got down at the door of the inn.

It was a curious tavern, the kind of drinking-den one finds in the suburbs of Versailles, simple but pretentious in appearance. A scarlet distemper brightened its façade from top to bottom, and over the garish color a marvelous sign stood out in golden letters:

THE PARADISE OF THE JANSENISTS.
RETREAT FOR PIOUS SOULS.
SALON FOR WEDDINGS. FAST OR MEALS AT WILL.

A facetious announcement, and a fry-cook who aimed for wit. Similar dives abound in the valley of the Chevreuse, and are habitual rendezvous for artists and men of letters.

Preceded by my conductor, I went in.

The first room of the "Paradise" was a sordid kitchen encumbered by tables and benches; a wine-merchant's counter occupied the back of the room. In front of a stove, a scullion was frying something, and behind the zinc a man in a blouse was asleep.

"Virgil! Hey, Monsieur Déchard!" shouted my driver. "A client!"

The man raised his head, revealing a rubicund face and blinking eyes. A florid nose, long hair and lamentable willow moustaches made him resemble some fairground clown. He seemed to me to be a trifle drunk.

"Here's a traveler," the coachman continued, "a Monsieur from Paris that I've brought you."

"A Parisian?" said the other.

He stood up immediately, took off his blouse, and appeared to us in a frock-coat. In an emphatic tone but with a thick voice, he intoned: "*Paris, brain of the world and ray of the empyrean!*" You're at home here, my master."

Bah! An Alexandrine for a welcome? I started laughing.

"I'd like a room for tonight," I said. "A good room, of course."

He nodded his head and with a fine gesture indicated his fetid abode: "*From the cellar to the loft, from its base to its crown, my palace welcomes you with a festival gown* . . . Ah, what richness of rhyme! One might think it were Banville. No *impedimentum, vulgo* luggage, Excellency?"

"No . . . I'd like dinner; what have you to serve me?"

"My God," he replied, in prose this time. "My Paradise is ordinarily a house of merriment, a castle of feasting, but look, of provender and reserves I no longer have any. A starveling band wound up here yesterday; it has devoured everything. Everything? I'm exaggerating. I can still offer the weakness of your stomach a garlic stew . . . come on, my seigneur, let's not be sorry: *garlic, at the feasts of the gods, was named ambrosia . . .* Toinette, serve your culinary masterpiece in the atrium."

Furious at having been duped thus, I allowed myself to be led into a banal drawing room, reeking with the odors of previous meals. A smoky lamp spread the fetor of its oil there, and horrible lithographs were hung over on the wallpaper, an entire salmagundi of poets.

"The Valhalla of the gods! I'll leave you in their company," cried my cruel trickster.

And, seeing me in his power, quite certain henceforth of his prey, he retired.

I was enraged, but what could I do? I was at the mercy of the innkeeper. *In truth*, I thought, *for want of thrushes I'll sup on my alexandrines.* A few morsels improvised during my journey will return to my memory. I therefore took my notebook, the habitual confident of my thoughts, out of my overcoat pocket and started to scribble furiously. I was more than half way through a sonnet when a hand fell on my shoulder and the ruddy face of the innkeeper leaned over me.

"Climbed on Parnassus!" he exclaimed. "A colleague, a poet!"

"I suspected as much, Master Virgil, and as soon as your first line . . ."

"You fled? Oh Monsieur, what a sacrilegious affront. Well, yes, I'm a poet, not to displease you: a former editor of the *Paillasse littéraire*—a long time ago in my youth; but always caressing the lyre; today, a fabricator of 'saws' for café-concerts, even an official supplier of one in Versailles. The famous *Rosière de Palaiseau* is the work of my genius. An entire artistic revolution! No more Parisian imports. I'm decentralizing."

He had rattled off his patter with such aplomb and such an enormity of boastfulness that I felt my anger ebbing away. He amused me.

"Does your copy sell well?" I asked him.

"Pooh! Literature doesn't nourish a man. Two or three francs a song and glory, but anonymous. Infamous Beotia!"

Meanwhile, the chambermaid had brought the masterpiece stew: burned brown, alas, exhaling aromas of garlic and perfumes of onion. My taverner poet cut two slices carefully, disposed them on my plate, and then put the dish back in the hands of the fry-cook.

"Now take the rest to the people in room number one. Serve them my Beaugency, which you can baptize Romanée, and feign indignation if they grimace. Understood? Good, turn on your heels."

He stuck a fork into my victual, casually, and shrugged his shoulders.

"Rotten, execrable dinner! But truly, it's not my fault. I wasn't expecting anyone today."

"Why no one today?"

"Eh? It's November the second, pagan: the day of the dead."

The day of the dead. Paying scant attention to Christian ceremonies, fundamentally a miscreant, I had not given that any thought. Nevertheless, I remained pensive for a few moments.

"However," said Déchard, "clients have come, and famous clients too. Guess who has the honor of sharing your grub up there." He paused, to produce an effect, and then slapped me on the shoulder familiarly. "The beautiful Clorinde, my dear . . . Clorinde de Villereuse in person!"

"Villereuse? A suburb of Geneva . . . damn, old Huguenot nobility!"

"A joke unworthy of you," he said, offended. "Villereuse or Batignolles, what does the name matter? But it's her, it's really her, the celebrated, the divine artiste!"

"Celebrated and divine! Why the extravagance of such epithets, Monsieur Déchard?"

He raised his hands with a stupefied gesture. "What, you, a Parisian and a poet, don't admire Clorinde de Villereuse?"

"I've never even heard of her."

"What a joke! The principal comic of the Alhambra . . . the Marquise?"

"You're much better informed than me. Why do you call her the Marquise?"

"All Paris designates her thus. The widow of a gentleman, the papers say . . . but you don't know her? Come, try to remember. The joyful performer who does such curious imitations in disguise: ministers, députés, professors, judges, anything goes. Your ignorance confounds me. Are you coming back from Pontoise? Go then, to applaud her; you'll be enthused. She sings, at present the *'Songe d'Athalie'*[1] to the tune of *'En Revenant de la Revue.'* Everyone writhes with laughter. An artiste of genius . . . yes, genius, Monsieur! Oh, if only I had such an interpreter in Versailles!"

Clorinde de Villereuse? I finally remembered: an old ham who paraded in eccentric costumes on the boards of the Alhambra. Many a time I had seen her image displayed on posters, and the theater reporters frequently advertised her. I had never heard her sing, though. Café-concerts rarely receive my visits, for their clowns have the virtue of getting on my nerves.

"Is she here in good company?" I asked.

"Good company? No, I suppose; she's dining with a bailiff."

"Not a very gallant tête-à-tête, although it's affirmed that . . ."

"And what a bailiff, Monsieur! That bandit Crochard, the most cunning and the most ferocious of all the bailiffs in Versailles. They're both shut away in a room—her lying in an armchair smoking cigarettes, him poring over his sky-blue paper. Oh, the rogue! It's necessary to see him scribbling kilometers of his ignoble prose: 'For legal expenses, a hundred and twenty-five francs . . .' Poverty, I'll wager, addressed to some poor devil."

"Or stamped paper that she's unleashing at her director."

"Via the ministry of a bailiff of Versailles? Impossible, colleague. You don't understand chicanery at all. I'm an expert; you have to be in my position. Judge for yourself . . . A little while

---

1 "Le Songe d'Athalie" [Athalie' Dream] is a passage from *Athalie* (1691), Jean Racine's famous tragedy.

ago, sitting outside my door, I see three marvelous heads go past; two miserable ragamuffins, real fairground louts, and an old she-monkey in a nun's wimple. The men perched the woman in a sedan chair and, hitched to the vehicle, they pull her like beasts of burden. The unspeakable trio set off for Port-Royal. Well, the beautiful Clorinde is doubtless on the lookout for their arrival, because she immediately makes a sign to her Crochard, who sets off on their heels. Escorted by the man in black, she follows the ragged porters at a distance, then they both come back to the hotel and the scribbling begins. It's those good-for-nothings that she must be after. But why?"

I got up. The verbiage had become tedious, and the incomparable Villereuse did not interest me. I left the drawing room, traversed the kitchen and stopped on the threshold of the tavern.

"Over there, I think, is the winding path that goes down to Port-Royal?"

"Winding path . . . the former pavement of the king?" objected Monsieur Déchard. "What irreverence! Yes, you only have to go down it, and beware of the bends. But the doors of the Abbey are closed now; you'd find a face of wood."

"I'm not, however, in the Jesuit era, and in exchange for a tip, the warden . . ."

"Incorruptible and ferocious; more Jansenist than Jansen! Besides which, he lodges right at the back of the enclosure, and you wouldn't be able to tempt his virtue."

"Too bad; I regret it. It's a beautiful evening, and seen by moonlight, those ruins . . ."

He interrupted me with a loud burst of laughter. "You rhyme to the moon, my master? Are you a Romantic, a disciple of Lamartine? *Often on the mountain, in the shadow of the old oak* . . . Pooh! Go and listen to Clorinde!"

And with that advice, so worthy of the *Paillasse littéraire*, my lover of gamy poetry returned to his den.

V

The night was limpid, transparent, and luminous in its azured pallor. The gray mist that had extended over the plain as the day declined had condensed into icy droplets; the sky was scintillating now, diamond-dusted with stars, and the whiteness of the moon was rising over the horizon.

With mistrustful steps, I set forth into the sunken path.

A disquieting rut! The thickets, stripped by the first frosts, brushed my face with their weeping branches, and on the ground, heaps of leaves exhaled the bitter scents of autumnal mildews. At every moment I bumped into stones that made humps in the slope, slipping and stumbling, digging in my cane in order not to fall. What, this was the road that Madame de Longueville's carriages had once followed when the white and blonde penitent went from convent to convent bewailing the sins of her amorous youth? What brutal shocks for the delicate limbs of the *précieuse*, and how piously she must have offered to heaven the bruises of those expiatory jolts![1]

In spite of the false steps, I felt energetic, and my indoor-sickness was active. What an amusing subject of a play for a dramaturge, that conversion of the amiable Urania, the devout dolors of the beauty with the beautiful hands! I was already drawing up my plan. One could show her rediscovering at Port-Royal, among the solitaries, some of the gallants of old, her adorers of the days of the Fronde, having become, in a spirit of penitence, manual laborers or domestics, gardeners or carters. One day, they find themselves face to face: a *coup de théâtre*, and . . .

---

1 The royal princess Anne-Geneviève de Bourbon (1619-1679) was the daughter of the Prince de Condé, and the wife of Henri II d'Orléans, Duc de Longueville; she was also the lover of La Rochefoucauld, and a leading member of the rebellious conspiracy known as Le Fronde; after the defeat of the Fronde she turned to religion and embraced Jansenism wholeheartedly; she protected the nuns of Port-Royal while she lived, but her elder son became a Jesuit and facilitated the abbey's destruction.

Hold on, what's this?

I had reached the bottom of the slope, and before me stood a high and broad wall. It extended into the distance, bearing my passage, enclosing a large domain. At hazard, I turned right. For a few minutes I went along the enclosure, sometimes marching through nettles, sometimes plunging into muddy potholes.

Suddenly, I stopped surprised. In the mud of that cloaca, a coupé of mysterious appearance was parked; the glasses were raised, and behind their windows I saw a man who was agitating, and seemed to be on the lookout . . .

It was a very elegant carriage, to be sure: expensive horses, harness in good taste, a coachman fur-clad like a boyar, armories on the doors. It had already been waiting for a long time, for the coachman was fast asleep and the "stepper" was pawing the ground with impatience.

I went by, and still the wall was to my left. Would it be necessary to follow that interminable masonry for leagues? I was about to turn back when I finally noticed a door fitted into the enclosure. Broad, with whitewashed panels, it resembled one of those massive coaching entrances that close Cauchois dwellings. That must be the entrance to Port-Royal.

My hotelier had lied; the door was not closed; both battens were open. I risked a glance inside. Yes, the ruins! But no warden—no one! My word, an adventure! And briskly, I headed for the abbey.

I found myself in a vast grassland, which descended at a shallow slope toward the narrow channel of a stream. The moon, having emerged from the horizon, bathed the undulating landscape with its milky radiance, and every detail of the enclosure—trees or fragments of wall, stood out in forceful relief. To the right, in an abrupt surge, rose arduous escarpments denuded of trees; in front of me, obscure curtains of poplars extended toward a building, and under their lacy blackness I perceived lamentable ruins: colonnettes with demolished arches, pillars discrowned of ogives, and tumulary slabs scattered on the grass. A pretentious edicule, an expiatory chapel, an entirely modern construction, dominated that debris. Further away stood a square of living hedges from which the spires of a centenarian fir-tree launched forth; finally, out there, under the foliage of the great wood, other hills fled into the depths of the distance . . .

And over all the sadness of that taciturn valley, over all the heartbreak of the formless ruins, over all that life sunk in death, the moon spread out like a pious shroud the white melancholy of its radiance.

I stopped, very moved. So this was Port-Royal-des-Champs, where, for sixty years the dignity, honor and the outraged virtue of the Christian conscience had sought refuge—this was everything that the butchering rage of Louis XIV had spared! I knew—no one is unaware—that in fear of a death sensed to be imminent, the King, already very old, had decided to extirpate the Jansenist heresy in its cradle. He judged it damnably contagious. Three times the executors of his will had undertaken the work of destruction. They had labored against the living—the nuns had been dispersed—and then against the dead; their coffins had been profaned; and finally against the stones themselves; church and monastery, they had razed everything. But I would not have been able to imagine such a complete annihilation of a noble and glorious thing.

And while I was gazing at it, sickened, strange connections were made in my mind. If the existence of a God is demonstrated by his power, what was the God of the Jansenists worth? In Pompeii, the ashes of Vesuvius had even left the houses of prostitution standing; at Pozzuoli, the earthquakes had respected the circus where the Emperor Nero cut the throats of captives—and the God of the Arnaulds had not even been able to preserve his altar! Oh, dementia of their folly of the Cross! What good, wretches, were so many tortures inflicted on your flesh, the oppressions of your liberty and the anguish of your hearts? The cry of your faith, the prayers of your holy hope, had all risen, then, to the indifference of the heavens!

Standing on the edge of the pasture, I evoked ardently the soul of things and the specter of humans. Here, to these hills, a Nicole and a Pascal had come to ask the silence to enable them to hear God more clearly; and here, in this valley, the daughters of Port-Royal had aspired to the mystical and imminent amours of the Spouse, following their hearts. Oh, if it had only been given to me to see the white form of one of those brides surge forth, or the unquiet phantom of some solitary, in order to interrogate them about the disillusionments of their tomb!

But no; around me there was nothing but mute desert: the desolation of a cemetery, abolished and devoid of tears.

Abruptly, I was awoken from my reverie; the bleak solitude had just been suddenly animated. In front of me, in the blackness of the shadow that extended over the grassland, I perceived a light; it came and went, swung and changing place; someone was searching, looking for something in the darkness.

Soon, vague noises became audible, blows struck against the ground; a spade grated and screeched on pebbles. At times the mysterious labor was interrupted, only to resume again immediately afterwards, methodical and monotonous. Then, in the intervals of silence, lamentations reached me, alternated and sobbing prayers. "*Miserere*," said a man's voice, and a woman's voice responded: "*Miserere*." In the distance, behind the walls of a farm, a dog howled desperately.

What was happening? My first impulse had been to return to the door, but, having reached the threshold, curiosity retained me. Thirty paces away, at the most, the curtain of poplars rose up; I slid into their cluster, and, moving toward the ruddy light, I saw.

Alongside the trees, a narrow meadow descended, closed by a trellis. Undulating and studded with mounds, the grass was verdant there, invaded by thistles, couch-grass or thorns, and in the middle of that fallow ground rose the white rigidity of a sepulchral stone. According to all appearances, I had before me an abandoned cemetery, some Jansenist field of repose, where, under the shelter of their church, the solitaries had wanted to sleep their final slumber. A lantern had been placed against the stele, and by its dubious light I succeeded in deciphering a few words:

Memory . . . profanation . . . Jean Racine.[1]

Racine! It was here, then, that the repentant lover of Champmeslé, the ravisher of Duparc, felled by Grace, detesting the sins of his amours and his pride, the expiator of his glory and voluntary murderer of his genius, had hoped to await the formidable appeal of Judgment! A hope soon disappointed, for he also had had to undergo the outrage of exhumation.

Not far from the cenotaph, three individuals were agitating, fantastically. One might have thought, on seeing them, of the macabre apparitions that the imagination of German Romanticism, the bizarre imagination of a Zedlitz or a Bürger, once loved to invent.

In the middle of the meadow, a woman was kneeling: a very old woman, dressed in a monastic habit and coiffed as a nun. She was motionless, her arms extended in the form of a cross, her hands open and her gaze lost in space. Next to her a tall man was disemboweling the earth with blows of a pick, and he had hollowed out a large hole. He was already sunk hip-deep, and, now handling a spade, was hurling earth and gravel out of the ditch.

At times, the woman seemed to extract herself from her ecstasy; she leaned over the projected earth then, and dug into it with her fingers, pulverizing it and spreading it out carefully, feeling, palpating and scrutinizing it. At times, too, she raised her head and took a deep breath, like a dog sniffing the wind, a bloodhound tracking.

---

1 The dramatist Jean Racine (1639-1699) had a turbulent relationship with Jansenism after being educated at the school associated with Port-Royal, where his aunt was the abbess. His affiliation was tokenistic until he married a devout wife in 1679. He broke with the heresy some while thereafter and attacked it, but returned to it repentant before his death. He wrote some of his finest tragedies for the actress Marie Champmeslé. His "kidnapping" of another actress, Mademoiselle Du Parc (Mari-Thérèse de Gorla), from Molière's company in the course of a quarrel between the two dramatists caused a sensation.

Stranger still, however, appeared to me to be the third member of the trio. Humbly prostrated, his head bowed, arching his back, he had laid his shoulders bare in spite of the cold, and was lashing himself with a rhythmic movement of the hand. His whip of cords rose and fell, lacerating the flesh and tracing violet furrows there. And while striking himself he recited in Old French the penitential psalm: "Have mercy upon me O Lord, for I am weak; O Lord, heal me, Lord, for my bones are vexed."[1] Every nine verses, however, the man interrupted his martyrdom, sighed dolorously, and repeated with a sob: "*Miserere.*"

What were they looking for, and for what horrible finds were they hoping? I was already advancing to interrogate them when I was obliged to hurl myself swiftly behind a tree; in the tall grave-digger I had just recognized my preacher of the previous day.

"Monsieur Silvat," the woman said to him, finally breaking her long silence, "my calculations were erroneous; we are working in vain. The artisans of the Antichrist have passed this way; let us dig further away."

The man with the pick-ax immediately emerged from his hole and joined her. Then, with the spasmodic gait of a blind woman, she took several steps forward, muttered a few words, bent down, appeared to sniff, and extended a finger.

"Here! Let's dig! I scent perfumes of sanctity, exhaling toward the heavens."

"Superfluous labor, Reverend Mother," her companion objected. "I will obey for the sake of obeying, but our hope will be disappointed. The profaners have made a complete harvest; nothing remains to glean."

An imperious gesture was the woman's only response, and meekly, Monsieur Silvat resumed work. He went to fetch a lantern, explored the soil, and his pick resumed excavating. The

---

1 Psalm VI. The author inserts a reference here crediting his translation to "Le Maître de Saci" (Louis-Isaac Lemaitre de Sacy, 1613-1684, the priest who translated the so-called Port-Royal Bible), but I have substituted the Authorized Version, which is not significantly different.

Reverend Mother—doubtless the lady of the stigmata—now leaned over the new ditch, still groping, still palpating, and encouraged the ardent toiler.

"Search, laborer of God, search, and you will soon have found! The treasure is here . . ."

Meanwhile, the administrator of the whip pursued the course of his lamentations. "Render me, Lord, the joy that is born of the Grace of your Salvation, and fortify me by giving me a spirit of strength."

The nun cut into the monotonous recitation brutally: "It's futile to cry 'Lord! Lord!' thus, since the demon fills your soul! Either you are worthy of being justified, in which case, obey the Grace, or you are one of the unfortunates whom God vowed to reprobation before birth, in which case, abstain from trying to tempt the Eternal. Your prayers outrage him even more than a blasphemy."

The penitent dropped his whip and sighed, discouraged.

The harsh sermonizer continued: "What good does it do, the prophet asks us, to flee before the face of the lion, if one encounters the bear, or if, having returned to your dwelling, you are bitten by the serpent? Such is your case, my brother. In order to flee the demon of pride, to escape the temptation of lust, you have sought refuge at the feet of the Stainless Lamb; but the viper has slipped into your cell and it has bitten you in the heart; the cause of your perdition is named Monique."

"My unfortunate child!" groaned the person thus criticized.

Angry laughter shook the treasure-seeker. "What! You dare to name 'your child' that daughter of fornication! Is it, then, a posterity blessed by God, that part issued from the adulterous woman? When I know that Monique is with you, my entire being rises up with indignation and disgust. You love her, you affirm? No, you only cherish in her the memory of your lubricity, the remembrance of your lust. Do you believe that because I am blind I cannot perceive you? When you look at her, it is not her that your eyes see; you seek in her face for the traces of her abominable mother. The work of your sin, Monique is the continuation of it . . . oh, you horrify me!"

"Mother Angélique-Marie," Monsieur Silvat intervened, severely, "you are too forgetful of divine charity. Be less acerbic."

There was a brief silence between them.

"Extirpate, then, that intoxication of your heart," the woman went on, softened somewhat. "Learn, finally, to suffer truly, and in a holy manner. Perhaps then, in spite of the enormity of your sins, the terrible God will receive you in his mercy. Invoke our ancestor; the blessed Claudine-Armande is omnipotent in Paradise. Imitate her example; after her conversion the holy penitent no longer wanted to know her family according to the flesh. Oh, my poor stray, you whom I venerated for a long time as a soul of election, on this pious Day of the Dead, before the tomb of our martyrs, for the last time, I adjure you! Have pity, my brother, have pity on yourself! Spare yourself the eternal Gehenna! Set aside courageously the troubling vision of your sin; stay away from the child of your adultery; your salvation is at that price."

"Abandon everything that I love!" moaned the suppliant. "Such a sacrifice is beyond my strength; God cannot demand it."

"Jephthah also loved his daughter, but Jephthah immolated her to the glory of the Eternal."

"A figure of the ancient law," objected the timid reasoner. "The new Law . . ."

"If it no longer demands blood, the new Law requires even more tears! Separate yourself from Monique; never see her again."

"Never again? Alas, what will become of her?"

"Our friends in Holland will collect the child of shame, that opprobrium of our race. They will deign to extract her from her idle life strewn with perils. Obey. She will soon depart and take the veil. I want it."

"A nun? She does not have the faith."

"If that is the case, let the mud go to the quagmire; return that Monique to her mother."

"To her mother? She still exists, then?" cried the kneeling man, in a tremulous voice. He stood up, shaken by frissons. "You lied to me, then," he continued, "in telling me that she was dead! That's bad, oh, that's bad of you. In the reclusion in which I'm confined, it's so easy to deceive me! She's alive! Oh, for pity's sake, tell me . . ."

"Think of your salvation," Monsieur Silvat interrupted. "The rest scarcely matters. Let me, Monsieur, speak to you without reticence. I'm a physician and I have been observing you for a long time. You're ill, very ill; your end might be imminent; don't think any longer about anything but God. If, tomorrow . . ."

He could not finish; a joyous clamor interrupted him.

"Alleluia!" cried the blind woman. "The treasure! We have the treasure! Look!"

And with both hands she brandished a bone.

The violator of tombs drew nearer. "Yes," he said. "A human maxilla."

"A relic of one of our Messieurs," declared the woman. "Let us keep it preciously."

She lifted the pretended relic to her lips, and then handed it to Monsieur Silvat, who placed the find in a casket.

"*Ecrabam!*" he said, with compunction. "Louis XIV's men have not dispersed everything; we can still reap."

His strange crop was now becoming abundant; with every spadeful, he threw up numerous bones. He examined them in turn, naming them one by one, and tarsals, carpals or vertebrae went piously to join the maxilla in the casket.

"We'll arrange them," said the old woman, "in the ossuary that our blessed Claudine-Armande once had hollowed out. Not all of them, however; with the smallest debris we'll make a nice reliquary, a pretty frame of embroidered velvet, festooned with gold braid, and we'll suspend it in the chapel."

Suddenly, she stretched out her head, appeared to sniff, and inhaled noisily.

"The reek of sin!" she cried. "Someone's spying on us!"

Immediately, the two men came running; they seized the blind woman by the hands and drew her away in a reckless flight. I saw them descend all the way to the bottom of the valley, climb the other slope and then knock on the door of the farm. It opened, and all three of them disappeared.

VI

It was late; my night-birds had flown and I had received a sufficient impression of Port-Royal; I therefore thought about going back to my inn. Still astounded, almost believing it to be a hallucination, I was about to emerge from the clump of trees when surprise stopped me for a second time. From the tenebrous profundities where I was so well hidden, two more curious individuals had just emerged: a man and a woman, who had been hidden in the shadows like me. They must have penetrated into the enclosure after my arrival, but, attentive to the spectacle of the seekers of relics, I had not heard their approach.

Having stopped in full moonlight, they were talking in loud voices. The man, dressed in a solemn frock-coat and a white cravat, was, in spite of that costume, of vulgar appearance; he had a nasty look about him—but the woman accompanying him seemed interesting to me.

She might have been about forty years old. Tall and lithe, although perhaps a trifle massive, in her nascent stoutness she had a magnificent presence and an imposing manner. From the distance that separated us I could not have made out the details, but the generous features of the face, starkly illuminated by the moonlight, seemed to me to be regular. The nose, however, was slightly curved, too aquiline. Over the forehead, undulating hair of an ardent blonde—the Venetian red so lauded by poets—was spread in broad tresses, in the Botticelli style. Was I mistaken? The majestic person seemed to me to be outrageously made-up. Her costume was very elegant, but garish, in dubious taste and of an indiscreet luxury: a shiny satin dress scintillating with jet, a sable mantle with guipure trimmings, a monumental Rembrandt hat shaded by a triple plume; enormous solitaires glittered in her ears. All the products of perfumers must have been spread over her person, so many heady emanations were distantly exhaled—the various stenches of sin that had so promptly alerted the blind woman. Shod in boots with very high heels, the lady was leaning on one of those walking-sticks with a golden pommel like those wielded by the Pompadours and Dubarrys of our operetta theaters when they come on stage to exhibit their cleavages.

They were walking past me, heading for the exit, without having perceived me. Every last word of their conversation reached me distinctly.

"I knew," she said, "that one day or another, we'd catch up with our man . . . what! You're leaving, my dear? Aren't you going to seize that piece of evidence?" With her finger, she designated the casket and the bones that half-filled it.

"Impossible, Madame la Marquise! I have neither an entitlement nor a warrant, and I don't care to receive a reprimand."

"Reprimand? From whom?"

"From the tribunal, of course."

The lady with the superb plume whipped the air with her cane. Then, in a chagrined tone: "A plague on your Dandin! We have there, however, a conclusive item of evidence. When will you send me your sworn statement?"

"Not before two days, at the earliest."

"Not before two days? Are you joking, friend? I require more zeal!"

"I have so many to write, at the moment, that I really can't . . ."

"Good, good . . . a truce on jeremiads. Lamentations always make me laugh. I'll give you twenty-four hours."

"Expedition in duplicate?"

"In duplicate: one for me, the other for my advocate."

"I'll give him his sworn statement myself."

"Quickly, quickly! We're beginning the dance. Instant request to the prefect first; then the application to the tribunal."

"You'll win the case, Marquise."

"I hope so . . . it's necessary to finish it."

She went back up the hill with a bold stride, and to spare her dress from catching on the thistles she had tucked it up brazenly. The gentleman of the witness statement craned his neck, risked a furtive glance, and then, stimulated, scratched his nape. She perceived the gesture, and immediately gathered her skirts.

"Don't be embarrassed! Am I to your taste? Gratis, at present, the spectacle."

"You're returning to Paris?" asked the lover of exhibitions, crestfallen.

"Not until tomorrow. I'll sleep at the château tonight."

"At Cernay?"

"The prince desires it."

"His Highness?"

"Why do you call him Highness? He's simply 'prince,' and that title is sufficient."

"The word Highness gives him pleasure, so I give him Highness. Since you're going to Cernay, Madame la Marquise, it would be very amiable of you to drop me on the way. I'm obliged to go to Dampere, and . . ."

"Granted! Zrelinsky's waiting for me in his carriage; you can ride on the seat."

Who was that marquise with the manners of a courtesan and who spoke the jargon of the lower orders so well? I was soon informed in that regard. As they went through the door her companion turned round; he saw me, and immediately called to me.

"Monsieur! Hey, Monsieur! You were here just now? Your name, in order that you can be cited as a witness."

His speech was insolent, his demand vulgar. I riposted in the same vein.

"My name? First, what's yours?"

"If you live in the vicinity you ought to know me. I'm Myrtil Crochard, the bailiff Crochard, of Versailles."

"Don't know, my dear Monsieur, and have no desire to know."

"A rebellion?" he said, in a menacing voice. "We'll be able to discover who you are, and constrain you to testify."

Good, a tile on the head![1] Was I about to have trouble with the law? Oh, no . . . adieu, then, Port-Royal; first thing in the morning. I'd be off!

Exchanging amenities thus, we had emerged from the enclosure. The carriage with the armoried panels was still parked.

"Clorinde!" cried an irritated voice. "Have you finished at last?"

At the same time, a head leaned out of the window, a head with a face as wrinkled as a crab-apple, evidently the "Highness," Prince Zrelinsky.

"I've been sat here for at least two hours," grumbled the peevish individual.

The lady with the red hair approached rapidly, and simpered.

"Oh, the nasty man! How he speaks to me! I couldn't come back any sooner—ask Crochard."

"Are you satisfied?"

"Delighted . . . but you, my prince, have you written to the prefect?"

"Your request has departed this evening; my letter accompanied it."

"In that case," said the bailiff, "everything will go smoothly."

"You understand, master idler," Clorinde insisted, "that it's necessary to hurry?"

"We'll be diligent, Madame de Villereuse. My office is at your devotion. May I climb up on the seat?"

"Mount!" said the Highness, dryly.

The man of law climbed up next to the coachman, and, jolted by the ruts, the carriage drew away slowly.

---

1 A literal translation of a phrase used metaphorically to signify a sudden stroke of bad luck.

VII

The next day I returned home in the afternoon. A good walker, I had covered the few leagues that separated me from Versailles briskly, in the early morning mist, through fields powdered with frost.

Certainly, I counted on returning to Port-Royal in order to interrogate the ruin further and extract other secrets therefrom, but the bailiff's threats and apprehension of the inconveniences of the law had caused me to get away as quickly as possible. It is an amusing thing to observe, the scant attraction that the spectacle of a judge in a toga and braided bonnet exerts in this land of France. I have known people who, in order to avoid the pleasure of "being summoned as a witness," asked their physicians for good certificates of illness, or even, buckling their valise, set forth to travel the world. I am one such timorous individual, and, having resolved to flee the assignation, I fled.

In Versailles, however, I had obtained more news of Madame de Villereuse and her protector. In the room in the restaurant where I had my repast, two young officers were talking irreverently.

"What a pain, my dear! Invited to go shooting with the prince the day after tomorrow, and unable to go!"

"To Zrelinsky's? He still hunts, in spite of his age?"

"Still a sure foot and a good eye, at seventy springs!"

"Will Clorinde be in the party?"

"Of course! She doesn't let go of her prey, and would like to be married."

"Bigamy, then? For it's said that she in the power of her husband."

"She'll divorce him—but the old fox won't marry her."

"He seems very smitten with her, though."

"Him? Not any more! The 'marquise' takes liberties; she has a carriage, a villa, a town house on the edge of the Parc Monceau, and still isn't satisfied. Zrelinsky's had enough."

"Has he finally perceived that the 'marquise' dyes her hair and paints her face?"

"Very mature, at present, the adored! Her lord and master, it's said, would like to savor fresher fruit."

"He no longer has teeth, but that's his age. So, rupture imminent?"

"Yes, very imminent, I believe; the household is falling apart."

And on those chaste metaphors, the officers, cigarettes in their mouths, had returned to barracks.

I returned to Paris the same day, and two o'clock was chiming on the clocks when I reached my abode.

"Josias! Anything new during my absence?"

"Yes indeed, Monsieur. The young lady of the other day has honored us with a further visit."

"Did she leave her name this time?"

"No—still secretive. She'll return today."

"As soon as she presents herself, my lad, have her come in."

Cards and letters were piled up on the table in the vestibule; I was congratulated for my victory of two nights ago. I picked up my mail and went into my study in order to read it. Right away, an envelope bearing the inscription *urgent* attracted my gaze: ministerial paper, large red seal, pretentious heading, *Théâtre de l'Idée*; a missive from Sant-Réal.

"My dear author," he wrote, "I've just visited your home, this evening of the third of November, at six o'clock precisely. I have an important request to present to you. Oh, don't put yourself on the defensive. You hold in your hand my fortune as a director and artiste."

That epistle made me grimace; I divined an indiscreet importunity. The vainglorious individual knew that I had credit with his Minister; he wanted to solicit some favor; academic palms, a red ribbon, even the Odéon; what was he about to request?

The sound of the doorbell interrupted my reflections. I heard Josias go to open the door; then my study door opened and the peasant stood aside to let a woman pass.

I stood up; at the first glance I had recognized the pretty face of my visitor.

VIII

"Monsieur Germain Surville?" she asked.

"That's me, Madame. Please come in."

Yes, the strange young person glimpsed at the theater! Having stopped on the threshold, she stood there, hesitant and embarrassed, doubtless wondering how to commence the conversation.

"What audacity is mine!" she said, finally. "I'm ashamed. I hope, however, that you'll excuse the incorrection of my conduct when you know the motive for my action."

A very soft voice, eyes lowered candidly, the pert embarrassment of a child caught at fault: I found her charming. But her speech was prepared, her words were precious, although timid; certainly my unknown woman was unaccustomed to society.

"Take this armchair, Madame."

"No, not Madame," she said, sitting down, "Mademoiselle."

Supple and slender, with a dainty figure and a distinguished aspect, she seemed to be very young. An unhealthy pallor emaciated her face, which was famed by ardent blonde hair. Her nose was a little too long, but beneath her delicate eyebrows, superb dark eyes shone with a feverish gleam. Her forehead was a little low, partly hidden, in addition, by a "virginal" headband. There were a few patches, however, on her pretty face. Above the brow-ridge, toward the right temple, there was a birthmark resembling the scar of a recent and profound burn. I could not help, on seeing it, regretting that the charm of that gracious physiognomy was thus marred. The young woman surprised my indiscreet gaze, for, blushing, she pulled down her veil to the middle of her forehead.

She was clad in a singular costume: a black woolen dress, a broad white collar, and the hideous headgear of a deaconess that had astonished me so. For footwear, vulgar shoes devoid of heels, although the ankle appeared to me to be delicate, the foot slender and well-arched. One might have thought her an ingenuous inmate of a convent, in uniform, in the parloir.

Finely gloved in black, and willingly showing her hand, the visitor was carrying a scroll of paper under her arm. *Oof!* I thought, *a woman of letters! The threat of poems, the peril of short stories, or even novels!* I waited, poorly resigned . . .

"Monsieur," she began, "I witnessed, the day before yesterday, the performance of *Le Nazaréen* . . ."

"I know. You were in the front row of the fourth gallery."

"Who told you that?" she asked.

"My police, dear child." And I added, trying to seize the hand that was exhibited with complaisance: "And my heart also."

That was insipid, and stupid, unworthy of a man of good education. The young woman recoiled sharply, and her eyes addressed a reproachful gaze to me.

"Oh, Monsieur!" she said, alarmed. "What do you dare to think of me, then? You believe me to be in quest of an adventure? You're mistaken—I'm an honest young woman."

"Pardon me, Mademoiselle," I said, confused by that merited lesson. "The late Boileau informs us that: 'The most stupid animal, in my opinion, is man,' and I have not belied his adage. What were we saying? You witnessed the performance of *Le Nazaréen?* I would have liked more auditors like you. Dare I, at present, ask your name?"

My pretty blonde seemed to consult herself, and then said, in a resolute tone: "Excuse me, but I must still conceal my name from you."

I examined her, increasingly intrigued.

"Your play, *Le Nazaréen*," she continued, after a brief pause, "is borrowed entirely from an opusculum signed Némo. That Némo, Monsieur, is my father."

"Your father! Némo is your father!"

"Oh, have no fear; no one has any intention of pursuing your plagiarism. Némo has been dead to the world for a long time, dead to himself—and, if you don't help me, dead to his daughter."

"Her use of the word 'plagiarism' had displeased me, but the heart-rending sadness of her final words had just transformed my vainglorious chagrin into interest.

"It's true," I said to her, crestfallen. "I have acted too much in the manner of our classics, and taken my wealth where I encountered it. Nevertheless, I believe that I have acted honestly; Némo's name has been proclaimed with my own, so I have nothing for which to reproach myself. Oh, Mademoiselle, what talent your father has!"

"Oh, yes, Monsieur," she exclaimed, shivering. "My father had talent, even genius. Alas, they wanted to stifle every flame in his life."

With a melodramatic gesture, the young beauty let her head fall into her hands, and I understood that she was weeping. Abruptly, however, she straightened up, and unrolled her scroll of paper.

"I'll arrive now at the objective of my visit. You know, Monsieur, the vast intelligence of the thinker who dared to write *Le Nazaréen*. Here, therefore, is the unpublished verse and prose of the unfortunate Némo, mere fragments, however, because his manuscripts have been unworthily burned. Not all of them, though! I was able, by stealth, to procure these various morsels; I carried them away to my young girl's bedroom, and I read them during entire nights. Magisterial work!"

While speaking, she was exalted by a surge of enthusiastic pride.

"Yes, Monsieur, magisterial. Admire, for example his marvelous sonnet overflowing with passion. In order to appreciate my father's value fully, it is necessary to listen to the poet in him, and I have a duty today to enable you to hear him."

70

The young woman stood up, threw back her veil, uncovering her forehead again, and came to stand in the middle of the room. Then, striking the pose of a tragedienne, she declaimed: "To the beloved!

> *Amour, sweetness of loving . . . I gazed at the skies;*
> *An immense frisson agitated matter,*
> *For the star to the star belonged entire.*
> *Troubled, from the firmament I turned my eyes . . .*
>
> *But the desire of April passed, contagious,*
> *Over the earth exultant with spring intoxication;*
> *Fecundating pollen fluttered like dust;*
> *A hymn of kisses rose up, religious . . .*
>
> *Suddenly, I cursed my bitter solitude,*
> *The desert of my days consumed in study,*
> *And the tomb in which, believing, I had tried to sink;*
>
> *The Tempter smiled in my bewildered soul,*
> *I loved . . . life was then rendered to my heart . . .*
> *Yes, you alone are alive, Amour, sweetness of loving!*

Well," she said, anxiously, "What do you think of that masterpiece?"

Masterpiece? Pooh! Rather banal inspiration, the verses of an amateur abusing adjectives, cadenced prose at the most. I was much better able to concoct a sonnet . . .

I approved nevertheless; much more than the paltry conceit of the languorous Némo, I had admired the talent of his interpreter. Harmonious and vibrant, she had recited the paternal madrigal with a consummate art of diction, developing the scansion incisively, detaching the epithets, rolling the *r*s in accordance with the Parnassian method: a laureate of the Conservatoire could not have done better.

"Bravo!" I cried. "An interesting piece! May one know now who the 'beloved' is?"

"I don't know her and I don't want to know her; she was always unworthy of such an amour."

The voice, so musical a moment ago, had become dry and harsh; her eyes were glistening malevolently, their gaze charged with hatred.

"If I've understood you correctly," I went on, "you're asking me to have these verses inserted in the revues with which I collaborate? Gladly."

"Oh," she said, "I dare to request from you much less and much more. Read, I beg you, the fragments I've brought you, and if you find them worthy of praise, then . . ."

"Then, Mademoiselle?"

"I will ask your permission to introduce you to Némo. He is being hidden, detained like a captive; but, conducted by me, they would not dare to expel you. Oh, Monsieur, if you knew what kind of man my father is! Noble, disinterested, magnanimous: an elite heart. How have they not appreciated the treasures of his soul? But no: genius, inspiration, pride in himself, they have tried to annihilate everything in him. And yet, the fire still burns beneath the ashes! Sometimes, when we talk about art or literature, I surprise a glint in his eyes; he still shivers in the breath of the Ideal! Assisted by you, I could revive that flame, which is on the brink of extinction; we could talk to him about his books, his talent, the vast hope that he has let go, and perhaps then he would begin to love life again!"

The naïve pathos of the tirade merited a smile, but the fervor of her prayer had moved me.

"At your orders, Mademoiselle. I have the ambition to oblige you and the desire to know my collaborator; you may introduce me to hm. One question, however . . . Némo is being detained as a prisoner? Why does he allow himself to be sequestered in that fashion?"

An atrocious emotion stung the young woman's pallor with livid patches, and the stain on her forehead became scarlet.

"They thought they were obliged to hide him," she stammered. "That reclusion was necessary for a long time . . ."

"Reclusion? Why?"

Weakly, she bowed her head, as if under an opprobrium. "Oh, Monsieur, Monsieur . . . you haven't guessed, then? Poor Némo has been convicted of a crime."

"Convicted?" I started.

"An iniquitous charge," she went on, "abominable and infamous, and I am finally rebelling against it. In my father's manuscripts you will find the story of his adventure and the sincere confession of his error. He wrote it for me alone; I confide it to you. Read it, Monsieur; read it carefully, and you, who describe the passions, will understand. It's a family secret that I'm delivering to you, but it's necessary. *Le Nazaréen*, according to the newspapers, will be performed throughout France, and perhaps abroad; he is entering into his glory. Sooner or later, you would have discovered our secret, and Némo would then have disappeared from the posters. I want the honor to remain to him!

"That, above all, is the motive for my action; I want to spare my father a supreme outrage . . . and then, I have confidence that you will assist me in the work of reparation and justice that I have resolved to undertake; I want my father to be rehabilitated. How? Oh, I don't know, I don't know . . . but that too, I want! You understand now my insistence on forcing your door. I don't know anyone in Paris; I live an entirely solitary life here. To whom can I address my request if not to you? Today, the wretched Némo has earned you a resounding success; you owe him a great deal . . . you will consider it a matter of honor to acquit your debt.

"Yes, together we shall go to find my father. What I dare not, he will dare; he will tell you his name himself. We shall lift up that collapsed soul, and, in saving him, and returning him to his daughter you will have accomplished, Monsieur, a good deed. Have pity! Help me, and I will bless you . . . I will love you for as long as I live."

Tremulously, she had seized my hands and was pressing them in a convulsive grip. I was bowled over.

"Your filial piety, Mademoiselle, will not have implored me in vain. I will read the manuscripts that you have given me, and I will soon give you my response. When shall I see you again?"

This time, she blushed and lowered her eyes.

"Oh, not here! You understand why . . . not here! Give me a rendezvous by an advertisement on the further page of a newspaper—*Le Figaro*, for example. Indicate a day and an hour and I will go to wait for you by the railings of the Observatoire."

She stood up, bowed to me awkwardly, opened the door and left. I accompanied her as far as the landing.

IX

The wall-clock in the antechamber indicated half past three; I was expecting Saint-Réal, so I went back into my study.

Now, seated at my desk, closing my eyes, tilting my head back in my armchair, I saw the blonde image again. What an interesting little creature! Audacious and timid; the modesty of a convent boarder and the affectations of an actress! She expressed herself elegantly in spite of the emphasis of her grandiose words and the formulae of an outmoded rhetoric. Learned, even a trifle pedantic, doubtless the result of the paternal education . . . pretty—my word, very pretty!—in spite of the bizarre birthmark on her forehead. And I could hear her too . . . every word, the slightest inflections of the melodious voice returned to my memory. "Help me and I will bless you . . . I will love you as long as I live . . ." Yes, yes, the surge of your filial prayer has stirred my heart delectably! One so rarely encounters souls smitten with duty in the depressing road that we travel every day!

74

I raised my head and interrogated myself curiously. What a sudden enthusiasm, my dear . . . ! Romeo's thunderbolt . . . ? No, for I started laughing at myself.

The daylight was beginning to fade; I lit my lamp . . .

Let's go, Monsieur Surville, to work!

I picked up the papers that the visitor had handed me, and I began to leaf through them slowly . . .

An elegant calligraphy; the writing of a young woman! She must have spent entire days and nights copying the originals. Dear child! The fragments were numerous; one could have formed two volumes with them. Prose and verse . . . several attempts at an impossible theater; a few short stories, moral tales in the taste of the eighteenth century; here incomplete sketches, there morsels that seemed to me to be finished. Talent everywhere, in spite of the slightly old-fashioned style of the scoria of Romanticism. A man disabused of Faith, the "unfortunate Némo," skeptical and Pyrrhonian—but what desolation in his heartbroken atheism, what a clamor of despair uttered toward the desert of the heavens . . . !

Aha! The story of his "adventure," the confession of his "error." What scholarly euphemisms, Mademoiselle, and what an ardent speech in your father's defense!

It was a long story, but truncated, scratched out in several places and interrupted by frequent lacunae. *The Perversion of a Soul*, one read at the head of the manuscript. A rapid glance sufficed, however, to convince me that the narrator had once lived his own narrative: the soul fallen into Evil was that of Némo himelf. A curious delicacy, moreover, did not allow any doubt to subsist in me.

To my daughter, for I owe her the entire confession of my sin . . .

I have collected my memories, in order to render them more precise, giving them the form of a journal. May she, in receiving the confession of my fault, not condemn her father too severely, and pity him rather than scorning him . . .

A solemn adjuration!

And without further delay, I leaned over the manuscript.

The Perversion of a Soul

. . . .
. . . .

Paris. Last days of April, 1874. Here I am, installed in my new apartment in the Rue Mazarine, and I have resumed my service with the Tribunal of the Seine. Judiciary rotation has taken me, this year, to the secondary chamber of the correctional police. There, I see displayed before the bar all the ignominies of the human soul: lies, theft, rapine, fornication and adultery; a repulsive spectacle, and yet, for me, fecund in useful information. Every day, it affirms me more forcefully in my faith; it demonstrates the verity of the terrifying dogma of our original fall, and the reprobation in which the Holy of Holies wants to maintain us, for the corruption of our first parents. How many times, on emerging from the audience hall, have I not cried with Pascal: "The human heart is hollow and full of ordure!" Then I bless God for being willing to enlighten me by means of the luminous doctrine of his efficacious Grace, for having thus distinguished me from others, preordained by their errors to the fall and damnation. I believe, I believe! Oh, if I could take my place among those rare creatures of election whom, for centuries, the Eternal has reserved for his glory!

My voyage in Holland has been nothing but a long delight. I visited Harlem, and then Deventer, and I have made contact with the Holy Church of our old Catholics. Why, then, the ultramontanism whose philosophy believes that it is humiliating us with the name of Jansenists? Why accept the insult, Monsieur d'Ypres? The powerful Jansen was Catholic, and we want to be Catholics in his image. In the two cities, our dear Church appeared to me to be living in edifying prosperity; some of our faithful have even established themselves in Gorcum;[1] it will soon be necessary to elect and consecrate a bishop there.

In Utrecht, our archbishop gave me the most affable of welcomes. He talked to me for a long time about the Christian glories of my family and the numerous miracles accomplished in olden times by the intercession of the blessed Claudine-Armande, my ancestress. "You are," he added, "an entire race of the just, children of Grace, always remain its indomitable champions." He also deigned to smile at the projects of my sister and to encourage them. We are going to revive the celebrated Brotherhood of the Stainless Lamb, in order to form catechumens therein. My poor Angélique-Marie's blindness prevents her from founding a convent of women and becoming its abbess, but she will be able to group around her cradle an increasing number of purified ewes. The archbishop has authorized her to don the habit of a nun and my sister has chosen the glorious livery of the daughters of Port-Royal. Thus, our family, like the Arnaulds, will have its Mother Angélique.

A delicate enterprise! In order to carry it through successfully, we have brought a priest of Sainte-Gertrude, a man already mature although recently emerged from the seminary of Amersford, Matthias Silvat. French by birth, the descendant of a lineage illustrious among our refugees in Holland, he will be the organizer and almoner of our brotherhood; he will also become the pastor of our true Catholics, abandoned without hope to all the temptations of Paris. An interesting and curious individual: mild to others, hard on himself; inflexible in regard to heresy, intractable in his faith. Knowledgeable in all sciences, he holds two doctorates from the University of Leyden . . . what hand, then, pushed that physician, already renowned, to quit his clientele,

---

1 The city of Gorinchem in the Netherlands was formerly known as Gorcum or Gorkum; it is celebrated in religious history for the hanging by Protestants during the Wars of Religion of nineteen Franciscan friars in 1572, who became known as the martyrs of Gorkum.

to disdain fortune and bid farewell to his vanities of glory? The hand of the One who leads you to the goal, if you obey, and who drags you if you resist.

How I envy that priest! I too once wanted to be a priest. While very young I traversed the seminary, but the new doctrines and the ultramontanism of the clergy of France horrified me. And then, on the point of receiving orders, I sensed all of my unworthiness. A terror of the Holy of Holies passed through my soul, and I returned, shivering, to the world. Thus, moreover, the greatest of our great Jansenists, the ally of my family, the blessed Pâris, once hesitated.

I asked the archbishop to impose a rule of life upon me; I desired to curb myself under a discipline like that to which the members of the third Order of Saint Francis are subject. Monsieur d'Utrecht gave me for a model the illustrious *Messieurs*, the old solitaries of Port-Royal: "Love of God, hatred of oneself." All virtue is contained in that simple formula. I shall imitate them. Humble? Yes, for I believe blindly. Poor? I shall strip myself of all my wealth. Chaste? I have always experienced the horror of the flesh.

"You are not thinking, then, of the sacrament of marriage?" the archbishop asked me.

"I'm too old, Monseigneur. I'm over forty."

The prelate joked with me amiably, and as he insisted, I had to reveal to him all the dolorous secrets of our house—the evil, produced by atavism, that our daughters . . .

(Here followed the first erasure, ten lines carefully effaced. The manuscript continued:)

Those two words, *atavism* and *degeneracy*, appeared unworthy to the prelate.

"The terms of a materialist!" he cried. "How dare you name thus a mark of election, a living miracle that the will of God perpetuates in your family?"

He is right. And yet I persist in avoiding marriage. I have a terror of Woman; I sense that a single one of her kisses might be sufficient to pervert my heart; my long judiciary practice has taught me too well to see in her the author of all our evils, Furthermore, two heritages combined could hardly suffice for the pious foundations that my sister is preparing. I intend to abandon all my property to her; better still, I will cede to her the patrimonial house that belongs to me, and which I occupy, on the Île Saint-Louis. Our truly Catholic church—*the* Church—will open there. And now, "Dieu ayde!" as one of our forefathers cried, at the first shock of battle.[1]

May, 1874. All is accomplished! I have made the entire donation of my fortune to my sister, by an authentic deed. Nothing remains to me except my stipend as a judge, which will suffice, I hope, to defray my alms.

I have been able to obtain from the government the authorization necessary for the existence of our Brotherhood. It is a first victory. But how many cabals already, how many muted machinations are perpetrated against us!

15 May 1874. Yesterday I received the most extravagant of visits, that of Monsieur Gédeon Manousso, who lodges on the first floor of the house where I live. An interested step, moreover. My neighbor is being pursued for the offense of assault and wounding, and will appear imminently before the chamber in which I sit. He came humbly to implore his judge.

Paltry, worn out and graying, his beard and hair unkempt, exhaling the stink of falsity in his smile as well as the gaze the

---

1 "Dieu ayde [au premier chrestien]" is the motto of the Montmorency family, who styled themselves the foremost Christian barons from the tenth century onward.

individual displeased me strangely from the outset. The culpable act for which he is reproached cannot be contested, and his story did not please me. Sieur Manousso is, it appears, a "scriptural" Jew who intrigues fanatically in order to found in Paris a temple of Caraïtes.[1] Until now my man had hidden his game so well that he was still a chazzan and had intoned his prayers in an orthodox synagogue, but his rabbi had discovered the fraud and had expelled the heretic ignominiously. A lively altercation had then ensued, a quarrel accompanied by insults and violence. In a fit of rage, the ferocious Gédeon had taken hold of his rabbi by the beard and, ripping it out, had lacerated his face; hence the correctional complaint and a demand for pecuniary indemnity: two thousand francs in damages. That is a costly beard! The advocates will be amused, and the tribunal too.

Any religious question solicits, not to say impassions me. I would have liked to know the philosophy and the dogmatics of the Caraïte schism, but Sieur Manousso, an Oriental originating I know not where, scarcely speaks anything but a Levantine jargon, and his bad French is Hebrew to me. He promised to come back soon accompanied by an interpreter.

In the evening I recounted the adventure to my sister and Monsieur Silvat. Immediately, our almoner became pensive. "'Scripturals' in Paris!" he cried. "It's God who has brought them! Freed from Talmudic superstition, rejecting the lies of the rabbis, they should be easier to convince. The reconciliation of Israel has always been one of our cherished objectives. Has not Pascal, speaking of the Jews, said: 'Their religion is likeable to me.' See Monsieur Manousso again, and strive to convert him."

I was rebellious at first, I raised the objection of my position as a magistrate, my situation of a judge facing a delinquent; but Angélique-Marie interrupted me violently.

"What about human respect, my brother? We do not tolerate it: Obey!"

---

1 The Caraïtes were a Jewish sect founded in the eighth century in what is now Iraq, whose distinctive beliefs are those outlined in the story.

17 May 1871. This morning I saw Gédeon Manousso enter my apartment preceded by his interpreter: a young woman, eighteen years old at the most . . . a gracious apparition! Face delicately oval, milky white complexion, large dark eyes with a velvety gaze, hair wound into Venetian blonde tresses, figure slim and dainty at the same time. Everything in that Shulamite seems made for charm and temptation.

Very surprised by such a visit I advanced an armchair and, addressing myself to the superb Jewess, I qualified her as Mademoiselle. Her companion started to laugh. "No, Madame . . . Esther Manousso, daughter of Zacharias Nessim, my wife. She was without a family and I married her in order not to allow a daughter of Israel to fall."

The most scholarly conversation was immediately engaged between us. In a soft, well-timbred, very musical voice the young lady explained the reasons of the quarrel again. I already knew them; her husband was in the wrong and I would condemn him. Rapidly, therefore, I turned the conversation in another direction, asking one or other of them to explain the doctrine of the "Scripturals" to me. With the assurance of a professor at the Sorbonne, Madame Manousso explained everything, and everything was understood. The Caraïtes are dissident Jews who reject the Talmud and only want to admit the reading of the text of the Old Testament. I took advantage of the dissertation to commence my work of proselytism. One by one I developed the most irrefutable arguments of our Christian dialectic: the prophecies and the figures. Manousso listened to me sardonically, pursing his mouth and caressing his chin. At the word "immortality of the soul" he interrupted me and said, impertinently:

"A soul? What, then, is a soul? Our books have never mentioned one. An importation of gentiles, a lie of idolaters later exploited by the rabbis. When the Eternal wanted to recompense our patriarchs, he promised them wives, children and numerous ewes and innumerable camels. Yes, certainly, the Messiah will come, but he will descend from the clouds, surrounded by lightning. Then there will be palaces more splendid than those of King David, harems as populous as that of the great Solomon. There!"

That vulgar theology horrified me. A Sadducee! Even worse than a rationalist philosophy! And while he was spouting those inanities the young woman became indignant and confused. With what religious attention she had listened to my words! What an ardent gaze she had attached to mine! The good seed, I was confident, had not fallen on infertile rock.

"I feel very emotional," she said to me when Gédeon got up. "The Christian God seduces me and attracts me. We'll talk about him, Monsieur; let me come back, I beg you."

※

19 May. She has come back, but alone. Why have I not spoken about these repeated visits to Monsieur Silvat?

※

28 May. My dear pupil is accomplishing rapid and surprising progress toward the faith. A little more time and Monsieur Silvat will be able to confer the sacrament of baptism upon her. What joy then, what pride for my heart! I persist, however, in keeping the adventure of that conversion secret. An indiscreet remark would offend us cruelly; stupid insinuations might perhaps hamper my work of proselytism.

Gédeon Manousso has not honored me with a second visit; he seems to want to abandon the soul of his companion to me. The information that reaches me regarding his character is deplorable. His turbulence as a sectarian will expose him to further unpleasantness. He insults and calumniates rabbis and Christians: a rogue. He is also accused, with reason, of usury. What a sorry husband, my poor sweet Esther!

❋

29 May. Sometimes, certain reflections of that ingenuous mouth embarrass and disconcert me; this morning, again, I felt some confusion.

"Is it true, Monsieur," she asked me, "that there is a question of reestablishing divorce in France?"

"Alas, yes . . . the gospel, however, reproves it in energetic terms. 'Whoever marries a repudiated wife commits adultery.' But one ought to dread everything in our impious century, and soon I fear, divorce will dishonor our laws. Why that question, dear Madame?"

She sighed, without responding, and her gaze was attached to mine for a long time. Very emotional, I looked away. Oh, no, I shall not confide to Monsieur Silvat the unnerving details of this conversion. In order to disguise my disturbance, I started a commentary on the Sermon on the Mount; my pupil interrupted me almost immediately.

"An admirable morality! You practice, Monsieur, the most sublime precepts." And when I protested, alarmed for my modesty, she went on, excitedly. "Oh, I know, I know. Issued from the most ancient nobility, you do not wear any of your titles, and rich, very rich, you have abandoned your fortune. Am I correctly informed?"

"Curious individual. You've opened an enquiry, then?"

"I know," she responded. Then, approaching my chair: "However, if you were to renounce celibacy, all those donations would become invalid because of the unforeseen arrival of a child?"

"Yes, doubtless," I said, laughing. "Article 960—but I'm not thinking of marrying. Stronger, Madame, than a president of the court, where have you studied your Code so well?"

"I'm very ignorant," she sighed, "and only want to know what you deign to teach me."

Ignorant? No, that humble person has a very distinguished intelligence, conversing with ease, having seen a great deal and read a great deal. Every day my astonishment increases. What, then, is the mystery of that life? When I interrogate Esther about her past, she weeps silently. Who is she, and where does she come from?

When my lesson in the catechism had finished we talked about literature. Immediately, she recited to me, in their own languages, monologues by Shakespeare, tirades by Manzoni and even Arabic poetry: "Kadidja, my rose all rosy, my lamb so white" and other trivia that Moorish singers intone while playing the marabba. And I only speak and understand my poor French! I was ashamed of myself.

"Are you a good poet as well as a perfect theologian?" she asked, suddenly. "Yes, I'll wager . . . well, dedicate a sonnet to me."

I must, therefore, take up arms against rhyme. Alas, alas, what folly is becoming mine?

30 May. Our religious instruction has been replaced today by a literary conversation. I showed my young scholar the sonnet that I had composed for her. She found it pretty and wanted to learn it by heart. "Amour, sweetness of loving!" she declaimed, in her singing voice—while looking at me.

2 June. Sieur Manousso has been condemned by the tribunal, and severely: a two hundred franc fine and six months in prison. In order to obey my conscience I pronounced a rigorous sentence. What am I saying? In the council chamber I spoke against him violently and thus obtained an aggravation of the penalty. My colleagues hesitated, however; they thought the condemnation excessive. No, the antecedents of that boor and usurer are too bad.

At the announcement of the judgment, Manousso got carried away with threats; nevertheless, he did not want to put in an appeal.

"Enough money for advocates," he said. "I've been duped, but I'll have my revenge: an eye for an eye, a tooth for a tooth."

Terrified, Esther came to repeat those words to me. What does the man hope for, then? Is he expecting me to commit a crime?

I simply announced the bad news to Monsieur Silvat, and made him understand that my hope of converting the Jew had been disappointed.

✳

4 June. Oh, torment, torture of my thought, jealousy! Yes, I'm jealous . . . jealous of a past that I don't know. What is it? It's hidden from me. And yet I suspect, but dare not divine.

For hour after hour I have tortured that woman in order to know her life: as always, a bleak silence or tears. She has, however, shown me her birth certificate and that of her marriage. Born in Algeria, she is twenty-three years old. Her father was a modest servant in a synagogue in Bône, and the marriage dates back two years. It was in Egypt that Manousso married Esther Nessim; I've seen the seal and signature of the Russian consul, for my Caraïte Jew is originally from the Crimea. But a dolorous secret still subsists. Why was the daughter of Zacharias in Alexandria? I questioned her ardently and even became irritated with her.

"You have, therefore, a fault to dissimulate from me, Madame?"

"And you, Monsieur," she replied to me, quietly, "are you truly without sin, to cast the stone at me thus?"

That is a confession, an entire confession, alas! A fault! And without modesty, that Manousso married the adventuress? Oh, the bestiality of the human heart, which degrades us and makes us pant with lust! But, you—you, wretch, how do you dare to reprove that man? Speak to me, speak to me, my conscience! Castigate all those lies that I have spoken for such a long time; the cowardly hypocrisies with which I have masked the turpitude of my passion! What! The corruption of that body and that soul, in exciting my jealousy, has inflamed my senses and spurred my desires! And that condemnation that I had pronounced, atrociously! I, the judge, am transforming myself into an accuser; I'm afraid to look at myself. Speak, then; are you not my safeguard, will you leave me to perdition?

No, I shall not see the wretched woman again. I feel myself debased by her, dishonored and despicable. O pride of my birth, pride of my stainless life, hope of eternal salvation, this is what has been made of you by a woman's smile and a few tears!

I love, I love frenziedly. The demon is victorious. He hallucinates me, he possesses me, he is wreaking violence upon me . . .

No, no, no! I must struggle, I shall triumph, I . . .

10 June. I have addressed myself to the One who pardons, and during my slow insomnias I have implored counsel desperately. And he has responded to me: "Why this trouble in the conscience, my poor and feeble child?"

"My Lord, my God, what ought I to do with the sinner confided to my care? She has detested her sins, washed them away with her tears, and asks to be curbed beneath your yoke. Is it necessary for me to reject her to the perils of the earth?"

"Timorous soul, what a strange ignorance of my Law! I am still the one who was so mild to the Samaritan woman; the one who repelled the Pharisees in order to welcome Mary Magdalen."

"My Lord, my God, what will society think of me?"

"What does society matter if I, who shouted down society, smile at you and approve of you . . . ?"

11 June. Well, so be it. For it's too much suffering. I have written and sent a note to Esther. It only contained a single word: *Return.* She came running immediately.

"Oh, cruel, pitiless heart!" she cried. "Your abandonment is killing me."

Suppliant, the penitent inclined her head upon my shoulder. Suddenly, she burst into sobs. Then, recklessly, I posed my lips on hers, and my soul passed entirely into my kiss.

20 June. The fall! The beloved is mine—entirely mine. Oh, her caresses are still burning me, the bite of her kisses is poisoning me like a venom.

10 July. The exaltation of this amour maddens me and frightens me. Esther no longer quits my apartment; she has attached herself audaciously, and is compromising us . . .

Yesterday evening, I engaged in a painful argument, almost a dispute, with my sister. Angélique-Marie reproached me for the rarity of my visits, my desolating lukewarm attitude, and my continual absences from their ceremonies. I replied bitterly and became angry with her. Monsieur Silvat listened to us silently, but he looked at me. What a gaze! When I got up to go he followed me to the staircase and then said, in a very harsh voice: "I'd like a conversation, Monsieur, a one-to-one conversation. I'll expect you tomorrow."

I won't go, and even if my sermonizer presents himself at my home, I'll forbid my door to him. They're both beginning to fatigue me with the intransigence of their zeal.

✳

20 July. An offense! This morning the postman handed me a registered letter. I took it, I looked at it: Monsieur Silvat's handwriting. I tore open the envelope; it contained a page cut out from the Vulgate.

Two men lived in the same city, one was rich, the other poor. The rich man had numerous flocks, but the poor man only possessed one little ewe, which he loved, etc. etc.

The parable of the prophet Nathan!

It's an insult, but the insulter will receive a lesson. I shall have a conversation with Angélique-Marie, and will tell her to choose between Monsieur Silvat and me. I want her to send that man away. Let him go, or I shall never see my sister again!

✳

20 October. Another outrage, this one abominable. Esther, in tears, has just brought me an ignoble newspaper article. Transparent allusions are made therein to our amours, to my name, to my family, to my character of judge and to the detention of Manousso. It is insinuated that I condemned that fellow in order to steal his wife! Who, then, has revealed to the pamphleteer the incessant tortures of my conscience?

"You see," sighed Esther, "that we are both compromised."

Yes, I feel very compromised; my adventure, which I hoped to keep secret, is rumored everywhere; the scandal has burst, published. Various indications warn me of a disquieting peril.

Yesterday I encountered one of my young colleagues, whose language and manner offended me cruelly.

"Bonjour, my dear Don Juan," he said to me. "Try to discover the author of the anonymous letters that we receive every day. You're being attacked with fervor and vilified."

Anonymous letters? I must expect for the reentry some virtuous admonition from my resident. He'll be wasting his eloquence; no, I shan't break my heart. I love, I love . . . someone unworthy, perhaps, but alas, amour inspires and does not merit.

16 November. Today, the day of the reentry of the tribunals, a painful humiliation. At the emergence from the "red mass" none of my friends came near me; they seemed to want to flee me, and the men of the court, prosecutors and deputies, affected airs of sly impertinence . . . My tedious chores will grip me again: long afternoons spent far from the one I adore. Brief separations, doubtless, but one of the sadnesses of absence is to blacken everything, and further darken our thoughts . . . and that Manousso will be released from prison in ten days.

18 November. I'm doomed! It's necessary to quit France, expatriate myself, and flee toward the unknown of another life.

This morning, the president of the tribunal summoned me to his study.

"You have strangely compromised your character of magistrate," he said to me, "and dishonored in a matter of days the entire existence of an honest man. A complaint of adultery is going to be brought against you. It's a defamation, I suppose?"

And as I maintained silence, dejected: "The fact is true, then?" he cried. "Yes, I'm only too certain of it. Who is this Manousso, who has formulated the complaint and demands justice? A man condemned by you? And you have seduced his wife? Oh, that's unworthy, Monsieur. An ignominy, a crime!"

Such a word irritated me; it was, however, only too just. I replied violently. The president immediately recalled my attitude in the council chamber during Manousso's trial.

"Yes, a crime," he went on. "Without your intervention, the wretch might have been acquitted. You have abused the good faith of your colleagues; I've received a protest from them that accuses you. Since you are a poor guardian of your honor, we have the duty to preserve ours. Here is a letter that I have drafted in advance. It contains your resignation. Sign it."

And I signed it. I was about to leave but the issuer of reprimands retained me.

"One more word, Monsieur. The court can't stop the pursuit; your crime is too flagrant; more than twenty newspapers have made allusion to it in order to attack the law; you're convicted by the public clamor. Will it be necessary for us to see you on the correctional benches? No; please spare us the scandal of your appearance. So, take some sage advice: quit France as soon as possible; disappear, and for a long time.

Frightened, curbing my spine under the shame, I ran to find Esther in order to tell her about the catastrophe. To my profound amazement, she uttered a cry of joy.

"There, dear friend, is a president who grants all my wishes! I was going to beg you to leave today. It's just in time! In four months I shall be a mother; you didn't know, I'm announcing it to you. My husband is going to be released from prison, and the wretch would kill me."

Then, becoming seductive and tender, "Amour, sweetness of loving," she murmured. "What will the rest of the world matter when you see your wife smile, and beside her, the child playing, your little child?"

"Come," I cried. "Let's depart. Exile . . . Hell itself, with you!"

✳

(Here there was a profound lacuna in the manuscript. The next pages transported the reader, six years later, to the city of Geneva.)

. . . .
. . . .

Geneva, 1 January 1881. What a funereal day of the year! The city is torpid beneath a shroud of snow; the wind, the icy Genevan wind, is making squalls howl, and under the grayness of a heavy fog, the waters of the lake convulse, all black. A bitter cold, and no joyous flame in the hearth, for want of money in my sad lodgings in the Rue Verdaine. I have amassed a few francs, however, hidden in a drawer, to buy toys for my little Monique. The poor thing seized the dolls with cries of joy. "How beautiful it is, how beautiful it is! And how I love you, dear Papa." I took her on my knees then and I gazed at her for a long time . . .

Yes, you really are my daughter, in you I recognize my race. From your mother you've received the velvet of your dark eyes and the golden silk of your hair; but the design and the expression of your face are of our family. Oh! What have I seen? At the summit of the forehead, that birthmark, that rosy mark . . .

(At this point, more erasures, several lines struck out.)

. . . Suddenly, Monique has become fearful. With a loud rustle of skirts, her mother has entered the room. And the child is in rags! Esther abuses me acrimoniously. Since the morning she has been making visits; she has not been received anywhere. The wife of a modest giver of lessons, a simple private tutor, does not count for anything with those Genevan millionaires. We are thought to be married, however, and I have not hesitated, alas, to declare myself a protestant. Two ignoble lies; but if I had confessed my veritable situation, the morality of these people and their Calvinist intransigence would have closed all doors to me. Oh, conscience, miserable science, you are completely dead in me!

"I've had enough of such martyrdom," Esther cried. "Let's

pack our trunks and leave. The limitation has passed; let's return to Paris and reclaim your name."

The limitation. With what cruelty my former colleagues of the tribunal condemned me for contumacy! A year in prison! They sacrificed me to appease the clamors of certain journalists, and in order to avoid the scandal of indulgence accomplished a scandal of atrocity. "The true prevaricating judge," Aguesseau informs us, "is the one preoccupied with public opinion." I shall not return to Paris, and I refuse to resume my name. Henceforth, in my perpetual exile, I no longer want to be known by any other name than Monsieur Némo . . .

Esther, disappointed in her hope, went out, slamming the door.

I deposited Monique on the parquet then, in order to return to my labor; and while I bent over my work, the child dressed her dolls and agitated her puppets. Laugh, darling, laugh in hiccups! Amuse yourself! But the most grotesque puppet, the lamentable Guignol, is really your unfortunate father!

Let's work! First, I need to finish the essay on religious criticism that I destine for the *Magasin Vaudois*. The small articles that it inserts and my Latin lessons are our only resource at present. Scarcely two hundred francs a month! Then I have to finish my drama, the dear *Nazaréen*. Oh, if a helpful theater could only accept it! Let's hope.

Geneva, February 1881. Le Nazaréen is finished, and I'm founding an ardent hope on my symbolic drama. But as I copied it, I felt a kind of fear of myself. What! Six years of incessant suffering have brought me to this point of skepticism and apostasy? The character of my Jesus of Nazareth detesting his humiliated illusions and regretting the folly of his Cross is a blasphemy . . . I have ceased to believe; all Christian faith has escaped through the wounds in my heart. Alas, there is no more balm in Gilead!

I shall take the play to the theater of Geneva. May the director give it a kind welcome!

❋

Geneva, March 1881. Refused. Even the actors are afraid of my thought. No matter! I shall appeal to the public; I shall have *Le Nazaréen* printed. Perhaps the Swiss newspapers will talk about my work and will want to render it a benevolent justice. Let's still hope; let's always hope!

Oh, if only I had the companion of my hours of anguish with me, the one who dissipates sadness by means of a smile and drinks up a tear beneath a kiss, I would feel more valiant for the struggle, less dejected by the defeat. But no; to each of my checks, scornful irony. Esther seems to take pleasure in envenoming my wounds.

"Another refusal," she said to me. "One must expect it. Are you finally cured of working for glory? Oh, I know: the Ideal! A meager pittance, my dear; meat much too hollow. Come on, throw all your philosophy and all your metaphysics, all your nonsense, in the fire. Write vaudevilles, café-concert songs, whatever you please, but earn money! Are you such a great man, then, that we must die of hunger, your daughter and I?"

Every day her character reveals itself shrewish, her language has become acerbic. Esther is disgusted with our life; she no longer loves . . . but I still love, and I still love her, desperately!

❋

Geneva, March 1881. Le Nazaréen has appeared as a pamphlet, printed in Lausanne, at my expense. No success in sales, not even curiosity. No newspaper or revue has taken account of it; the most disdainful silence reigns over the unknown Némo. A preacher, however, has insulted me from the height of his pulpit, and pastors have slyly maneuvered against me. So the doors that once stood ajar for me have been brutally closed, and the "impious" professor has been dismissed from the homes of several of my pupils.

Who will render us the old pagan law and all its liberty? Indifferent Olympus permitted Epicurus to dispute its gods, and the pontiffs maxima did not condemn the atheist Lucretius or torture him with hunger!

Geneva, March 1881. Big news: Manousso is dead. He had quit France to return to his Orient and found a Caraïte church in Syria; the constant folly of that other madman! The newspapers inform me that he has just been assassinated in Damascus by a fanatic of his species in a brawl with orthodox Jews. I dare not say: "Peace to his soul," for he did not believe in that chimerical hypothesis either. The wretch! He will not receive flocks, nor palaces, nor the harem that seemed to him to be the recompense of the true believer. Let him sleep in repose in the harsh maternal bosom of the earth, in which our first seed was formed, and which will annihilate us entirely.

I want to write to Damascus, to the Russian consul, to obtain information.

Geneva, May 1881. A copy of the official death certificate has arrived. Yes, Manousso is dead. I shall, therefore, marry your mother, Monique. You will no longer be the child of adultery, my darling, the daughter of my shame and my abjection.

Geneva, 20 July 1881. I'm married! The purely civil ceremony was accomplished at the French consulate in Geneva; no priest intervened in our sad espousal. The Judaic fanaticism of my wife—how she had lied to me!—would have liked the consecration of a rabbi. I resisted. No church, no temple, no synagogue! I want to put myself in unison with the philosophers of my homeland. Married civilly, me!

So, Mademoiselle Nessim is ornamented with the title of Marquise that she coveted so much. On emerging from the consulate, the daughter of Zachariah was exultant with joy . . .

Marquise! Well, no, Madame, I shall not drag from one hovel to another the glories of my family. When one gives private lessons at three francs apiece, it is necessary to know that one is not a marquis. Tomorrow, I shall resume my humble pseudonym, Monsieur Némo, the writer, Monsieur Némo, the petty pedagogue.

Geneva, August 1881. Violent arguments with Madame! Madame would like me to annul the consented donation to my sister; she invokes article 960: the fact of the arrival of a "legitimate" child. Not yet, and not ever. A dangerous litigation might be engaged and further scandals; another dishonor would attain Monique, the innocent child.

Geneva, 10 September 1881. Dolor after dolor, opprobrium upon ignominy! A sweat of shame rose to my face today; the repulsive secret that Esther Nessim had always hidden from me has finally been revealed.

This afternoon, I heard cries and mocking laughter under my window. I lifted the curtain and looked out. In the street, children were accompanying with jeers a grotesque individual, a Levantine Jew clad in a ragged caftan. The man was going from house to house, asking for an address. Soon he penetrated into the house where I live and rang at my door. I went to open it.

"What do you want?"

The Jew examines me and then he pronounces my name—that of my family.

"That's me. You have something to say to me?"

He takes a letter out of his overcoat and presents it to me: "So, you are the second husband of Esther Nessim, of the *Biondinetta?*"

His air is mysterious and the messenger intrigues me. I ask: "Was Manousso murdered, then?"

"Murdered? No. He provoked death, because he wanted to die: a suicide. You can guess why? The imbecile was still in love."

A suicide! An act of despair because I had stolen his wife! I have blood on my conscience! And I look at the red seal on the folded letter, fearfully.

"Take it, then," the man insists. "Take it and read."

"What does this paper contain?"

"The dead man's wedding gift to you."

With a solemn gesture he hands the letter to me, bows and retires . . .

I should have torn it up. I had the weakness to open it. My dementia gripped my heart. I love, I love and I am jealous!

The envelope contained ten pages written in Damascus by Manousso.

To the iniquitous judge, said the first line, *as soon as he has married the adulterous woman . . .*

There followed a long account of the vagabond existence that Esther had led before her marriage in Egypt. At sixteen, that daughter of a rabbi had fled the paternal house in order to conceal a first fault, and had joined a troupe of traveling actors. Simultaneously a performer and prostitute, she had roamed Asia Minor, Syria and Egypt, climbing on stages and singing in Moorish cafes. That was the explanation of the Shakespearean tirades and snatches of poetry that had charmed me so much: fragments of roles heard from the wings. No talent, in any case, the hateful revelation affirmed; nothing but a success of the shoulders and the hair—the Biondinetta, as she was called. It was in an Alexandrian theater, the Zizinia, that Manousso encountered her; she was among the performers there. The Israelite had been so smitten with her that he married her, but, shamed by the other Caraïtes, he had been obliged to quit Egypt to seek refuge in Paris. And I, who . . .

Oh, imbecile dupe I had not divined! The end of the shameful story had nothing to teach me. It told me about the despair of the deceived husband, the impotence of his rage and his abominable project of vengeance. Dishonored by me, the man had wanted that in my turn I should know dishonor

My hand, he wrote, *has emerged from the tomb in order to slap you.*

And while I was reading and rereading the denunciatory pages, confounded, Esther came into my room with Monique. Made-up, her lips reddened with carmine, her eyes enlarged by kohl, clad in garish clothes bought from the second-hand dealer, she was coming back from the garden of the bastions. Since she has been a Marquise, Madame parades her pretentious idleness every day. She leaned over my shoulder and, wheedling, asked me for money for new clothes.

"Money! Go back to the Zizinia. You'll find it on your boards."

She straightened up, stupefied.

Then I showed her Manousso's letter. Esther recognized the handwriting, and immediately understood everything.

"A petty infamy, Monsieur, but very belated; I'm married."

"So you've lied to me, Madame . . . lied by your silence and lied by your tears."

"Lied? A nasty word. I played my role well, that's all."

She went to stand in front of the mirror, and powdered her face with a nonchalant hand. "So be it! I don't contest anything. Be indignant, curse me, it doesn't matter. The miserable clown whose confidences you've received hasn't deceived you. Yes, at eighteen I was worth more sequins than the centimes that all your philosophies will ever earn. I was in vogue; I was the Biondinetta. A nice name, isn't it?"

She approached my armchair.

"But you don't know everything, my dear . . . and it's necessary to know everything. From the first day I encountered you, you pleased me. Amour, no. You wouldn't believe me. But your blazon had seduced me. To be called in Paris 'Madame Gédéon Manousso' is a poor regale for an ambitious soul; but to figure on the armorial, to wear 'sinople on the mountain clouded with silver'—that was what tempted me. I had nevertheless to use skillful maneuvers, and I had to maneuver. Do you recall those anonymous letters, those newspaper articles that attacked you? Well, it's your humble servant who had them written, or who inspired them. And it was also me who revealed to Manousso his humorous misfortune. I knew my man, and knew him to be brutal, violent and desirous of a scandal. I had also studied you carefully. If a scandal burst, your scruples would oblige you to flee with me. Was I mistaken? No! We're in Geneva."

In that mocking tone, her language exasperated me. Gathering together the little money that there was in the house, I flung it in the wretch's face.

"Get out of here and never come back! I'm throwing you out."

Tranquilly, she picked up the banknotes and a few louis that had fallen on the floor.

"You're throwing me out? No, it's me who's quitting you. I've been waiting for a long time for a propitious occasion; you've furnished me with one; thank you. One last word, however: divorce doesn't yet exist in France, and, I hope, never will exist. Let's separate, if you wish, but I keep your name. Marquise I am, Marquise I'll stay. Adieu."

Addressing an insolent reverence to me, she opened the door and left. From my window I watched her descend the Rue Verdaine slowly, heading for the gardens of the lake. A carriage passed along the shore; Esther climbed into it and disappeared; she had not even turned her head.

Then, understanding the horror of my life, broken forever, I uttered a cry of despair. "To die! Oh, to die!" And I collapsed on the floor.

I must have been unconscious for a long time. A warm sensation of tears and kisses finally made me open my eyes. Night had fallen, but in the darkness I heard a sob. Tears had moistened my hands, and a soft voice appealed to me:

"Father, father! Don't die . . . you still have me."

Monique! Also abandoned, you, the timid, loving creature! And suddenly, I felt the desire and understood the duty of living. "My child! My child!" I got up, I hugged the neglected child and embraced her convulsively.

Geneva, 11 September 1881. Come back! I forgive . . . I have forgiven, in the name of our child . . .

Geneva, 14 September 1881. Four days ago, Esther disappeared. How has she not understood that my mouth might have cursed her but my heart will always idolize her?

Devoured by anxiety, I addressed myself to the police; they have furnished me with the most deplorable information. By her behavior in public the wretch has become an object of scandal. They found the coachman of the carriage she took on the evening when she went away never to return. The man was able to give them a few indications. Esther was taken to a villa on the road to Hermance, inhabited during the season by a rich foreigner, doubtless some former acquaintance of the theater. She stayed there for more than an hour, and then returned to Geneva, got out at the railway station and took the train to Paris.

Gone! And her child is desolate, interrogating me and calling for her!

Saint-Gingolph, 3 November 1881. "Joy, joy, tears of joy!"

And I too uttered the clamor of delight, the cry of divine ecstasy into which, for an entire night, Pascal collapsed when, thunderstruck by Grace, he saw the dazzle of the Amour that consumes! Yes, my Jesus, would I have been able to find you if, taking pity on my misery, you had not summoned me to you? I have detested my sacrilegious follies, and a ray of your Light has descended on my blindness . . . I believe, I believe! I am disabused!

Yesterday, the second of November, seeing my dear Monique etiolated by chagrin, I wanted to distract her.

"Let's depart, darling; we too are going to travel."

Nothing retained me in Geneva. Professor Némo no longer had any lessons to give; his belated marriage merited him too many just reproaches and he lost his last pupils. And I felt myself becoming an object of ridicule.

Toward midday we took the ferry to the Savoyard coast. I did not get off until Saint-Gingolph, the first village in France. Four hours of rolling and pitching had wearied my little girl; scarcely were we out of the boat that she asked me to rest. I therefore went to sit down on a bench on the solitary pontoon, and there, taking her on my knees, I saw her fall asleep.

The air was keen, traversed by frequent frissons, with an autumnal bite, but a cloudless sapphire sky extended the profundities of its azure. And the child slept, to the lulling sound of the waves lapping the shore with the soporific monotony of their song.

What a soothing quietude there was around us, and what a torpor in my thoughts! On the other side of the lake, on the Vaudois shore, Montreux extended the already rusty verdure of its gardens, the terraces of the Kursaal, the garish distemper of its hostelries and the slender blackness of its church. The sun was declining and its oblique rays spread a crimson blaze toward the sparkling town. But, darker on the declivities of the hill, Glyon was staged, misted by the nascent vapors of the dusk, and the Avants huddled in their ring of fir-woods. Up above, finally, dominating those tormented undulations, the Dent de Jaman pointed toward the blue of the sky the dazzling whiteness of its recent snows. The landscape emitted a reposing charm, a melancholy voluptuousness . . .

Oh, how sweet it would have seemed to me, at that moment, to be holding a beloved hand in mine, and listening, the two of us, to the harmony of that speaking silence . . .

Abruptly, I woke Monique and got up.

We followed then the broad road to Simplon, which traverses the village and plunges into the land of France, going to terminate at the gates of Paris. With what fearful emotion I perceived your flag, your colors, O fatherland, now that my harsh exile could come to an end! My penalty has now expired and I have expiated cruelly before God . . .

God? What word, unlearned for a long time, had I just pronounced? And then the ringing of a bell, so soft and so plaintive, passed through the evening mists. People were praying in the distance, in the pious church that I glimpsed above the thatched roofs of the hamlet . . .

Yes, yes, the second of November, the feast of the Dead; the dolorous day sacred for Catholic souls, in the land where a beloved tomb is not a tomb but a cradle of hope. And I, who, for so many years, no longer remembered, seized Monique's arm and drew her toward that appeal. On the steps of the portal, however, gripped again by my philosophism, I stopped, hesitant. But the bell rang and rang, still inviting, still appealing. I went in.

It was a poor little village church, with whitewashed walls and rustic benches aligned in the nave; a humble edifice made to receive the humble. The salvation had just commenced, and on the altar, amid the candles, stood a silver monstrance. The bitter rustic voices of the children of the catechism were singing at that moment a good old canticle to the Virgin, the *Souvendez-vous*. An old tune, banal poetry; but each of those notes and each of those couplets penetrated me profoundly. A hymn to mildness, tenderness and purity . . . "Remember, our Mother . . ."

Our mother, did they say? A simple myth, assuredly, nothing but a symbol: the Isis, the Demeter of the Christians; but how much more touching is your face, O Mary!

". . . That one never has recourse to you without the prayer being granted . . ."

Always and forever the cry of human distress! They too, the believers of ancient Egypt, where the devotees of the temple of Eleusis, invoking the emblem of suffering, had begged. Had they been heard? They affirmed it, at last . . .

Oh, what if the supreme Bounty, the emanation of the Being of Beings, could radiate as far as me? If, enveloping with pity the ingenuous weakness, he deigned to take in his mercy the wretched child, the timid creature abandoned by her mother!

I put Monique's hands together and put her on her knees.

"Pray for us both, darling . . . and pray too for her. . . ."

Her: the one whose name I no longer dared to pronounce.

The little girl looked at me surprised; she had never been taught to pray.

And in the clouds of symbolic incense, crudely and heavily cadenced, the naïve song rose up and up, imploring . . .

But then a sudden flight of my thought carried me far away from the present moment toward the days of innocence of my culpable life. Through the fog of years elapsed I saw once again the placid and religious college where my adolescence had been spent: the past, a dear past disappeared forever. I too had repeated those same canticles, had loved the Virgin, so loving, had implored the Mother of forbearance. Oh, the mystical happiness of my childhood: the vigil of Noël and its midnight mass, when my infantile voice made itself so soft, as if not to trouble the sweet slumber of the newborn! "Come let us adore him; unto us a child is born . . ." And the Alleluias of Easter, so joyously cadenced, clamored triumphantly; and the beautiful evenings in the month of Mary, when, in the scent of lilacs and roses, in the great flowering garden, we went one by one toward the odorous altar where, crowned with flowers, the Virgin opened her arms to us . . . !

Finished, all that—those passionate surges of the heart, that blaze of amour, that ecstasy, that rapture of the entire self—finished, finished! I no longer believed . . .

In the church, however, a moving silence had fallen. The celebrant had quit his place and, mounting to the altar, had just grasped the monstrance. He turned to us, and above the inclined heads, the priest raised his God.

I was still standing. Suddenly, I felt something like a powerful hand descending on my shoulders; brutally, it curbed me toward the flagstones. "On your knees, philosopher! Silence your pride and your blasphemy! Faith, faith without arguments! I am the certainty according joy and peace. Believe and adore, and you will stand up again justified!"

What happened then? I don't know . . . I closed my eyes; my heart had ceased beating; my breast rose up convulsively; my entire being was gasping with suffering and bitter voluptuousness; a word, always the same, emerged from my quivering lips:

"Pardon! Pardon!"

When I came round, I was alone with Monique. The church was now deserted; but in the darkness the humble night-light of the sanctuary was shining, like a living symbol of the faith remaining in the darkness of my soul. I got up, having become valiant, and to me also a voice seemed to say: "Console yourself; you would not have looked for me if you had not found me."

. . . .
. . . .
. . . .
. . . .

I shall go to ask for refuge in my sister's house; I shall beg her to reconcile me with God; she will have pity, and, weeping beside the man who weeps, will want to take care of my child.

X

There the dolorous romance of that Perversion of a Soul ended. Too abruptly interrupted, it did not give any details of the return of the penitent to his family, or the welcome that the scrupulous Angélique-Marie had been able to spare him, or the austere Monsieur Silvat. But the imploring step that Némo's daughter had taken edified me fully in that regard. It was, in any case, a cry of protest, a plea, a speech for the defense, an appeal interjected by a father before the conscience of his child. He revealed himself there tender and weak, but also honest, in spite of his heavy sin. In addition, a sentiment of desolate fatalism traversed every page of the heart-rending narration: the absence of any notion of free will, the latent belief in two supernatural forces, one evil and the other good, demonic or divine, determining human action, constraining it to sin or repentance. And, thus tossed between the Devil and God, Némo, hallucinated by amour, appeared as a miserable stake that the two powers were disputing. Jansenism, perhaps; Manicheism above all . . .

A sonorous burst of voices, and the noisy opening of my door suddenly made me turn my head; standing on the threshold of my study, like Don Carlos at the tomb of Charlemagne,[1] was the actor Saint-Réal.

He was admirable to behold: nobler than a Frederick, as correct as a repertory milord. Shod in varnished boots, pearl-gray trousers and brightly gloved, he was strutting in a superb frockcoat with a shiny lining. My man had explored the hothouses and boutiques of many horticulturalists, for a rutilant geranium

---

1 In Victor Hugo's *Hernani* (1830), the Don Carlos in question being the Holy Roman Emperor Charles V, or Charles Quint.

was glistening in his buttonhole in spite of the season; the flower bloomed pompously, like a ribbon of the Légion d'honneur. And what bearing, what an Olympian head! His hair, dyed crow-black, was bouffant, curled with tongs, and over the blue of his glabrous face a "soupçon" of make-up was perceptible, a dusting of rice-powder. The crimson satin of his cravat was ornamented by a Roman *victoriat*, and camped over his ear, his balloon hat had all the dandyism of Bolivar. In the right eye, a monocle made the face grimace—but what a sardonic grimace! The rictus of a lion: the "superb and generous" lion of the menageries of 1830.

"Here I am!" he said, in a cavernous voice. "At your orders, Seigneur!"

For a few seconds I peered, wonderstruck, at that emulator of Brummel.

"What elegance, Saint-Réal! Irresistible! To what sort of conquest are we going this evening?"

He braced himself like an antique hero, and caressed an absent moustache. "To the conquest of the Golden Fleece! And you hold our destiny in your hand."

Familiar and protective, he had the mania on certain days of addressing everyone as *tu*—authors, actors, and actresses above all; he was a ham of the olden days.

"Are you ready?" he said. "We're going to debauch at the Restaurant Mauret."

I went to fetch my hat and overcoat, and then took the arm of the actor and went out.

At Mauret's the meal was noisy. Saint-Réal talked in a loud voice, exalting his glory, evoking memories of his past. He had known Bocage, Ligier, Rouvière, Chilly, Mélingue, Saint-Firmin, Saint-Ernest and other saints more venerated behind the footlights than beneath the flames of church candles. "Nourished on the marrow of lions, all those giants! Kneaded with the prose of the likes of Gaillardet, Bouchardy, Félicien Mallefille and Victor

Séjour. Oh, child, child, what decadence! Vile insects, your actors of the present day! And your fashionable authors, what a joke!"

Every time a woman came in to dine, my man adjusted his monocle and stared impertinently. "Look at that! What a swoon! She recognized me. A rendezvous in a wink!"

Finally, over dessert, he lowered the tone and became mysterious. Then, stretching out his forehead between two bottles, like Choppard, the so-called Amiable, in *Le Courrier de Lyon*: "Enough bagatelles! Let's talk seriously. I have secret designs for you. In a little while, we're going to the Alhambra; I've reserved us a forestage box."

"Always unparalleled," I said, annoyed. "But why the Alhambra?"

"We need to hear the celestial Clorinde . . . you know, the 'Marquise' . . . I'm introducing you to her divinity this evening."

"What's the point? I'm unfamiliar with her clowning, and I can't bear her genre of talent."

The visit appeared dangerous to me; the lady might recognize me, and I remembered the odious Crochard. I was firmly determined not to go.

"The beautiful Clorinde," Saint-Réal went on, "has written me an urgent letter, and I've been to see her at her town house. Head and blood! What sumptuousness, and what a dream, my poet. I came out ectasized . . . The Marquise desires to sup with you, for she's the noble lady I mentioned to you the other evening, but you took flight like a peasant. Guess what she desires. I'll give you a thousand. She wants to play the Magdalen of the *Nazaréen*!"

I started. That veteran of revues reciting my alexandrines!

"Amazing!" Saint-Réal went on. "I'm still astounded. And yet, I didn't dismiss it. You can grasp my reasoning. Clorinde can pour over me the riches of California. Her engagement at the Alhambra is coming to an end, and you understand that with her comic genius—*virtus comica!*—she refuses to spout any longer in the racket of tankards and pipe-smoke. Why does she want to play a role in your *Nazaréen*? A whim and a mystery. She won't obtain it, but I'm attaching the chariot of my fortune to her. You'll compose an Aristophanean comedy for her; we'll exhibit her grimace and harvest the maximum. What do you say, Manlius?"[1]

He swallowed two small glasses of cognac one after another, and clicked his tongue.

"I'll go on . . . Clorinde is richly maintained by a Galician prince, a sumptuous seigneur whom she maintains under her charm. This evening, he'll be in his idol's dressing-room, and the idol has given me a rendezvous. She'll introduce us, and— listen carefully—I'll say to the noble protector: 'My prince, a fair exchange: I'll carry to the clouds the worthy object of your amours; in recompense, pour a few drops of your Pactolus into my pocket. Paris has a thirst for great Art, slake it. Help us to erect in mid-boulevard a temple consecrated to the religion of Beauty, an edifice with the magical title: Théâtre de l'Idée. Hence, a commission, O Maecenas! A rich affair, to boot; the placement of a father of a family. With two names on our poster: Princesse Clorinde and Saint-Réal, a gentleman of the stage, the public will be attracted, and one will multiply one's capital tenfold. Here, in addition, is Monsieur Surville, the illustrious author of *Le Nazaréen*, who is burning with desire to write a masterpiece for your dear marquise. Don't hesitate . . .' Tomorrow, I'll go to see my notary, and within three days we'll have signed the contracts."

He finally stopped, his tirade having rendered him breathless, and squeezed my arm. "Eh! Is that well stitched up? Have you understood?"

Yes, certainly, I had understood, and far too well. A fraud— five hundred thousand francs, at least, thrown into a pit; the apostle of great Art seemed to me to be turning thief.

---

1 Sant-Réal's reference is to the protagonist of the tragedy *Manlius Capitolinus* (1698) by Antoine de La Fosse, Sieur d'Aubigny.

"And Clorinde is in on this fine conspiracy?" I asked.

"It's her who has the honor of its invention."

I shook my head, determined not to appear in the affair. "Well, no, I refuse."

The pontiff of the Idea looked at me, furiously.

"So that's a friend! That's the man that I've dragged out of the dirt, and now he's rejecting me! Oh, human turpitude! But nothing surprises me. Anyway," he said twisting his napkin, "let's still go to the Alhambra. You'll hear Clorinde, and you'll reflect . . ."

He asked for the bill, settled it without checking it, threw a five-franc tip on to the plate and got up. Preceding me, my "gentleman of the stage" traversed the room. He marched with his head high, effacing his shoulders, developing his torso—magnificent. As he passed by all the diners turned round; the cashier contemplated him ardently, and the sommelier, the waiters and the doorman all murmured his name.

XI

Without addressing a word to me, Saint-Réal headed for the café-concert. He cursed and muttered in angry asides, and his cane bruised the sidewalks furiously. I accompanied him silently, and we arrived thus outside the Alhambra.

On the walls of the façade enormous posters were displayed, the garish colors of which attracted the gaze and assaulted the eyes of passers-by. A woman was depicted there, life-sized, clad entirely in red. Her low-necked dress and the gloves that went up to her shoulders were red, and her perforated shoes revealed scarlet stockings. Even the hair had ardent tones, and on that yellow mane was the crown of a marquise. Atrocious attire, but a figure even more surprising! With a lewd gesture, the splendid individual was raising her hands to the level of her lips, making a kind of loud-hailer, and seemed to be hurling some lascivious joke at the public. Vignettes framed that illumination, showing the singer in her various employments, and placards lavished her name extravagantly.

Saint-Réal examined the poster and approved. For myself, I was resigned. The last words of his roaring anger returned to my memory: "You'll hear . . . and you'll reflect." A threat to my *Nazaréen*! Better to make myself small, to be wily with that potentate, ready to make my escape at a favorable moment.

With his majestic stride he traversed the peristyle; I followed him sulkily.

Our box was a forestage ground-floor situated next to the iron door that gave access to the wings.

"Usherette!" cried my Buridan. "Director Saint-Réal's box!"

At the sound of that thunderous voice the door to the wings opened slightly and a head appeared in the embrasure—a face with a graying red beard. The curious individual emerged immediately and advanced, making the most obsequious of bows. Doubtless a dignitary of the Alhambra, he was dressed in a frock-coat and a white cravat; the universitarian ribbon displayed its violet brightness over the lapel of his coat.

"It's you, Monsieur Léoné?" said Saint-Réal, in a protective tone. "Always prosperous and flourishing. You look like a young patriarch!"

The other grimaced a smile; then Saint-Réal introduced us.

"Monsieur Surville, one of my authors . . . Monsieur Isaac Léoné, stage-manager. Dear Léoné . . . what news in your tabernacle?"

The dignitary of the Alhambra raised his arms to the heavens, and then, in a despairing tone: "Imminent catastrophe! Nine forty-five and Madame Clorinde hasn't arrived yet."

"A fine! It'll be paid for her, anyway."

"Yes, certainly, the prince is an excellent banker. But she abuses. Yesterday, again, she didn't come and I had to make an announcement. Oh, if you'd heard the racket in the hall!"

"Sudden illness?"

"No, forgetfulness of her duties."

"'Do your duty and leave it to the gods,' Corneille, Monsieur Léoné. Personally, I'm fond of my classics. And speaking of the classics, a question. Is Clorinde still parodying the 'Songe d'Athalie'?"

"Alas, no; she intends to serve us a dish of her own invention, and we're very fearful."

"Tell us your fear."

"Well, this is it: the 'Songe d'Athalie' to the tune of *En revenant de la revue* always brings the audience to their feet; it's the nail of our presentations; however, the ambitious lady is weary of such success. At present she needs tragic effects."

"Great art? What presumption!"

"She'd like to imitate two renowned artistes simply by reciting a sonnet. Will the public understand it?"

"Dangerous, my handsome Léoné, dangerous—and how! Why do you put up with such caprices?"

"We have such need of her! A spoiled child, my cousin."

Sant-Réal looked at him in surprise. "Villereuse is your cousin? You're related?"

"On the distaff side, and even closely, Clorinde is my niece, in the Breton mode."

"Oh, Breton! Why, then, does she deck herself with the title of marquise?"

"It's entirely her right. The widow of a gentleman! But excuse me, Messieurs; I'm awaited on stage."

And, quitting us with the finest of his confidences, the stage manager launched himself toward the wings.

"Palmed with silver, decorated with violet!" muttered the envious Saint-Réal. "A fellow that I knew when he was a candle-snuffer! But protected by La Villereuse. Thanks to her prince, she can obtain anything . . ."

Having thus vented his bile, the Apostle of the Idea went into the box.

In the hall, the public was agitated and stormy. Ten o'clock had chimed, and the star had not appeared. Lewd singers and generic warblers succeeded one another for twenty minutes in the midst of the din. "Enough!" they cried. "Clorinde! We want Clorinde!" In vain the Falcon of the troupe had sighed all the languors of a *Viens dans ma gondole*; in vain also, the principal comic had tried the irresistible effect of his ballad *Panama*. Nobody listened. On the floor the tankards struck the tables, and in the boxes, ladies and gentlemen who had come to hear the "Songe d'Athalie" stamped their feet or tapped their canes. The first part of the program came to an end and the curtain was lowered. Soon there was a tumultuous din, a deafening racket. One might have thought it a madhouse before a storm, a menagerie of hungry beasts demanding their fodder.

Suddenly, the curtain went up, and a handsome monsieur in a Venetian leotard advanced toward the prompter's nest.

"Young Serafino," my companion told me. "He'll warble a ballad. No talent."

A roar of protest greeted the pomaded head.

"Mesdames et Messieurs," the young Romeo commenced, "a sudden indisposition has overtaken our comrade . . ."

"No, no!" interrupted a voice from the wings. "She's just arrived!"

And the stage-manager exhibited himself in front of the stage in his turn.

"A little patience, please! Madame Clorinde is at your orders. You're going to hear her in a new creation."

But the public was very discontented; it is a tyrant who does not like to be kept waiting, and this evening, the casual attitude of its favorite exasperated it. The orchestra intoned a triumphal march, and Monsieur Léoné reappeared in order to suspend a placard:

Clorinde—the sonnet—first performance.

Silence was immediately reestablished. Saint-Réal adjusted his monocle, and nudged me with his elbow. "Here she is! Let's applaud . . ."

It was really her, finally. With the deportment of a queen, the actress advanced toward the public and bowed, smiling. She was clad in the same scarlet costume that illuminated the posters, and in her hair a diadem with fleurons scintillated, the marquise's crown.

I examined her curiously. She appeared to me, under the stage lights, much less beautiful than in the moonlight. Plumpness was already softening the face, and a few wrinkles were hollowed out in the whiteness of her make-up. The nose was poorly shaped, but the dark eyes were scintillating, superb, provocative and disquieting.

Sparse applause saluted her entrance; she was being held in rigor.

"Mesdames et messieurs," she said, visibly surprised by that lack of enthusiasm, "today we're going to strive to be serious; I'm going to recite you a sonnet."

Ironic "ohs" and "ahs" responded to her announcement. Unmoved, she went on:

"Yes, a sonnet, don't be displeased. But this is how I recite it. Without augmenting the price of your places, I'm going to transport you to two theaters, and enable to admire two stars, tragedy and parade, tears and laughter . . . pay attention, aim your opera-glasses."

Immediately, the orchestra attacked a muted tremolo, and the comical speaker came to place herself over a trap-door. Briskly, the initial costume was withdrawn, and the parodist presented herself in a tragic peplum. Then, in a warm, harmonious, well-timbred voice, she commenced:

> *Amour, sweetness of loving . . . I gazed at the skies*
> *An immense frisson . . .*

At that moment a strident volley of whistles resounded under the chandelier; Clorinde stopped, stupefied . . .

At the first words of the sonnet, I had risen to my feet; I had just recognized the lines that Monique had recited to me.

Under the stage, however, the scene-shifter had not heard anything; he continued the undressing; the frolicsome star was now exhibited in a short skirt—but her first quatrain was not finished, and the effect was spoiled; she made a gesture of chagrin. Wanting to catch up, she skipped two lines, grimaced, in order to pass from the sublime to the grotesque, and forgot her line. Mocking laughter immediately greeted her lapse, and simultaneous cries of impatience: "Enough! Enough! Something else!"

Alarmed by such a welcome, the actress looked at the orchestra leader, making him a sign to interrupt the music. Suddenly, a tremor of rage shook her. Resolutely, she advanced to the edge of the stage and addressed the whistlers with a gesture of bravado.

"Load of imbeciles!" she cried.

A noisy clamor responded to that insult; the entire audience was on its feet.

"Apologies! We want apologies!"

"Bah! Apologies!"

Slowly, Clorinde had quit the stage, shrugging her shoulders and sniggering. The curtain had immediately come down, and the musicians had already quit their lecterns. The entr'acte had commenced, but the racket continued, furiously.

Saint-Réal appeared very content, and was rubbing his hands.

"Bravo! Well sung, nightingales . . . ! She's ours . . . ! Let's run now, to console the poor thing."

"I'm going to go to her dressing-room," I replied. "I need to speak to her without delay."

"You've reflected, then, Surville? I forgive you. But have you really understood? What do you think of my serenade?"

"What! It's you . . . you, who paid those whistlers!"

"Me alone, and that's enough."

"Good God, why that cabal?"

"O holy innocence! After such a scandal, the Alhambra will let the star go; we'll collect her on the wing."

XII

The star's dressing room was an elegant boudoir populated with rare trinkets and perfumed by heady odors. In his munificence, the gallant Zrelinsky had done things nobly. The walls of the sparkling candy-box, lined with mauve satin, and the Venetian chandelier with opaline fleurettes, reflected its azure light. There were mirrors everywhere, of all shapes and sizes; the beautiful Clorinde was able to study her slightest poses and prepare the most expert plastic effects. On the dressing-table adorned with lace, two superb bouquets of crimson roses expanded in Japanese vases, and, suspended by poppy-red ribbons, twenty photographs were pinned to the drapes, representing the Marquise in her various costumes, from the famous nacarat dress to a short skirt, the supreme attempt of her inventive genius.

Escorted by Saint-Réal, I went in. Collapsed on a divan, Clorinde was agitating like an epileptic and moaning to cleave the soul: "Whistled! Me, whistled!" she sighed.

A rich vocabulary of fishwife language accompanied that lamentation, but the flood remained grammatical, in conformity with syntax, and even dotted with scholarly terms: "Vile blackbirds," said the desolate woman, but she added: "Dense Béotians! Islets of Messina!" Assuredly, the lady must have practiced for a long time with a devotee of our classic authors.

On his knees before her mistress, a dresser was making her respire salts, while Monsieur Serafino, the well-curled tenor, was lavishing his consolations upon her amorously. Why, then, was that amiable Italian reeking of cassoulet, and pronouncing his tendernesses in the purest accent of Saint-Gaudens? Also next to her, Monsieur Léoné was agitating tearfully.

"Come on, cousin . . . a good gesture. It's necessary to make apologies."

"No and no. I maintain the word 'imbeciles.'"

"But they'll break everything, tear everything to pieces! And the director is absent!"

At every minute good comrades were arriving, with heartbroken expressions, but smiling at the corners of their lips.

"It's an indignity, my dear . . . !"

"Never have you shown such verve . . ."

"There was a cabal . . ."

"In your place, I'd rather cancel . . ."

A young and sprightly monsieur was also agitating in the dressing-room, with familiar gestures and protective words, going from one young actress to another and pinching their chins.

"The advocate of those ladies, Maître Onsyme Samuel," murmured the ever-informed Saint-Réal.

But the one that I had remarked immediately was Prince Zrelinsky. Lounging in an armchair, with his hat on his head and a cigar in his mouth, he was observing impassively and silently. That apparent indifference seemed to exacerbate the dolors of the starlet. She rebuked the insensible individual continually in ungracious terms.

"Well? You're not saying anything? God, my God, what a man! When you've finished infecting my dressing-room! Smoking is prohibited!"

A vain appeal to the regulations; the cigar did not quit the princely lips. Exasperated by that arrogant silence, she attempted a *coup de théatre*. "Dishonored!" she exclaimed. "My artistic life is ruined! I want to die!"

At those words the Havana left the protective lips momentarily.

"Cruvelli, Penco and Alboni herself heard whistles, and yet they continued to live."

"Oh, if you're going to recite us the memories of your youth, let's arm ourselves with patience; we're about to go back to the Directoire."

The admirer of the ladies of olden times did not protest against the impertinence, but a contraction of anger emphasized the creases of his face. He was a tall old man, elegant and haughty in manner. Although bald and furrowed by wrinkles, he carried his age with a swagger; his figure was still svelte and broad-shouldered; powerful biceps testified to the habitual usage of violent exercise. His Slavic face had character. Long white moustaches fell to either side of his mouth, and gave the old man the classic physiognomy of a Polish magnate. He would have been superb in national costume, ornamented with a red cloak, shod in scarlet boots and coiffed in a chapka, but alas, trousers, the frock-coat and a hideous cylinder replaced everything that was picturesque. At least he wore them with the fashionable elegance of an English gentleman. His advancing lip and charm were viciously sensual; his narrow pinched nostrils denounced a dryness of heart. A libertine, without a doubt, but a libertine in the grand manner.

Saint-Réal, meanwhile, had approached him and, inclining very humbly said: "I have a rendezvous with Your Highness, I believe."

For his only response, the "Highness" put his thumb to his hat; but Clorinde had perceived us and had immediately stood up.

"Let's go, all of you," she said to the crowd of her comrades, "I have to talk to these Messieurs. Samuel, stay, and you too, little Serafino."

"Monseigneur," the apostle of Great Art commenced, as soon as the door was closed, "Madame de Villereuse has just discovered, alas, how close the Tarpeian Rock is to the Capitol. She . . ."

"Pardon me," the prince interrupted. "Remind me of your name . . . Saint-Réal, I believe . . . well, Monsieur Saint-Réal, I don't appreciate fine speeches. I know only too well what they cost. Diets and their orators have caused the ruination of my homeland."

"Samuel," said Clorinde then, alarmed by that poor start, "explain the affair more simply. The prince doesn't seem to understand, although I've told him about it three times."

The sprightly advocate approached the Galician, and sat beside him.

"This is it," he said. "It's a matter of an interesting and lucrative enterprise, a placement. After this evening's abominable adventure, Madame Clorinde cannot, must not remain any longer at the Alhambra. Now, an impresario of renown, the artiste Saint-Réal . . ."

"And Monsieur Serafino is also in the band?" the prince interrogated, dryly. Caressing his moustache, he stared at the Romeo of Saint-Gaudens, to whom the imprudent Villereuse had just addressed a wink.

"Yes, certainly," affirmed the starlet. "A fine talent! Serafino is family."

Gallantly, this time, Prince Zrelinsky inclined before her. "I knew, Madame, that you were the fortunate mother of an eighteen-year-old daughter, but I did not know that you had other children."

"Serafino isn't my son," replied Clorinde, quivering with fury. "He's a comrade, a . . ."

"Good, good! One might have been mistaken . . . in that case, dear Madame, I have to talk to you seriously . . . very seriously. I'll expect you at my home; would you care to come without delay."

He got up, and then addressed us: "As for you, Messieurs no need to persist. Your enterprise is just a filibuster; seek elsewhere for your dupes."

Without lifting his hat, he gratified us with a little gesture of disdain, lit another cigar, went to the door and left.

"What insolence!" exclaimed Clorinde, trembling with rage. "And people think that I'm fortunate."

"Alas," sighed Maître Samuel, "thus sang the Favorite. But calm down. Thanks to me, the other affair is taking a good turn. It's ready; we'll finish it the day after tomorrow. I still need the bailiff's statement."

"Crochard has promised me to be diligent . . . and then, we have a witness, isn't that true, Monsieur Surville?"

Aah! I had been recognized. What did they want of me?

"But for the moment," Clorinde went on, "I'm at the present hour. I'm afraid . . . oh, very frightened. My Zrelinsky must be meditating some bad turn."

"What do you fear?" asked the advocate.

"Everything, with such a rogue. Monseigneur needs ingénues now. Arnolphe wants an Agnès, Don Ruy a Doña Sol; he'll marry, if necessary, stupid old man! Fortunately, I know his vices, and I have my plan."

"What plan, without being indiscreet?"

"Curious! Mariette, my wrap. My carriage is down below; I'm running to join the personage."

Enveloping herself in a long ermine mantle, Clorinde headed for the door of the dressing-room. Resolutely, I barred her way. She had addressed me; I intended to interrogate her in my turn.

"Just a word, Madame!"

"No, I don't have time. By the way, Monsieur Surville, I desire to play in *Le Nazaréen*."

"Very honored. We'll talk about it."

"Agreed. I want it."

"What a peremptory order! Well, one question."

"Quickly, quickly, please! I have to go!"

"The sonnet, the innocent cause of such a fine racket; is it an unpublished work?"

"Absolutely unpublished, and addressed to me. It's my property."

"You make noble usage of the gifts addressed to you. Who is its author?"

"What does it matter to you?"

"It matters a great deal. His name, and you'll play in *Le Nazaréen*."

"You demand it? So be it!" Then, in a slow voice, emphasizing the orders and stressing the syllables: "The Marquis de Montmesnil . . . and he's my husband."[1]

---

1 An assiduous historian, Thierry must have known that the Breton surname

❋

The next morning I went to the advertisement office of *Le Figaro*. I took a note to be inserted without delay in the next day's edition:

The person who came the day before yesterday to the house of M. S***, Rue Chanoinesse, is urgently begged to be, today, 5 November, at the rendezvous indicated by her.

XIII

At the extremity of the Luxembourg gardens, in the heart of the Latin quarter, is a solitary path where lovers of great silence can meditate at their ease. It is the shady and too short avenue that extends toward the railings of the Observatoire. Discreet and taciturn, although surrounded by movement and noise, it makes one think of one of those promenades that extend from the gates of cities in the Orléanais region. One does not see there, it is true, boule players or citizens drinking cheap wine directly from the bottle, and yet I believe that I am breathing there a little of my natal air, and recovering the vast peace of our Blésois villages. In the days of heat-waves, a few children play there, and students might work or flirt, but during the autumnal mists and the frosts of winter that somnolent corner of busy Paris is rarely visited even by idlers. It had always charmed me; it attracts me today because the modest pathway has become for me a dolorous cemetery populated by tender memories and painful remorse.

It was there that Mademoiselle de Montmesnil—I could name her now—had arranged our rendezvous. It was raining. All morning the November fogs had extended all the melancholy of

---

Montmesnil, more commonly employed by a Canadian branch of the family, was a variant of Montmeny, and his use of it presumably connects with the early citation of the motto of the Montmorency family.

their grayness over the city; the muddy avenue was deserted and I waited nervously, marching agitatedly beneath the dripping branches.

What was happening within me? I felt that I was incapable of analyzing myself, inapt to comprehend myself. Why that sudden passion for a woman barely glimpsed? What was the irresistible force drawing me toward her: a violent and sensual constraint of my will, a sort of magnetic attraction? Amour? Yes, certainly, everything in Monique de Montmesnil had fascinated me: the beauty of her face, the elegance of her manner, the distinction of her intelligence, the qualities of her heart, and her admirable devotion to duty. But amour, veritable amour aureoles the beloved creature with the ideal and surrounds her with a pious respect. Personally, I only experienced vulgar desires and coarse appetites. "Would you marry the daughter of the Marquise?" I had asked myself that very morning; a mocking snigger and a shrug of the shoulders had been my only response. The libertinage of my life, the custom of facile abandonments had stifled all delicacy in me. Accustomed to adventures, I believed it to be an adventure. This one was perhaps more unexpected, more romantic, more intoxicating than the others, but that was all. Oh, if I could grasp that pale and unhealthy face, caress with full hands the blonde undulation of that hair, place my lips on that forehead and its rosy birthmark!

That unhealthy ardor was combined, moreover, with the strangest of sentiments: a sort of fury, of philosophical jealousy. I divined in that young woman a life of struggle and suffering, an incessant daily martyrdom: they wanted to constrain her to enter a convent. Some of the words overheard at Port-Royal came back to memory. "She will soon depart and receive the veil," the seeker of relics had signified. "I want it!" You, Monique—you, a nun by constraint or surprise? I revolted against the idea. No silent cloisters and monastery vaults; she was made for human amours: you shall not have her!

Midday! Swiftly, I crossed the road; I had just perceived Monique hastening to our rendezvous.

She was still costumed in her graceful uniform, but soiled with mud and soaked by rain. Too poor, no doubt, to offer herself the luxury of a carriage, the young woman had made the long journey on foot. I ran to meet her.

"You've had pity on me," she said to me, extending her hand to me. "Thank you, oh thank you, Monsieur."

Ardently I seized the black-gloved fingers and squeezed them in a passionate grip. "Mademoiselle de Montmesnil, I was impatient to see you again!"

By virtue of an indiscreet malice I had decided, as soon as I spoke, to salute her with her name. I immediately regretted that impropriety. A blush of confusion reddened the pale face; Némo's daughter pulled her hand away violently.

"What, you know!" she stammered. "You . . ."

"Yes, I know. Monsieur your father is the Marquis de Montmesnil."

"Who told you? Speak, speak! How did you discover our secret?"

"Very simply, Mademoiselle. The day before yesterday, at the Alhamnra."

"At the Alhambra?" she said, terrified.

"Madame de Villereuse declaimed before the public the sonnet that you had recited to me. Very surprised, I had myself introduced to . . . that artiste, and she is the one who revealed to me what I know."

I deliberately omitted the detail of the burlesque comedy that Clorinde had given us. Very pale, the young woman was silent, but her eyes were examining me anxiously.

"It's ignoble," she murmured, finally, "to sell to the crowd the most intimate secrets of her heart. Infamous woman!"

Infamous woman? That was her mother.

"Yes," she went on, "you know my dolorous secret. The daughter of a prostitute and a judiciary convict—such is my lot down here! And it's to make me party to your unfortunate encounter that you've given me such an urgent rendezvous?"

"What bitterness in your words! No, but I have to warn you about a menacing danger. Mademoiselle de Montmesnil, they would like to constrain you to take the veil."

I told her then about the conversation I had overheard at Port-Royal. She listened impassively; the dementia of the seekers of relics did not seem to astonish her.

"I don't fear them," she said. "For a year my aunt has been persecuting me, but I'm resisting her. No, I won't be a nun . . . never, never!"

"What if you're abducted?"

"Abducted? I'll flee their convent. You don't suspect all the energy of my will. In any case, you understand now the ardor I'm deploying in order to reconquer my father; weak as he is, he would protect me. Have you read the manuscript?"

"With passionate interest. The poor fellow! How I excuse him."

"He was in love."

A convulsive shudder agitated her frail person; the patch on her forehead stood out, very red.

"And the other fragments?" she said. "What do you think of them?"

"I admired them greatly. I am at your orders; dispose of me."

Going back up the avenue, we took a few steps in silence.

"One question," I said, stopping. "Is it necessary to speak to Némo about my evening at the Alhambra?"

"No, no! Don't do that! Until the last few days, my father believed that Esther Nessim was dead. The poor man has been maladroitly disabused, but he still doesn't know about the extravagances of that woman. Out of modesty and respect, I never mention her to him; don't kill him today with the shame."

"We'll only talk about *Le Nazaréen*, then."

"A purely literary conversation, you promise me? I had to confess my escapade, my audacious approach to you. Oh, I was scolded, but so mildly! And I feel happy! When I told Némo about the resounding success his play obtained . . . pardon me, his and yours . . . I saw a gleam of pride shining in his eyes. The most saintly kind of pride, that of the creative artist for his creation, suddenly revived his heart. And then, the announcement of your visit seemed to cause him a sensible pleasure. Poor father! A distraction in his solitude! Come, then, help me to break the dungeon, the moral *in pace* that sequesters him! Again, I implore you! Oh, Monsieur, Monsieur, acquit your debt thus, and merit all my blessings forever."

I looked at her, shivering. She was truly beautiful, with her long lashes, in which tears pearled, and the fugitive incarnadine that tinted her cheeks.

"How I shall love your father," I said to her, taking her hand again, "since, Mademoiselle, I love you."

She threw herself backwards, looking at me fearfully. Her pale face had become very hard; her lip curled scornfully.

"You love me?" she said, bitterly. "By what right, Monsieur, do you mock me so cruelly?"

"Me, mock you? I love you."

"Enough, I beg you. I am not one of those one marries, much less one of those one debauches!"

XIV

The mist that had enveloped Paris since dawn had become a streaming rain; we were soaked to the skin by it.

"Let's take a carriage," I said to Mademoiselle de Montmesnil.

But she made a kind of fearful gesture. "What's the point, Monsieur. The route to travel isn't long. Let's walk."

Evidently, my overly gallant manners had frightened her.

"So be it, Mademoiselle. Let's risk the cold shower. Where are you taking me?"

"Not far from your dear Cité; to the Île Saint-Louis."

"On foot? In this deluge? Divine bounty!"

"Divine bounty!" she said, with a harrowing laugh. "That's an attribute of God, alas, that I've scarcely known."

In order to shelter her better under my umbrella, I had offered her my arm; we were now descending the Boulevard de Port-Royal. Sometimes, I risked a glance at my companion, and as her gaze met mine, I saw her blush. Sometimes, with a feeble pressure, I dared to squeeze her elbow; I felt her shudder then, but she immediately withdrew from the excessively familiar embrace.

Walking in that fashion, we had reached the Rue Monge and the somber bulk of Saint-Médard loomed up in the mist.

"Monsieur Surville," she said suddenly, "let's stop in that church."

"In that church? Why?"

"In order to understand the existence of my father and his odious martyrdom, it's first necessary to know the history of my family."

"I obey; let's go into Saint-Médard. The old sanctuary of your Jansenists?"

"Yes, entirely filled with the glories of Deacon Pâris. There, also, one of my ancestors sleeps, the blessed Claudine-Armande."

Like a country church, the miserable parish church of that poor quarter only shows its disparate ugliness in half-light. Never before had I visited that famous oratory of the Convulsionnaires; the inelegance of the edifice, the asymmetry of its structure, shocked me immediately. In the nave, pseudo-Gothic pillars in the bastard style of the sixteenth century; in the choir, heavy columns with Doric capitals dating from the reign of Louis XIV, and in the prolongation of the apse a neo-Grecian rotunda like some Pompeiian bath, or like the dreary milking shed of Rambouillet. On the walls, no work of art, not even any architectural curiosity. I stopped, nevertheless, before a stone frame, a modern sculpture, but symbolic and suggestive of the poor parish: the infant Jesus in his stable, shivering under the winter wind. *Behold the God of the poor,* said a Latin inscription. *Jesus on his bed of straw: run to him.* But today the appeal seemed to be inviting the poor, the starvelings of the Saint-Marcel quarter, in vain; the church was almost deserted; only the doorkeeper and a priest in a surplice were walking, conversing in low voices.

Preceded by Monique, I walked along the aisles. Level with the transept, a lateral door opened to the left, through which she went, in order to enter a corridor. We were now walking along a sinuous path strangled by high and oozing walls. Above that enclosure the branches of a few trees spread, branches twisted by old age and corroded by moss; an acrid odor was exhaled by that dampness.

"The charnel-house of Saint-Médard," my companion said, "the place that witnessed so many marvels. Let's try to penetrate it."

At the turning, however, the wall stopped and gave way to a house, doubtless the presbytery; no apparent door permitted access to the courtyard. Disappointed, Mademoiselle de Montmesnil went back to the nave. The two men were pursuing the course of their conversation there. She advanced toward them.

"Can one, Messieurs, visit the ancient cemetery?"

"What cemetery?" asked the doorkeeper. "I don't know."

At the same time he looked at the young woman and, re-marking the strangeness of her attire, exchanged a mocking glance with the priest.

"You don't know the tomb of Deacon Pâris!" Monique cried. "Without ever having seen it, I can take you there. It's situated behind the apse, against the exterior wall, a little to the right. Once, a slab of black marble . . ."

"And what do you want with your Deacon Pâris?" the priest interrupted sniggering.

He was a young abbé, freshly molded by the seminary; a youth of the church with a doll-like face and pretentiously curled hair. His manner and the persiflage of his tone displeased Mademoiselle de Montmesnil, who returned his insolence.

"What does it matter to you? Simple curiosity or pilgrimage. Have I asked you to convert me?"

With a gesture of compassion the abbé shrugged his shoulders. "You're a Jansenist, then? Well, dear Madame, one doesn't address prayers here to heresy and schism. We don't tolerate your sacrilegious jokes today."

And very impertinently, the impetuous ultramontanist went back into the sacristy.

Mademoiselle de Montmesnil was momentarily nonplussed. I observed her anxiously; was that woman really in full possession of her reason and lucidity?

Did she divine my thought? Yes, undoubtedly, for with a grim exaltation, she said: "You believe me to be mad, Monsieur? Mad . . . mad . . . perhaps. Who can escape the heredity of her family?"

A sinister confession! And in what a tone of rage it had been pronounced!

We went back through the church toward the exit; again the young woman stopped.

"Look," she said.

Her finger designated a funerary stone framed in the pavement of the floor; I approached. The stone, roughened—worn down, it seemed to me by kneeling—still allowed the sight of an inscription surmounted by armories.

"Can you read it, Monsieur?"

"I'll try."

And, leaning over the epitaph, I succeeded, not without difficulty, in deciphering it. At first sight it appeared to me to be written in the lapidary style customary in the eighteenth century, but certain words were bizarre and not in conformity with the ostentation of humility that our forefathers lavished on tombs. This is what I had read:

D.O.M.[1]

Here lies, in the assurance of eternal bliss, the very noble lady Claudine-Armande Pâris, when alive the spouse of Messier François Lesueur, Marquis de Montmesnil, counselor and president of inquests in the Court of the Parlement, born in Paris on the twenty-fourth day of May in the year of salvation 1708, and who died in the joy of her Lord on the fifth day of November 1739. God has her soul.

"Bravo!" Monique approved. "You have all the mastery of a professor at the École des Chartes.

"Who was that Marquise de Montmesnil?"

"A paternal ancestress, the Blessed Claudine-Armande, as she's called in my family. She entered into 'the joy of her Lord.' I want to believe that, because that person preordained to the bliss of the Elect has bequeathed nothing to her descendants but misfortune and opprobrium."

"Is your house of Montmesnil very ancient?" I asked, alarmed by that hateful intonation.

"Very ancient. Nobility of the robe worth as much as any nobility of the sword. One of my ancestors received in the fifteenth century the *garde des sceaux de France*, and under Henri III the land of Montmesnil was raised to the status of a marquisat.

She had raised her head, her eyes were shining, and her bosom swelled with pride.

"You have my father's manuscript," she went on. "You know now his error and his repentance, his fit of revolt followed by submission; but alas, you don't know all our miseries. The most atrocious of penances is being imposed on him today—the same kind of life that his ancestress, Madame Claudine-Armande, lived."

"Tell me what I don't know, but above all let's get out of here. We'll be better off outside, to talk at our ease."

---

1 *Deo optimo maximo* [To the Very Good and Very Great God] was an inscription frequently found on French tombstones.

"You're right. Since they've bolted the cemetery, our visit is pointless. This church, in any case, and its sepulchral stone, have nothing more to tell you."

The rainstorm had cleared the sky, and timid rays of sunlight were sliding through the prisms of the clouds. Adjacent to the nave, bordered by the Rue Monge, there was a pretty square; the downpour had chased away the strollers; we went to take refuge there.

XV

"So," said Monique, "the person whose tombstone you deciphered was named Claudine-Armande, Marquise de Montmesnil. A demoiselle of a very good family, but less illustrious than our house, she was the daughter of Monsieur Séverin Pâris, counselor of the Grand Chambre."

"A relative of the famous deacon?"

"His first cousin. She was, according to our family traditions, an elegant woman, rather coquettish and very prominent in society. Oh, it wasn't her who, at eighteen years of age, was decked out in my hideous costume, this nunnish outfit that I'm obliged to put on. A portrait shows her to us pretty: pale and blonde with large dark eyes . . ."

"Yours!"

"Spare me your jokes. I can easily imagine her in a frilly skirt, with a beauty spot at the corner of the mouth, powdered with a suspicion of frost, chatting and flirting with young counselors or genteel abbés, haunters of alcoves. At seventeen she married a man already mature, Marquis François de Monmesnil, the president of inquests, also a counselor of the Parlement. You know, Monsieur, that our nobility of the robe is only ordinarily allied with people of the robe. A brilliant marriage, assuredly; beauty in the wife, fortune in the husband, as well as antiquity of family and personal merit. In the Pâris family, however, certain devotees criticized the union. My ancestor Montmesnil was a learned man, an honest magistrate, but perverted by the spirit of the century, a great reader of English philosophers, scarcely a deist, a rationalist and a libertine . . ."

"A man of the Regency!" I interjected, finally able to get a word in.

"We're in the early days of the Fleury ministry," the learned young person rectified.[1]

"Very well! In the time of the likes of Grécourt and Piron. In those days, men and women of high society regaled themselves with atheism and obscenity."

"I know, Monsieur. Let's pass on. Yes, it was an epoch of shameful and brazen immorality, of ostentation in all insolent lust. So, materialism in her hearth, deportment among her best friends, my poor ancestress lost her head. She was, moreover, a flighty woman of rather weak intelligence. Did she commit faults of conduct? I don't think so. In spite of the difference in their ages, she loved her husband tenderly. In order to please him she affected the most provocative impiety and, pushed by her, Montmesnil, the deist rationalist, became a resolute atheist. He was weak of character, vain, and much too loving, like all the men of my family. Their house on the Île Saint-Louis was soon the rendezvous of all the strong minds, petty libertines and petty miscreants that the Regency had fashioned. Every week, on days of reception, they philosophized there around the table, mocked embroidered and sang the God enigma. 'The infamous Montmesnil suppers, a devil's sabbat,' groaned the devout. But, devil's sabbat or Platonic banquets, the cynical meetings were very popular. The irreligon of Madame Armande had earned her a fine renown; Voltaire mentions her eulogistically in his correspondence."

"And what did the saintly deacon think of the antics of his cousin?"

---

1 Cardinal Fleury (1653-1743) became Louis XV's chief minister in 1726; he was a notorious persecutor of Jansenists.

"No earthly rumor reached as far as him. Ignored by men, he always lived ignoring them. It was then the most ardent phase of the quarrel born of the bull *Unigenitus*, people of the efficacious Grace and people of the sufficient Grace, Jansenists and ultramontanists, were tearing one another apart ferociously. I must seem very pedantic to you, Monsieur; there are, alas, question which it is impossible for me to ignore. The Pope had declared 'false, heretical and blasphemous' the doctrine of Port-Royal; for eighteen years, Port-Royal itself had no longer existed, but the Jansenists still refused their submission. That stubborn resistance exasperated the Jesuits. Excited by them, Louis XV's minister, Cardinal Fleury, attempted to constrain the rebel convictions, and his persecution raged violently. Futile rigors: one cannot imprison the public conscience; a great pity for the martyrs of Grace gained the populace, and among the people pity is rapidly transformed into devotion.

"It was at that moment that Deacon Pâris died and was buried in the Saint-Médard charnel-house. Jansenist since childhood, he had exhaled toward his God a Jansenist soul; his last words were to proclaim his faith. A pious pamphlet that served as my catechism tells us how that man lived, passionate for suffering, that madman of the Cross, a voluntary expiator of the sins of the world; laboring his flesh with blows of the whip, clad in sordid rags, sleeping on rubble in a hut open to all the winds, only eating crusts, the refuse of bakeries; distributing in alms the mediocre salary of his manual labor; disdainful—or rather ignorant—of all knowledge and yet having something better than science, since he had love.

"But the world that the recluse had fled fearfully came to assail him in his coffin; alive, he had passed through life doing good; dead, he was made to do evil. The pursued Jansenists needed miracles, and popular miracles; poor Pâris furnished them . . .

"Is it necessary, Monsieur, for me to remind you of the extravagant marvels, the contagion of frenzy that was produced over the grave of that other Lazarus? The entire city ran to it, above all the crowd of the weak, paupers without assistance, moribunds without hope. The deacon was invoked, and suddenly the blind recovered sight, the lame threw away their crutches, the paralyzed began to gambol. The populace lavished hosannas upon him. Jansenism had found its patron saint of poverty . . .

"The Jesuits were stupefied, and on their insistence the cardinal minister decided to close the cemetery; but the Parlement caught wind of the plan; it did not like the Jesuits and decided to protest."

"The remonstrations! The famous remonstrations that the king received in a bed of justice . . ."

"One morning, after the audience, Monsieur le Premier had my ancestor summoned, the president of the enquiries. 'The new miracles are being ardently discussed,' he said to him. 'Investigate the affair, but discreetly.' My ancestor's well-known skepticism had merited him that choice. Certainly, he could not be accused of Jansenism!

'At dinner, the president announced the news to his wife. 'My God, dear Madame, the deacon your cousin still does things his own way. Parlement has delegated me to open an enquiry; I'll be going to Saint-Médard shortly.'

"'I want to be in the party,' replied Madame Claudine-Armande. 'I need some amusement.'

"They climbed into a carriage and arrived at the Saint-Médard charnel-house. A print that you can see represents my ancestor traversing the crowd. Laced up in his ornate coat, cane in hand and his hat under his arm, he has a grandiose air beneath his three-tassel wig. My ancestress accompanies him, perched on high-heeled brodequins, pompous in her flower-patterned dress. Around them are the rabble at prayer: poor people sitting on the cemetery wall telling their rosaries; Jansenist priests with emaciated faces singing litanies; and, crawling on the ground, atrocious to see, browsing grass and eating soil, the demented throng of the convulsed.

"The president had a passage opened. 'See,' he said to his wife, 'the deadly effects of fanaticism! The enlightenment of our philosophy ought to . . .'

"He could not finish. Madame de Montmesnil had uttered a cry of pain; she had fallen heavily to her knees. Her dilated eyes were staring fearfully; an expression of horror contracted her features; a sweat of effort was trickling down her cheeks. Her husband tried to pick her up, but in vain. Her body was inert, icy, as rigid as a cadaver; she was breathing, however. Someone ran to fetch a physician; he confessed that he did not understand it. And while the investigator lamented, the crowd proclaimed the miracle. 'The efficacious Grace! The overwhelming Grace! An ecstasy! Alleluia!'

"It was necessary to carry the sick woman away in her posture of prayer, still kneeling. She remained thus for twenty-four hours, in spite of remedies. Finally, Madame de Montmesnil recovered consciousness, and her first words were to request a confessor, but a Jansenist—no one but a Jansenist. Claudine-Armande had gone mad, the most incurable kind of madness: mystical dementia. She recounted that as she approached the tomb, mocking, her cousin the deacon had snatched her soul away, and in order to purify it, had plunged it into the flames of purgatory; then, that baptism of fire having been accomplished, the blessed Pâris had deposited his relative on Calvary . . .

"The recipient of the miracle was pregnant. Two months later she gave birth to a son, and the child she brought into the world bore a stigma on the forehead: the bleeding wounds of the crown of thorns."[1]

---

1 Author's note: "See the curious volume of the counselor of the Parlement Carré de Montgeron and the story of his sudden conversion by physical prémotion before the tomb of Deacon Pâris: *Verité des miracles opérées par l'intercession du diacre Pâris*, 1737." The reference is to Louis Basile Carré de Montgeron (1686-1754), the most outspoken defender of the Convulsionnaires; when he tried to present a copy of the first volume of the cited work to Louis XV, Fleury had him arrested, and after a brief spell in the Bastille he was exiled; he completed the second and third volumes

"A simple case of pathology," I interjected. "But what a practical joker, your deacon saint! What did the president do then? Did he continue his investigation?"

"The inquest was conclusive; it only remained to be converted, and he was converted. They dismissed their domestics, sold their silverware and distributed the product to the poor and to the prisoners. Transforming the reception rooms of her house into a hospital, Madame de Montmesnil confined herself to a mansard, a filthy attic under the eaves. There, clad in a hair shirt, fasting and sleeping on the floorboards, she died twelve years later. In my family we call her the 'Blessed' and implore her in our distress. She also operates petty miracles; however, I can offer no guarantees.

"Her husband, in any case, had preceded her to the tomb. By virtue of conjugal amour, the atheist philosopher had become a fervent Christian, a militant Jansenist. One day, in full Parlement, he dared to speak sharply to the king. Louis XV was holding a bed of justice and the scandal was enormous. Montmesnil reproached him for his mistresses, the depravity of his court and his persecutions of the holy. He was imprisoned in the Bastille the same evening. He died there."

"And what became of the stigmatized child?"

"Oh, let's not talk about him. He was a sorry individual, fanatical and debauched, a monstrous mixture of superstitions and vices. At his baptism he had received the name of Dieudonné, a name the heads of my family have borne since then, but the Devil alone directed his conduct. His entire life was nothing but a lamentable absurdity. By day he gambled and ran after prostitutes, in the evening he slipped into clandestine assemblies in which Jansenist enthusiasts gave one another 'help.' Sad illuminates, Monsieur, our last champions of Efficacious Grace: their grotesque extravagances would have frightened Pascal.

---

of the *Verité*, published in 1741 and 1747, in prison in Valence. The word "prémotion," which I have left untranslated, is unusual and might have been coined by Thierry, who often improvised new words.

"Dieudonné de Montmesnil frequented those secret meetings. There, in spite of the police, people delivered themselves to the most infamous practices. To hasten the coming of the precursor Élie, children and women were beaten and tortured, nuns were crucified. 'We want to repair the infamies of the world,' those fanatics claimed. 'God is pleased by bloody sacrifices.' And my credulous ancestor aided them to shed blood. He martyrized himself in order to redeem his sins, but, the day after his tortures, he resumed his sins more enthusiastically. Nevertheless, late in life he married, in order to wed a visionary of his own species . . . and it is him, Monsieur, who transmitted his mother's insanity to us, him who bequeathed us the defect of his degeneracy."

Monique de Montmesnil had curbed her head dejectedly. She was beautiful thus—weak and desperate. I sensed by desires stimulated further.

"What absurd words are you daring to pronounce, Mademoiselle? The charm of your face, the brilliance of your intelligence, the . . ."

"What does it matter, Monsieur? All of that can be annihilated in an instant. The fatal dementia, the heredity of all my family, terrifies me. I know it, I sense it lying in wait, menacing. It has already seized my aunt; my father is struggling in its grip. So I shall never marry; it's necessary that our wretched breed disappear. Yes, I ought to enter a convent, but I don't have the faith. In truth, can I believe in a God who, for the salary of a conversion, gratifies an entire family with the most atrocious madness?"

And clenching her fist, in a mute blasphemy, she extended her arm toward the church of Saint-Médard.

"In addition," she went on, "for a surplus of good fortune, I have my personal ignominy: my birth."

Her birth! Another imprecation against her mother! For several seconds, she was absorbed, silently, in anguished thought. Finally, she got to her feet.

"Now you know the history of my family. Come; nothing of what you are going to see can astonish you any longer."

XVI

It was a house in one of the streets of the Île Saint-Louis, superb in its structure but dilapidated, almost falling into ruins. It was still standing, however, and still magnificent among the old magnificence of the somnolent quarter. The fronton of its façade, the mascarons surmounting its windows, the balconies with balusters, the timid sketches of festoons and the absence of shell-work indicated the date of its construction sufficiently: the majestic houses built in the final days of the reign of Louis XIV. But its appearance of decrepitude, its mossy and disjoined stones and its crumbling moldings also declared the present poverty of the dwelling or the carelessness of its inhabitants.

"The Hôtel de Montmesnil; salute, Monsieur!" my companion announced. "It was bought by our ancestor the president shortly after his marriage. It's here that his little philosophical suppers took place, here that the existence of God was disputed between the romanée and the champagne. Today you see a temple of sanctification. Look, nevertheless, at those fauns, those heads of grimacing sylvans. Do they not have the air of devils jeering at their new employment as archangels?"

"They do, in fact, seem ill at ease, scenting the font . . . the headquarters of your Jansenists, I suppose?"

"Yes and no. We are the lost children, almost the heresiarchs of the Doctrine. The archbishop of Utrecht broke off all connection with our schism a long time ago; he thinks us too dangerous. But we have our prelate, Monsieur de Gorcum."

"Why do you employ the word schism?"

"It explains our situation in regard to Jansenist orthodoxy. My aunt is a reformer; she wanted to found her little Brotherhood, the expiators of the Stainless Lamb, and also to revive the sect of the Vaillantists."

"Pardon me, but I don't really understand; what is that phenomenon, a Vaillantist?"

"An Elysian, if you prefer. Curé Vaillant was another maker of marvels in the last century, a kind of Saint Pâris, but of discreet miracles. A marvelous prophet, although deprived of humility, he proclaimed himself a forerunner of the precursor Élie. He was imprisoned, stupidly; Charenton ought to have been his Bastille. It was him, the rival of another visionary, Frère Augustin—a reincarnation of the Bishop of Hippo, that one!—who regulated the method of 'helpful beaters.' They were the evangelists of the pretty devotees who were whipped, twisted with pincers and crucified in the secret assemblies. Better than that: they pushed impudence as far as wanting to be adored. A worthy heir of my ancestor Dieudonné, my aunt Angélique-Marie has always admired that theology of the rod. She has unified the two sects and amalgamated their deliria. From Frère Augustin she has taken the Stainless Lamb, from Vaillant . . ."[1]

"The efficacious cudgel . . . One question, please: What do the police say to this?"

"The police? They have always let us alone. Mad as my aunt is, she has found disciples for her madness. Her propaganda has recruited followers in Paris, and even in the provinces. The Elysians were once fairly numerous; they have not disappeared entirely. To tell the truth, the leaders of Jansenism reprove us, but Madame Angélique does not care about their remonstrations. She has the soul of a sectarian, inflexible in her principles, ferocious in her convictions. In addition, she has beside her an illuminate even more fanatical, Monsieur Silvat . . ."

"Oh, that one I know: a charlatan."

---

1 "Frère Augustin" was a convulsionnaire leader who split from Vaillant's sect, as the story says. His baptismal surname appears to have been Cos. An elaborate account of his activities can be found in *Lettres théologiques sur les convulsionnaires* (1739) by Louis-Bernard La Taste, and a briefer and more hostile one in *Le Naturalisme des convulsions dans les maladies de l'épidemie* (1733) by Philippe Hecquet. Thierry had surely read both.

"No, a convinced believer. Having suffered a great deal, he is determined to make suffering a dogma and a voluptuousness."

"Perfect: an esthete! Why does he not reserve his pleasures for himself?"

The door of the house was closed. Mademoiselle de Montmensnil raised the knocker and let it fall three times.

"One stroke for Jansenius," she said, sarcastically, "one for Saint Pâris, and *bang!* for the blessed Claudine-Armande! Prayer in action, as in Tibet; it's our pious custom."

A youth with the casual manner of Master Josias, my domestic, opened one of the battens slightly.

"*Ave*, my sister," he said. "You've been absent for a long time again, and earned me a stern scolding. I sinned in letting you go out the other evening and the guard of the door has been taken away from me. Oh, Sister Monique running the streets at the risk of her soul! What does this Madianite want with us?"[1]

"One of our friends. He has a rendezvous with my father."

With a suspicious eye, the youth inspected my attire.

"No! The livery of society! This man isn't one of ours . . . ! I'll go inform Mère Angélique."

He had extended his hand toward a bell-cord hanging next to his lodge, but he changed his mind. "I daren't disturb her; she's in full mortification."

"Well, let her mortify herself. We have no need of her presence. Come, Monsieur."

The scrupulous concierge closed his huge door again, then followed us with his gaze, anxiously.

"What espionage!" claimed Monique. "One can no longer approach my father without my aunt immediately coming running. And what amenity! What do you think of her fashion of addressing everyone as *tu*?"

"I'm very edified by it."

---

1 I have left "Madianite" as it is in the original, although it is more usually rendered in English as Midianite. It refers to the descendants of one of the sons of Abraham, some of whose womenfolk annoyed Moses in *Numbers* 31.

"A usage borrowed from the visionaries of Saint-Médard. All brothers and sisters before the Eternal! Everyone is *tu* in Paradise, they say."

A stone staircase with sculpted banisters rose up under the vault, but the steps were dusty, and age-old mildew was spread in layers over the walls. The broom and the duster had assuredly been less frequently employed than the "helpful rod" in the house of the "Stainless Lamb." On the first floor landing a door was open, garlanded with foliage of painted paper: a vulgar decoration, reminiscent of the crèche or the needlework-room on feast days.

"Go in here," Monique said to me. "I'll go inform my father, and he'll see you soon."

The room into which I entered had once formed a vast and sumptuous reception gallery. The woodwork, once gilded, alternated there with mirrors and oval frames were carved in relief above the panels, but an infamous distemper now plastered the elegant moldings, the mirrors had disappeared under gray paper, and the frames gaped, deprived of their Amours. No chairs or armchairs; the only furniture was a few benches; the libertine drawing room had been converted into an austere chapel.

At the back of the gallery stood an altar in the rococo style, on which was embossed the emblem of the Stainless Lamb. On the altar was a tabernacle between two candles, and a crucifix, a curious and veritable work of art. Its Christ, carved in a single block of ivory, did not extend his loving arms over Jerusalem, the gentiles and the world; he raised their contortion directly toward the heavens. All Jansenist desperation appeared in that sinister and disconcerting symbol. The Redeemer showed thus that the dew of the divine blood had only flowed for the rare elect. His convulsed face was atrocious to behold, not with suffering and agony, but with anger and menace. There was no forgiveness, or even pity in his gaze; that vanquisher of Sin must hate the sinner.

Along the walls various paintings had been suspended: first, a Deacon Pâris in a ragged soutane, and, placed before that image, the founder of the Élianite sect, Curé Vaillant. A caption bore his name. That missionary of the Precursor, with the banal face of a country bumpkin, was exhibited on the canvas in the costume of a High Priest of Israel, with the cidaris, the ephod and the tablets of the Law for a rabat: a grotesque and modern daub. The most amusing of the paintings, however, was a reduction of Michelangelo's Vatican fresco, a sort of parody, sincere and convinced. Standing in the midst of clouds, one saw the Son of Man hurling into the abyss those accursed by his Father. They were falling in clusters, but those damned souls did not have naked torsos; they wore Jesuit robes, or Sulpician soutanes. Kneeling to the right of their Avenger, the Jansenist elect were contemplating blissfully the work, so long anticipated, of holy revenge.

Outside, I perceived the branches of a few trees; the interior façade of the house overlooked a garden. I approached an open casement, and a curious spectacle was offered to my gaze. On the grass strewn with leaves, sticky and drenched by rain, an old nun clad in white was marching back and forth, she was dragging herself with difficulty, weighed down by a cross that was trailing along the ground. Marching beside her was a sort of slattern in a nun's wimple, holding her arm; the old woman was blind. She stumbled and fell continually; then her companion whipped her with strokes of a thong, helping her thereafter to lift her cross again—and the mortified woman continued her Calvary . . .

I had immediately recognized the woman of Port-Royal, Mère Angélique-Marie des Cinq Plaies, the expiatrice of the sins of France, Monique's aunt.

Monique! How sweetly that name sang at present in the depths of my soul! Monique! Since her lamentable confidence, a tumult of new sensations was agitating within me, and had turned me upside-down. My brutal desires were combined with a nobler emotion . . . Monique, dear Monique, with the dolorous smile attracting kisses; Monique, whose tears my lips longed to dry up!

Was that compassion for the abandoned, the charm of a young women so distinguished in intelligence and so valiant of heart? Yes, I felt that I loved her . . . that I loved her passionately.

I was at that point in my dithyramb when a lateral door opened and a long, thin body slid into the chapel: Monsieur Silvat! Even more haggard, stiff and ragged than on the parvis of Nore-Dame, he was carrying a beggar's satchel over his shoulder.

"Monsieur Surville!" he cried, stupefied. "Who can have introduced you here?"

"Mademoiselle de Montmesnil."

"You know her, then?"

"I have the honor of knowing her; I have even come—not to displease you, to render a visit to her father, Némo."

The face of the sectarian expressed an intense apprehension.

"And it's her . . . her who brought you to the penitent's cell? I find that very daring."

"Why daring?"

"She is interrupting the meditation of a purifying solitude, compromising the salvation of that soul, and impudently violating the rule of our discipline. Where did you encounter her?"

"What does it matter to you? I had the pleasure of talking to Mademoiselle de Montmesnil, and, seduced by her rare qualities, the nobility of her soul, the distinction of . . ."

"No! By concupiscence!" he said, harshly. The term was brutal; it revolted me.

"Measure your language better, I beg you."

"Dare, then, to descend into yourself. We, vulgar savages, know nothing of your gallant hypocrisies. Mocked and jeered by society, we dare nevertheless to tell society the names of its sins. Yes, conscupiscence—or rather, the Devil's spur. I say the Devil, my poor Monsieur!" He uttered a long sigh, the sigh of a disappointed lover or a deceived husband. "Mistrust Woman! She is our perdition!"

I was about to respond harshly to that enemy of feminism when Mademoiselle de Montmensnil finally reappeared.

"My father is waiting for you," she said to me.

"And I shall accompany you," declared Monsieur Silvat, formally.

"Your presence is superfluous. My father desires to speak to Monsieur alone."

"No, my dear girl, that's impossible, Mère Angéqlique is at prayer, and I have the duty to replace her with regard to you."

"Odious tyranny! We are no longer in a humor to support it henceforth, as you will see!"

Preceded by Monique and followed by our watcher, I went up to the second floor, which served as the commons of the house. The domestics' rooms had been transformed into cells; placards indicated their new destination and placed them under pious patronage: Saint-Cyran, Arnauld, Singlin, Nicole, Saci, Pontchâteau, Quesnel, etc.—all the venerables of Jansenism. At each door Monsieur Silvat paused and slid his scrutinizing glance into the room; an adjutant in service could not have inspected his barracks better. Almost all the rooms were unoccupied, however; only three women coiffed as nuns were working there; evidently, the community of the Stainless Lamb recruited few adherents.

"Sister Euphémie," said Monsieur Silvat to one of them, "You are to prepare the apartment of honor tomorrow. Monsieur Gorcum will arrive in a few days."

"His Grandeur is paying us a visit? Alleluia!"

Having reached the last of the rooms, the scrupulous inspector wanted to pursue his inspection. Monique prevented him from doing so.

"Pardon me, my dear Monsieur; this is my home. One does not go in."

Without insisting, he inclined his head and passed on. Finally, we arrived at the end of the corridor. There stood a mason's ladder, which it was necessary to climb. It ended at a door. Mademoiselle de Montmesnil opened it and turned to me.

"The abode of the blessed Claudine-Armande, and the cell, the *in pace*, in which my father is detained."

"His remorse ought to be sufficient to sequester him there," replied Monsieur Silvat dryly.

"His remorse . . . and also your captation of our entire fortune. Come, Monsieur."

The door that she indicated to me, a narrow and low cat-hole, was partly blocked by a wooden beam and rubble; one could only get through by bending the spine. I therefore extended my head in order to squeeze into that hole worthy of a pig-sty, but I had to recoil in disgust. A nauseating odor had seized my throat, a noxious mixture of leather, rags and ordure.

"Is that you, Monsieur Surville?" exclaimed a voice. "Come in, please. I'm delighted by your visit."

XVII

In a fetid cupboard only a few feet long and broad a man was crouched on the floor. He was repairing shoes, and the fragments of their parings were making the hovel stink. And what a hovel! It was a verminous attic wedged under the roof. Daylight descended into it through a skylight, but the frame had been nailed shut and air only penetrated through gaping cracks between the tiles. In the summer months the cubby-hole must be a steam-bath, in December an ice-box, and a cloaca during rainstorms. A ragged mattress from which the reek of seaweed escaped served the recluse as a bed. The garments and linen that Monsieur de Montmesnil had doubtless laundered himself were drying on a rope. In a corner of the room a faience stove could still be seen, a brazier, a pitcher, and a crust of bread: the kitchen and larder of mortification. Not a single book, no furniture save for a stool—but a whip was suspended from the wall, with thongs tipped with lead.

The man who was crouching in that corruption appeared to me to be about sixty years of age. His cadaverous face was shaven like that of a cleric, and long curls of gray hair fell over his neck, and even over his shoulders. At intervals he coughed—a dry, convulsive, disquieting cough, and his brief respiration grated like the sound of a rasp. The head was still beautiful with intelligence and distinction. The gaze—of very dark eyes—shone, mobile and feverish; the vast forehead, slightly receding, indicated thought, but the excessively short chin would have denounced to the examination of a phrenologist the weakness of the will, a deplorable absence of character.

Hammering, plying an awl, and drawing thread coated with wax through the holes, that poet, that philosopher, was repairing an old shoe.

"Sit down," he said to me, indicating the stool. "My cell isn't magnificent, but the great Bossuet informs us: 'Fortunate is he who has been able to find his refuge.'"

"Fortunate! Are you truly fortunate, Father?" asked Monique, sadly.

Monsieur Silvat, meanwhile, had slid behind us, and approached the mender of footwear. "I've brought you your quotidian task, Brother, and here is our supper."

He dropped his satchel, and then took out a few battered boots, crusts of stale bread and two carrots. "Your task," he went on, "has been furnished to us by the shoemaker of the Rue des Deux-Ponts; various breaches to sew; it's urgent work. As for our supper, it's meager this evening. Yesterday's repairs were poorly done; they were refused. Where was your mind, then? Nevertheless, my slippers—oh, I take no pride from it—brought me forty centimes. I put four sous into the works of the community; the surplus of the money sufficed for our pittance. No treats today, of course; no fresh bread or salad . . ."

"You arrange them well, our treats," said Monsieur de Montmesnil, smiling. "Yesterday, my daughter seasoned your dandelions with a little oil; you, with horror, steeped them in water."

"In such an occurrence, the blessed Pâris did the same. He avoided the sin of gluttony."

"Absurd mortification! How can salad oil offend the Eternal?"

"And yet it offends him! Don't philosophize! God orders that always, always, we must master the beast. So I've asked our baker not to furnish us henceforth with any but prison bread—bread mixed with straw. The saintly deacon wanted no other. But that baker only prepares orgies for the flesh; we'll look elsewhere."

"How difficult it is to accomplish one's salvation," sniggered the penitent.

"Don't laugh! Fine words, bad character! I therefore picked up a few crusts, the refuse of the bakery; I've dipped them in water; with the two carrots they'll suffice for our feast. I authorize, however, the use of salt."

"*Sal sapientiae* . . . That of your wisdom is sufficient for me."

Without objecting to that further pleasantry, the master-cook approached the stove and commenced lighting it. Monique's father addressed a gesture of impatience to him.

"No, please, wait. You can cook later. I have to talk to Monsieur Surville."

"Converse, my brother, converse at your ease. How can my presence hinder you? Furthermore, the daylight is declining, the time will soon come to recite the evening office together; your conversation can't last for long."

"It will be prolonged for as long as is necessary," retorted Monsieur de Montmesnil.

The bearer of the satchel straightened up, scandalized. "Think hard, poor soul! You're about to disobey grievously!"

"Disobey whom?" asked Monique.

"The rule of reclusion imposed on him by our founding Mother."

"My aunt," riposted the young woman, "is not in command here. This house does not belong to her."

"How does it not belong to her?"

"My father's donations were annulled by my birth. Will it be necessary for me to address myself to the tribunals?"

"She's right," said the former magistrate, timidly. "The Code is formal, and . . ."

"I know a law more formal still, my brother: the Gospel. It orders putting one's wealth in common, without even the hope of taking it back."

"The *mutuum date?* My God, Monsieur Silvat, your commentary is bold.[1] We'll talk about that later. For the moment, leave me."

But the illuminate did not go.

"More spirit of revolt!" he growled. "In truth, Monsieur, I dare not understand what is happening within you. Three days ago, the demon entered your soul again. Your daughter, I declare, is your perdition. It's necessary to send her away."

"Separate me from everything I love? Try, then!" cried Monique.

"Calm down, my child," said Monsieur de Montmesnil. "If you don't have the vocation, your scruples will be respected. And you, Monsieur Silvat, a truce on indiscretions. Withdraw."

The order was peremptory, the voice irritated, the gesture imperative. Recoiling then, step by step, the apostle of communism headed for the exit. He was making violent efforts to refrain from anger, but his jaundiced and meager face was trembling with indignation.

"What, sin upon sin! Pride, indolence, rebellion: all mortal. Hell has entered into the cell of the Blessed. A sacrilege! Well, so be it, I shall leave you, in order not to aggravate your guilt. I shall retire. But I must and will inform Mère Angélique. The wretch, the wretch! He is returning to his vomit!"

Finally, his long spine plunged into the cat-hole and disappeared.

---

1 The Biblical instruction *mutuum date nihil inde sperantes* is usually construed to mean that it is prohibited to charge interest on money loaned.

XVIII

"Good, Father!" applauded the young woman. "I've finally found you again! Yes, you're at home here. Believe me, clean this house!"

But the violent altercation had sapped all the energy of the debilitated individual; now he seemed frightened of himself.

"I fear," he said, "having committed an iniquity. After all, the worthy Monsieur Silvat is the director of my conscience; he believes that he is accomplishing a duty."

With a mechanical movement, the penitent had resumed his work, and was sewing again.

"That's not how you spoke this morning," Monique said to him. "What a sudden reversion! Yesterday, you were indignant against their despotism; you . . ."

"Yes, undoubtedly! Our friends sometimes abuse their authority, but always by virtue of an excess of pious zeal. So . . .

He could not finish; a fit of coughing cut off his voice and shook him with convulsions. Very frightened, Monique ran to him.

"The wretches! They're going to kill him! At any price, I want to get him out of their hands."

And, in tears, she sustained the weak head, wiping away the sweat of anemia, wrapping her arms around the sick man like a mother at the bedside of that aged child. The coughing gradually eased and the suffocations ceased.

"My days are counted henceforth," he said, sadly. "My hour is imminent; daughter, let's not think of anything any longer but the work of my salvation."

Monique, meanwhile, had addressed a glance to me, a mute plea imploring me to speak.

"Monsieur de Montmesnil," I said, then, "Mademoiselle your daughter has been kind enough to confide to me various fragments of your manuscripts. I have read them with attention. Several of them seem to me to be remarkable, and I have the design of publishing them."

"Remarkable, those mediocre rhapsodies? You're joking, Monsieur? Your newspapers would be very good to insert today what they rejected yesterday, with reason."

"A reformable bad judgment, dear Master; we're going to appeal. The revue for which I write, *La Minerve*, will publish them, I assure you."

"You hear, Father? Justice will finally be rendered to your talent. Oh, if you pulled yourself together, if you would deign to reignite the flame that they want to extinguish within you—what a joy for your child!"

"Well, yes," he said, sighing. "God put into my soul the religion of Beauty, the cult of the Ideal . . . Oh, my enthusiasms of old, those quiverings of my entire being when a noble thought or a melodious verse carried me away in space and in dream, what became of you . . . ? Alas!"

"You'll rediscover them, Father! The artist, the poet, is only asleep, not dead in you. Already, thanks to Monsieur Surville, your superb drama has conquered the public; tomorrow, your name on the poster will reveal . . ."

"Don't do anything, Monsieur!" he cried, fearfully. "Let Némo remain Némo forever. You're talking to me about *Le Nazaréen?* That work of infamy, that blasphemy, was born of my despair, and now I hope . . . I hope! To obey the divine Master I have made myself poor in spirit. Look: I'm no longer anything but a laborer, a maladroit artisan, too often inept. Oh, Monsieur, if I had to compose a book, how different it would be today! I would formulate my act of faith. The heart is the father of eloquence; perhaps I would be eloquent, perhaps I . . ."

He interrupted himself, and put his hand to his left arm, which he squeezed violently.

"Always and forever the hateful *me!* Pride, the dementia of my pride, I will be able to impose silence on you!"

But his gaze belied his words; his eyes were shining, burned by an interior flame not yet stifled; poorly resigned to voluntary stupidity, that humble individual was rebelling against humility.

He was suffering atrociously . . . However, he made a visible effort to constrain himself to the renunciation of all vanities

"I criticize you severely, Monique, for your indiscretion. Monsieur Surville must bring back the manuscripts and we will destroy them pitilessly."

"Too late!" replied the young woman. "Several pieces of verse are in press and will appear."

She was lying, but what a pious lie! For myself, I was following anxiously the peripeties of the combat engaged between those two souls. I believed that I was witnessing the most poignant of dramas: Life at grips with Death, and delivering the supreme assault against it . . .

Alarmed by that announcement, Monsieur de Montmesnil had raised his head.

"What verses are you talking about, my daughter. It isn't, I imagine . . ."

"The sonnet: *Amour, sweetness of loving* . . . Yes, Father, it's urgent that the author is known."

The mortifier got up with a start, "Oh! Not that one! A cry of ignominious lust! Not that one!"

"How you still love!" murmured Monique, dolorously.

"No, no, I no longer love! Ashes and dust, that memory is extinct! I no longer love, I no longer want to love."

Intense shudders agitated his meager body, and for a second time he squeezed his arm, angrily. Soon, drops of blood reddened his rags and trickled along his hands. I was frightened; the expiator was wearing on his flesh a bracelet garnished with spikes, and to suppress the revolt of ancient desires, he was martyrizing himself . . .

I no longer want to love. The poor fellow! He still adored.

Poor Monique looked at me, consternated. I no longer understood. Why, having forbidden me the slightest allusion to the parodied sonnet, was she speaking about it with that audacity?

"What!" Monsieur de Montmensnil said to me. "Is it, then, to induce me to temptation that you are honoring me with your visit? Can we not talk about something else?"

He had become very mild again; the torture of his flesh had calmed the frenzy; now, while plying the needle, he was smiling.

"About what is it necessary to talk to you?" his daughter asked him, with chagrin.

"About you, darling . . . isn't that true, Monsieur?"

"About . . . me? An uninteresting subject, alas."

"Oh, the dissimulation! The pretty mask of innocence!"

She blushed, and moved swiftly to the back of the room.

"Dear Monsieur," the ex-magistrate went on, "are you, by any chance, a relative of a Monsieur Surville that I once knew, the general counselor of Loir-et-Cher, a former prefect and . . ."

"My regretted and venerable father, Monsieur."

"Excellent family! Grandson, then, of a colonel of the First Empire?"

"My grandfather, died a Maréchal de Camp under Louis-Philippe."

"I know: one of our old brigands of the Loire, faithful to his Emperor! Although hardly a Bonapartist, I've always appreciated the devotion to memories . . . yes, a very honorable family! You know who we are: an ancient line of parlementarians; counselors of the Grand Chambre, five presidents *à mortier*, one Chancellor of France; but unfortunately, no more fortune. How did you meet Monique?"

"Mademoiselle your daughter must have told you . . ."

"An improbable story, much too romantic a fiction. No matter! God, by secret ways, directs our actions and leads us to his ends. You're only occupied with literature?"

"The theater above all. I'm making a name for myself there."

"No excess of pride, my dear Monsieur Germain! The theater, moreover, is a damnable work. Couldn't you find a better employment of your intelligence? We'll talk about it again."

My dear Monsieur Germain? That language, that counsel, that investigation of my person and my parents? I had finally guessed. In his candor, the naïve fellow imagined that I had used a subterfuge in order to entertain projects of marriage.

My visit must appear to him to be so bizarre! He took me for a suitor . . . so that was why he had welcomed me joyfully, and why he had sent Monsieur Silvat away so insistently!

Still smiling, he looked at us by turns. His eyes seemed to be saying: "Well, well, you're understood, amorous Monsieur. Smitten with my daughter! You have good taste. And in accord with her you've forced my door in order to ask for her hand? Come on, courage! What are you waiting for? Present your request; commence your courtship. But it will be necessary to convert, of course; I don't want a miscreant as a son-in-law."

Surreptitiously, I observed Monique. The pallor of twilight falling from the high skylight enveloped her slender figure with a nimbus and aureoled the purity of her face; she was very seductive, the pretty blonde, caressed thus by the last rays of daylight. A flux of blood rose to my face; I closed my eyes, as if dazzled—but I kept silent. Me? Marry the daughter of La Villereuse and this convict? What a burst of laughter in the newspaper; what reprobation in my family! And yet, I loved her . . . yes, I loved her!

I have reflected a great deal since then, interrogated myself, and, alas, analyzed myself. "Simple concupiscence," the disdainful Monsieur Silvat had declared.

Slow minutes went by without speech, while the rumors of the city reached us in a confused murmur. Suddenly, the rolling of a vehicle on the pavement of the isle became audible, and stopped outside the house. Almost immediately, blows resounded at the coaching entrance; it grated on its hinges and an argument commenced in the street . . .

At the church of Saint-Louis, the angelus rang.

Monsieur de Montmesnil, meanwhile, examined me with surprise, no longer hiding his disappointment. Why this obstinate silence? What was I waiting for in order to formulate my request?

"You have nothing to say to me, then?" he said, finally.

I bowed my head without responding. He understood then that he had been cruelly mistaken.

"Six o'clock," he said, dryly. "It's necessary for you to retire, Monsieur. I must . . . what's that noise?"

Strange outbursts of voices were now filling the house, cries of protest to which menacing abuse replied.

The recluse listened anxiously. "Why that racket?" he asked.

"Nothing out of the ordinary," Monique replied. "Everyday insanities: some noisy meeting of brothers and sisters of the Stainless Lamb, that's all."

"No, no assembly has ever taken place before nine o'clock in the evening. This disorder is bizarre! As for you, Monsieur Surville, since I cannot know the motive for your visit, I won't retain you any longer."

Very haughty again, having remained too much a marquis, that emulator of Deacon Pâris! The counselors of the Grand Chambre, the five presidents *à mortier* and the Chancellor of France had transmitted their soul to that soul, so vainly mortified; the holes in the penitent's rags allowed glimpses of the most damnable pride.

He raised toward his daughter a gaze charged with reproaches, simultaneously chagrined and angry.

"You, Monique, return to your room and await my orders; I'll summon you shortly. We need to talk, Mademoiselle; you are in great need of being recalled to duty."

A paternal reprimand in prospect! But the young woman did not obey. I had inclined before her, and I was about to take my leave of the sad Némo, when she retained me with an imperious gesture.

"Stay! I have recourse again to your assistance. And you, Father, please listen to me."

"No! We'll talk later. For the moment, I need to say my prayers."

"Your prayers! Truly, I admire you! You put your conscience in repose so easily!"

"What is this speech?" cried the old man, stupefied. "What is this tone?"

"I am imploring Monsieur Surville not to leave; his presence is necessary to the conversation I'm demanding."

"Necessary!"

"Indispensable even. He can talk to you about my mother."

Again, as if projected by a shock, Monsieur de Montmesnil got to his feet.

"Pardon me," said Monique, "for reawakening thus an abominable memory, but I have to. You were allowed to believe for a long time that my mother was dead, and I have associated myself with that charitable lie. Three days ago you were disabused, and you are suffering cruelly. Well, it is necessary to arm yourself with courage in order to learn the truth, Monsieur, the whole truth."

In the penumbra of the room, the recluse agitated anxiously

"You told me just now, Father, that you were going to recall me to my duty. I don't know it what respect I can have failed, and I am ready to explain my conduct. But—excuse my frankness— dare I ask you before then whether you really believe that you are accomplishing yours?"

"An impious speech, my daughter. What does it mean?"

"The care of your salvation absorbs you; that's all well and good. You weep for yourself, but do you ever think of groaning for your child? Oh, I know: God before everything, the family afterwards. An obstacle to salvation, an opportunity for sin, the family! Illustrious examples abound that put your conscience at rest. I know them, for I too am stuffed with pious reading. Saint Mélanie abandoned her son to public assistance in order to travel the deserts of the Thébaïde; Pascal reproached his sister for cherishing her children too much; your Deacon Pâris refused to receive his brother even on his deathbed; I could cite many others. Such are your models; you proclaim them saints; I call them monstrous. And that is why I hate your teaching, why . . ."

"Enough, I beg you! What have you to tell me on the subject of your mother?"

"That, then is where all your thoughts are going? She is your obsession, your demon and your God!"

"Monique!"

"However, they're going to separate us, and you scarcely seemed moved! Oh, don't protest! My aunt's decision is irrevocable, and you, out of weakness, are letting her do it. Personally, I don't want to be a nun . . . I don't want it, you hear me? I shall flee their convent! What will become of me then? I'm a minor; into what hands will it be necessary for me to fall? Dare to respond . . . into my mother's hands! Monsieur Surville, tell Monsieur le Marquis de Montmesnil what Madame la Marquise is at present!"

I felt very ill at ease; the brutal sortie impressed me painfully. What, was this the daughter of Némo, previously so admirable in filial tenderness? Her language was harsh, her voice aggressive; she was mocking mercilessly. But, by a curious effect of that violence, like a recalcitrant horse reanimated by the whip, the slumped body of the penitent stiffened under the invective.

"Speak, Monsieur, speak!" he growled grimly. "I'm listening."

"I prefer to inform you myself," the young woman replied. "Monsieur will interrupt me if I exaggerate. Well, in spite of bolts and grilles, I've been able, on a certain evening, to escape from here. I wanted to know, and I know. I've seen my mother on her stage . . ."

"On her stage!"

"Saluted by the gibes of the crowd, greeted by the quips of an entire audience. Poor, poor Father, today she's a comic singer, a café-concert travesty!"

A gasp of dolor, and also of rage, rose up in the increasing obscurity of the cell.

"And what degradation!" the pitiless Monique continued. "How they parade, how they clown, at the Alhambra! A good métier, apparently, since Madame possesses a house and travels in a carriage! Can you see me sleeping under the same roof, in the silks paid for by her admirers, eating the suppers offered to her by her Prince Zrelinsky? Pardon me, I'm being vulgar at this moment, very vulgar, but I want to be. And that still isn't all. They're mining money with your blazon, they're making litter of our family honor. Today the newspapers call her 'the Marquise'; tomorrow they're going to say 'La Montmesnil.' Will it be necessary for me to bear an infamous name? Tell me, tell me! You're a gentleman, you're a husband, and you're a father. What do you decide?"

And while she detailed as she pleased the heart-rending truth, Esther Nessim's husband went back and forth in his attic, stopping abruptly and abruptly resuming his march. Cries of anger and words of menace hissed between his teeth.

"The wretch! Why isn't she dead? Oh, if I could, if I were able to punish . . . !"

"Punish, then, Father. Surge forth before the face of that wretch; enjoin her to modify her life, and if she refuses, appeal to the law. Divorce: let's finish it. For fear of scandal, don't accept the ignominy. Come, let's quit this house of dementia, the tomb of our reason. We'll come back when you've swept away the band of evil lunatics that oppress you and debase you. Come! Not tomorrow, but this instant! Before being a saint, know how to be a man! The first of our duties is still our human duty!"

Without responding, the Marquis de Montmesnil continued marching, feverishly. A violent combat was agitating in that soul in torment. To whom would the victory be? To his God, demanding the absolute sacrifice of all passions, even honor? Or to his daughter, who, in the name of honor, was reviving all passions?

Meanwhile, the tumult in the house was increasing. I recognized the voice of Monsieur Silvat, who was protesting indignantly. Imperiously, another voice was responding to him.

Finally, Monsieur de Montmesnil appeared to make a decision. He went to take down a garment hanging in the cell, and then, putting it on, he said: "Let's go."

"Where are you going?" a mocking voice suddenly interrogated.

I turned my head. Before the door of the cell, a white form had surged forth: a woman, who, extending her arms, blocked the narrow passage. We had not heard her coming, and in the blackness of the falling night, she had loomed up, a spectral and hieratic apparition

"What fear!" she said. "Your speech was less sober just now. Is the angel of extermination standing beside me? Answer me: where are you going?"

"In accordance with our pious habit, Aunt," Monique said to her, "I suppose you were listening. It is, therefore, pointless to question us. So, no scandal, Madame, and let us pass."

Without responding to that challenge, Mère Angélique came into the attic. She advanced with assurance, her head high, proceeding at the automatic and jerky pace customary to the blind. There was no hesitation, no groping, in her step; she seemed to be able to see in the dark. Like a phantom she traversed the room and stopped in front of one of the wooden panels covering the wall. Stretching out her hand then, she began to feel, to search, and abruptly, under the activation of a spring, one of the panels opened. Acrid scents of mildew spread through the gaping hole.

There was a mysterious redoubt fitted into the wall, a hiding place, low but deep. Three altar night-lights were sizzling inside, and by the light of those lamps I glimpsed masses of earth and human bones. Skulls, tibias and femurs were stacked up there, forming an ossuary. They must have been dressed devotedly, for, carefully washed, they were gleaming like polished ivory.

"Behold our holy catacombs," said the blind woman, in a solemn voice. "You know them, my brother. It's also the undiscoverable retreat that the Blessed Claudine-Armande had fitted out for our martyrs. Many of our champions of the Grace, tracked by the police, found their refuge here; one of them even lived there for an entire year. My brother, in your turn, a danger threatens you. This refuge is open to you, but are you worthy of this refuge?"

"A danger?" asked Monsieur de Montmesnil. "What?"

"Answer me first—without mental restrictions, without Jesuitical reticence—you'll know thereafter. And hurry up, for time is pressing. So, you're returning to the corruptions of the world . . . have you reflected?"

"I've reflected. My resolution is irrevocable."

"Dementia! Monique is accompanying you?"

"No power can detach me from her."

"Except God, I imagine! And, in revolt like you, she's refusing to take the veil?"

"She refuses, since she has no vocation."

"That's perfect. Have you reflected that you're ill, very ill, and already in the grip of death?"

"I know that; I have, therefore, to preoccupy myself with the future of my child."

"Rather than your salvation? Always dementia! And to whom do you count on leaving your heritage, this familial house sanctified by our ancestors? To the intruder, your daughter?"

"She is a Montmesnil."

"For you, perhaps, but not for us. So, you're disinheriting us, and soon, when you are no longer, Madame Esther Manousso and her worthy lineage will be able to install their turpitudes in this house of prayer! What will become then, Monsieur, of your sister's foundations, our Church, reconstituted here, this shelter that I wanted to offer to those who share our faith? You're silent? So, we're condemned by you . . . Dementia!"

She paused briefly, and then raised her voice again. "Have you reflected on the scandal that will burst forth tomorrow? You're thought to be dead, among the dead, and the prevaricating judge, the infamous magistrate, has long fallen into human forgetfulness. But tomorrow, on seeing you again, the impious will be exultant; the Enemy will triumph, your opprobrium will spring forth upon our doctrine and dishonor it . . . Have you reflected?"

"I've reflected that I was a bad father; I've repented."

"Dementia, dementia! They're right. One final word, my brother. Have you reflected that you're dooming your soul without remission? The demon is lying in wait for you; his spur is ready; the old temptations are going to assail you again? The woman, the . . ."

"And if I want to be punished . . . finally to avenge myself!" cried Monsieur de Montmesnil, quivering.

"Avenge yourself!" exclaimed the blind woman. "There is it, then, his veritable dementia, his filthy and shameful folly: lust! She's inciting him to crime now! Well, since God rejects you, let men take you back, and let them be able to keep you!"

Violently, she replaced the panel, traversed the room for a second time, and returned to the door.

"That's your decision?" she said, again. "Yes? Then let the Eternal judge us!"

Suddenly, leaning through the hole, she shouted: "Monsieur Silvat! Enough lies! Come on, you others. He's here. God is delivering him to you."

A rising noise responded to that appeal; precipitate footfalls resonated on the floor below. Soon, the ladder grated and two men irrupted into the attic. One of them, a candle in his hand, was lighting their way. I recognized him; it was the bailiff Crochard. The other, who was wearing a tricolor sash, had to be a commissaire of police.

Motionless in the rigid whiteness of her costumes of an abbess, Mère Angélique-Marie, was standing on the threshold. As they entered, she bowed.

"Salut, Messieurs. God has sent you. Is it not written: 'You shall treat the madman in accordance with his madness.'"

"Where is the Marquis de Montmesnil?" demanded the man in the sash.

"There he is, Monsieur le Commissaire," replied the bailiff. "That's him; that's really him; I affirm it."

Monsieur de Montmasmil marched toward them. "Yes, that's me. What do you want with me?"

"Doctor!" shouted the functionary. "We have him. Come in!"

At those words, three new individuals penetrated into the room: a young physician accompanied by two acolytes.

"Pay attention!" he said. "Mystical folly, a bad madness."

He cast a glance around the verminous attic, perceived the fragments of leather, the shoes, the satchel, the crusts of bread and the whip, gazed momentarily at the strange marquis clad in repulsive rags, and then, coaxing, mild and insinuating: "This poor, this dear Monsieur! One is ill, then, very ill? We're going to cure you."

Immediately, the two orderlies rushed upon the old man, knocked him down and briskly placed a gag over his mouth.

"But this is infamous!" moaned Monique. "What crime have we committed?"

"The law of June 1838, section II, article 18," declared the commissaire. "Internment as a measure of public safety."

I tried to intervene. "A monstrous abuse of power, Messieurs! An illegal act! How dare you . . ."

"Who are you? Relative? Friend?"

"A friend, and I protest."

"Address yourself to the tribunal. For myself, I'm executing my duty. Notorious folly, dangerous and duly established by the formal statement of a ministerial officer."

"By my statement, Monsieur!" sniggered the bailiff Crochard. "Extravagances and violation of a sepulcher. You were, in addition, cited as a witness."

"Furthermore," added the commissaire, "the placement was made at the request of the family."

"What family, pray?" demanded Monique, exasperated. "Tell me, what family?"

"At the request of the spouse, Madame Noémi Esther, Marquise de Montmesnil."

"Of . . . of my mother?"

And the young woman collapsed, weakly. Her head buried in her hands, she wept heart-rending sobs.

Meanwhile, the orderlies had lifted up Monsieur de Montmesnil, who had, in any case, abandoned all resistance. Preceded by the physician and the bailiff Crochard, they took their new inmate downstairs; the old nun went out behind them. Soon, I heard the door of the house open and close again. Cries and the laughter of assembled idlers rose up from the street. A carriage drew away, and everything entered into repose again.

"Where are they taking my father?" Monique asked the police magistrate.

"To Sainte-Anne first; afterwards, I don't know."

"I'll go to join him."

"Impossible. I have the mission of taking you to Madame your mother."

"Me, to the home of . . . that woman!"

"My instructions are formal."

Suddenly, the most bizarre of changes took place in the young woman's attitude. With a decisive movement, she wiped her eyes; all flame of hatred was extinguished in her eyes, and her mouth began to smile.

"I'm at your orders," she said. "Yes, I'm in haste to embrace my mother."

"That desire honors you, Mademoiselle. Let's go."

"Is it really necessary for you to accompany me?"

"Such is my duty."

"Oh, Monsieur. Leave me the merit of my urgency."

She seemed so ingenuous, so desirous of obeying, that the functionary hesitated. "If you promise me not to flee . . ."

"Flee? All my heart is going out to my dear Maman. I have no other refuge than her love."

"Sagely spoken. You'll go, without delay, to Madame de Montmesnil's house?"

"Yes, and again yes. I swear it on oath."

"So be it; I accept your word. Do you know her address? 19 Avenue Velasquez."

"I know. A sumptuous house; a palace."

"Don't make me regret this act of weakness. I'll yield to your desire."

She readjusted the disorder of her poor costume; then she addressed herself to me: "Monsieur Surville, you know Madame de Villereuse; take me to her home."

Accompanied by the police commissaire we finally quit the cell. The Hôtel de Montmesnil had recovered its quietude, and nothing in its devout silence could have indicated the banal but dolorous tragedy that had just been accomplished here. On the first floor, however, at the entrance to the chapel, Mère Angélique-Marie was waiting. Monsieur Silvat was standing beside her, and five other aged nuns were arranged in a line. On hearing us coming she advanced and then, bowing her head humbly, she said:

"Pardon me, Monique; I had to act in accordance with my conscience. It was necessary for us to save that soul."

"I hate your God as much as I despise you!" riposted the young woman.

And, taking hold of my arm, she drew away impetuously.

XX

In the street, the police commissaire quit us in order to return to his red lantern. I had been obliged, however, to tell him my name, forenames and qualities: "Journalist." The magical virtue of such a word earned me the most affable of smiles.

Now Monique and I were alone.

"Seven o'clock," I said, looking at my watch. "Let's take a carriage, and hurry."

Yes, but in the desert of that quarter there was not a fiacre to be found. At a rapid pace we went along the Seine, descending the Quai d'Orléans. Grim and self-absorbed, Mademoiselle de Montmesnil marched without addressing a word to me. Sometimes, however, she uttered an exclamation of hatred, and then started to snigger; she worried me.

"We're going, Mademoiselle, to draft a request to the court and first thing tomorrow, I'll . . ."

"Superfluous effort, Monsieur. Madame de Villereuse has too much influence."

"What influence? Prince Zrelinsky? He won't be able . . ."

"Futile. We won't obtain anything. Oh, what a charming country, where a gallant man is the only power that is revered!"

The statement was angry, beyond measure, but cruelly true. I did not dare to protest.

"What kind of man is this Prince Zrelinsky?" she asked me.

"I've only caught a glimpse of him. An insolently rich monsieur, a palace in town, châteaux in the country, entire kingdoms in Galicia."

"Describe the individual to me. Ugly and repulsive, undoubtedly? Afflicted, I'm told, by eighty springs?"

"No, not yet. An old man, but well conserved, a sprightly old fellow full of vigor."

"Truly?" she murmured, with a nasty laugh.

And she fell back into a bleak silence.

Finally, on the Pont Louis-Philippe, I stopped a cab. Twenty minutes later it deposited us in the Avenue Velasquez. During the long journey we had not exchanged a single word. At number nineteen on the elegant thoroughfare stood a dainty bijou residence in the Renaissance style: the magnificent gift of the magnificent protector. A vast courtyard preceded it, fitted out as a flower-garden, and the windows of the upper stories overlooked the somber trees of the Parc Monceau.

"Here we are," sighed my companion. "How many times I've wandered in these gardens. I hoped to perceive my mother; I saw all too much of her."

They were watching out for our arrival, for the door was open and a domestic stationed at the gate. He ran to the door of our fiacre.

"Mademoiselle Monique?" he asked.

"That's me. Would you please announce me."

"Madame la Marquise is still at table, but she'll receive you."

"Oh, she deigns to receive me . . . Madame la Marquise. How generous!"

The footman looked at me with the fearful hatred with which liveried personnel eye policemen, recorders of misdemeanors and compilers of legal documents. "Madame is expecting you too," he told me. I was assumed to be one of the commissaire's agents.

"Don't come in," Monique begged. "Leave me alone with my mother. I'll come back as quickly as possible. I have another favor to ask you."

She leapt on to the sidewalk and I dismissed the carriage. Preceded by the grandiose lackey, Mademoiselle de Montmesnil traversed the courtyard and went into the house. Her pace was tranquil and decided, the stride of a good soldier going into battle. She paused at the top of the steps, turned round, and made me a gesture of supplication. "Please wait for me," she seemed to be saying.

The Galician magnate certainly lodged his lovers gallantly, and his sumptuous gift must have done him great honor at the Jockey Club or the Agricole. For a few minutes I admired the pretty design of the house: the balusters on its Italian roof, the pink marble of its colonnettes, the fine medallions with symbolic deities, the falling arabesques of its sculpted foliage, and then I commenced the most enervating of sentry duties. I went slowly back and forth, stopped at the edge of the park, retraced my path to the entrance to the Boulevard Malesherbes. There was no one but me in the solitary avenue.

My nascent passion was already making me suffer, and uncertainty anguished me. What was happening up there in the marquise's drawing room? With what indignant abuse, what scornful invective, must the young woman be lashing the courtesan! And with the aid of my imagination I represented the scene, a fourth-act situation: Monique standing, imperious and menacing, reproaching her mother for all the turpitudes of her life—and the mother kneeling, curbing her head beneath her child's disdain.

Half an hour . . . an hour . . . went by. Impatience took hold of me, an impatience made of anxiety. Weary of pacing back and forth, I went to station myself at the railings of the house.

In the courtyard, a coachman was washing the wheels of his caleche, scraping, brushing and rubbing, while chatting with a maidservant. The terms that they were using reeked of the stable and the sink.

"Tell me, Mademoiselle Mariette, is the little one still up there?"

"Still, Monsieur Arthur. Madame's retaining her to dinner."

"Pretty, but what a costume! What's happening? Jeremiads?"

"Not at all. Tears of happiness and 'Maman, my dear Mamans'. An innocent. They're chatting in the boudoir now and they sent me to the parlor."

"Secrets? That's humiliating."

"One is very sly now; one has secrets. What are you doing? Are you working?"

"I'm washing my vehicle."

"Don't knock yourself out . . . ruination here . . . we're going to be sacked."

"You're joking!"

"It's settled. Everything will be sold. Before long, the crash."

The coachman threw away his brush and drew nearer to the young woman. "The Pole's going to let us go, then? A quarrel?"

"Too right! Three hundred thousand francs of debts; our banker is closing his cash-box."

"So they don't love one another any more?"

"Old as he is, the prince can still see clearly, and in spite of her pomades the Marquise is stitched with wrinkles. To Les Invalides, darling! And on to another."

"Shh! Here's the kid."

The door had just opened. Monique came down the steps of the veranda. She was bare-headed, and was holding a piece of paper in her hand. She ran to me.

"Quickly, Monsieur Surville . . . for pity's sake, quickly, to Sainte-Anne. Give this letter to the director. It recommends my father to him, and he'll be at liberty soon."

"You're not accompanying me!" I cried, astonished.

"No, no . . . I can't . . . I don't want to. It would be necessary to see the poor man, and I'd never dare to confess to him . . ."

A frisson cut off her voice.

"You're frightening me, Mademoiselle. Finish, then, finish . . . confess what?"

"Well, here it is . . . I've been obliged to conclude an ignoble bargain. That man . . ." She hesitated again, and finally uttered a lamentable laugh. "That woman demands that I please her prince . . . enough to become a princess."

Had I really understood? I replied with an imprecation, but Mademoiselle de Montmesnil had already hurtled back into the gallant house.

XXI

There was amusing chatter in the social high-life of "All Paris" when the news spread toward the end of December that Prince Zrelinsky was going to marry. The announcement of the noble espousals first appeared in a gossip paper, a habitual furnisher of public malignity.

Noisy rumor in Paphos, said the *Indiscrétion Boulevardière,* with its malevolent preciosity. *One of our princesses of gallantry, until recently a star in the firmament of the Alhambra, is about to feel the sweetest sensations of maternal joy; Madame la Marquise is marrying off her daughter. What daughter? you ask me. Oh, but another child of mystery, lost and found for the circumstance. Eighteen years old, pale and blonde; immaculate ermine, the daisy of daisies. As for the husband, don't search: the most intimate friend of the household!*

The edifying hymen will be perpetrated far from Paris, in one of the manors—we were about to say mesnils—belonging to the amorous septuagenarian.[1]

Although no names were pronounced, the venomous article did not allow any doubt to subsist. Other journals, in any case, confirmed the news. Mademoiselle de Montmensil was becoming Princesse Zrelinska.

Without surprising me, that shameful marriage made me indignant. For two months I had not seen the young woman again, for in spite of repeated visits, her door remained closed to me. And yet, with what ardor I had accomplished my mission, deposited in the hands of the director of Sainte-Anne the letter committed to my care, and even insisted on seeing his new inmate. Wasted effort, in any case, futile steps; I had run into an administrative refusal. Monsieur de Montmesnil was being held in the most rigorous secrecy.

War-weary, I had then written to Monique. A fortnight of feverish waiting, and finally, a brief but poignant response:

Thank you for your precious amity. Alone, down here, Monsieur, you have had compassion for me. Be blessed!

Thanks to the credit of which the prince disposes, my father has finally recovered his liberty. I nourished the hope of transforming his life; another illusion disappointed. In spite of my insistent pleas, he wanted to resume all the tortures of his reclusion. No one can visit him at present—not even his daughter; he has not understood.

When you receive this letter I will have already quit Paris; I am going to my unknown destiny. Adieu, then; forget us. Adieu again, Monsieur, and forever.

---

1 "*Mensnil*" is an alternative term for "*Manse*"—hence the wordplay.

On receipt of such a letter I ran once again to the Avenue Veslasquez. Alas, the house was closed, the windows shuttered. Gone!

In despair, I returned to work, that victorious remedy for all dolors, but I asked my thought for absorption in vain. Vagabond, it carried me on Monique's tracks, out there, toward the snowy plains of Bug and Styra, which were probably going to keep the new wife forever. O torture, unspeakable torment of an amour that no longer has youth and its facile forgetfulness! I was in love now, with the implacable passion, the atrocious frenzy that sometimes wrings the human heart as the first gray hairs begin to grow. And I suffered. Yes, I, the libertine, the seeker of ephemeral adventures, was jealous—jealous of an old man. How I detested him, that ignoble individual, that trafficker of virgins, that buyer of young women!

I became ferociously grim, unsociable and uncivilized. Everything exceeded me, irritated me, and caused me enervating lassitude: soirées, the theater, reading, and work above all. I forbade my door to my dearest friends; they boasted too much about their mistresses; I sacked Josias brutally; he had mocked me one day on the subject of "the demoiselle." My only pleasure at present was wandering in the eloquent solitudes that reminded me of the beloved: the muddy avenue of the Observatoire; the deserted arches of Saint-Médard, the funereal back-streets of the Île Saint-Louis. There, I rediscovered the absentee; I walked timidly by her side; I listened to her confidences, I smiled at her heart-broken smile.

And December finished sadly. Sadly, too, the new year commenced. Around me, however, Paris was agitating joyfully, and already the carnival was in full swing. Tickets to theaters or concerts and invitations to dinner arrived in quantity; I refused them all, preferring the gray bleakness of my thoughts, the assiduous haunting of my blonde-haired phantom.

"Amour," a philosopher has said, only too well, "only establishes its power by destroying that of our reason."

XXII

One morning I went to knock on the door of the Hôtel de Montmesnil. I wanted to see the father of my fugitive again, interrogate him and make him talk about his child. The door, as usual, was carefully shut. I lifted the knocker and let it fall three times: one blow for Jansenius; another for Deacon Pâris, and *bang!* for the blessed Claudine-Armande—poor Monique's innocent joke.

To my great astonishment it was my former domestic Josias who came to open the door.

"You, my lad! What are you doing here?"

For several seconds I contemplated him in amazement. Humble, unctuous, steeped in mildness, modestly lowering his eyes, he wore the same costume as Monsieur Silvat: a maroon coat, but brand new. It yawned, much too large, around his meager frame and fell all the way to his heels.

"Yes, it's me," replied the solemn simpleton. "Monsieur threw me out for no reason; he committed the iniquity, and Judgment will be harsh for him in the Valley of Josaphat. I lament and am consoled; I have found my land of Canaan."

"Bah! You're now of the Boîte à Perrette,[1] Monsieur Josias?"

"Boîte a Perrette? I don't understand the wit of libertinage, the only one that Monsieur is able to use. I'm waiting here for the imminent arrival of the Prophet."

"What prophet?"

"Élie. He will descend from Heaven to constrain the rich to share with the poor. The Thousand-year reign will commence.

---

1 The Boîte à Perrette [Perrette's Money-Box] was created in 1695 by Pierre Nicole, so named because he had allegedly confided funds to his maidservant Perrette, in order to aid persecuted Jansenists, which she hid in her milk-jug. The story is surely apocryphal, echoing one of Jean de La Fontaine's most famous fables, but the fund in question did give much-needed support to many Jansenist causes.

No more poverty. I shall soon have an income."

"By the Great Book! My compliments . . . in the meantime, what is your employment in this house?"

"Don't address me as *tu* any longer; you're not of our tabernacle. The door has been confided to me; I . . ."

He interrupted himself; a man in a violet soutane had just penetrated under the vault in his turn; the youth ran to meet him.

"Monseigneur! Oh, Monseigneur! What are your orders, Monseigneur?"

The man thus devotedly welcomed was an individual about fifty years old, short, stout, paunchy and red-faced, with a vermilion mouth, curly hair and a jovial expression. His burlesque appearance was reminiscent of one of those joyous faiences that Delft manufactures in order to cheer up drinkers of faro and pipe-smokers.

"Ah, Paris!" he said tearfully, out of breath. "Detestable Sidon! Sinful Nineveh that Jonah himself could not have converted! What impiety! Just now, I was mocked in an omnibus!"

"A sacrilege, Monseigneur," growled the young man.

"I forgive them. Has the invalid requested my assistance?"

"Not yet, alas; but Mère Angélique is with him and preparing him to receive you."

The man with the porcelain face looked at his watch, a very ecclesiastical old silver turnip.

"Only ten o'clock; let's go to the kitchen."

"The triduum is for ten-thirty. Monsieur will say the office in a new ornament; it has just been brought. We've also received the miter, the crosier and the mosette."

"Camail, little manikin, it's necessary to say camail. 'Mosette' is an expression of the Roman heresy. I'll go to admire it later; I'll go to the kitchen first."

"Your Grandeur need not disturb himself; I'll run there and . . ."

"No, I want to give counsel to the sister cellaress myself. I've ordered a German delicacy, hare in preserves, a difficult condiment; I've brought her the recipe. And I have to address complaints to her; her beer is very bad and your Schiedam poisons me. Schiedam is, however, the inspiration of thought. Oh, France, France, a harsh country!"

He sketched a gesture of benediction and, waddling on his short legs, left the vestibule.

"Who is that monseigneur?" I asked the boy.

"Our prelate, Monsieur de Gorcum."

"A Janenist bishop?"

"Jansenist? I don't know that word. No, Catholic following our rites, a high priest of Élie and a precursor himself; a saint, Monsieur Justus."

"Delegated, no doubt, by the Archbishop of Utrecht."

"We no longer know the heresiarchs of Utrecht. The true Church, today, is us."

"He has come to visit his archdiocese of Paris?"

"Yes, to absolve a great sinner and harvest some alms."

Very good. *Absolve a great sinner*—I had understood.

"What has become of Monsieur de Montmesnil?" I asked.

The young porter addressed a mocking glance to me; he divined the motive for my visit.

"The penitent is very poorly, in a desperate state."

"What are you telling me? I want to see him."

"No, you can't come in. My instructions are formal. No one can approach the penitent."

"Yes, my lad, I'll talk to him. You'll announce me, and I'll be received."

At the same time I tried to slip into his hand what Bazile calls "the argument without reply,"[1] but he jibbed, refused the money, seized a bell-cord and rang it violently. At that appeal, Monsieur Silvat came running.

The heavy gluttonies habitual to Monsieur de Gorcum must

---

1 Bazile is a character in the opera known in English as *The Barber of Seville*.

have been unknown to that drinker of clear water; he had never seemed stiffer, more fleshless and more worn out than on that cold January morning. And what an outfit! His coat was coming apart at all the seams, the holes in his trousers were patched with string. Jacqueline Pascal had once reproached her brother for the neglect of his mortifying attire. What would she have thought of this one?

On perceiving me, he frowned. "Monsieur Surville again! What do you want?"

"To visit Monsieur de Montmesnil."

"You're asking the impossible. He can't receive you."

"Why?"

"The rumors of the world importune him."

"Get away! A little frankness. You've tightened the sequestration."

"Sequestration? As you please. I have an absolute scorn of words."

It was pointless to try to convince that stubborn jailer; I attempted nevertheless to obtain some information.

"I've just learned that Monsieur de Montmesnil is ill."

"Very ill; in extremis. We're beginning a triduum for him."

"He's dying? Have you informed his daughter?"

"His daughter? What's the point? It's her who's killing him."

Creasing his forehead and pursing his lips. Monsieur Silvat brought his hand down in a gesture of malediction. That insult made me indignant.

"Abominable speech, Monsieur! The noblest of women, worthy of all your respect!"

"Even when she wants to marry her mother's lover! An edifying marriage! The 'noble woman' has broken her father's heart; he's dying of it today!"

"Unfortunate man!"

"Oh, no superfluous compassion! Let us rather rejoice. The soul sick for so long is cured henceforth. He has finally known veritable dolor, and is purified entirely. Monsieur Montmesnil preferred his daughter to God; now he only loves God."

"Ah! And it's you, Monsieur, who announced the ignominious news to him?"

"Me. The shock was rude: a cry of amazement, then a faint. But when the sinner came round, the dolor had taken effect; he had grasped the meaning of the proof, and had understood that all terrestrial affection is only vanity, chimera and deception."

"Salvation by torture, then?"

"Another word, Monsieur Vaudevillist."

"All morality would reprove you."

A disdainful laugh agitated the aged sectarian's skeleton. "You make me feel pity, you false scholars! Morality, Monsieur, is the knowledge of duty, with the sole end of Eternity."

At that moment, the Bishop of Gorcum returned to the porch. He was emerging from the kitchen and was going to the chapel to admire his miter and camail. With an imperious gesture, monsieur Silvat enjoined him to approach.

"*Epulabatur quotidie splendide!*" he cried. "The orgy of the evil rich, the existence of a Harlay de Champvillon or a Cardinal Dubois! Are you truly one of us? No, for you make a scandal and abuse our Mère's illusions! Think hard, Monseigneur: Élie lived on wild honey and Saint John nourished himself on locusts."

"I shall try to imitate them," murmured the drinker of tankards, humbly. And, contrite, curbing his back under the criticism, he went upstairs. Monsieur Silvat followed him with his gaze, and then exhaled an angry sigh.

"That, a successor of the apostles? The heir of Pavillon and the Soanens? I still prefer our clergy of Utrecht; they will come back to us. Josias, ring a knell."

He turned back to me, and pointed at the door.

"One last advice, Monsieur Surville. You bring doubt and the spirit of revolt here; entry to this house is forbidden to you in future."

XXIII

Thrown out! Josias, with a feigned expression of compassion, closed the heavy battens on me. In the street, I waited for a few minutes listening. What was happening up there? The bell was now tolling slowly, and the groan of a harmonium descended from the first floor. The odious Silvat was certainly not sparing the effects of his mortuary display, and the expiator Montmesnil would be able to witness his own funeral while alive.

I drew away, furious. Oh, the rogues, to treat me like that! But patience; I'll be able to fustigate you in my newspaper; I'll have my revenge, Messieurs the Efficacious! Yes, Molière, your Tartuffe must have been a Jansenist.

Vituperating thus, I went into a café, breakfasted with a mediocre appetite, and consulted myself. What should I do? Monique's father was dying; I had to inform his daughter as soon as possible. But how? Where to send a telegram? In what part of the vast world was Princesse Zrelinsky traveling at present?

After long hesitation I decided: Let's go to see Clorinde; perhaps she's returned.

A perilous step, however. Esther Nessim was a woman fond of scandal. Perhaps she would want to penetrate to the moribund by force, install herself in the Hôtel de Montmesnil as mistress and render the horror of the death-throes even more atrocious. Yes, the danger was certain—but what other course of action could I adopt?

It was scarcely midday; I leapt into a carriage.

My fiacre stopped at the gate of the Parc Monceau; the causeway was encumbered; it was impossible to go forward. The Avenue Velasquez, ordinarily so calm, presented an unusual animation that morning. Joyful events must have occurred there, for concierges and servants were grouped on the sidewalks, gazing and joking. All eyes were aimed at the Villereuse house, and the name of the "Marquise" was running from mouth to mouth.

"There she is!"

"No, she wouldn't dare appear!"

And there were loud jeers, servants' chatter, insolent gibes.

But the diva's house seemed far less cheerful. No more coachman in the courtyard, no caleche. The gates and doors were open, and several removal wagons were parked in front of the façade. Men in the livery of auctioneers were coming and going, carrying furniture and wrapping up chandeliers, paintings, drapes, crystal and porcelain: an entire exodus. A notice stuck to the wall furnished me with the key to the enigma promptly: *Sale by legal authority. Execution of seizure.*

Bah! The "crash" that the maidservant Mariette had announced. You've been seized, Madame la Marquise. How lamentable!

No domestic to announce me; all of them had fled to other kitchens. I traversed the courtyard and penetrated into the house. Under the veranda the most superb garments were displayed in piles: linen and lace, city outfits and theatrical costumes; the entire wardrobe, including the rutilant scarlet costume that had once been the Parisian's joy, the pride of the Alhambra. Such a relic falling into the hands of Madame la Ressource! O vanity of vanities of glory!

They had, moreover, arrived in swarms, the ladies of the Rue de Provence or the Boulevard de Batignolles, the second-hand dealers and clothing-sellers. Curbed over the packets of garments they were palpating, weighing and calculating, as meditative as in a sanctuary. From one group to anther a monsieur of rather ignoble appearance was strolling, his hat on his head and his pipe in his mouth, apparently the supervisor of the seizure.

"Don't touch, Mesdames . . . wait for the sale. The exposition is for tomorrow."

"Is Madame de Villereuse here?" I asked him.

"You'll find her upstairs. She's raging, and enraging us."

Ah! She was "raging." A bad state of mind to be able to comprehend me . . . I went upstairs and arrived in a drawing room, entirely stripped bare. No one. At hazard, I called out.

At the sound of my voice, a voice replied from the next room: "Is that you Crochard? You've taken your time coming! At last!"

A heavy sigh, and then a rustle of skirts, and the beautiful Clorinde appeared.

No, alas, it was not the providential Crochard. The unfortunate woman looked at me, consternated. She did not recognize me at first, and I had to remind her of my name.

"Good, good," she said. "I can place you now: Monsieur Surville, Saint-Réal's friend. You have to talk to me? Come into my bedroom."

Lugete, veneres! [1] It was heartbreaking to see the bedroom of an antique amorous woman. No more garniture on the mantelpiece, carpets on the floor, curtains on the windows. Denuded, devastated, pillaged: the abomination of desolation. For all furniture, a bed and an amusing dressing-table in a corner, a costly ornament in the Pompadour style. Two old saxe palm trees framed a looking-glass, and Incas, sons of Monsieur Marmontel, sustained the candelabras: a pricy curiosity for the lover of bric-à-brac. Clorinde had planted a chair in front of the two marvels and there she was waiting, wild and untamed, like the dragon of the Hesperides, protecting her final treasure.

So many emotions, moreover, had not returned her youth. Puffy, blotchy and spotty under her make-up, the Marquise was no longer anything but a lamentable ruin. With a grand gesture she indicated the whole disaster of her bedroom.

"What a catastrophe, Monsieur! Seized, sold, reduced to the hospital! And all my daughter's doing."

"What!" I said, adopting an expression of sympathy. "Madame your daughter, Princesse Zrelinska, was unable to prevent such a misadventure?"

She agitated in her chair and addressed a black look to me. "There is no Princesse Zrelinska! You must know that . . . are you making fun of me?"

---

1 "Weep, the lustful"; the full quotation from Catullus is *Lugete, O Veneres Cupidinesque*, approximately "Weep, O lustful Venuses" (although most translations do not render it that way).

"Making fun of you, Madame? Certainly not. I too was once exposed to such disgrace and, 'unfortunate, I learned to lament misfortune.' So, no Princesse Zrelinska?"

I had gone very pale; surprise and joy were gripping my heart.

"No, Monsieur. An infamy of my child! I'm disappointed in the dearest of my maternal ambitions."

"The prince recoiled, then, before the odium and ridicule?"

"Odium? Ridicule? Let's not moralize. Men are men and we know how to govern them. Yes, the prince desired the marriage ardently. The modest enticements of Mademoiselle Monique had charmed, conquered and subjugated him; he loved her and he coveted her. I showed myself to be a clever psychologist, as you others say: I knew him so well! But damn! A fortnight after her father was set at liberty, my Saint Touch-me-Not of a daughter ducked out of it and signified a formal refusal."

"The marriage was impossible; Mademoiselle your daughter was obeying the injunctions of her honor."

"Of her honor!" she cried, furiously. "One talks about honor when one has income, and we haven't . . . Yes, mocked, duped, turned over, and by the craftiest of ingénues! So, look: the prince is abandoning us, he's taking his revenge. It's abominable, Monsieur! A child who allows her mother to be murdered thus! A daughter for whom I had consented to the harshest, the most humiliating of sacrifices! That's her gratitude! I've received the recompense of King Lear!"

"Blow, winds!" I murmured, smiling. "You cataracts and hurricanes, spout . . . I tax you not, you elements with unkindness; I never gave you kingdom, call'd you children!"[1]

"An idea!" she said, interrupting the Shakespearean invective. "You ought, my dear author, to translate and put in verse the dolors of *King Lear*. I'll play Cordelia for you."

Cordelia? That body already obese, that face hollowed out by wrinkles! I could not repress a shrug of the shoulders.

---

1 *King Lear* Act III, Scene 2; I have substituted the actual text rather than back-translating Thierry's version, which is probably taken from a rather free French translation.

"An ingenious idea, Madame; we'll talk about it . . . but for the moment, I have to talk to you about a rather important matter . . ."

"Nothing is more important than my artistic career."

"I am bringing you grave news; Monsieur de Montmesnil is on the point of death."

She got up abruptly.

"How do you know? Bah! It's the hundredth time that announcement has been made to me . . . and always a hope deceived."

"The news is exact. I've come from the Île Saint-Louis."

"In fact," she said, sitting down again, "I forgot—you know the saintly man; Monique told me about your visit. Ah! He's dead? Too late, Monsieur Surville, much too late. Always my habitual luck. Six months sooner, and I would have been able to marry my prince, and I wouldn't be under the bailiff's claws. But . . ."

She did not finish her complaint. The movers had just come in. Clorinde immediately marched toward them and barred their way.

"What do you want? Nothing more to take! This bed remains mine and can't be sold. Article 592 of the Code of procedure."

"And the Pompadour furniture that I perceive over there?" riposted the agent of the seizure.

"It's my dressing table. Instrument of artistic labor, my means of earning a living, thus unseizable. Reread your law."

"I know it, and I'm carrying out my orders. Go on, you men, take it away."

Chagrined and indignant, Clorinde protested. "A referee! I demand a referee!" But the fellows had heard it all before. They mocked her insolently and got carried away. For a few minutes there was a scene as repulsive as it was burlesque. At the noise of the quarrel, the lady traders had come running and took sides against the rebel. The whole society that had been smiling humbly a little while before at the courtesan's money was now laughing at her in her distress.

Dismissed and humiliated, the beautiful Clorinde finally went back into her bedroom, but suddenly uttered a burst of laughter.

"'Man is an apprentice, dolor is his master.' Truly, I don't believe myself and would have thought myself more philosophical. What were we saying? Monsieur de Montmesnil is about to die? Alas, we're all mortal; I can't do anything to return him to life."

"You have, at least, a duty to fulfill; have your daughter summoned."

"She isn't in Paris. What can one do at such a moment? Mademoiselle Monique has remained in Nice; she's hiding there and does well."

"Then give me her address, Madame, in order that I can inform her as quickly as possible."

"You? What touching interest! A beautiful soul this Monsieur Surville! But don't go to any expense. The slut won't disturb herself for so little."

"You're insulting her, Madame."

The hateful creature started to snigger. "And if it pleases me to avenge myself? To prevent the child from collecting her father's last sigh? To give her thus a great chagrin and remorse?"

I started, indignant. "Be careful! Your daughter won't forgive you. You have great need of her. Prudence!"

"So be it!" she said. "Let's practice nobly the forgetfulness of insults, let's bow our head." She exhaled a sigh, like the whine of a beaten dog, crawling, and then resumed bantering. "Let's resign ourselves, but morality for morality. Dare I, Monsieur Preacher, implore your protection?"

"My protection? Why that word and that ironic tone?"

"Mademoiselle Monique—your friend—will soon inherit the Hôtel de Montmesnil. Perhaps, if you recommend me, she'll deign to abandon it to her mother. Les Invalides for my old age! Come on, don't be annoyed; I'll do it."

She took a dainty pencil-holder from her bosom, and then, placing a wad of stamped papers on her knees, started writing on the back.

"Excuse the dirty rag; I don't have any other paper to offer you. They've taken everything, except these love-letters. A shameful pillage! Here's my dispatch: 'Monique de Montmensil, Villa des Glycines, Nice-Montboron. Your father is dying; come.' Succinct, but precise, isn't it? Personally, you see, I can't leave here, so send the telegram yourself. Tomorrow, if all this turmoil permits, I'll go to see what's happening on the Île Saint-Louis. Now leave me . . . I can see Crochard."

The bailiff from Versailles, in fact, the counselor, the friend of the day of proofs, had just shown his face through a gap in the door. He was shaking his head sympathetically with a melancholy smile, a sad confession of his impotence. Perhaps an idea of genius relative to a referee and opposition had germinated in his fertile brain; perhaps, too, the man of law was slightly drunk.

I left the house, and a few minutes later I had sent Clorinde's dispatch. I drafted a second one, emotional and respectful, to implore the fugitive to hasten her return. Having accomplished that duty, I went back into the Parc Monceau and walked through the trees for a long time, thoughtfully.

So, you're free, Monique, free to allow yourself to be loved. My wife! Yes, my wife! I was no longer hesitant now. But I wanted our marriage to be discreet, almost clandestine, accomplished above all far from the ignominious presence of your mother.

And what if, perchance, she refuses her consent? Well, we'll depart together; I'll be able to convince you to flee with me. Enlaced with one another, we'll seek clement climes for our amour, in order to live there together until the day when you can legally receive my name . . .

Romance, an absurd romance, at my age! But alas, the most delirious passions are still those that come to assault the heart of a man at forty. Oh, how little I was thinking then about all the chimeras of glory recently pursued so ardently and so voluptuously caressed!

And, walking thus through the deserted pathways, marching beside the absentee, conversing with her, I lived until dusk in those mirages, in the delights of a dream. I saw myself carrying the beloved away toward the mysterious refuge, the charming nest of our amours, a white and pink villa, out there, in the dentellate shadow of the Apennines, amid the troubling scents of jasmines and lilies, somnolent, to the cadenced rhythm of the waves . . . The living reality of illusion! On that bitter winter evening, the gusts of wind were chilling my face, but I found it caressant, with the tender mildness of spring. January was dusting the silence of the great trees with frost, and yet the birdsong of April as singing in my soul.

Finally, as night fell, I returned to my lodgings. Here I found the hoped-for response:

Departing in all haste. Will be in Paris tomorrow evening. Will you be at the station? Monique.

Monique! A chaste rendezvous, as of old. And she had signed, smiling at me through her tears, with the only name that my heart gave her.

XXIV

The express coming from Nice arrives at the station in Paris a little before six o'clock. At half past five I was already on the disembarkation platform.

Since the morning an anxiety had obsessed me: would the intractable Silvat dare to close the door to us? I recalled his insulting words: *No one can approach the penitent . . . his daughter has killed him . . . As for you, Monsieur Surville, our house is forbidden to you . . .* No! Impotent threats! I was determined to fray a passage for us. And, striding resolutely under the smoke of the hall, my eyes aimed at the host of lights that were shining in the darkness outside, I waited for the first glance that might perhaps inform me of my destiny.

Six o'clock! The electric bell rang; a distant searchlight dotted the obscure profundity of the track with white, approached, became enormous; three blasts of the whistle, an exhalation of steam from the engine, and the train arriving from Nice glided, screeched and grated over the rails. A blonde head was leaning out of a window. I ran to open the door; Monique leapt lightly down on to the platform.

Her! At first, the pallor of her face and the austerity of her attire surprised and saddened me. The young woman was still clad in black wool, as poor a garment as on her departure; only the bonnet of the deaconess had disappeared from the somber costume.

With a passionate movement, I seized her hands,

"You! You . . . ! Finally!"

But she recoiled swiftly.

"My father? Tell me about my father!"

"Monsieur de Montmesnil is very ill. I've been forbidden entry, but yesterday morning, he was still alive."

"Let's hurry, Monsieur. Let's arrive . . . oh, let's arrive in time!"

She launched herself toward the exit, and only stopped in the courtyard. I could scarcely keep up with her, so feverish was her agitation, so rapid her stride. Slightly offended by her indifference in my regard, I set out in quest of a cab, and my fiacre soon stopped in front of the traveler.

"Climb in, Mademoiselle; I'll accompany you, and won't quit you again."

Her fingers leaned on my hand; she had already hoisted herself on to the footstep when she threw herself backwards violently.

"No! You frighten me too much!"

Good God, what a welcome! She had, moreover, played the same comedy three months before, during our rendezvous at the crossroads of the Observatoire. It was discourteous, insulting, and even vulgar. Wounded, and cruelly disappointed, I inclined, in order to take my leave of her.

"If my presence importunes you, I'll withdraw. I'll come to seek news tomorrow. I . . ."

A bizarre laugh interrupted me, and the young woman burst into sobs. Very astonished, I looked at her with more attention. Alas, how changed she seemed! Her thinner face resembled a wax mask; the haggard eyes were gleaming in their orbits; the pink patch on her forehead had expanded strangely, and three other livid marks were designed at the hairline. What was that?

Monique had wiped away her tears, but spasms were shaking her, and between two frissons she placed her hand on her breast as if she were stifling.

"Don't leave me," she begged. "You're the only friend I have. For pity's sake, don't abandon me!"

The plaintive expression of her voice and the humility of her pleas bowled me over.

"Why did you offend me just now? Tell me, why? I love you so respectfully!"

"Forgive me!" she implored. "I'm suffering so much! Disgust for myself and terror of others!"

In silence, we went down the steps leading to the Boulevard Diderot. We went at a rapid pace along the quays of the Seine, heading toward the Île Saint-Louis. On the bridge traversing the canal she stopped suddenly and leaned over toward the blackness of the stagnant water.

"I've always been scornful of the suicides of grisettes . . . but I understand them now; I even approve of them."

"Is it you," I exclaimed, "you, Monique de Montmesnil, who is speaking thus?"

She started to laugh, and continued the progress of her feverish march.

"A problem to solve," she said to me, suddenly. "Where shall I stay tonight?"

"At the house in the Avenue Velasquez, I suppose. Your room must have been prepared."

"In that evil place? No! I count on resuming the cell where I lived for such a long time. I'll find a few clothes and a little linen there; they'll suffice for me."

Hmm! That respect for abandoned clothing appeared at least dubious to me.

"In any case," I said, "a traveling costume is easy to constitute, and this evening . . ."

"No again! I haven't brought any money. In any case, I've been left in absolute destitution."

"Not prodigal toward you, Madame your mother!"

"She intends to punish me. Poor woman!"

She appeared, however, to have calmed down—but her artificial gaiety was hard for me to bear.

"You, so worthy of happiness," I sighed, "and yet so unfortunate . . ."

Without responding to me she slid her arm gently under mine; her hand brushed my hand, and I felt it pass like a caress.

"Who informed you, my dear Monsieur, of my abode in Montboron?"

"Madame de Montmesnil."

"Name her Villereuse! What, you've seen her again! To interrogate her on the subject of her daughter? Oh, how indiscreet! So you were thinking about me?"

"I love you, and my amour maddens me. Yes, I've seen her again, but in painful circumstances . . . in the house put to pillage, everything seized and sold."

"Seized and sold! How you must have laughed, Monsieur; I laughed at it myself. In the clutches of the bailiff, the beauty! An amusing adventure! You have caused tears, you will weep! The talion of eternal justice."

"A little more indulgence. The poor woman is suffering in her turn."

"She's suffering? Yes, in her vanity and her need for luxury. Is that suffering? I hate her! If I'm wrong, let God judge me!"

"I understand your just grievances only too well. Your mother has created irreparable woes."

"Yes, I hate her, and yet, I only asked to be able to love her. Oh, to love, to love!"

With a convulsive pressure, her fingers had seized my hand and they squeezed it, twisting it violently; her arm leaned against my breast; soon, languidly, her head leaned against my shoulder and her hair brushed my face.

"Monique! Monique, my adored!"

But suddenly, she pulled away with a violent effort, recoiled, uttering a shrill plaint, traversed the road and started to run, as if afflicted by a sudden madness. I caught up with her promptly.

"Leave me!" she cried. "Go away. I've already told you: you frighten me!"

Then the bizarre burst of laughter, immediately followed by the explosion of sobs.

Very alarmed, I drew away, a few paces, but firmly resolved to follow her at a distance. She was marching with insensate gestures, sometimes stopping in order to draw breath, and then turning her head, looking to see whether I was following her.

Having reached the Hôtel de Montmesnil she stopped, retraced her steps and came to meet me.

"You don't understand anything?" she said to me, wildly. "It's forbidden to me to be able to love! God, the cruel God of my family, doesn't permit it!"

XXV

Although night had fallen a long time ago, the door of the house was wide open, and the windows of the façade were shining in the snowy darkness. The voices of men and women could be heard, alternating with the melodies of a harmonium. Soon there was a vigorously rhythmic chant, and soon languid adagios sighed by the muted organ. Someone was dying to the sound of music in that convent of dementia.

The young woman went under the vault. I followed her.

At the bottom of the staircase, Monsieur Silvat, very brisk and very busy, was giving orders to Josias.

"A night of delight!" he said. "Let's leave our doors open. Let the gentiles be welcomed by us. It's necessary that the skeptic sees and is convinced. The seer is going to enter into ecstasy!"

Nevertheless, on seeing us, he attempted to draw away—but Mademoiselle de Montmesnil ran after him.

"My father! Where's my father?"

"Reconciled! Justified at last! He's in the chapel now."

"Cured!"

"Yes, of the cancer that was corroding his soul . . . of his sin."

"He's alive! Oh, God be praised! I want to see him."

"So be it. This morning, still, I would have forbidden you to approach him, but at present I have no fear. He won't recognize you any longer."

"Dying! And you didn't inform me! What atrocious infamy!"

"Our infamies according to men are our glory in the eyes of God. Come."

And preceding Monique, he went up the stairs.

"What's happening here?" I asked Josias.

"Everything and everyone in joy, Monsieur. The sinner has finally received the gift of Grace; he's justified! This afternoon he was brought down to the chapel. There, following our pious custom, he made his public confession, detested his error and received our sacrament; then he lost consciousness."

"So you've triumphed! My compliments. Why such brilliant lighting?"

"Why? A necessary precaution against the demons of the night. It's the moment when those prowlers slip to the bedside of the dying to devour their souls. So the floor and walls of the chapel have been sprinkled with holy water, candles and torches lit . . . the crawling dogs, the lucifuges, won't approach. In any case, Mère Angélique is mounting good guard."

Meanwhile, the music was becoming more languid; the voices fell silent and the organ modulated an enervating solo. Sometimes, however, a dry click came to interrupt the melody, a woman's cries responded to it, immediately followed by vibrant burst of laughter.

"What's that noise, Josias? Why those clamors and those fits of joy?"

"The great help, Monsieur. The bruising help is being administered."

"Right, I can guess. The old practices of Saint-Médard."

"Our holy beatitudes. Monsieur Silvat has restored the worship in its integrity."

"And who are they martyrizing up there?"

"Martyrizing? Monsieur is joking. It's the sweetest kind of voluptuousness. Mère Angelique has resolved to rise toward the Lord in order to implore him in an ecstasy. But she's only as yet in the supreme languor; they're accelerating the rapture."

"What kind of ecstasy is your Mère Angéhique experiencing today, then?"

"The salvation of her brother impassions her. Holy among the holy, she has decided that she will flex the rigors of the Terrible Being."

"But I thought the decrees of your God were immutable. Elect or reproved, he knows you and preordains you for all eternity."

"Undoubtedly; but he has certain accommodations for us. Furthermore, Mère Angélique proclaimed this morning that a Montmesnil cannot be a reproved."

"This, Josias, is a spectacle that I must offer myself."

"Go up, Monsieur; you have permission. You'll find our postulants and our Messieurs gathered there. Your impious eyelids will finally be unsealed. It's a miracle to see, a marvel to hear.

A marvel to hear, a miracle to see . . . I had no need of his exhortation to seek to rejoin Monique. Accompanied by the brother doorman, I went up.[1]

---

1 Author's note: "See, on the subject of Convulsionnaires, their practices and their fashion of provoking ecstasy, the curious *Recueil des Prédictions* of Marie-Anne-Elisabeth Fronteau, the celebrated Jansenist Sister Holda. Five

In accordance with Monsieur Silvat's orders, entrance to the chapel was permitted to any curious individual, open to any gentile; I therefore slipped into the cenacle. The sumptuous drawing rooms, once decorated by President François de Montmesnil, were resplendent with light. Chandeliers, candelabra and girandoles had been illuminated, and if not for the actors I might have thought that I was in the foyer of some provincial theater. The floor, however, was moistened with holy water and a heavy perfume of incense—the odor insupportable to demons—took me by the throat and went to my head. Certainly, the wanderers in space, the vagabonds of the darkness—ghouls, lamias, empusas, larvae and lemurs, as an exorcist would have named them—had only to remain tranquil. If they risked an attack, beware of the burns of the aspergillum!

On the steps of the altar I immediately perceived the Bishop of Gorcum, Monsieur Justus. He was enthroned on a gilded armchair, a miter on his head, magnificent in the magnificence of his brocade cope. To his right and his left were seated two deacons—where had they sprung from?—in scarlet velvet dalmatics. For such a "night of delight" the officiants had put on festival ornaments. His Grandeur seemed to me to be bored and sullen, doubtless ashamed of exhibiting himself on such a grotesque and

---

volumes taken from her manuscripts, Paris 1822. See also, although it is not a Jansenist work, *La Vie et les Révélations de la soeur Nativité*, the description of her combat with the devil and her conversations with God. The book has, at any rate, always been suspect to the Catholic Church." Sister Holda's "ecstasies" commenced in 1733, according to a two-volume reprint of 1792; the same edition claims that Marie-Anne Fronteau was born in 1730 (and died in 1786), which would make her three years old when her career as a prophet began. The five-volume work cited is signed by Louis Silvy, in whose house in Paris Jansenists were still meeting in the 1810s and who later bought the domain of Port-Royal-des-Champs, to which he retired. The extent to which Silvy invented the prophecies he attributed to Sister Holda is undeterminable. The other work cited, which actually refers to "la Soeur de la Nativité (1731-1798)" is a four-volume collection of prophecies made by Clarisse-Jeanne de Royer in an "Urbanist" convent, and assembled by Charles Genet in 1819; again, the extent to which he invented them is undeterminable, but the collection has been recently reprinted.

lugubrious stage. Come from afar in order to absolve a great sinner in person, Monsieur Justus had perhaps been unaware until today of the monstrous practices of this house of insanity. Caught in a trap! And the florid prelate was sighing piteously. He kept quiet nevertheless, resigned to suffering all the miracles and also imbursing all the gifts.

Benches had been arranged along the walls in four rows. Israel had hoped for numerous visits, an entire invasion of Madianites and Philistines to convert. Alas, the infidels had not come, and on the benches, widely spaced out, were a dozen individuals of fantastic appearance. They were the new "Messieurs" of this burlesque Port-Royal; they appeared to me, for the most part, to be good-for-nothings and beggars. Nevertheless, they remained meditative, devoutly silent, captivated by the horror of the ceremony that was taking place at that moment Perhaps among those Élianites, those millenarians, there was some somber dreamer pursuing a mystical chimera of social renovation; perhaps also, there was some soul in distress, believing that he had finally found his way, and wanting to annihilate Doubt under Absurdity. So I refrained from smiling at the sight of those illuminates and their ragged penitents. Seven aged nuns with tubular headgear completed the personnel of the new Jerusalem, the stainless flock ranged in the cradle of the Stainless Lamb.

Much less comical, however, was the other half of the tableau. In the middle of the chapel Monsieur de Montmesnil's body had been exposed, still clad in his rags. Four assembled planks formed his bed; a wooden block was his pillow; ashes and earth—earth brought from Port-Royal—took the place of a mattress and blankets. The poor man was in his death throes. His face, emaciated to the point of fleshlessness, was a greenish white, and his motionless eyes were already iridescent with the vitreous reflections that are one of the indications of death. Unconscious of the sinister parade in which he was playing the leading role, he lay inert, like a cadaver. However, he was still breathing, and his strangled gasps traversed the rare silences of the harmonium. Monique was kneeling beside him and, bending her head, applying her forehead to her father's face. In spite of her heart-rending dolor, I experienced a dull irritation against her. Why did she not put a stop to the sacrilegious farce?

A saddening exhibition, a pretentious parody of a pious usage sometimes practiced in the primitive Church . . .

And I turned my eyes away. My attention, moreover, was quickly absorbed by another spectacle. Mère Angélique-Marie des Cinq-Plaies was at that moment enraptured in the empyrean. In order to ender her visit to Paradise, she had donned her most beautiful attire: the white habit with the scarlet cross of the abbesses of Port-Royal. Placed to the left of her brother, the blind woman was standing upright, rigid, her head high, her arms extended in the form of a cross. Was that the "supreme languor" or some morbid catalepsy? She seemed to me as if petrified. No movement agitated her body, no muscle budged in her contracted face. Very ugly, stitched with wrinkled, yellow and parchmented, she reminded me of the colorless mummies that grimace in Bordeaux in the crypt of the Tour Saint-Michel. On her forehead a profound violet-tinted crimson mark was hollowed out, doubtless the first of the five marvelous wounds that had merited her name. Two more scars also showed on her hands, but the blood was not flowing from those miraculous stigmata.

All eyes were turned toward the expiatrice, all bodies stretching in order to see more clearly. Prostrate before her, Monsieur Silvat was contemplating her with veneration. Did he truly have the faith, that physician, that doctor of the University of Leyden, whom a mysterious vocation had brought into this devout lunatic asylum? Yes, and soon I had no doubt about it: he believed . . .

He believed, and he wanted to oblige us to believe. But this evening, his *compelle intrare* appeared to me to be primarily exercised by the rod . . . Next to him I observed a strong fellow armed with a massive club, who was waiting, meditatively. He was one of the "helpful brothers," distributors of ineffable voluptuousness. The "messieurs" were silent, but a morbid agitation was shaking the female witnesses. Already, several of those women were writhing convulsively, moaning and begging:

"Me! Me too . . . ! Help! Consolations! Felicities!"

"The howlers," Josias said to me. "They're uttering the same clamors of desire that the pilgrims of the Grace once did at Saint-Médard."

Meanwhile, the minutes were flowing by, and the gate of Heaven was slow to open. Impatient to accelerate the rapture, the helpful brother made as if to resume his caresses; a gesture from Monsieur Silvat stopped his hand.

"Enough! The eighth echelon is now crossed; the ecstasy is about to commence . . . Venerable Mother, can you see?"

"I can see!" murmured the nun; and abruptly, she collapsed on the floor.

"On your knees, the rest of you!" ordered the organizer. "Heaven is about to speak to the earth."

Everyone hastened to obey; the harmonium fell silent, and there was a profound silence.

"Spouse of Adonai, rose of Sharon, tabernacle of Cedar," Monsieur Salvat went on, "deign to describe to us the sidereal splendors of the palace that the Elect inhabit."

Then, in a voice that was very low at first, but mounting gradually, in halting words, breathless and gasping with terror, the ecstasized individual commenced:

"White, oh, very white! Radiant whiteness . . . ! Sun . . . ! Red, also . . . ! Fulgurant crimson . . . ! Lightning!"[1]

She hesitated, searching for terms, and then resumed in a plaintive, tearful tone, soon desperate:

"But I'm blind! I don't know colors! I can't describe! I can't, I can't! God, my God! What, still blind, even in the splendor of

---

1 Author's note: "It is well-known that recent experiments have established that for certain blind people, 'white' and 'red' express an idea of physical beauty; 'black' and 'blue,' on the contrary, signify ugliness."

your palace? Be clement, open my eyes . . . ! I have given myself to you, in order to see . . . in order to see you! Open my eyes . . . ! Ah . . . ! I can see! The blessed Claudine-Armande, my saintly ancestress, has descended toward me; she is speaking to me, she is encouraging me. Deacon Pâris is also by my side; he has taken me by the hand; he is guiding me . . . No, no, my two patrons, for pity's sake, let's stop; I'm afraid! Out there, in the infinite distance, what dazzling light . . . God!"

And, gripped by fear, she buried her face in the mass of earth that was covering Monsieur de Montmesnil's body. The Bishop of Gorcum shrugged his shoulders; Monsieur Silvat perceived that, and addressed us:

"The same vision, my brothers, as that of the apostle Saint John on the rock of Patmos: 'His head and his hair were white like wool, as white as snow; and his eyes were as a flame of fire.'"[1]

Then, satisfied with his commentary, the skilful exegete looked at the bishop with a wrathful expression. Reprimanded in that fashion, the excessively skeptical Monsieur Justus lowered his eyes. But already the blind woman had raised her head; her face expressed an unspeakable bliss; she was smiling, she was even singing.

"I can hear! If God is all Light, he is all Harmony . . . oh, too happy, my soul! Drink long draughts from the torrent of voluptuousness; intoxicate yourself with celestial inebriations . . . What a canticle! What an endless melody! Organs, flutes, oboes, violins. Three seraphim are singing a motet; Paradise takes it up in chorus. I recognize the voices of the nuns of Port-Royal; our Messieurs of the Desert, our priests of Saint-Médard make themselves heard and respond to them: 'Glory, glory, thrice glory to the One who has sanctified us by martyrdom!'"

"An exact description," observed Monsieur Silvat. Saint Augustine in his *Manuel* has depicted to us at length all the floods of harmony that fill the blissful palaces: 'Here resound

---

1 *Revelation* 1:14; I have inserted the A.V. text rather than back-translating Thierry's version.

harps accompanied by cantilenas; there organs spread their fluid sounds like honey.'"[1]

The explainer could, however, have dispensed with such erudition; no one was listening to him. A current of dementia passed through the assembly; in their turn, its members intended to play their part in the eternal serenade offered to Jehovah. The women uttered bizarre cries; the great hysteria raged contagiously; one might have thought oneself among the agitated of the Salpêtrière.

"Mewlers and barkers," Josias told me. "Very advanced in perfection. The Spirit first makes them sing the alleluias of animals."

Discordant and tumultuous, the charivari was prolonged for a few seconds, but abruptly, everything stopped; the seeress had just uttered a howl.

"Aaah! There she is, the maleficent Beast, the Tenebrous, the Temptress of filthy passions: the Enemy . . . black and blue . . . there she is . . . Pooh! What odors of fornication! She exhales all the stinks of Hell!"[2]

"The demon!" exclaimed Monsieur Silvat, alarmed. "Quickly, a prayer! The prose of the exorcism."

The harmonium immediately commenced a prelude, and quivering voices began to sing the most extravagant prayers.

The peril was indeed becoming menacing. From one moment to the next, the visionary's terror augmented; very agitated, she was now crawling on her hands and knees. Her face projected forward like a dog at bay, sniffing, grunting and growling, she abused the Enemy: the demon scented, perhaps perceived:

1 The reference is to a collection of translated works by St. Augustine first published in France in 1502 as *Le Manuel Saint Augustin*, one of the earliest French texts printed in that country.

2 There is an ambiguity here intrinsic to the French language: because the noun *bête* [beast] has the feminine gender, the pronouns associated with it are automatically rendered as *elle* without any necessary indication of sex. In the earlier report of Mère Angélique-Marie's visions, therefore, I translated *elle* as "it." In the present instance, however, for reasons that will become obvious momentarily, it seems more appropriate to employ "she."

"Get away. Get away! Yes, I know her, You have the name Leila, the prince of the vagabonds of the night.[1] Empusa, lamia, siren! You put on the figure and body of a woman. It is you who come to assail and put in temptation monks and cenobites. *Vade retro!* You shall not eat this soul . . . ! Listen, listen! Can you hear her, the devouring Beast? She is prowling, at this moment, around our cenacle; she is searching, she is examining, she is ferreting. *Vade retro* . . . ! What, stopping before the house of God, your Lord? I find that very bold, accursed one . . . ! She is recoiling . . . get away . . . ! Ah, she's going to enter, she's coming up . . . No! The singing of our canticles has terrified her; the odor of sanctity is suffocating her; she is still hesitant . . . Ah! Ah! She's approaching . . . back . . . ! God! God . . . ! Here she is!"

A clamor departed from all mouths; I turned my head swiftly. On the threshold of the chapel, Clorinde de Villereuse was looking at us insolently.

XXVI

In spite of her recent misfortunes and the pillage of her wardrobe, she was still elegantly clad: blue satin skirt, velvet mantle, hat with black plumes—"black and blue," as the ecstatic had depicted her.

"May I come in?" she asked. "Yes, I imagine! I'm the Marquise de Montmesnil."

"Go away!" Monsieur Silvat enjoined her. "Your presence here is a profanation."

"No, and no. Phrases. I shan't leave!"

---

1 The use of the name Leila in this context is puzzling; it had been used in England as a female forename in a "romance" by Isaac d'Israeli and a novel by Edward Bulwer-Lytton, but neither character is demonic. Demons do figure large in James Paton's poem "Leila," but the eponymous heroine is an innocent. It is probable that Mère Marie-Angélique is referring to Lilith, Adam's demonized first wife.

She took a chair, and without paying any heed to the objurgation, installed herself near the altar. There, playing with a lorgnon, tranquil and smiling, she started to examine the face of the moribund. Her attitude was odious, revolting in its provocative cynicism, and yet Monique remained silent, still kneeling.

A solemn silence had succeeded the rumors of the initial alarm. All the tremblers were reassured: the devil was only a woman. For myself, I was following with anguish the prologue to the drama that was about to begin: the world and its corruption daring to assail a justified soul! It was like a living and brutal staging of the mystical combats that had been raging in the penitent's cell for so many years.

Monsieur Silvat, however, had risen to his feet, and, quivering with a holy fury, advanced toward the intruder; suddenly, he stopped. Plaintive words and suppliant sobs had just escaped the lips of the dying man.

"Amour," he moaned, "sweetness of loving!"

". . . Of loving one's neighbor in Jesus Christ," rectified the Jansenist. "You hear, Madame? He pardons you."

The pardon of the Christian? No, personally, I had recognized it . . . sensual poetry, the sonnet so ardently carnal; the verse that the prevaricating judge had written at the moment of forfeiting his duty! Oh, power of delirium that is able to extract from the heart its most intimate thoughts. He cherished . . . he still idolized . . . and he was appealing to his perdition.

A sentiment of poignant pity seized me and distressed me. My gaze fixed on Monsieur de Montmesnil, I no longer took my eyes off him. Had he clearly perceived the presence of the "beloved"? Why was he, who had not even recognized his daughter, shuddering like that? Frissons were shaking him in convulsive spasms; while gasping, he was agitating; his arms were making feeble efforts, as if to embrace, as if to enlace. With a start, he raised his head, and suddenly uttered a cry of distress.

"Come! Come! Let's go! Exile . . . Hell . . . with you!"

They were the passionate words, the words of infinite tenderness that he had pronounced, recklessly, before his condemnation and his flight to Geneva. So he was seeing once again the distant days, he was reviving gladly his life of sin and tearful illusions; his long remorse had only ever been a long regret."

"Amour," he murmured again, "sweetness of loving!"

Then, a tearing sigh; the head fell backwards, and the rattle immediately ceased; Monsieur de Montmesnil was dead. He had died in an ardent appeal to human sensuality, recaptured by his sin in a last assault of terrestrial temptation: woman, the enemy, was triumphant.

"Satan, you have vanquished us!" declaimed the seeress, collapsing on the floor for a second time.

"Yes, vanquished!" said Monsieur Silvat, in his turn. "The Abyss is exultant! One damned soul more!"

And as the Bishop of Gorcum intoned a *Miserere,* the grim predestinator cut off the psalmody.

"Sacrilegious supplications! No outrageous insistence against the Verdict! The prayer for the reproved is an offense to God."

"The sinner seemed, however, to be very repentant," objected the conciliatory Monsieur Justus.

"No matter!" riposted the sectarian. "He was one of those souls destined to the demons; the Son of Man did not die for those!"

Then, with an imperious gesture, he designated the door to us.

"Everything is consummated! Withdraw!"

"No," said Monique getting to her feet. "I am in my home. I'm staying."

XXVII

On the injunction of Monsieur Silvat, the chapel was promptly evacuated. The entirely pagan end of Monsieur de Montmesnil, in spite of the prayers and of the exorcism, had produced a disastrous effect. Everyone was making reflections, ironic and malevolent commentaries; a breath of skepticism was blowing through the house. Hearts still hesitant, those people, in their lukewarm zeal, were beginning to doubt Mère Angélique and her credit with the Eternal. A miracle became necessary, a splendid marvel, in order to reaffirm the faith shaken in the conscience of all those reasoners . . .

For myself, in spite of my emotion, I was only thinking about a means of obtaining a decisive conversation with Monique. At any price, and that evening, I wanted to talk to her despair, to show her the devotion of my amour, perhaps to convince her. "Is not the ability to console," a moralist has said, "already to be able to love?"

Yes, but it was necessary to rejoin her in great mystery, in order to avoid compromising her. While meditating some skillful strategy, I was going down the steps of the staircase when Madame de Villereuse approached me. Without any concern for the slightest propriety, she was returning to the Avenue Velasquez.

"Finished, quite finished, this time," she sighed. "Would you believe it, I feel distressed."

"Do I believe you, dear Madame? One would never know the treasures of tenderness that your smile conceals."

"Don't mock. Yes, I'm quite shaken. The poor fellow! How he loved me!"

"A fine triumph over the good God! I congratulate you on it."

"Poor illuminate! I feel remorse. Perhaps I didn't understand him?"

Her remorse, however, was of short duration; an importunate companion, remorse!

"By the way," she said, "I was going to write to you. Big, very big news, my dear! Our friend Saint-Réal has found capital, and he's going to found his theater. I'm expecting a creation from you, the principal role of a great lover."

"Oh, I know, Marquise. A role as a mother has never been your employ."

"Too much wit," she said, dryly. "A quip that will make Monique laugh. She has need of distractions; go and cheer her up, then, as quickly as possible."

Firmly resolved not to quit the place, I took my leave of the sensitive Clorinde and retraced my steps.

The few dozen fellow-travelers, strangers to the community and simple followers of ceremonies, were only withdrawing slowly. In the street, Josias was supervising their departure, and at that moment he was chatting to one of them outside the door. The opportunity was therefore propitious to carry out the plan that I had traced. It seemed to me to be easy of accomplishment: to await the exit of the last stragglers and then to go back up to the chapel in order to rejoin Monique there. I did not doubt that the dear mourner would spend the night keeping vigil over her father's body. Perhaps I might still bump into the terrible Silvat or even Mère Angélique, but too bad; I would explain myself. Mademoiselle de Montmesnil was presently in her own home and I was only obeying her injunctions.

Well reasoned! But where to hide? Over there, at the extremity of the vault, extended protective darkness, a silent garden; a spacious and tranquil hiding-place; in the winter frost, no one would come there to sigh at the stars. Rapidly, I slid toward that darkness.

I now found myself in the discreet enclosure situated behind the interior façade of the house. It was there that I had perceived the expiatrice abbess, some time before, walking and stumbling under the burden of her cross. The night was dark, opaque and very misty; I could scarcely glimpse the white skeletons of trees powdered with frost or the snowy undulation of the lawn. Chestnut trees spread their branches at the entrance to the garden; I went to hide amid the thickest branches.

Nine o'clock chimed. Oh, what a frenzy of amour mine was becoming! Was the contagion gaining me of that house of insanity?

House of insanity: yes, certainly. And yet its extravagance no longer surprised me. Old readings came back to my memory, and in comparing, I understood. A Jansenism that had become vulgar, the noblest doctrine sadly debased—but true Jansenism, all that! In the words of Monsieur Silvat I rediscovered, exaggerated to the point of absurdity, the ancient instruction of Port-Royal, the faith of an Arnauld or a Quesnel, not to say a Saint Augustine. There was all the despair, and all the terror, of their theology, their desolating fashion of explaining the mystery of our destiny:

A creator God who had taken his creature in hatred; the Son of Man who had not died for all humans, and the blood of Redemption departed at the whim of an inscrutable caprice; fatalism, produced by divine arbitrariness, the sole and unique master of all our actions; the preordination of the sinner to his sin; reprobation attaining the reproved before birth—the reproved being almost all of us; the practice of God by virtue of the sole attraction of the ideal God declared impossible—or, rather, offensive, blasphemous to God; the dolorous crippling of the meaning of life and the misunderstanding of human dignity; the deliberate annihilation by the vilest martyrdom of our intelligence, the mother of our pride; the most imperious sentiments of nature suspect or condemned: no family born of the flesh; the piety of a daughter or the tenderness of a father declared dangerous for eternal salvation; this poor world becoming, finally, the purveyor of Hell, and consequently that Hell transformed into a kind of human pantheon, since independent virtue, philosophical wisdom, science, genius and glory all had to be swallowed up therein . . .

In brief, a logical affliction of insanity, of exacerbated Calvinsim: a Christianity in delirium.

Yes, I recognized Jansensim in those same buffooneries that had made me indignant or made me smile a little while ago: the repulsive staging of the death-bed, practiced several times at Port-Royal; the contortions of the convulsionnaires, worthy emulators of the barkers of Sant-Médard, and even the invective addressed to the demon, the crawling dog that had dared to sniff Deacon Pâris at prayer one evening. That, therefore, was what had become, in being combined with the popular, of the soul of a Nicole or a Pascal! In deserting philosophical solitude, it had at the crossroads the soul of a Curé Vaillant, Oh, that one, in his trivial vulgarity, the multitude had understood! Bizarre Jansenists still met in our provinces, even in Paris; religions are so slow to die.

And it was the death-throes of that degenerate faith that the fanatic Silvat intended to revive today. Better than a prophet, he was a psychologist, for he had divined that the human heart is thirsty for marvels and he had procured a harvest of them. Woeful Jansenism! But alas, the one had fatally to engender the other. The apposition of the Holy Thorn curing Marguerite Périer of her lachrymal fistula contained within it the therapeutic beatings of the "helpful brothers," and on the parchment of his amulet Pascal, exalting his hallucination, had inscribed in advance all the visions of an Angélique de Montmesnil . . .[1]

Lamentable theology, but so full of verity! Who among us has not sensed seething within his being the morbid ferments of human corruption? Yes, whatever its name might be, "original sin" exists. In our day, the term has been changed; we say "atavism," but the implacable fatality has remained the same: the heredity of vices; transmission of instinct; degeneracy of an entire race; moral defects of ancestor to often reproduced in their descendants. Original sin! Oh, nullity, nullity of human wisdom! After so much philosophizing, to return today to the Judaic revelation, that familial solidarity proclaimed by the Decalogue! Is it necessary, then, for us to cry with the Manichean: "Birth, thou art an evil!" or to envy the sad aspiration of the Buddhist, the repose of our intelligence in the annihilation of Nirvana?

---

1 Marguerite Périer was Blaise Pascal's niece, who was allegedly cured of an ocular malady in 1656 by the application of a thorn from the crown of thorns, an alleged relic then in the possession of the Abby of Port-Royal: a supposed miracle that helped to provoke numerous conversions.

Quarter past nine. By the saintly deacon, what cold! A mantle of ice fell over my shoulders. And that Josias had not reentered his lodge! The coaching entrance was closed again, however, and the last catechumen had departed a long time ago. But no, the idler was walking back and forth under the porch. What was he waiting for? Oh, if the rigid Monsieur Silvat had been able to see me in my agitation with what a scornful mouth he would have shamed "the spur of concupiscence"—the only term by which he deigned to qualify amour.

Slowly, the successive minutes went by; the lights in the windows of the façade were extinguished; silence, and perhaps quietude, was already making the house torpid. I was about to emerge when a sound of voices caused me to withdraw into the shadow. At the bottom of the stairway Monsieur Silvat was giving orders to Josias.

"Our Mère Angélique and Sister Euphémie are going to depart for a long voyage. You'll go to fetch a carriage for them at half past ten. I shall accompany them to the railway station. Watch, then, and await my return."

"Our Mother is absenting herself?"

"She is abandoning this house never to return. Satan is expelling us. We are transporting our tabernacle to the Israel of Holland."

"To Gorcum?"

"No, to Utrecht. I have broken all relation with Monsieur Justus this evening. That man does not have the faith."

"So we're quitting our homeland?" sighed the sentimental Josias.

"What is your fatherland? Personally, I only know one: the Celestial City."

"Amen," murmured the doorkeeper. "I understand, but I have so much need of the Grace."

"Believe blindly, and perhaps it will descend. Now, to your work. I shall go to meditate in my cell."

"Where should I inform our Mother?"

"At ten o'clock, upstairs. She is praying in the blessed Claudine-Armande's attic; I shall join her there. Go."

What a subordinate amenity, and above all what an abuse of "me," the hateful "me." But Brother Josias did not take offence. Nevertheless, he delayed going and appeared to be emotional.

"Father," he exclaimed, "reassure my conscience. I feel very troubled, for I've stumbled upon a scandal."

"A scandal here? Speak."

"Mère Angélique is not going to attend her brother's funeral?"

"No; eternity separates them forever."

"What will be done with Monsieur de Montmesnil's body?"

"His daughter will dispose of it. A Roman ceremony or civil burial, as she pleases."

"Poor demoiselle. Is she going to keep vigil until morning?"

"If the sinner weeps over the sinner, it is of no importance to us. It is written: 'Let the dead bury their dead.'"

And, hard, stiff and arrogant, having discarded any mask of forbearance, Monsieur Silvat left the vault, traversed the garden and went to his cell.

XXVIII

Alone! So, abandoned by everyone, Monique would remain alone. I was patient for a few more minutes, and then, with precaution, risked emerging from my hiding place. On the stairway, thick darkness, but on the first floor there was a thin thread of light. Like a thief in the night I made my way toward it.

No sound except, at intervals, a few sobs. Her! And yet, I hesitated. I was gripped by a scruple; I heard a kind of appeal of my conscience: "What audacity is yours! To want to talk about amour at such a moment! At least respect her tears. Go away." No: a momentary indecision. "Dare then!" replied another voice. "Take advantage of the opportunity; seduce her despair.

She is weeping? Be able to weep with her, and you will captivate her heart."

The doors had been closed; I opened one quietly and went in.

On the threshold, I stopped, seized. My first sensation was one of vague terror, so sinister did the aspect of the chapel seem to have become. The wax candles, chandeliers and standard lamps had been snuffed out, and like a symbol of filial piety, still faithful in the abandonment of all, a single tallow candle was burning next to the recumbent body. Its flickering flame accentuated the hardness of the motionless face, and in his cadaveric rigidity, Monsieur de Montmesnil was frightful to behold. But the flame only illuminated a narrow space around the litter; the rest of the gallery extended its profundities in compact darkness.

I was not mistaken; Monique was really alone. She was still kneeling, curbing her head toward the mortuary bed. At the sound of the door she stood up, alarmed.

"You, you? Don't come in. For pity's sake, don't come in!"

"I'm a friend," I said to her. "I've come to share your trouble."

"Leave me!" she said, wildly. "Everything separates us henceforth. I feel broken, annihilated. The hand of God has descended upon me."

She interrupted herself, changed her mind, and made me a sign to advance.

"Oh! What's that? Come quickly, look. My father is still alive!"

I approached. Illusion! The body was already icy. Sadly, I shook my head.

"Yes, yes! He's still alive!" Monique insisted. "Why are you deceiving me? I just saw him shudder. Your presence here makes him indignant!"

Again she leaned over Monsieur de Montmesnil, examined him for a long time, and then finally got up, with a distraught expression.

"Dead!" she exclaimed. "He didn't even recognize his daughter!"

"We arrived too late, my poor friend. His thought, already obscured, couldn't . . ."

"But he recognized . . . the other . . . the abominable woman . . . his perdition! He recognized her, and wanted to put his arms around her! An end, entirely happy! But what voluptuousness, then, is amour, since it is stronger than death-throes, and transforms the death-rattle into a sigh of delight?"

Abruptly, she uttered a cry, raised her fingers toward her hair and pulled her veil over her forehead. In the penumbra in which we were standing I could only see her eyes clearly: ardent eyes burning with fever, shining with an unsustainable glare. Bewildered, I seized her hands.

"Monique!"

"Go away!" she said, struggling. "Spare me! No sacrilege!"

Vain efforts. I tightened my grip.

"*Amour, sweetness of loving,*" I murmured to her, leaning toward her face.

She moved her head away and looked to me fearfully. "Accursed! He dares to make the dead speak! You're infamous!"

But she was no longer resisting, and, as if subdued by a magic formula, she abandoned her hands to the pressure of mine. Then, making her recoil slowly, I only stopped at the extremity of the gallery. We were now completely enveloped by darkness, silent in a profound and lugubrious silence. Passionately, my eyes sought her fascinating eyes, the haunting of my days, the vision of my nights; but she, shaken by frequent spasms, kept her gaze fixed on the distant flame.

"Don't push me away," I said. "You've said yourself that your only friend, henceforth, is me. Indifferent and odious to your mother, or rather an orphan, you . . ."

"I have nothing else to do but become your mistress!" she cried, hurling a burst of laughter at me.

She freed her hands and recoiled a few paces.

"Monsieur Surville, consoler of the afflicted and my unique friend, do you believe in the demon?"

"The demon? Why that question?"

"Because it's necessary to be driven by the devil to want to suborn a poor young woman weeping over the body of her father."

Her words were insulting and her voice scornful; however, she was no longer moving away. She appeared to be suffering cruelly; her agitation increased; her respiration became halting; a dolorous rictus contracted her mouth.

"So many emotions are killing you," I said. "Let's go."

But she did not hear; her haggard eyes were following the oscillation of the funereal light in the distance; and she was still laughing, laughing convulsively.

"His mistress!" she said, after a long silence. "What ignominy of thought at such a moment! His mistress!"

"No, not that word! It debases amour! Marriage will soon permit us . . ."

"Come on, enough hypocrisy! I'm not one of those that one marries; you know that very well. Yes, your mistress: I've read that word in your gaze. So be it, it doesn't matter to me. If you love, I will love. But I want amour . . . human amour, in spite of God! Monsieur Surville, you whom the devil sends me, do you believe in God?"

This time, I made no response; the incoherence of her speech was beginning to alarm me; an increasing anxiety took hold of me, a mysterious fear.

"No," she replied, "you don't believe in him. Personally, I'd like to flee him. God? I only know him by virtue of the harm that he does me, incessantly. I've just expelled from here his most fervent adorers, the wretches who tortured my father for such a long time. Well, he's seeking to avenge them. Look, he's torturing me; he wants me to yield; I won't yield. Me, a nun! Ha ha ha! But it's you I love—you alone. Do you hear? Do you understand? I'm scornful of you, but I love you: you, desire you, sin . . . Take me away . . ."

I had to sustain her; fainting, she was about to fall.

"What exaltation, Monique! What harm are you talking about?"

"Atrocious . . . oh, atrocious! The harm of my family! He claws me, he digs into my flesh . . . Your mistress? I accept! I abandon myself. We'll leave together. We . . . we . . . ah . . . ! The divine kiss!"

What was she saying? With a furious movement, I enlaced the young woman, and placed my lips on her forehead . . .

"Loving! Sweetness of loving!" she sighed, as if in ecstasy. "God . . . !"

Suddenly, I recoiled in horror; my mouth and my fingers were stained with blood. And suddenly, also, she uttered a scream and collapsed on the floor.

"Monique! Monique!"

No response. I tried to lift her up; she was unconscious. I ran to fetch the candle that was burning next to the litter, came back, and stopped, fearful.

Inert and rigid, exactly like a corpse, she was lying on the floor, her arms in a cross. But her convulsed head was raised, projected forwards; her dilated, fearful, enormous eyes were staring into space. Five large rips appeared in her forehead, vermilion red, which designed a sort of crown . . . hideous, hideous to behold! Two more wounds had also formed on the backs of her hands, and a pink sweat was trickling drop by drop, from those wounds . . .

Catalepsy!

However, confused sounds, a strange stammer, emerged from the grimacing mouth.

"Amour," she stammered, "sweetness of loving . . . ! God . . . !"

I ran to the door and called for help. In response to my cries footsteps were heard and soon Monsieur Silvat, guiding Mère Angélique, entered the chapel.

On perceiving me he addressed a gesture of indignation to me, but without giving him time to launch into invective, I pointed at Monique.

He advanced, and raised his arms to the heavens.

"The revenge of God! A miracle! Reverend Mother, a splendid miracle! Satan, the victory remains ours!"

Guided by him, the blind woman approached the cataleptic, bent down, felt her forehead and palpated her hands. In her turn, she uttered a cry of triumph: "The stigmata! Our glorious stigmata! Yes, yes, the revenge of God!"

Transported, she embraced her niece, kissed the suppurating wounds devotedly, and addressed words of tenderness to her, words of mystical exaltation.

"Be my daughter henceforth; be the child of my tears! I have wept so much for your father! You, a veritable Montmesnil, an elect, the heir of our sanctity? The Eternal be blessed! What are you saying? The sweetness of loving God? Yes, the infinite sweetness; there is no other amour down here. Repeat, dear child, say and say again your canticle: I listen to it with delight . . . My dove, my immaculate rose, my pretty saint! You belong to us; we shall be able to snatch you from the earth!"

"Let's hurry," enjoined Monsieur Silvat.

And, lifting the paralyzed body, he carried it out of the chapel. Mère Angélique went out with them.

My first impulse had been to follow them, but on the threshold it was necessary for me to stop.

"Where are you going, Monsieur Surville? Your indiscretion astonishes me. Go back inside. I'll rejoin you in a moment."

Not doubting that someone would return promptly to bring me news, I obeyed. So many shocks had exhausted me. I went to sit down on one of the benches in the chapel . . .

And time went by. Weary of waiting, I picked up the candle and started examining the objects suspended from the wall. Jansenist paintings; I recognized them . . . Wait! What was that?

It was, handwritten in a golden frame, a citation of Saint Augustine, a famous phrase from the *Soliloquies*:

"Lord, when I consider the souls that you have chosen, I remain stupefied, and cannot penetrate the profundity of your designs. Those whose names you have inscribed in the Book of Life cannot perish. Destining them for your Temple, you wash away their corruption with your own hands . . ."

Bizarre, so bizarre, that text, in such a circumstance. It seemed to me truly to apply to Monique . . .

"They fall, and are not wounded; their very sin enables their salvation."

Their salvation? Oh, but no! The god of the Jansensists would not steal a beloved woman from me! I ran to the door; it resisted; I had been locked in. I called out. Nothing budged in the house . . .

Finally, toward midnight, Monsieur Silvat reappeared. Furious, I ran toward him.

"Where is she? Tell me. Where is she?"

"Gone. Beyond your reach. You will never see her again."

✳

. . . .
. . . .
. . . .
. . . .
. . . .
. . . .

Never again? Yes, I have seen her again, alas, and I was bowled over by the shock of my sudden encounter.

What events had been accomplished in four years! The sale of the Hôtel de Mensnilmont and the disappearance of its inhabitants; the death of Prince Zrelinsky; the marriage of the beautiful Clorinde with that other beau, the actor Saint-Réal; and also, my repeated successes on the stage, my growing reputation. I am almost famous, now; I have earned a certain fortune. We would have been so happy together, my love!

Four years, and silence! Despair first, bitter sadness, then pensive chagrin, soon the charm of regrets. An ever-increasing fog blurred, today, a too-distant image. Have I, then, forgotten? No. Veritable forgetfulness is a shroud that one never lifts, and I sometimes loved to tear the shroud in order to contemplate my memories. I evoked then the gracious phantom of the young woman with the blonde hair, the flames of her dark eyes, the unhealthy pallor of her face, the seductions of her heart-rending smile; I gazed at her and remained thoughtful . . .

Oh, why have I seen her again?

It was near the city of Utrecht, in the spring of this year, that chance put me in her presence. I had come to the university city where, I believed, new victories awaited me. Its theater, although very modest, was putting on one of my plays with great publicity: my work of predilection, the dear *Nazaréen*. But as soon as I arrived it was necessary to retreat. "Translation is treason," and that, fashioned to the taste of his homeland by my colleague Octavius Bloysmans, pastor, journalist and dramaturge, was nothing but a frightful carnage of my thought, a massacre of my work.

That day our rehearsal was prolonged and stormy. Lamentation of the author, criticism of the impresario, sniggering of the actresses—nothing was lacking the preparations for the fête. Exasperated by those shameful mutilations I went out, making a scandal; but on the Vredeburg Monsieur Boysmans joined me.

"Why so much fury?" he said to me. "My cuts are indispensable. We're in a religious city here."

"Get away! Your university? I thought it in full rationalist movement."

"Well, yes, our future advocates, our student pharmacists or veterinarians—very philosophical. But our theologians! In any case, an entire population of believers, reformed or Catholic, not to mention the Mennonite, the Moravian, the Jansenist, the . . ."

"Jansenists? Are they numerous?

"Enough to cause annoyance. Archbishop, chapter, priests of Saint Gertrude—more than is necessary to cry scandal."

"An entire colony, then?"

"Yes, a few thousand faithful. Have you seen their quarter? No? Well, pay it a visit. Go see those curious houses, huddled in the shadow of their church, those mistrustful doors, those suspicious windows: humble lodgings, ostentatious in humility. Fanatical and very intransigent people."

"What a speech for the prosecution, my revered friend! However, Monsieur Calvinists, they're your distant cousins."

"No, I protest. Too idolatrous, and we liberals want to overturn them. Personally, for example, I'm a pastor, but fundamentally quite agnostic. Oh, it isn't your Jansenists who will go to preach in the world the Gospel of the new humanity, the religion without dogmas, the Christianity of Reason."

Very Protestant, my timid translator. I made him that observation; he was content to smile.

Conversing thus we had emerged from the old quarters to reach the promenades. In front of us the Maliebaan developed the perspective of its sixfold pathway, and we were chatting, idly under the branches of the greening lindens. Dusk was falling, a Dutch spring evening charged with moist effluvia, those blue-tinted mists that the grass and the turf emit. The twilight was already misting the distances of the city, and, surpassing its floating grayness, the tower of the Dom sent us the sound of its carillons. Everything in the roseate plain was restful, languid, and soporific.

Sitting down under the scents of the nascent flowers, we had resumed our conversation.

"A very curious work, your *Nazaréen*," Boymans said to me. "It will make its tour of the Netherlands; I'll take responsibility for that. Have you thought about Germany?"

"I've thought about it; an adaptation is in preparation for a theater in Dresden."

"It'll succeed there. Yes, a work of high range, but so scantly French! How, in a land where everything is a joke, have you felt that rationalism so full of tears? One would think that a Christian soul, long fervent but finally disillusioned, whose dolorous blasphemy . . ."

He interrupted himself and stretched out his hand.

"Look! You were talking about your Jansenists. Well, look over there! There's a curious specimen . . . it's the stigmatized!"

At the extremity of the Mall I perceived, heading toward Utrecht, two young nuns in black dresses, coifed with tubular headdresses, without veils. They were about to pass in front of us.

"What stigmatized?" I asked, suddenly emotional.

"One of your compatriots, a simple convert in a Janensist community of our city, but a miraculous one, even more surprising than Palma d'Oria or Louise Lateau.[1] Every week, on a fixed day, she falls into ecstasy, receives the stigmata and proclaims the sweetness of loving God. People come to see her from ten leagues around; few conversions, though; a futile marvel. The Protestant mocks and the Catholic mistrusts. In any case, a poor girl, almost an idiot, she's ordinarily confined in the infirmary."

The two sisters had now drawn level with us. One of them—doubtless the stigmatized—was dragging herself painfully, leaning heavily on the arm of her companion. They were talking to one another in French; the chatter of a nurse, talking about tisanes and cataplasms . . .

Shivering, I stood up.

Monique!

But I fell back on my bench. Oh, the disgust! The monstrous apparition! A face stitched by scars, a purulent mask, all wounds . . . nothing but a wound!

With a bewildered gaze, the invalid looked at me. Did she recognize me? Yes, for I saw her shudder and hasten her pace.

She passed by.

---

1 Louise Lateau and Palma d'Oria are both prominently featured in *Les Stigmatisées* (1873) by Antoine Imbert-Gourbeyre. The author, a physician, accounts for their "ecstasies" and physical symptoms as instances of hysteria. His study was quickly supplemented by two books by William Alexander Hammond, published in 1876 and 1879, which put more emphasis on the "fasting" of the two young girls in question, whom modern retrospective diagnosis would probably qualify as anorexic.

THE POMPEIIAN FRESCO

The fourth species of demons is the most redoubtable. Cunning and perverse, they frequently take pleasure in donning feminine form.
Trithemius, *The Book of Questions*, cited by Del Rio (*Disquistiones Magicae*)[1]

I
A Première in Monte Carlo

. . . And *Leucosia*, the lyric drama by my friend Marcellus, finished, very quietly defended by the timid bravos of the "petty symbolists." Was it a success? Certainly not.

It had pleased me, however, in spite of its nebulous mysticism, that original and sometimes powerful work. Besotted with ultra-wagnerism, inventing for his own part the most complex

---

1 Trithemius (Johann Heidenberg, 1462-1516) was a Benedictine abbot whose students included Cornelius Agrippa and Paracelsus, and who became a legendary figure in the pseudohistory of occult science as a result of second-hand reports by them and others. His *Steganographia*, published long after his death in 1606, had a considerable reputation—among people who had never read it—as a handbook of magic, but it is actually the founding text of the science of cryptography. The demonological text credited to Trithemius by the Jesuit Martin Delrio (1551-1608) is certainly apocryphal. The highly fanciful *Disquisitiones Magicae* was first published in three volumes in 1599-1600, and became a key reference text for later demonologists. The French title attributed to it in the body of the story is presumably credited to a fictitious translation.

harmonies, a composer of religious music and an author of interesting oratorios, and also an independent, intransigent, decadent poet, the "neo-Christian Marcel Lautrem, had written the libretto and the score. "Me, I say, and that's enough. Make way for the young!"

Make way for the young! Now, the thirty-three springs of my friend Marcellus, his combative articles in the revues of the Saint-Sulpice district, the conclusiveness of his thought and the virulence of his pen, his fashion of attacking, insulting and mocking Voltairean philosophism—in sum, a glory well established under the Arcades of the Odéon and the speechifying brasseries of the Latin quarter—all merited the tall fellow in fine title of "young." But, O God of Pindar and you, classical Euterpe, what complicated and apocalyptic artistry!

"Blondel," the illuminate in question had said to me, "no one has yet dared what I am going to attempt in Monte Carlo. My *Leucosia* is intended as a war-cry uttered against Woman."

"Against Woman? What blasphemy! You'll be whistled."

"It doesn't matter. I shall state my thought entirely. Woman is our perdition. Woe betide the insensate who listens to her! He will hear the Voice of the Abyss."

"A voice that has often charmed me. Bah, my dear: Hercules and Omphale; Samson and Delilah; old, very old stories!"

"Stories ever new. What! The strength, the honor, even the genius of a man at the mercy of a sigh of his mistress? I rebel! So, a religious, not to say superhuman drama, my *Leucosia* is metaphysics in action. I celebrate therein the end of sin and the death of the flesh . . . You're smiling? Why? I am the Paladin of the Soul."

"Paladin of the Soul? Metaphysics in action? Admirable! Will you be understood?"

"We shall see."

Alas, I had seen: an entire audience sniggering. Here and there, it is true, a few adepts of Symbolism, fine esthetes with doll-like faces quivering on their orchestra armchairs; but in the boxes and on the balconies, Grand Dukes, pachas, Yankee oil barons, Guatemalan generals, ladies from Pimlico, baronesses from the Marbeuf quarter—in brief, the upper crust of Monte Carlo—scarcely seemed subject to the charm of metaphysics in action. That hymn exhaled toward the Ideal bewildered the courtesan and the gigolo . . .

For myself, a naturalist painter, the truculent lyricism of Marcellus frightened my prosaic brain; this, in the style of a reporter, is what I believe I had divined:

In the Emerald Grotto of Capri, under the sun of Sorrento, in the imperial times of the pacificator Caesar Claudius, the Siren Leucosia[1] attracted the people of Campania by means of her voice. She sang, and enamored the pagans of the Italian shore sailing toward her in order to hear her better. All received a good welcome, for the genre of demoiselles to which Sirens and Oceanides belong is never exclusive or prudish. Sweet talk, caresses, enlacement of the lady, rapture of sensual ecstasy, then engulfment in the waves, nothing was spared those suitors. Ever unsatisfied, the fun-loving Leucosia stocked her harem thus—or, rather, the melodious donzelle was a symbol: Evil, the attraction of the Flesh, seduction, sin, Woman . . .

So, the lustful Parthenope had dressed in mourning: Justinus, the prefect of the praetory; Cecina, the vanquisher of Parthia;

---

1 The name Leucosia is attributed to one of three sirens (the others being Parthenope and Ligeia) by Lycophron in the poem *Alexandra*, allegedly written the third century B.C.—the only work by that prolific author to have survived in its entirety, and considered apocryphal by many modern scholars because of references datable to the second century B.C. The name was attached to an island by the pioneering geographer Strabo in the first century B.C.; he was fond of variants of the legend of the Sirens and employed names attributed to them liberally and fancifully. Although the narrator's account is vague, and perhaps unreliable, Marcellus seems to conflate Leucosia with Parthenope, whose body was said by Lycophron to have washed up in the Bay of Naples.

and Agathokles, the favorite aede of Apollo. Jurists, pontiffs, and above all philosophers, had gone joyously toward the Siren's kisses, and not one of them had returned. The abomination of desolation! Every day, in plaintive processions, young women, wives and mistresses climbed the steps of temples inhabited by helpful simulacra. "Take pity on our husbands, Athene, inspirer of wisdom, and you, virginal Artemis, defend our sons against impurity." Futile sobs! Eros is the most powerful of the gods; nothing can blunt the spur of concupiscence; the Abyss continued to receive its prey.

Now, here come the pallors of the dawn, and traveling over the moving immensity of the seas, a man has appeared, grim in aspect and repulsively ugly: a cynical Diogenes in rags. His beard is already going gray and his head is shaven in accordance with the rite of the pastophores, priests of Egypt. Isis, O good goddess, will you have compassion or the plaintive city? But no; in his robe of coarse muslin, this vagabond of the waves will never adore the idol, lover, wife and mother. He is yet another symbol: Lazarus, the friend of Jesus, the revenant from the realm of the dead, the precursor of resurrections: Lazarus, who personifies disdain for Woman, scorn of the Flesh, the victory of the Soul, Renovation . . .

Leucosia has seen him, and the desire to defeat that insolent chastity has bitten her courtesan's heart; she appeals:

> *Spreading under the heavens a strange clarity,*
> *You whom the waves rock and the wind caresses,*
> *O pale voyager, come to the enchantress!*
> *The insatiable Eros tortures and oppresses me;*
> *The reckless Siren is all voluptuousness.*

He approaches . . . Now, at the entrance to the grotto, in the religious silence of attentive Nature, the ascetic in the monastic garb has raised his voice:

It is the ineffable Amour, it is Jesus who brings me;
He has taken pity on human decadence;
Disappear! Obey the pure God, the strong God,
And daughter of Death, finally reenter death.

But the brave Leucosia mocks him, strives to tempt him, opens her arms to him:

I am Death, you say? Those name me life,
Who expire, loving, beneath my kisses.

Vain efforts! Lazarus has traversed the tomb; he knows that woman is its provider, and his horror for that auxiliary of Satan bursts forth in invectives:

Cause of our misfortunes, reason of our sins,
Perdition of the world, Woman, I hate you!

Brutally, he extracts himself from the embrace, rejects the suborner, constrains her to bow her head, and then, extending his hands:

Flesh still palpitating, body of ignominy,
Astaroth, Leucosia, whatever be your name,
Go seek your lovers in Hell, O demon!

An exorcism! And suddenly, the form of the charmer is transmuted into light vapors; impalpable fluid, she dissolves, evaporates into thin air, and disappears. Meanwhile, Leucosia is still singing, but her words of lust have become religious canticles. "Hosanna! Glory to the triumphant Christ, to the Amour born of suffering, to relentless desire, to endless happiness; to the sole kiss of the Eloah . . . !" Pan, old Pan is no more; the times are accomplished; the Stainless Lamb is about to reign over the earth.

Such was, in a dry analysis, the gist of the curious poem, a sort of Medieval mystery with philosophical pretentions. Too original an essay, it often poured into extravagance, but already the young talent of Marcel Lautrem announced a master musician.

And yet, I judged the work of that neurotic unhealthy; his "neo-Christian" mysticism had an indecency as pagan as the libertinage of Apuleius, and the revolt of a heart in distress seemed to be struggling in the grip of an indomitable passion . . .

Paladin of the Soul? No, poor fellow, you too—I had divined it, comrade—were in love, and indignant in loving; the spur of sin was tormenting your being, and the "Voice of the Abyss" was calling you, menacingly, naïve detractor of Woman!

II
The Siren

The curtain was raised again, and, more solemn than an archimandrite, the monkish Lazarus marched to the front of the stage.

"Mesdames et messieurs, the lyrical and symbolist drama that we have had the honor of performing before you is the work of Monsieur Marcellus."

A few bravos saluted my friend's name; the glabrous decadents and the dainty esthetes applauded with gloved hands, but murmurs, shushes and even whistles quickly stifled that excessively discreet enthusiasm. Immediately, a clamor rose up in the hall: "Diva! Diva! Diva!" They were demanding the Siren.

Lazarus went back into the wings and then reappeared, holding his comrade by the hand. She pulled away abruptly and went alone, at a nonchalant pace, to stand on the edge of the stage. Then, for several minutes, there were hurrahs, bouquets, wreaths and sprays of flowers; the play had just suffered a lamentable fall, but over the debris, Mademoiselle Diva was triumphant, and not modestly.

During the three acts of the interminable mystery, I had studied her at length. She intrigued me. Diva? What was that mythological and pretentious name? Where did she come from? In what theater had she been heard before? I had interrogated my memories in vain; they told me nothing. Diva . . . ?

A very pretty sinner, that "daughter of the bitter wave and the azure gulf," but too ignorant of the couturier and the corset-maker, and decency, not to mention simple self-respect! Decked out in a clinging leotard, crowned with seashells, garlanded with seaweed, with no other jewelry than a ring with coupled pearls, she exhibited with a savant immodesty the harmonious design of her provocative form. Diva . . . ? Why, then, with her golden hair, her dark eyes charged with impure promises, her sensual lips and their enigmatic smile, did that young barely-dressed individual resemble those libidinous figures at which I had once peered in the hiding-places of the secret Museum of Naples? To see her displaying her apparent nudity, one might have thought her one of those lascivious images that decorate certain atriums in Pompeii: the Aphrodite Pandemos or the Venus Meretrix, ancient patronesses of courtesans. Strange, in truth! But damn it, goddess or woman, she was very beautiful, and Beauty, according to the ancients, constitutes a morality by itself . . .

And it was not to the superb music, a rare morsel of the studio, that so many bravos were addressed; they were acclaiming, above all, the cantatrice. What an amiable voice! Soprano or contralto at will, sometimes the Nereid recalled Christine Nilsson by her crystalline and vibrant trills, sometimes Alboni by her velvety basso profundo. A Siren in the body of an Aphrodite? Where the devil had the impresario Rodriguez discovered such a heady marvel? Diva . . . ? A great artiste, that unknown! With what splendid notes she had lunched her audacious challenge to the importunate reciter of nonsense, the apostle of "the chaste and strong God":

I laugh at your God, I who am Sin!

Meanwhile, the recalls succeeded one another: "Diva! Diva!" She came back for the third time, flanked by her impresario, the lively Carlos Rodriguez, dispenser of small Monegasque pleasures. A delirium shook the hall; the whole audience was on its feet; the men were tapping their canes or stamping their feet; on the balconies, the women were waving their handkerchiefs. But, superbly indifferent, the goddess scarcely deigned to incline her chin. "Well, yes," she seemed to be saying, "you find me beautiful; I am, in fact, very beautiful. You love the richness of my voice; my voice, I know, is magical. Now then, which of you, Messieurs, Princes, Grand Dukes, wants to acquire the Oceanide? Calculate, determine your prices, make your bids. A petty royalty! How much for the Siren . . . ?"

At that moment, Bob Davison, the American billionaire stood up in his forestage box and threw a sapphire necklace at the feet of the charmer. Had she found her taker? Yes, doubtless, for she raised a knowing gaze toward the sumptuous Yankee; then, winking, she gratified him with a smile. Davison immediately went out.

Finally, the enthusiasm calmed down and I quit the hall. At the cloakroom there was much talk about the Diva, and even more about the sapphire necklace; courtesans great and small formulated envious commentaries; Englishmen and Americans, all the "businessmen" were jealous of the good luck of "big Bob," the sultan of tinned goods and seasonings—but the misunderstood Marcellus, his Lazarus, his *Leucosia*, his poem and his music, were only the butt of gibes.

Poor fellow, this, then, is what it had cost you to dare to attack Woman! In spite of your invectives and your symbolist audacities, not to mention your rare talent, she had triumphed, and the very rubble of your play was a kind of pedestal for her.

III
The Confidences of Mademoiselle Hortensia

I was already descending the steps of the Casino when I suddenly found myself face to face with Maxence Groeben.[1]

Everyone knew that spiteful and redoubted chronicler, a virtuoso of malicious criticism, a demolisher of renown, the terror of the singer and the actor. Doubtless to sneer at the princely elegances of the nabobs and the hospodars, he had come to the theater in the simple costume of a patron of cabarets: gray coat, yellow shoes and a Bolivar sombrero, even more negligent in his attire than the late Gustave Planche of such Bohemian memory.[2] He was surrounded; people were paying court to him. Juvenile leads or noble fathers, several actors were drinking his words, and dainty actresses were assassinating him with their fluttering eyelashes. The great man was savoring his glory, bracing his bad shoulders, sticking out his chest, striking poses, and holding his crimson-cheeked head high.

I saluted him. "Are you content?" I asked.

"Yes, certainly: a black oven. But Rodriguez was right to open his door to the noisiest of the esthetes. Heard, judged, condemned!

---

1 It is not a coincidence that the name "Maxence" is frequently employed by Jean Lorrain as that of the viewpoint character of many of the anecdotal short stories he contributed to *Le Journal* while living in Nice in 1902-04, especially those featuring cynical *femmes fatales* reprinted in *Fards et poisons* (1904; tr. as *Fards and Poisons*). Groeben is, in part, an obvious parody of Lorrain, whose most famous work, *Monsieur de Phocas. Astarté* (1901; tr. as *Monsieur de Phocas*), is a lurid account of an erotic haunting that the eponymous protagonist tries hard to resist—but Lorrain would never have attacked symbolism as Groeben does.

2 The witty art critic Gustave Planche (1808-1857) was a pillar of the *Revue des deux mondes* for many years, alongside Gilbert-Augustin Thiery's father. Planche attempted to reconcile Classicism and Romanticism by celebrating the common features of their attitude to human passion rather than their differences.

Do you know this Marcellus?"[1]

"A school comrade. We inhabited the Villa Medicis together."

"What? You, a former Prix de Rome, the painter of realities, the Raphael of the absinthe-drinkers, the modern Titian of the dancing-girls of the Moulin Rouge?"

Me . . . *Olim in Arcadia*.[2] I was even a pupil of Paul Baudry."

"So that's why you try to sketch so much. No, humans aren't perfect. Well, tell your Marcellus that his esthetic is now worn out, old hat and fastidious. Greeks and Romans, Capri, Lazarus, an Oceanide? Verses instead of rhythmic prose? All that reeks of the old school, Monsieur Blondel. Again and always "pompier art." Besides which, a Siren! What sort of female is that? I've never embraced a siren, although I've traveled the sea."

"Symbolism is very fashionable, and its apostles . . ."

"Cripples! They don't understand anything of their epoch. The dawn of the great day is rising; Revolution is rumbling and menacing around us; writers, painters or musicians, we should all be uttering the cry of social revolt. Stand up, the accursed of the earth, stand up the convicts of hunger! Oh, if our Marcellus had put our proletarian poverty on the stage; enabled to clamor in their beautiful popular language a gang of laundresses or a crew of masons, vituperated the bourgeois, the well-to-do, the gambler, I would have applauded. But bah—what good would it do us to reform our mores? A monk! Your friend is too clerical, and although the Catholic periodicals proclaim him a genius, I protest, I . . . hey, you over there, by what right do you offer yourself my head?"

He had interrupted his lecture to shout at a hairy and long-bearded lanky fellow, who had planted himself before us,

---

1 The Villa des Medicis was the site of the school attended by winners of the French scholarships known as the Prix de Rome: bursaries that allowed students of art, music and architecture to spend three years in Rome, and sometimes longer, at the expense of the State.

2 *Olim* is usually translated into English as "once upon a time"; Blondel's reference recalls Nicolas Poussin's famous painting "Et in Arcadia Ego" [I have also lived in Arcadia].

had aimed his Kodak and had taken a photograph of the glory of journalism. The man with the mane smiled, and told us his name: Numa Heurtebise, director, editor-in-chief and artistic reporter of the *Phare de Montboron.*

"Don't move, Monsieur Groeben . . . good, it's done. My rag will possess the portrait of the king of kings of critics. Now, talented colleague, let me interview you . . . oh, don't forbid it; I'm more tenacious than a horse-fly, and I'm hanging on to your coat-tails."

He took out of his pocket a pencil, pen-knife and notebook, the apparatus of his literature, and started to scribble: "So you say, *Leucosia*, a valetudianarian and childish poem, reactionary and clerical music. As for the Siren . . ."

"Oh la la, what chirping!" exclaimed the mocking voice of a small woman with a face plastered with make-up.

Heurtebise immediately introduced her: "Mademoiselle Hortensia Lavandou, alias Niniche, my unchaste friend, a generic singer at the Villefranche Eldorado. Style, throat and gesture! Truly, dear master, this incomparable child merits academic palms."

"A Siren, Diva?" Mademoiselle Niniche continued, mischievously. "No, truly, my princess, let me laugh or pass me a bottle of salts. First of all, her name isn't Diva but Esther Mosselman. I know her; we've both rolled around the café-concerts of Tunisia."

"Unknown, in fact, at the Conservatoire," observed Groeben. "Even unknown in the editorial offices. She's nonetheless one of our future stars. Splendor and purity of voice, method and diction, she lacks nothing."

"Luck, Monsieur, that's all! No one threw her orchids or sapphires when she was cooing *Stella confidente* at the Garibaldi in Tunis.[1] Destitute, then, up to her shoulders, poor thing—yes, in the blackest poverty, Messeigneurs. After every ballad Esther went from table to table holding out the begging-bowl, but the

---

1 *Alla stella confidente* [Bright Star of Love] (1870) by Vincenzo Robaudi became an immensely popular song, accompanied by the violin.

silver scarcely fell into it. Her Grrrreat Art—I'm vibrating like her—bored the drinkers. Me, I obtained much more success with my travesties. I danced the jig, and the cadis, the agas, the bachaghas . . ."

"Good, good, we can guess the rest. Tell us about Mademoiselle Diva. Did she also charm the cadis?"

"That poseur? She played Mademoiselle Orange-Blossom. Excuse me . . . In any case, a good guard was kept around her virtue. 'Palace archers, on watch!' And they watched."

The actress's chatter amused the other actors; even Groeben deigned to smile. "The vestal of the Moorish café," he said. "A nice title for a piquant short story. Go on, Mademoiselle Hortensia, you're furnishing me with copy."

"Too honored, dear master! But you'll carve me a little adver-tisement with it. I'll spill . . . so, every evening, an Uncle Killjoy brought Esther to our dive, watched her better than a mother hen, and then, when the lights went out, took her home. An amusing fellow, clad in a ragged soutanelle, coiffed with curly side-plaits with an astrakhan bonnet, chatting to his infanta sometimes in Italian and sometimes in an unknown language. We called him Mardochée because . . . because . . ."[1]

"Has she found her Assuerus?"

"Her ape? No, that animal only prospers in Tunisia. Anyway, the Sicilians, the clientele of the Garibaldi, claimed that that Mosselman brings bad luck. Don't go near her, if you're supersti-tious; she has the evil eye."

"*Gettatrice?* What stupidity!"[2]

"She has the evil eye! Study her carefully. With her hair, more

---

1 I have retained the French spelling of Mardochée [Mordecai], the uncle of the eponymous heroine of the Biblical book of Esther, and have also retained Thierry's spelling of the name of the Persian king Assuerus [Ahasuerus in the A.V.], who marries Esther and employs her influence to institutes a series of massacres of the enemies of the Jews.

2 The legend of the Evil Eye was well-known in French literary circles by virtue of Théophile Gautier's novella *Jettatura* (1856). *Gettatrice* is the feminine version of the equivalent Italian word.

red than blonde, her cadaverous pallor, her perfidious smile, her mendacious and cruel gaze, doesn't she seem the daughter of some demon? I imagine that one must encounter several specimens of that genre in Hell. And to think that such a witch will soon be getting married!"

"She's taken you into her confidence?"

"One doesn't know her any longer—but I noticed the engagement ring she's exhibiting on her left hand. Scrap metal, moreover, a horror that Cydalie, my cook, wouldn't want. Assuerus can't be juggling with millions. If I knew the name of the future husband I'd write to the unfortunate, advising him to make himself scarce as quickly as possible. *Les Amours du diable!* There's a play that has never succeeded."[1]

"Bravo! The punch line!" cried Groeben. "Thank you, lovely child and good little comrade. Thanks to you, I have my next article."

Brazenly, Mademoiselle Hortensia came to camp under the chin of the eminent man. "Such is my information, dear master. Are you satisfied with Niniche? Yes. Then grant her for recompense the honor and pleasure of a modest kiss."

With a protective hand, the "dear master" tapped the floury cheek of the little monkey and then, breaking through the circle of admirers, he headed toward the gaming rooms.

IV
Esther Mosselman

So much chatter had delayed me: half past eleven already! Wanting, nevertheless, to shake my comrade's hand, protest against the injustice of the public and comfort a defeated warrior, I went to the artistes' entrance.

---

1 *Les Amours du diable* (1859) is an *opéra-féerie* with music by Albert Grisar and words by Henri Saint-Georges, but Niniche is presumably using the title generically.

An elegant victoria was stationed in front of the perron, harnessed to spirited high-steppers. Their "gentlemanly" coachman, surely called Tom or Jim, was sitting motionless on his seat, but the footman, less correct, had gone to chat with the concierge.

"Who do you desire?" the woman asked me.

"Monsieur Marcel Lautrem."

"Lautrem? Don't know him."

"Marcellus: the author of the new play."

"Oh, I know . . . the musician with long hair who declaims and rants while he walks . . . an escapee from Charenton!" the lady added, turning to the lackey.

She too had noticed my symbolist's bizarre appearance, his exuberant gestures and his vocal outbursts, the air of an inspired prophet: symptoms of neurosis that amuse idlers but make physicians anxious.

"Monsieur Marcellus hasn't come to the theater this evening."

"Get away! You're mistaken, Madame."

"He hasn't come . . . perhaps forewarned of his lack of success."

"Where can he be found?"

"At the Villa Ravel, I imagine . . . but stand aside, please; you're blocking the passage."

Three people were descending, at that moment, the sinuous staircase that led to the actors' dressing-rooms. A monsieur in a white cravat led the way: a short and obese quinquagenarian, with a clean-shaven face in the fashion of New York or Chicago. He was well known to me: Davison, the Bob famous in all the grocery stores of the New World, the richest of the *nouveaux riches*, an emperor among the powerful kings of corned beef and hams with trichinosis. Diva was following him, in civilian costume now, but in an old costume seemingly bought second-hand. Behind her, a colorless apparition, came a skeletally thin man with a graying beard and a hooked nose. By the black woolen overcoat, oiled hair, side-plaits and fake astrakhan bonnet, the air and attire of a patriarch of Israel, I divined Uncle Mardochée. Curbing his stature, worried and muttering, Esther Mosselman's chaperon was holding a green velvet jewel-case, the symbol and color of hope.

Soon, in her second-hand clothing, the Oceanide went past me, and I was able to look her almost in the face. Yes, a strange creature; she reminded me of one of those Pompeiian frescoes of maleficent divinities, devastating Venuses whose triumphant immodesty was an entire symbol for antiquity. Her face had a classic and admirable perfection, but her mouth was parted cruelly; her dark eyes, flecked with gold, were gleaming provocatively, cunning and malevolent. *Gettatrice!* I understood the terror that the Sicilians of the Moorish café had felt.

Meanwhile, Davison had launched himself toward the carriage and had opened the door. Haughty and tranquil, magnificent in her indifference, the cantatrice installed herself in the vehicle, and then wrapped herself up warmly in her furs.

"Where is it necessary to take you now, Miss Syren?" asked the American

The gold-flecked dark eyes looked at him ironically. "First to the villa you mentioned to me; afterwards, we'll see."

"All right. Drive on, Tom. Palais des Glycines." And he tried to hoist himself into the victoria. Very arrogantly, however, "Miss Syren" stopped him with a gesture.

"No! I'm not your property yet; let's draw up our little contract first. Business, dear Monsieur, is business."

"Indeed? Even in amour?"

"In amour above all. Come and join me in a little while at the Glycines; we'll sign, and then . . . then I'll be all yours, Robert."

"Oh, my love, my sweet, my flower of Beauty!"

With that, Bob Davison inclined gallantly, and then drew away whistling a joyous "Yankee Doodle." He too understood music—the melody of the dollar, at least.

Mosselman, however, remained standing on the sidewalk, and continued to mutter.

"Get in the carriage, quickly, Uncle Jeremiah," Diva enjoined him. "I need your advice to draft the final clauses of our agreement."

She was expressing herself now in the Levantine Italian that many Caraïte Jews employ. Their jargon does not much resemble the harmonious language of the Transteverines, my former models; nevertheless, I was able to understand it.

"Esther," growled Uncle Killjoy, furiously, "do you think that I saved you from the slaughterhouse to make you a Delilah?"

"Delilah was worth as much as Judith. Anyway, I appreciate them both. Get in the carriage; you can moralize tomorrow."

"Goïm flesh! Solomon said . . ."

"Spare me your Solomon and his babble. The affair is good; I'll conclude it."

"He said: 'Gain acquired by sin steals the soul from those who receive it.'"

"Sin? But, absurd speechifier, I'm Sin personified."

"Wretch! Heart of Astaroth! Here, this is what I think of your Philistine!"

Brandishing the jewel-case, he threw it on the ground and then kicked it away with his foot. A sapphire necklace escaped from it, but at a gesture from Delilah, the domestic picked up the item of jewelry.

"*Dourak!*" clamored the Mosselman niece, angrily. "Another prank of that sort and I'll send you back to Kherson to savor the pleasures of a pogrom."

At the word "pogrom" the patriarch with the side-plaits uttered a cry of desolation. "My sons! Ephraim, Manassé . . . ! My joy, my pride! They killed them!"

Petty Russians, doubtless, the two Mosselmans must, before their vagabondage, have had inhabited the land of orthodoxy that is so harsh to the Israelite, the pitiless country where the God of forgiveness is nothing but a ferocious executioner for Jacob, and where the Cross of Mercy looms up in Jewish eyes more menacing than a gibbet. They had fled, but the old man was seeing again in his mind's eye one of those abominable massacres that are the opprobrium of Russian civilization: an entire fanaticized people rushing against the accursed houses, pillaging, burning and murdering.

"My sons, my poor sons!" he groaned. "What infamy of you to remind me of their death. The pogroms! But they also killed your father, progeny of tears and blood!"

"The horses are getting impatient," sniggered Esther. "Have you finished your play-acting?"

"And the other . . . the other who is waiting for us?" continued the plaintive Mosselman.

"He'll wait; I can do without him henceforth."

She took from her finger the engagement ring that Niniche had remarked, and held it out to the sermonizer. "You can take his jewelry back to him. Or rather, go offer the ring to a second-hand dealer in Nice. The pearls are rather fine; demand two hundred francs for it."

"Ignoble! But that's ignoble, Esther! He loves you to the point of dying of it, and you . . ."

"Words. Many other Celadons have loved me, do love me or will love me; it matters little to me, Furthermore, in driving that Christian to despair, the ridiculous note-cruncher of religious music, I'm associating myself with the work of our common vengeance. Ah, you're smiling now; your obtuse brain has understood. I have something else to tell you, a secret that will render you more malevolent to that Amalekite than a Joshua or a Samuel. Get ten or twelve louis for the ring, then, and I'll make you a gift of it. You can offer that money to the kitty of your Zionists, or if you prefer"—she uttered an insulting laugh—"buy for your sordid rag some nice sepulcher in the Valley of Josaphat."

Then, like a beaten dog that comes to lick the hand that whips it, the "Uncle Jeremiah" curbed his spine and slid next to his niece.

The carriage drew away and I set forth for the Villa Ravel anxiously. Alas, I had divined who "the other" was, the ridiculous note-cruncher of religious music who was waiting for Diva too confidently.

V
Astaroth

With his ascetic thinness, his blazing eyes and his blond hair and beard, Marcel Lautrem resembled one of the ecstatic individuals that Fra Angelico represented. The son of poor Bretons from Morbihan, he was born on the Île des Moines, the land of desolation relentlessly swept by the torment and filled by the howls of the voice of the Atlantic, which is licked, bitten and gnawed away by the currents of yellow foam, the ebb and flow of the Savage Sea. All the women there are clad in black, all wearing mourning for some beloved . . .

His mother, the widow of a long-haul captain, a fervent soul even in that land of fervent Catholics, had nourished the ambition of offering to a seminary the last-born of her five children, of making him a "rector" of a parish. Thus, she had impregnated him with Christian faith, as well as Celtic superstitions that the intelligence of her favorite son, her dear little Marcel, preferred.

"Every evening, to the sound of the waves," my friend confided to me later, "Corentine[1] told me terrifying stories: Saint Renatus resuscitating among the dead in order to receive baptism, or Saint Corneli changing a cohort of pagan legionaries into granite."

For a long time he had believed all the old tales, the terrors of the populace: the dead who appear and implore masses; the crawling dog that is glimpsed prowling round a house of agony; the witches who transform themselves into crows and fly to the heath where they abandon themselves to the great Sabbat Goat. But "the Spirit blows where it wants to blow," and the musician Lautrem had followed another vocation. Having come to Paris he entered the Conservatoire, to emerge with the first Prix de Rome.

1 The name of the Breton saint Corentin of Quimper, after whom Marcel's mother is presumably named, signifies "tempest" or "hurricane."

At the Villa Medicis, that Breton-speaking Breton displeased. Our boarders found him eccentric in humor, unsociable, concentrated within himself and too misanthropic, making himself old among the young. Personally, I had linked myself with the tall pale fellow whose emaciated features reminded me of the legendary face of the *Poverello*.[1] We never knew him to have any mistress; he had been nicknamed the Joseph of the Pincio, and while, joyful in living, all our future great men went on the spree and had many flirtations, he frequented churches, went to mass and intoxicated himself with sacred music. Old Allegri, and you, ancient Palestrina, how many times Lautrem tried to make me understand the desperations of your *Requiem*, the sublimities of your *Magnificat!* Very literate and classically cultured, he read a great deal, but works of mysticism or books of extravagance. Often, his lamp remained lit far into the night; often, too, when he had extinguished it, the sound of his footsteps was heard resonating. He went back and forth, dementedly, in the midst of the thickest darkness; we also called him "the nyctalope," and some claimed that he was a somnambulist.

One evening, entering Lautrem's room unexpectedly, I surprised him poring over an ancient and dusty quarto, a bookshop curiosity that he had just bought. He had not heard me knock on his door, and I was astonished by the fear that his gaze expressed. I touched him lightly on the shoulder; he started, uttered a cry and closed his book.

"What a stupid joke!" he stammered. "I thought it was the invisible hand tormenting me again. Oh, you can boast of having scared me!"

"Always your absurd nervousness, Marcel! What is that venerable book? A Grimoire?"

"No, the treatise of a very sagacious demonologist: *Les Enquêtes Magiques* by the theologian Del Rio. A savant, suggestive work! It has demonstrated to me a few human appearances that certain demons love to put on."

---

1 *Il poverello* was the nickname of Saint Francis of Assisi.

"You'd do much better, my handsome friend, to meditate on Voltaire's tales."

"The sniggering of that vile ape has always made me indignant; I prefer my doctor of Salamanca. I wanted to know; thanks to him, I know."

"More fortunate than Montaigne!"

"Montaigne? The ancestor of Monsieur Homais? I detest him as much as your great Pascal cursed him."

He stood up, very agitated, took a few steps and then sat down again. "Blondel," he asked me, "do you believe in the mysterious and redoubtable phenomena of second sight?"

"What do you call second sight?"

"The clear vision of our obscure becoming."

"You know my sentiments of a hardened rationalist."

"So much the worse for you, and I feel sorry for you; personally, I'm less skeptical. Well, magic spell or miracle, an invisible hand has recently led me to confront my destiny."

"In the home of what necromancer, credulous young man? In the lair of what pythoness?"

"A bizarre adventure has recently traversed my life. I wanted to conserve the secret of it, but it weighs upon me. You're my only friend; advise me, then, or rather, tell me whether I've gone mad."

"Good! I divine . . . a story of amour! Finally!"

"Yes, amour . . . abominable amour; satanic amour. Don't laugh thus; I tell you that I've seen my destiny; I've seen it, and I'm afraid."

Stretching myself out on the sofa, I lit a cigar, wanting to listen without interrupting. The night spread out around us, and in the grayness of the dusk I only glimpsed a long body agitated by frissons. Timid at first, as if ashamed, Lautrem's voice gradually became louder, and the terror that it contained soon gained my Voltairean heart. I have conserved an ineffaceable memory of that troubling evening.

"Last month," Marcel recounted, "one Friday, the eve of the Assumption, finding myself in Naples, the idea came to me of going to visit Pompeii. I desired to invoke in that city of the dead a contrasting thought of life, to search there for the subject of a drama, human and fantastic at the same time. I therefore ate breakfast in haste—a frugal meal, for my purse was crying famine—and soon the train deposited me at the Torre d'Annunziata. Having entered Pompeii by the marine gate, I hastened to dismiss my guide; his chatter fatigued me, and I had the intention of wandering at will. The Forum, its temples, the Curia and the drapers' market did not retain me for long; I pushed on further and launched myself into the Villa della Fortuna.

"What a day! The heat was overwhelming; beneath the sky the radiance of an implacable sun was streaming; in the abolished city the silence extended of what is the mute irony of human effort, the mystery of the afterlife, and its terror.

"In the distance, in the churches of the Annunziata, the bell of the Angelus began to ring; midday chimed. Suddenly, I felt a faint pressure on my shoulder; a hand had just settled there, which caressed me gently. I turned my head. No one! The street and its borders of gaping houses extended, deserted . . .

"Surprised, even frightened, I wanted to retrace my steps; the pressure became painful; fingernails dug into my flesh; I was constrained to obey . . .

". . . What was that . . . ?

"The memory returned to me then of an ancient prayer of our Catholic liturgy: 'Lord, drive away from our route the demon of noon.' In the hours when the sun is flamboyant, those sorts of demons, theurgists affirm, love to crawl in ruined castles or over the rubble of towns; they take pleasure in mocking what humans call life. But bah—three years at the Villa Medicis have rendered me philosophical, and I started joking: 'Try someone else, old puppet, grotesque scarecrow of my childhood; you won't scare me in the least today. I . . .'

"The laughter stopped on my lips; the claws lacerated me; I also experienced the sensation of an atrocious burn. 'March! March!' And I marched. The hand became less rude; it guided me . . .

"Thus led, I went into the Cardo, traveling the rich quarters of Pompeiian elegance that rose up toward the Porta Vesuvia. Laborers and masons had gone to take their siesta; the solitude extended into the distance, terrifying; I was alone, desperately alone, with the invisible companion . . .

"But then a recently-exhumed house attracted, fixed and fascinated my gaze, Two columns with Tuscan capitals formed a peristyle for it, and to either side of the atrium I perceived painted murals. I approached. Immediately, a faint whistle, the ignoble invitation of a procuress, became audible; someone was summoning me. 'No, no!' And I hastened to pass on. Then the hand that was gripping me nailed me to the spot. It was there . . . there . . . that I was being enjoined to enter . . ."

"Are you joking, Lautrem?" I interrupted. "I didn't know, my dear, that you were such an imperturbable trickster."

"Spare me your pleasantries. Blondel, and don't have any kind of padded cell prepared for me. I don't believe, absolutely not, in the demons of noon; under the torturing claws, I even took account perfectly of being the victim of a hallucination. Are you satisfied? I'm reasoning like you, as a materialist, as a petty Holbachian. But I ought to confide to you a sad family secret. Often, in my childhood, I was prey to similar vertigoes. My father, in the course of his voyages to Hong Kong, had contracted the vice of opium, frequented smoking dens and died in a hospital demanding the dream, howling to obtain his blissful visions. Alas, had he bequeathed me one of his cerebral defects? I'll continue my story . . .

"Advancing, I examined curiously the two paintings that flanked the narrow peristyle. They represented Sirens, one playing the double-flute, the other holding a lyre and singing; both of them bore in their marine coiffures a bizarre diadem, the mitella of affranchised Syrian women. Corroded by the ashes, crumbling in places, the paintings were in a pitiful state. In spite of such degradation, however, a word written in Greek capital letters could be read: the word LEUCOSIA

"Leucosia? Was that the name of the Siren or that of the courtesan who had come, sheltered by the cento of scarlet linen, to offer her temporary hospitality to anyone and everyone? I was informed very quickly. The atrium into which I penetrated was nothing but a sickening obscenity. Lubricious emblems and priapic filth decorated the perimeter, and on the steps of the tablinum the triple figure of a goat had been erected on an altar. That brothel was a kind of clandestine temple in which filthy initiates had once adored some infamous divinity, Pandemos, Venus Athor or Mylitta . . .

"And the sun darted its rays at my head; the stucco and the coruscating marble sent me blinding sparks, and still, the nails of my companion obliged me to gaze . . .

"Then an appearance of life seemed to traverse the death of that deserted city. I heard, vaguely, a strange murmur floating in the air, of the cadenced voices of woman; a rhythmic chant similar to some nuptial canticle; the sound of flutes, harps, sistra and crotales. Someone called to me again; softly, tenderly, my name was pronounced: 'Marcel . . . ! Disdainful Marcel . . . ! It's finally necessary to love . . . ! The hour of espousal has come . . . ! Enter the sanctuary; Astaroth has chosen you, Marcel."

"Too emotional, having expelled all dread, I sought the eyes of the suborner, the procuress of the gilded words . . .

"Eh! Over there, what was that chamber in which a superb fresco was shining?

"A profound cella paved with indecent mosaics, it was a mysterious chapel in which a bronze tripod stood destined to receive incense. To the right and left, the walls were ornamented with delicate quadratures, the exquisite work of Magna Graecia that one often encounters in Pompeiian villas: birds and foliage, interlacements of roses, halcyons or doves, pecking one another under the frisson of myrtles. A hieratic fresco occupied the back of the sacellum all on its own: well-conserved, that one, for I was easily able to decipher the votive inscription:

Ven . . . Ast . . . Leucos . . . : To Venus, Astarte, Leucosia.

"That Venus was none other than Astaroth,[1] the patronne of Sidon and Tyre, the symbol of carnal Beauty, the inhabitant of the "high Places," the idol to which Jezebel, the abomination of the Eternal God had burned incense. Phoenician, or perhaps Jewish, the hetaira with the siren voice, Leucosia, coiffed by a Semite mitella, had opened her house to the adorers of Astarte. They were numerous in Italy, for the vanquished Orient had conquered its conqueror by means of its divinities . . .

"For a long time I remained as if in ecstasy. The master painter, the author of that fresco, must also have believed in Astaroth, and the lubricity of his brush had been nothing but an act of faith. The Tyrienne seemed still to be alive, as in the days when the Lydians, the Lalages and the Asiatic Phormions came to burn perfumes to her, and then practice her rites. Like a golden mantle, her tawny hair fell all the way to the ground; the features of her pale face were admirable in their purity, and the forms of her body blossomed impeccably. But what ferocity there was in those sensual lips, that laughing mouth, those dark caressant eyes!

"Standing up in her triumphant nudity, leaning one hand on the conical stone, the emblem of Ela Gabala, generator of worlds,[2] Venus surged from the waves to become the lust of Nature, and Nature addressed the cries of its desires to her. Fauns, sylvans, tritons, images of humanity in the fields, in the woods, on the seas, surrounded the Anadyomene, imploring her

---

1 The name Astaroth is prominent in demonology as the name of a prince of Hell, but the name is a derivative of that of the Phoencian goddess Astarte, which is itself a variant of the Babylonian Ishtar. It was Astarte who was associated with Sidon and Tyre, but she was probably not the Asherah to whom the Biblical Jezebel "burned incense," whom Marcel also gathers into his syncretic composite

2 The nickname Elagabalus, given posthumously to a demonized Roman emperor and often corrupted to Heliogabalus was derived from a Semitic word for god and an Arabic word for mountain, separated here by Thierry.

to open her arms. And while I contemplated her in the rapture of my entire being, the imprecations of the prophets of Iaveh, interpreters of the Most High, the Most Pure, the Most Holy nevertheless returned to my memory: 'Gods of filth, gods of ordure . . . !'

"Suddenly I felt faint; my gaze was obscured; my legs buckled beneath me; heavily, I collapsed to my knees. Then—frightful hallucination—I saw, in spite of my closed eyelids . . . yes, I saw Astaroth detach herself from the wall, advance slowly and place on my head her fingers chilled by the cold of the Abyss.

"'Salut! You want to ignore me, but you will know me. We shall find one another again, for in spite of Golgotha, the Beast will always reign over the world. You will learn then that, vivified by me, every living thing obeys my law. Your soul will strive to flee me; but, having passed into your flesh, I will devour you entirely. You will love, you will love, you will love; subject to dolor, struggling against opprobrium, accomplishing sacrilege, committing crime, disappearing into dementia . . . yes, you, whose disdain outrages me, will have no other God henceforth but me . . .'

"She had spoken; and over my forehead, my eyes and my mouth I felt, bewildered, the chill of long, long kisses . . . I had received the baptism of the Beast; I belonged to her . . ."

Lautrem interrupted himself, very emotional, still shivering at the memory of his vision.

"When I came to," he went on, "I was lying n a mattress and a warden of Pompeii was moistening my temples. '*Ebbene!*' said the man; we'll get away with a slight faint. But in future, Monsieur Frenchman, beware of sunstroke.'

"Such, Blondel, is my adventure. It might appear ridiculous to you, but I find it atrocious; it terrified me. Don't mention it to anyone."

I promised him an entire discretion, while lavishing my advice upon him. Why did he not seek a wife or mistress? But he shook his head.

"No, I'm afraid of Woman. I sense that if I have the misfortune to fall in love, my passion will be exclusive, furious, delirious . . . And besides, I intend to become a great artist, and talent is only acquired at the price of chastity.

"An overly mystical soul, my dear! The mentality of a monk."

"That's probable, and I've missed my vocation. Expect, however, some day to receive this news: Lautrem, the illustrious composer, has entered into religion."

"Amen, immodest Mozart. I wouldn't choose you for a confessor."

"Ah," he sighed, putting his hands together, "a picturesque convent under the sky of Naples, at Punta Campanella or on the hills of Umbria, in places where his brethren, the birds, gave their celestial concerts to the *Poverello* of Assisi, that will be the holy refuge for me, the port sheltered from all storms! There, at least, I shall be able to laugh at Astaroth."

"She will follow you everywhere poor friend, for Astaroth is none other than yourself."

After that, my friend's late nights became more frequent, and I often surprised him studying his demonic grimoire, Del Rio's *Enquêtes Magiques*.

After my emergence from the School I returned to Paris and, richer in ambitious hopes than income inscribed in the Great Book, I worked furiously for eight years. I had ceased all relationship with my visionary; absorbed by labor I no longer even thought about him. Meanwhile, his name had become celebrated in the Latin Quarter. Under the pseudonym Marcellus, Lautrem battled in several juvenile revues, an apostle of the Ideal, attacking men and things, proposing to reform everything: poetry, fiction; painting, philosophy and the theater; prophesying the triumph of the Beautiful, which is to say, God, and the defeat of Woman, whom he called, ungallantly, the Beast. The excessive formulae of that mystagogue, the acrimony of his polemic, his renewed dithyrambs or insults worthy of Lammenais had acquired him a noisy renown. I also knew that, devoting himself to sacred music, Marcellus had made oratorios heard at the Colonne and other Spiritual Concerts. The inspiration of that other Palestrina was praised: a genius, affirmed his admirers. But so much turbulence in a debutant had seemed to me to be in poor taste; true talent, I thought, is more modest; besides which, scratch a comrade and you will often find an envious person.

Envious? No, but I knew my own merit perfectly. The closet where I worked, on the Boulevard Montparnasse, appeared to me unworthy to shelter Armand Blondel, and I dreamed there of magnificent studios, town houses in the Renaissance style and a palace built in the Plaine Monceau. In order to acquire a little money I abjured, not without a few sighs, the religion that I had been taught in Rome: the cult of Louis David, the adoration of Monsieur Ingres. An adept of the new art, a painter of democracy, improvising myself as a naturalist, impressionist, verist and open air painter, I consecrated my canvases to magnifying human labor: roofers, diggers, shop assistants, midinettes, publicans, secretaries of trades unions and municipal councilors. I was something of an arriviste. My famous painting *Rosière et Cocotte*, an amusement of the Salon of 1896, enabled me to know the first intoxications of glory.

The art critics were moved. *The talented Blondel . . . Blondel, the young master humorist . . .* The City bought that badinage, and enlivened a hall in the Mairie with it. The merchants of the Rue Laffitte risked themselves to the staircase of my roost; commissions arrived to decorate the brasseries of the Pigalle quarter; a little more time and I would figure in the Album Mariani![1] But so much effort had wearied me. Toward the end of autumn

---

1 *L'Abum Mariani, Figures contemporaines*, containing illustrated biographies of famous people, was published annually from 1894 to 1935. Named after the inventor of a stimulant drink based on alcohol and coca leaves, it was primarily a means of advertising the liquor in question.

my physician scolded me severely. "You work too hard! More jaundiced than a Carmelite! Go inhale the breezes of the Côte d'Azur." Good advice; I would find many ridiculous things to draw out there. I packed my paints and prepared my flight to the costly land of the sun.

On the day of All Hallows, the eve of my departure, I had an unexpected encounter.

Returning to my studio at about five o'clock in the afternoon I was going up the Boulevard Montparnasse. Night was falling, a foggy November night traversed by the north wind; icy mists floated over the tedious avenue; rusty carrot-top trees were shivering in the icy blast, under a gray sky harboring snow; everything announced the imminent bites of winter. At Notre-Dame-des-Champs the bells were sounding the Salut; the light of the brightly-lit stained glass widows stood out against the blackness of the fog, and the silhouettes of a few devout individuals were hastening toward the appeal. A subject for a paining—*Evening Mass, a study in the manner of Rembrandt*—immediately came to mind. I went into the church.

The Salut had just commenced. In the distance of the choir, illuminated by a profusion of candles, the monstrance was radiant on the altar, but the nave was only feebly illuminated and the aisles extended, turned and disappeared under the profundities of shadow. *What a science of scene-setting*, I thought, *and what an eloquent symbolism there is in these Christian basilicas: wretched humanity lost in semi-darkness, with no other illumination than faith!*

Soon, the great organ was heard, modulating a prelude; then a woman's voice rose up toward the vaults, magnificent, passionate and troubling, in which the desire vibrated to be absorbed in divine love. *Ecce panis Angelorum* . . . O Jesus, she said, you are the voluptuousness of angels; I am hungry for your flesh; I am thirsty for your possession! But while she was singing, so recklessly worshipful, a memory obsessed me. That melody was familiar. How many times I had heard it at the Villa Medici when at the end of the day, Lautrem's harmonium had exhaled its mystical prayers. Very intrigued, I questioned the doorkeeper who was standing nearby at the edge of the church.

"Is not the author of this *Panis Angelorum* Marcel Lautrem?"

"Marcellus? Yes. We often play his music."

"Who is the singer?"

"I don't know her name. A fine timbre! A true warbler, a nightingale of the woods. Everything here is first-rate, Monsieur; one wouldn't find better at Saint-Roch."

The functionary with the braided bicorn hat felt the zeal of his house, chauvinism for his parish.

"Do you know Marcellus' address? I'd like to write to the master composer and congratulate him."

"Spare yourself the expense of a postage stamp; he's here."

He indicated a man who was kneeling on the paving-stones, plunged in the shadow of a pillar. It really was my comrade and school-friend, but I had difficulty recognizing the handsome Marcel of the Villa Medicis. He had aged strangely. A few white hairs were peppering the thickness of his blond beard; the top of his head was clear; several graying locks showed among the excessively long hair that he wore thrown back over his shoulders, and his devastated face announced the storms of a soul subject to torments. Putting his hands together and raising his head, he was listening to the crystalline notes fly, smiling, his eyes closed, motionless, like some image of a contemplative saint, rapturous, languid and ecstatic.

The *Panis Angelorum* finished; the singer sighed a heart-rending *Amen*; she fell silent, and the liturgical prayers resumed in the choir. I approached Lautrem then, and named myself. He looked at me with a distracted gaze, like a somnambulist snatched abruptly from the bliss of a dream.

Finally, he recognized me. "Blondel! I'm glad to see you again, comrade . . . so you frequent churches, Monsieur Rationalist!"

"Only too glad, illustrious Marcellus, to have experienced that temporary whim. Your *Panis Angelorum* is a superb work."

"Pooh! But what an interpreter! Have you ever hear a more delectably seraphic canticle? A marvelous artiste!"

"'A living harp attached to her heart,' as Musset said of La Malibran."

"I don't want to be Musset, and you're offending me. A massacrer of verses, a flat speaker of commonplace things, rhyming diabolically and making money, the clown, out of something sacred: dolor! And what abject sensualism there was in that drunkard, who needed absinthe to cure him of having loved. Ignoble! Oh, I've demolished him! But let's go out for a moment; we're troubling the meditation of the faithful."

Preceding me, the blasphemer of the divine Musset crossed the threshold of the church, descended the steps and stopped before the façade.

"Yes, Blondel," he said. "What a voice, what a soul, what intelligence of the noblest of the arts! You're right, another Malibran. And it's me that has discovered her!"

"You're talking about the cantatrice, your interpreter? I share your enthusiasm. Passion, ardor . . ."

"The ardor of a neophyte! She was Jewish, wretchedly Jewish, and it's me again who converted her. Unknown to her family, an uncle as ridiculous as fanatical, she desired to receive baptism. Now she's Christian, a good and fervent Christian; now, we can marry." He sighed dolorously. "Artistes' espousals, comrade: paradise perched on a fifth floor in the Rue Vavin. My wife will give singing lessons; I shall compose oratorios; and we shall live very happily in a love-nest of kisses, canticles and prayers. Yes, a blessed household: the heavens come to inhabit the earth."

He had declaimed his conjugal dithyramb with such ironic desolation that I looked at him in amazement.

"Why are you marrying, Lautrem?"

"Why?" he said, angrily. "Because I'm in love and it's driving me mad. My scrupulous conscience forbids me a mistress, so I'm marrying!"

Very material in his conclusions, that protagonist of spritualities! And for a second time he reeled off the insane theories with which he had often regaled me at the School: Woman was Evil; woman dragged man to perdition; but man ought to take pity on her and fashion the soul of such a pernicious creature.' Marcellus told me then that he was about to have a symbolist opera performed in Monte Carlo, his latest work.

"*Leucosia!*" he proclaimed. "The seduction, the appeal of the Abyss! Perhaps you'll recognize therein the speech-maker Lautrem. He is represented in Lazarus, an apostle of the Ideal. Oh, if only I too could escape the sepulcher that attracts me!"

The icy night enveloped us; the wind was blowing bitterly; a snowy dawn was fluttering in the air; I was numb with cold. A knell began to toll in the belfry of Notre-Dame-des-Champs. It announced for the following day the Feast of the Dead, and at long intervals the bells wept, lugubrious, monotonous and enervating. *De profundis*, they said. O living for an hour, are you thinking about eternity? *Die irae!* What will you respond, wretches, to the Judge appearing in the clouds?

An insult to human life, effort, action and hope, the funereal ringing exasperated me Good, good, and enough! While awaiting the Requiem, and then the marvelous trumpet of the archangel, let us collect from the rapid hour the rare moments of fugitive joy . . .

But Marcellus could not hear anything or feel anything; perorating under the frost, shaking his graying mane, agitating his long arms like the feet of an enormous crane-fly.

"Blondel," he asked, "do you recall my sinister adventure in Pompeii?"

"The demon of noon, the house of the Siren, Astaroth the giver of kisses?"

"You will love, she announced to me; henceforth, you will have no other God than me. Well, the damned creature is accomplishing her threat. She is devouring me: I'm in love . . . in love . . . in love. . . . Malediction!"

The doors of the church had just opened; the mass was over, and to the final modulations of the great organ the faithful were beginning to emerge.

"Excuse me for quitting you," said Lautrem. "I'm going to rejoin my cantatrice; we're awaited n the sacristy."

He launched himself toward the portal, but on the steps he continued shouting at me: "*Au revoir*, then, dear friend. Go to Monte Carlo! You'll hear my *Leucosia* and, knowing me, you'll understand it."

❋

His *Leucosia?* Well, yes, I had understood it; I had even seen Esther Mosselman climbing into Davison's carriage.

VI
Theurgy and Occult Powers

Established for six weeks at Cap d'Antibes, working or idling, I had not seen my friend again. He, in any case, was installed far from the Golfe Juan, near his Monagasque theater in the Villa Ravel, an amiable caravanserai frequented by actors, dramaturges and musicians. Having run to Monte Carlo to applaud *Leucosia*, I had scarcely had time to procure a room at hazard. That lodging was situated near the pension; I headed in that direction.

Midnight had chimed, but in the realm of roulette, people stay awake and go to bed very late. Cafés, brasseries, restaurants and all the cabarets where gypsy fiddlers are rife remain illuminated until dawn. The victors of Trente et Quarante make merry there; the vanquished come to drown their sorrows and meditate some infallible system. I thought, therefore, that the Villa Ravel would still be open. Its guests, authors and actors, were doubtless having supper with Marcellus, consoling him in their fashion: scratches or pinpricks.

To my sharp disappointment, the pension appeared to be asleep; its shutters were closed, its lights extinct. In the moonlight, however, in a small garden planted with pretentious palms, I perceived a man collapsed on a bench. He seemed to be waiting, his head bowed, hiding his face in his hands, perhaps weeping. At the sound of my footsteps, Lautrem ran to open the gate, looked at me, nonplussed and disappointed, and then put his arms around me.

"Thank you Blondel! Your visit does me good . . . oh, my poor friend, how I'm suffering!"

He returned to his bench. I sat down beside him.

"So you didn't attend the performance of your *Leucosia*?"

"No, I couldn't. My nerves, these wretched nerves, which make me suffer so much! I experienced all the cowardice of a conscript before a battle."

"I understand; stage-fright, the bane of actors. A well-known phenomenon."

"But I hid near the theater in a clump of bushes, and friends came to inform me, act by act."

"They must have told you that your music . . ."

"Let's not talk about my music. Lamentable fall, burlesque collapse, sentence, conviction without appeal. They've done me the honor of treating me like Berlioz . . . imbeciles! How many idiots does it need to compose an audience?"

He wiped away the sweat pearling on his temples, and then, in a grim voice: "What do you think of Mademoiselle Diva?"

The question embarrassed me. Had I the right to devastate further a man already wounded so cruelly?

"Mademoiselle Diva? She was greatly applauded."

"I know, I know. Bouquets, wreaths, a sapphire necklace, yes, I know everything. Ignoble indecency, I was told, was it not? In a leotard! Exhibiting, displaying her nudity under the opera-glasses of flashy foreigners, lovers of prostitutes. Creature! I had forbidden her formally to dare such an ignominy. Why has she infringed my orders? Mademoiselle Diva forgets a little too much that she is going to be my wife . . . my wife! An Esther Mosselman, my wife!"

"Are you firmly committed to this marriage, Lautrem?"

But he was not listening to me, letting his anger off the bridle.

"After all, it's my fault; I'm submitting to the punishment of my weakness. I should never have permitted my fiancée, a neophyte who claims to be ardently Christian, to go on the boards. But she begged me so much that I gave in. A man is so wretchedly cowardly when he's in love! And then, that play *Leucosia* no longer belongs to me; I've made a gift of it."

"Who has exploited you? Your publisher?"

"No, Mademoiselle Mosselman. Formal donation. My fiancée is poor; I thought I ought to constitute a dowry for her."

His stupid credulity revolted me. "You love that demoiselle recklessly, then?"

"Yes, I love her!" he said, excitedly. "But you've heard her! What power of seduction, what charm, what infinite tenderness in the cry of her soul! And you ask me whether I love her!"

In truth, I no longer knew what to think. Sometimes he was outraged by the woman, calling her "creature"; sometimes he talked about her with the devotion of a believer . . . naïve Lautrem . . . ! The "soul" of Mademoiselle Diva, the former singer of the Garibaldi. I tried to disabuse him.

"Before accomplishing the irreparable, dear friend, you ought to obtain information."

"What's the point? I know, Esther has confessed to me, sincerely, the sorrows, the tears, the indigence, not to mention the temptations, of her life. She has told me about her childhood in Kherson, the murder of her father, killed in a pogrom, her flight, her vagabondage from one country to another. To earn her bread, the bread of bitterness of which Dante speaks, she sang in Egypt, in Tunisia and in France, and it was in an infamous concert-hall in the Parisian suburbs that I discovered her.

"You would dare to choose her for your wife?"

"Yes, since I love her. Rousseau married a servant; Auguste Comte picked up and sheltered for a long time a filthy whore of the Palais-Royal. How many educators of our human thought there are whose conduct appears to us to be irrational! They were in love, that's all! But why were they in love? Yes, why . . . why . . . ?"

He started marching back and forth in front of me, opening the garden gate, advancing into the road, interrogating the solitude and the silence in vain.

"Have you ever read Del Rio's book?" he asked me, abruptly.

"Who's Del Rio? You're bewildering me, Marcel, with your question."

"Forgetful memory! The celebrated demonologist I studied at the Villa Medicis? Well, perhaps Del Rio furnishes us with the key to our enigma. Listen to this: 'The second species of demons is the most redoubtable of all. Spirits of corruption, they take pleasure in putting on feminine form, and, women in body and women in perversity, cause the damnation of the imprudent who allow themselves to be charmed.' Do you understand now?

Was he mad? Was he trying to mystify me? Yes, doubtless, for he started to laugh.

"An amusing explanation, isn't it? Astaroth sending me the siren Leucosia, or, rather, incarnating herself, in order to perpetrate the work of her vengeance! On such a premise I might perhaps have built a fine romantic tale, the pendant of the good Théo's *Albertus*,[1] but our epoch delights in naturalist platitudes; my story would not have obtained any success; I renounce it."

And he laughed, and laughed. Then, in a breathless voice, the author of *Leucosia* developed abstruse theories of demonic

---

1 *Albertus* (1832) by Théophile Gautier is a narrative poem about a young painter who falls in love with and sells his soul to a witch who, ugly by day, is metamorphosed into a beautiful woman at midnight. It shares the blithe irreverence of many of the poet's early works for themes he was to treat with much greater intensity later in his career.

possession for me. Since the day when, in Eden, the tempter had perverted man, Satan had pursued that prey furiously. Hellenizing or Christian, humankind had always believed in spirits: good or evil, they direct our actions, often uniting with our body. Lautrem cited me Socrates, inhabited by a benevolent demon, the inspirer of his philosophy; the second Brutus and the Caesar Julian who were subject, on the contrary, to infernal hauntings, the one an apostate, the other a parricide. The praetors and prefects of Severus or Diocletian, kneeling in the ditch of the tauroboles, inundated with blood, received there the baptism of the Beast, absorbed it in person and got up persecutors of Christ. The Middle Ages had believed entirely in possession

"Luther, the abominable Luther," he cried, "conversed with the Devil; at Wittenburg he even threw his ink-well at his head; Richelieu had the nuns of Loudun exorcised to liberate them from incubi; Shakespeare had an entire faith in the power of ghosts, or revenants; Pascal hid under his garment an amulet that kept the demon away; Racine witnessed black masses, and when La Montespan lay naked on La Voisin's satanic altar, she represented the belief of the Great Century!"

"A time of ignorance, your Great Century. Voltaire did it full justice."

"Voltaire? A guttersnipe! He produced our députés and our ministers. Fine progeniture! I, who don't draw a salary from the budget of the Republic, believe in the haunting of occult Powers as firmly as the most illustrious of our forefathers believed in them."

"Their theurgy was an insanity."

"Insanity, theurgy? It's the most attractive of the sciences. Many a time, during winter evenings, I pored over the writings of a Trithemius, a Lancre or a Bodin! Stupid people, you'll object to me, credulous visionaries. Not at all; they made me aware of the state of my soul, revealed to me what Possession is. Truly, our physiologists, pathologists, neurologists and other pedants of barbaric inflection amuse me or make me feel pity. 'The great neurosis, autosuggestion; we'll care for you.' Well, Messieurs of the Salpêtrière, care for yourselves! Try, when you're in love, to cure your amour! Oh, amour . . . amour . . . !"

He stopped; sobs strangled his voice. The night was nothing but a dazzle of starlight; a breeze perfumed with the scent of mimosas brushed us with its caresses; unfurling over the sonorous rocks, the sea sent us its powerful harmonies; around us everything was appeasement, quietude, the sweetness of living—and yet, he was weeping.

Suddenly, Marcel started; a man was standing before us, observing us silently.

VII
Uncle Mardochée

He had slipped into the garden without making a noise, with felted footsteps, like Death, the thief of whom the Gospel speaks.

"Monsieur Mosselman?" cried Lautrem. "Alone? Where is she? You've come to announce a misfortune to me!"

The Caraïte shook his head; then, sniggering, and with a strong Hebraic accent: "Solomon the sage of all sages, said: 'Do not plot evil against the man who is faithful to you . . .' *Raka!* Monsieur Marcellus, you have not meditated that proverb."

"Where is she? You're killing me."

"Die, then! I won't come to deposit a pebble on your sepulcher."

The vulgar gibe revealed such an intensity of hatred that I observed Mosselman with astonishment. By the light of the gas that was burning outside the villa, I saw a face white with fury, eyes illuminated by rage and quivering lips. Was this the man who had been moved to pity, a little while ago, by Lautrem's amour? What could Diva have told him, to produce such a fit of wrath in that apathy, resigned until now?

He marched toward us, and folded his arms. "So, you have abused our poverty in a cowardly fashion, and profited from our distress? That's ignoble, Monsieur!"

Lautrem looked at him, bewildered.

"What do you mean, my dear Mosselman?"

"Oh yes! 'My dear, my good, my excellent Mosselaman . . .' Are you going to regale me again with your flattery? Futile! Keep your holy water stoup for other dupes. Esther has finally confessed everything to me."

"Esther? I don't understand this enigma."

"Truly? So little intelligence? You understand me very well."

And he started to weep over his "rose of Sharon," his "lily of the valley," his "dove," his "stainless ewe," whom an impure gentile had not hesitated to soil.

"Lies!" Lautrem interrupted. "I have always respected your niece. Christian and Catholic, I have a notion of honor."

Mosselman extended his fist in the gesture of a fanatic. "Honor? Honor understood in the fashion of your rabbis, suborners of consciences and buyers of children! Yes, Monsieur, Esther has told me everything. Slyly, and unknown to me, betraying my confidence, you have obliged a daughter of Israel to suffer the opprobrium of your baptism."

"I haven't constrained her. And then, what does it matter to you? She is going to become my wife."

"What does it matter to me . . . ? Monsieur, Monsieur, you Christians have burned my dwelling, pillaged my heritage, massacred my brother and my two sons, valiant men, the hope of my house! Without them, life is more desert to me than the sands of the Horeb. They have killed me! They obliged us, my niece and me, to wander the face of the world, starving, weeping over all the rivers of Babylon. Perhaps you think I love my executioners? I hate them; I hate them! Esther Mosselman, a Christian? A renegade, her, who consecrated to the true God the blood of her family? Abomination! On the imminent day of the end of the world, in the Valley of Josaphat, when the exterminating

Archangel asks me: 'What have you done with your brother's daughter?' ashamed and bowing my head, what shall I reply? Esther, a Christian? No! Rather see her dead."

Grotesque, but nevertheless tragic, tearing at his beard, stamping his feet with rage, the Millenarian was becoming menacing. I ought to have kept quiet; all grief is respectable. But that Judaic fanaticism irritated my freethought, and I thought it useful to intervene.

"Enough play-acting, Monsieur Mosselman. Are you repeating a role learned at the Palais des Glycines?"

He started insulting me in my turn. "I'm not play-acting; I'm weeping, I'm suffering, insulter of tears. Mind your own business and let me torture in my fashion this exploiter of poverty."

"Marcel," I said, taking Lautrem by the arm. "I dared not tell you the truth. Arm yourself with courage; it is cruel. Mademoiselle Diva is, from this evening on, the mistress of Robert Davison."

"You're lying, Blondel . . . ! Oh, pardon me, pardon me! But I'm enduring martyrdom . . . no, I can't, I don't want . . ."

"I've seen the person for whom you're waiting, strutting in the billionaire's carriage."

"The man of the sapphires? Prostituted!"

"A very vulgar word. You had nothing to offer her but your talent' Mademoiselle Esther has preferred the millions of Assuerus."

"Assuerus will at least permit her to worship her God," growled Mosselman. "He has made a formal contract to that effect."

"Perfect. Rather a courtesan than a Christian wife! Has Uncle Mardochée signed the contract?"

A vivid blush reddened the old man's cheeks. How many times on their boards had singers and actresses addressed that ignominious insult to him! Mardochée! A glorious name, however!

Indignantly, the Caraïte came to stand before me. "Uncle Mardochée?" he clamored. "Look at me, them; see these gaping shoes and these threadbare garments, my pallor and my flesh-lessness, testimony to a stainless poverty! Do I seem infamous? Uncle Mardochée? Oh, when we have reconquered Jerusalem and rebuilt the Temple, when the kingdoms of the earth belong to us, when the torrents of Judea are no longer anything but milk and honey, when the Son of the Star appears, triumphant and vengeful, then you gentiles, you the impure, you Christians, you goïm, you rabble, will come to kiss the sandals of the Uncle Mardochées!"

He took from his overcoat a letter that he had brought, threw it into the garden, and then completed cutting his victim's throat: "There's your regulation dismissal, Marcellus! You, Monsieur whose name I don't know, but who is so well able to insult old men, I leave you the spectacle of tears and the gnashing of teeth. I enliven myself in advance at the thought of the cowardice that you are about to understand."

He continued to look at us for a few moments, confronting the abhorred Christians that he had just reduced to silence. Finally, having consummated the holocaust, insolent and majestic, the sacrificer made his exit with slow steps. He proffered many imprecations, and drew away, still cursing.

VIII
Mademoiselle Diva's Sobs

Meanwhile, Lautrem had picked up the letter, and, standing under the gas-lamp, he read it. At times, a rictus contracted his features, and hisses punctuated by ironic cries escaped from his lips.

"Read this sickening thing, then," he said, holding the paper out to me. "Amuse yourself, Blondel."

He let himself fall back on to a bench, tilted his head back, ad closed his eyes. I read.

Impregnated with heady odors, it was a rather long epistle that Diva addressed to him. She had composed it, impudently, in the Palais de Glycines, for a vignette of the sumptuous habitation decorated the first page.

✳

Marcel, my Marcel, I have doubtless caused your tears to flow; I am weeping myself in writing to you.

The amour that constrains to amour every beloved creature—an admirable line of Dante, which I have only been able to understand thanks to your lessons—has commanded me to my duty. You are poor; your fiancée brings you nothing for a dowry but poverty, and I do not want, friend, my poverty to render your poverty more painful. I would experience painful remorse in seeing your genius sink in the turmoil, cares, vulgarity and quarrels of an indigent household: your wife advertising for pupils under the sun, the rain or the snow; reentering the lodgings irritated; lamenting her labor and her fatigue; taking your reveries in hatred; and you, seeking in vain the inspiration that would have fled. Glory, dear great artist, ought to be your only spouse; I, being paltry, am sacrificing myself . . .

Don't curse me. The passion that made us both delirious was always noble and chaste; let its pure memory remain the consolation of our dolor. And yet, Marcel, remember! Remember that evening in September when I nearly abandoned myself to your desire. Sitting at the piano, I was singing Schubert's *Adieu*, the melody from which such poignant sorrows emerge, the ballad that our forefathers loved so much in the days when people were able to love:

> *Adieu, until the dawn*
> *Of the day in which I have faith . . .*

And suddenly, recklessly, you put your arm around my waist, and then posed on my lips the burn of your kiss. Quivering, I fell into your arms; I wanted to be yours, yours, Marcel . . .

entirely, utterly! But you respected me . . . and now I bless you, Monsieur, for the delicacy of your honor . . .

Oh, that *Adieu* by Schubert, the cry of hope! It is still singing, and always will sing, in my memory . . .

In the name of your unique kiss, Monsieur, in memory of my only weakness, will you deign to grant a prayer? Thought, our scholars affirm, can traverse space to unite with another thought. Well, later, when the image of your wretched Esther no longer evokes suffering or rancor in you, in the evening, in your room, sometimes sit down at the piano to modulate the cords of my melancholy *Adieu*. Wherever I am your voice will reach me; your thought will rejoin my thought, and then . . . oh, then. I will know that I'm forgiven.

Esther Mosselman, henceforth Diva.

That repulsive parody of Musset's *Rappelle-toi* made me indignant. What audacity on the part of such a hussy to talk thus of abnegation and sacrifice! With her ridiculous story of telepathy, "Esther, henceforth Diva" allowed the calculations of the game to be divined all too clearly. With womanly perversity, she was refusing to let go of her prey: a scheming courtesan, she was preparing the lover's pardon.

"What do you think of that sentimental pathos?" Lautrem asked.

"Pathos or dangerous deceit. Your Diva isn't certain to conserve her American for long; she's keeping a door of reentry in your heart."

"Evidently! Manon Lescaut and her lover. But I'm not a Grieux."

He tore up the epistle and threw it on the gravel.

"There! Are you satisfied? Summary execution! You see me quite calm, Blondel, even indifferent. No cowardice, no gnashing of teeth, as that old rogue Mosselman was hoping for. And yet, what ingratitude! I fashioned an intelligence; I could not create a soul. Esther knew nothing; I taught her everything: music and literature, the comprehension of the Beautiful, the art of moving crowds, the means of forcing applause. This is my recompense! But bah! Let's not talk about it any more; let's treat her as a dead woman; let's forget her; forgetfulness is also a shroud."

"What are your projects now? Returning to Paris?"

"No, certainly not. *Leucosia* isn't an irreparable defeat, and I want my revenge. The role of the Siren had been rehearsed in duplicate. The other singer has merit; she'll replace the demoiselle of the sapphire necklace without difficulty. And tomorrow, or rather this evening, I shall deliver a second battle. After Waterloo, Austerlitz! Will you come to applaud me?"

"Impossible—I'm awaited at Cap d'Antibes; I have a rendezvous with an English lady to finish her portrait there."

"Well, well! You're painting portraits now, Monsieur Impressionist?"

"The Boucher genre! A former Prix de Rome is apt for all employments."

"Alas! Even that of Jocrisses of amour—example, Marcellus. I'll come to visit you soon."

"Agreed! I'll retain you to lunch."

"With your model? A pretty woman, no doubt? Yes . . . does she too have golden hair, blazing eyes, the mysterious pallor of . . .'"

He picked up the letter that he had torn up and looked at it: "Schubert's *Adieu!* Inept words, tearful melody, infantile music! How was I able to find pleasure in listening to such platitudes? When I return to Paris I'll burn that lachrymose ballad. Ha ha! What a folderol for grisettes, that *Adieu* by Schubert!

And his convulsive hands crumpled, twisted and tore Diva's letter again. Nevertheless, he slipped the debris into his pocket.

Two o'clock in the morning chimed; I stood up.

"I'll quit you and return to my inn. Are you going to bed, Marcel?"

"Why? I'm not sleepy. The night is warm; the gentle warmth of the breeze will calm my nerves; I'll stay in the garden until daybreak."

"You're shivering with fever."

"Me? I'm trembling, but with cold."

"And you talk to me about the warmth of the breeze?"

"Permit me to accompany you to the door of your hotel."

He took my arm; we left.

IX
Schubert's *Adieu*

The road that we followed, a rather steep slope, ran alongside the railway, and beneath the whiteness spread by the moonlight the dominant curve of the embankment was clearly distinguishable.

Inclining his head, weary and bleak, as if dazed, Marcellus now maintained a grim silence. Violent frissons shook his tall frame; sometimes, poorly repressed, a sob lifted his bosom; his feet, having become leaden, trailed heavily: it was definitely the crisis that Mosselman had announced. Heart-rending as it was, that excessive chagrin nevertheless appeared to me to be ridiculous. Suffering is passable when the regretted object merits regret: the Institut, for example, the red ribbon, not to mention a first medal at the Salon! But to martyrize oneself for a banal story of a woman—what ingenuousness of youth or senility of old age!

So, while marching beside that taciturn individual, I thought about my own affairs.

Are you not tired, Armand Blondel of still selling naturalist studies at a low price? Declare a bankruptcy, then, of the esthetics of poverty; transform yourself into a portraitist for the usage of high society. A painter of women, understanding their need to please, you'll imitate Boucher, Greuze or Fragonard; your complexions will become lilies and roses; your eyes charged with languor will be designed in almonds; your mouths will resemble strawberries, your low necklines will form white and vaporous cascades. In addition, what velvets satins, malines and Alençons to finish with minute care! The daubers of the Butte will be indignant; at the Chat Noir the Montmartreans will call you an illustrator for fashionable newspapers, an artist on porcelain. So what? Will that prevent the clientele from arriving? Jennys from Indianapolis or Bellas from Frisco will come running to your studio. Go on, my lad, exploiting feminine coquetry is the short cut to fortune. Follow the example of the specialists, the painters for Americans, and the wads of banknotes will soon be splitting your wallet; you'll even be able to construct your Renaissance town house in the vicinity of the Bois de Boulogne . . .

A strident blast of a whistle and a start on the part of my companion caused that amiable dream to vanish. The train for Genoa was quitting Monte Carlo station. It soon passed us, and in a cloud of dust the three lanterns of the last wagon displayed their sudden redness. They shone for a moment, diminished in brightness, and disappear.

Laustrem had pulled his arm away abruptly. Advancing his head, his features contracted, he extended a finger in the direction of the fleeing object; hiccupped words and moaning words hissed between his teeth.

"There . . . ! She's there . . . ! Gone!"

"No! Mademoiselle Diva is sleeping tranquilly, in her bed at the Palais de Glycines. Tomorrow you . . ."

"Gone! I saw her . . . ! She was leaning her head against that man's shoulder . . . he had his arm around her . . . he was embracing her . . . Oh! Infamous! Infamous! Go! I'll be able to oblige you, even in the arms of another, to think about me!"

He pivoted like an automaton, and then started to run, going back up the slope that led to the Pension Ravel. Anxiously, I followed him.

"Lautrem! Marcel!"

No response; but again, his heart-rending laugh: a laugh of frenzy.

Having reached the Villa he traversed the garden, climbed the perron, opened the door and closed it again. Thank God, he had gone back inside . . .

But suddenly, in the silence of the sleeping house, the sweet and plaintive sounds of a piano were heard. Chords: a prelude; a well-known ballad . . . Schubert's *Adieu!* No window was illuminated, however; all the blinds remained dark.

Could Lautrem see in the dark?

> *Adieu, until the dawn*
> *Of the day in which I have faith . . .*

And beneath Marcel's fingers, vibrant now, but by arpeggios, trills and modulations, the melody continued to moan:

> *. . . The day that will again*
> *Reunite me with you.*

The poor fellow!

That night, the widowed Madame Ravel's boarders must have cursed music and musicians.

X
Disappeared

Twenty-four hours after that adventure, the *Phare de Montboron*—director, editor-in-chief and artistic reporter Numa Heurtebise—published the following article:

> *Amusing news, new amours! A star of song has just been transformed into a comet. Mademoiselle Diva has flown toward Occidental skies, attracted by a sun with golden rays of the first magnitude.*

Last night, Mlle. Esther Mos*** and M. Robert Dav*** took the train to Genoa that calls at Monte Carlo at two thirty-five a.m. We are, as always, very well informed, and here is the proof:

In the waiting room, Mister Bob, less grim than Lazarus, crumpled Leucosia a little, and Leucosia gazed at him with the covetousness of a Siren. Will she soon devour him? The betting is open.

P.S. Singular coincidence. The prince of symbolism, Marcel Lautrem, the famous Marcellus, has also gone toward the unknown. He is sought in vain in the plain and on the mountain. Like the Siren, has the author of Leucosia *evaporated?*

A superb gift, we offer the opera-glasses of Nostradamus to anyone who can discover that second hairy and fleeting star.

When I took cognizance of the venomous little paper it had been hanging around for several days in the lounge of my hostelry at Cap d'Antibes. I rarely read blackmail rags, but the prudish Englishwoman, my model, had drawn my attention to Monsieur Herurtebise's humorous prose. His article had, moreover, obtained a considerable success. In Cannes, Nice, Beaulieu and Monte Carlo no one was talking about anything but the "shooting star," the "sun with golden rays" and the "prince of symbolism" so abruptly let go. People were talking about it, and laughing.

Very intrigued, I went to the Villa Ravel, where I interrogated waiters, the manageress, actors and actresses. "Marcellus . . . ?" They had no news. Some claimed that Lautrem was running in pursuit of his Diva, others that he must have killed himself. All, moreover, were pitiless for a noctambulist who gave them concerts at three o'clock in the morning.

"Was the second performance of *Leucoisa* a revenge?" I also asked.

"There was no second. That pretentious ineptitude did not feature on the poster again."

Vae victis![1] The Gallic motto remains, alas, very French.

Less harsh to the vanquished, however, the manageress of the pension gave me some vague indications.

"Monsieur Lautrem settled his weekly bill; afterwards he went out and hasn't returned. Poor man!"

"Where do you suppose he could have gone?"

"One of our clients affirms that he saw him board the one-thirty train—the one that goes to Genoa, Rome and Naples."

"In Italy? Without even taking his luggage?"

"Such a strange monsieur! In any case, fled or suicide, he's disappeared."

A few months later, having returned to Paris, I did not spare my research. I went to the lodgings in the Rue Vavin where Marcel had resided; I questioned the curé, the curates, the doorkeeper and all the authorities of Note-Dame-des-Champs; I asked for my friend at the various editorial offices of the critical periodicals of which he was the Ruskin as well as the Veuillot; none of them could tell me anything.

Ten years went by. In my turn I acquired a Parisian renown, and, what was better, numerous cosmopolitan clients. A painter sought after by women, especially Americans. I quit my studio in the Boulevard Monparnasse in order to install myself in an elegant town house in the Avenue du Bois. In the course of my successes, however, my thought sometimes evoked the image of Lautrem. To what country clement to the ideal had his whim taken him? Or rather on what indifferent beach had the waves of the Mediterranean deposited his cadaver?

Already, however, in the Latin Quarter, no one any longer knew that name of such turbulent glory. Esthetes, decadents,

---

1 "Woe betide the vanquished!"

symbolists and the "young" had ceased their deafening racket; grown old and gray, they had become peevish classicists, pontificating La Harpes or sniggering Villemains, and the unrippable shroud of forgetfulness enveloped the memory of my poor Marcellus entirely.

XI
Agreeable Awakening

. . . That morning I had got up morose. The Renaissance town house that had been constructed for me in the Avenue de Bois had only been inhabited for six weeks, and already many irritating snags had come to assail me: the architect, the electrician and the upholsterers were demanding money. The day before, on my return from the Volney club, I had found a bailiff's summons on the nickel plate of my vestibule, and the insolence of the sky-blue paper made my lips tremble again and my fists clench. *Notification to sieur Blondel (Armand) to appear before Messieurs the Magistrates to hear himself condemned to a payment of fifteen thousand francs, etc. etc. in accordance with the law.* The law? A bad joke! And I wanted expertise! Even the frightful black man had not taken care to hide his chicken . . .

Sitting at my window, between two caryatids in the style of Jean Goujon that decorated my dwelling, I was gazing sadly at the August sunlight gilding the grass of the avenue. Fifteen thousand francs, under pain of a lawsuit! And American commissions were yielding so poorly at the moment! Oh Blondel, imprudent Blondel, why did you want to do violence to your fortune so quickly? Flemish tapestries, Italian stained glass, credenzas, dressers, Spanish panoplies—all my magnificence had become odious to me.

Two light raps on my door drew me out of such a painful reverie; discreetly, my domestic slipped into the studio.

"The postman is downstairs, Monsieur, with a registered letter."

Good! Another compliment from an entrepreneur, some mason's vulgarity. And, like Orestes, I cursed creditors, the implacable Eumenides.

"Have the man come up."

The postman entered, smiling—they all smile, hoping for the gift of a cigar—and handed me a letter . . .

Oof! I breathed out; no limousine literature.

Scented with bergamot, it was a dainty satined envelope, *franco bello* Italian, bearing the stamp of Sorrento . . . armoried seal, princely crown, feminine handwriting; what was that? I dismissed the post office employee, not without having gratified him with a Havana, broke the seal and, very intrigued, I read:

Dear Monsieur,

Last spring, finding myself passing through Paris, I had the opportunity to hear your glory newly celebrated. Until then, I had appreciated the art of the portraitist poorly, willingly sharing the disdain of Pascal—a sophist, just between us, the neurasthenic author of the *Pensées*. But thanks to you, on the thirtieth of April, the day of the private view at the Palais des Champs-Élysées, my eyes were opened to the evidence and I found my road to Damascus.

In hall A-B, several groups of visitors were surrounding a painting, a portrait of Baronne Elias in a nacarat satin gown. The men were nodding their heads with a connoisseur air, the women were ecstatic, playing with opera-glasses and uttering little admiring cries. "What a brush that Armand Blondel has! My dear, there's no one like him for capturing a resemblance."

Your name was familiar to me. During my long sojourn in the United States I had noticed two of your masterpieces: the slender tragedienne Fanny Patterson, costumed as Ophelia, and, under the furbelows of a Watteau shepherdess, the plump Mrs. Sheppard, the divorced wife of the cheese king. Each of those paintings had cost five thousand dollars: first rate talent; I knew your price.

Well, Monsieur, I value you much higher. What would you say to forty thousand francs for a full-length portrait of a Neapolitan princess? Very enticing, isn't it? And you accept. But I impose my conditions. Being neither the thin Patterson nor the fat Sheppard, nor the red-faced Baronne Elias, I don't want floating draperies, baskets or farthingales, much less a nacarat gown. I demand—don't rebel—simple nudity. My desire might appear surprising to you; this is the reason for it:

Recently, while visiting Pompeii, I admired a suggestive fresco: Venus emerging from the waves in order to impose her law of Amour on Nature entire. According to my friends, I resemble her in a gripping fashion. My Venetian hair, my mat complexion and my dark eyes are those of the goddess, and as for the rest of my person, I leave to initiates the care of its description. Now, the simplicity of that Anadyomene seemed to me to be becoming; her uncomplicated attire would make the most of me, and a skillful brush would be able . . . you will take my implication; furthermore, we will talk . . .

Forty thousand francs, Monsieur! Hasten to come. I have need of that portrait, for I want to have it reproduced in various illustrated Italian periodicals. I await your telegram. Let me know the day and hour of your arrival; my carriage will come to fetch you at Castellammare station.

Princesse D. Campofiori.
Palazzo Sirena. Sorrento.

P.S. My Parisian bankers, Winckelrield Rutli and John Meurisier père, *Comptoir Bâlo-Genevois*, are informed of your visit. They will send you ten thousand francs on account, including travel expenses. You will sign a receipt for them.

That letter was somewhat cavalier, not to say extravagant; I consulted myself. But damn it! A lawsuit in prospect, lawyers, advocates and experts to pay, and so much money to receive! In any case, a long sojourn in Sorrento, even under the blaze of the height of summer, enticed me. Attractive excursions! I would visit the convent of La Campanella, Positano, Amalfi, the medical Salerno and the imposing Paestum. What sketches to make, what curious figures to draw!

Yes, but what sort of princess was this unknown D. Campofiori?

Desirous of being informed, I went to the offices of the *Comptoir* and asked for Monsieur Rutli. He was absent; it was his associate who received me.

XII
The Advice of the Sage

The son, grandson and great-nephew of Genevan bankers, Monsieur John Meurisier (why John?) is, as everyone knows, a fervent pietist. Born in Haute-ville in the sanctifying shadow of the massive bells of Saint-Pierre, he has imported into Paris all the ardors of his Momierism[1] and the blessings of the Eternal God pour down upon his house; he has just obtained, in Morocco, the concession of the mines of Sidi Abdallah.

On penetrating into his office I was edified, for the venerable sanctuary had nothing of the furniture of dentistry too frequent in the offices of our potentates of share-issues. A bust of Calvin on the mantelpiece; verses from Scripture along the walls: an Osterwald Bible very much in evidence; portraits of illustrious Swiss, but pure and sinless; no Jean-Jacques, Fazy or Mermillod,

---

1 The Momiers were a Genevan Protestant sect whose adherents—notionally, at least—celebrated the Spirit of Mercy and had egalitarian sentiments. Persecuted by orthodox Calvinists for no reason that anyone else could understand, they reacted intransigently.

but Bonnets, Saussures, Simonde-Sismondis, Pictets, Amiels and even, I believe, a Monsieur Naville; one could have believed that one was in the home of a pastor of the Reformed Church. An obese sexagenarian with a ruddy face from which fell a cascading Coligny beard, Monsieur Meurisier *père* initially welcomed me in a surly fashion; even the elect are sometimes in a bad mood.

"What do you desire?"

I pronounced my name, and he immediately became amiable.

"I greatly admired, Monsieur Blondel, your portrait of Baronne Elias. An interesting person! Her husband, an intelligent financier, does a great deal of business with our Comptoir.

"Very flattered by your eulogies! Can you, Monsieur, give me some information on the subject of Madame la Princesse Campofiori?

"Gladly. She's the widow of Prince Gaetan, a pleasant fellow, but overly fond of the wings of the theater, who committed suicide. 'The madman lives and dies in accordance with his madness,' the Proverbs of Solomon inform us."

"Suicide? Not very serious people, the Campofioris!"

"Very serious and honorably rich; they're our clients."

"But the Princesse?"

Monsieur Meurisier looked at me, surprised.

"You're embarrassing me. Certainly the poor woman doesn't possess any of the virtues that scripture demands. In the course of her dissipated—let's not mince words, libertine—existence she has spun many other things than the distaff of a Rebecca. In any case, you undoubtedly know her: Esther Mosselnan, the celebrated Diva!"

The name Mosselman made me shudder; it evoked such distant and dolorous memories.

"Mademoiselle Diva the singer?"

"Singer? An admirable cantatrice, my dear Monsieur, the foremost lyrical artiste on the United States: five hundred dollars a performance."

"Damn! The price of one of my sketches."

"A widow at present, our prima donna is returning to her amours; La Campofiori will soon be heard on the boards of San Carlo. 'The dog returns to its vomit,' the Proverbs also inform us."

Not very gallant, the Momiers' comparison! For myself, I was astounded. A princess! Such adventures are not rare, and all our young pupils of the Conservatoire hope to become, one day, a duchesse or marquise. But a princess, that Mosselman, the companion of Hortensia Niniche, the former singer of the Garibaldi!

Something else intrigued me: what had become of her Davison?

"Mademoiselle Diva is an old acquaintance," I said. "I was present at her debut. Was she not whisked away thereafter by a rich American?"

"Yes, by Bob, the stout Davison. He married her, and killed himself."

"Him too? Your client doesn't bring good luck to the conjugal bed."

"Pooh! Only two husbands—far fewer than the daughter of Raguel.[1] But on the other hand . . . we wouldn't have tolerated such conduct in Geneva."

"Oh, I know all about the modesty of your immaculate city. Why did Davison kill himself?"

Monsieur Meurisier remained silent for a moment; then, emphasizing his words, he said: "He didn't kill himself . . . he was assisted to die."

"By whom? Mademoiselle Mosselman?"

"I don't accuse the poor sinner. She justified herself before men; alas, what will become of her before God? My brother Josias, the pastor of Cully, always calls her Astaroth. Esther . . . Astaroth: two forms, he affirms, of a single name. Our ministers

---

1 The daughter of Raguel, in the *Book of Tobit*, was Sarah, whose seven husbands were killed successively by the infatuated demon Asmodeus. As the book in question is excluded from Protestant Bibles, it is perhaps surprising to find it cited by a Momier.

of the Holy Gospel are more learned than your curés, and Josias is a scholar of Hebrew."

He swelled with pride, after he had launched his Calvinist crossbow-bolt, like a good Genevan, but his revelations perplexed me.

"Your princesse isn't very estimable," I told him, "so I need time to reflect."

The austere Meurisier shrugged his shoulders and placed his hand on his Bible.

"Reflect? Money, no matter how dirty it may be, is money. Who spoke thus? Solomon again! Listen, then, to the advice of the Sage: Monsieur Blondel, go to the cashier's desk."

I followed the advice of the Sage, pocketed my ten thousand francs on account, and a few days later, an express train carried me toward Naples.

XII
The Pierrot

A tiring journey! Thirty-six hours of jolts, curvatures, dust and smoke; but at last, Italy, *O terre felice e lieta*, under your sky, what intoxication of sunlight and azure! I did not stop anywhere; even Rome, that old and dear acquaintance, could not retain me . . .

There are too many engineers in the land of marvelous masterpieces! Even more barbaric than ours, those messieurs of the straight line have sacked, demolished or dishonored everything. In the Intangible City, a sanctuary that ought to have been inviolable for them, they have constructed tubular bridges, and even American "skyscrapers."

The art of the Bramantes or the Primatices appeared impractically old-fashioned to them, and they preferred to imitate our Parisian Durands, the Michels of Berlin, and above all the Yankee Jonathan. O Chicago, city of superb pork-butchers, with your bank offices, your negro hostelries, your gigantic chimneys, your thirty-story roosts, your lumber-room where busy businessmen swarm, how beautiful you must seem to them! They have not been able to accomplish the work of their vandalism everywhere, though; sometimes their love of the banal has only profaned by halves, but the Appian Way, cut today by railway lines and bordered by walls, resembles some street in Bagnolet.

> *Thus everything flees and everything passes;*
> *Thus we shall pass ourselves.*

I arrived in Naples on the thirteenth of August; I did not linger to muse; Chiaia, the Via Toledo and Posillipo no longer have any secrets for me, so I climbed into a suburban train and descended at Castellamare at two o'clock in the afternoon.

A caleche was waiting in the station forecourt. Its coachman, a burly fellow from the Riviera, was wearing English livery, but his companion on the seat was decked out in the most picturesque fashion. To see his bonnet of scarlet silk, his bouffant shirt with a turned-down collar, his broad belt, his short trousers and escarpins, one might have thought him an Opera Masaniello celebrating the return of the dawn: "Friends, the morning is beautiful . . ."[1] I scarcely recognized the Campofiori rig.

"Pay attention, Cecchino!" said the man in English livery. "Here's the Frenchman!"

Cecco, a youth about fifteen years old, leapt to the ground and came to meet me. "*Eccellenza!*" He installed me in the vehicle, and then they resumed chatting:

"Run to warn the Pierrot that we're about to depart."

"Where shall I look for him? At the Café de l'Indépendance?"

"No, more likely at the lottery office. The draw was made yesterday; his numbers didn't come up and our good-for-nothing will have gone to pick a quarrel with the Lotto employee."

"*Disgraziati!* He'll make us late, we'll no longer encounter the padre.

"Is poor Gigi very ill, then?"

---

1 In Daniel Auber's opera *Le Muette de Portici* (1828), also known as *Masaniello*.

"*Ahimé!* Teresa is desolate. My little brother is bewitched."

"*Per Dio!* She's lodged her child in the house of the she-devil."

Masaniello gratified the "she-devil" with a filthy insult, and then ran toward the town in search of the Pierrot . . .

And time went by. The sun was burning; the horses were restless under the bites of horse-flies, while a verminous rabble, clear-sighted blind men or active paralytics, a dozen beggars harassed me with their plaints. Finally, Cecco came back, shouting and cursing.

"Here he is! He was tranquilly drinking his vermouth in the Café Cavour."

"Always on credit! He owes money at every trattoria in the region; three hundred lire at least. Who'll pay his debts? *La lupa!*"[1]

"Idler! Witch's ruffian! Even more crapulous than those of the *Mala vita!*"[2]

Soon I saw a man of very noble appearance appear, a tall and handsome man of about thirty with very curly hair, whose turned-up moustaches seemed to be menacing the sky. His foppish face might have seemed a trifle Moorish, but a layer of white make-up tried to render him irresistible. Coiffed in a fur hat with a pheasant plume and shod in varnished boots, he was dressed in a white flannel suit, and in the buttonhole of his jacket there was the crimson, saffron and azure of an astonishing decoration. Evidently, this was "the Pierrot." He advanced nonchalantly, holding his head high and bracing his athletic torso, twirling his swagger-stick, singing in a baritone voice, vocalizing. "The flash of her smile . . . *Il baten del suo sorriso* . . ." He sang, with many flourishes, a refrain from *Il Trovatore*, the ballad of the amorous Count di Luna.

---

1 The literal meaning of *lupa* is "she-wolf," but it is more often used to indicate an inmate of a *lupanar* [brothel].

2 *Mala vita* [Rotten Life] (1892) is an opera by Umberto Giordano, which employs Neapolitan popular songs and the Neapolitan dialect, based on a play by Salvatore di Giacomo. Its downtrodden heroine, Cristina, is a prostitute; it does not end happily.

With a theatrical gesture, like d'Artagnan lifting his plumed hat, the decorated monsieur saluted me.

"The illustrious Blondel, I believe . . . the guest of our dear Diva?"

Cultured language, choice epithet; one might have taken him for an ambassador. I bowed.

"Our beautiful Princesse," he went on, "has delegated me to receive you. She would have liked to lodge your glorious person in her palazzo, but excessively numerous friends are occupying all the rooms, so we have retained you an apartment at La Cocoumella . . . a magnificent inn, Monsieur, a former Jesuit convent!"[1]

"The good Fathers knew how to treat themselves well . . . go, then, for your convent."

"Permit me, now, to introduce my humble individual. His name is less famous than yours, but it is known. Angelo di Sant'Angiolo, the baritone."

"Artiste at San Carlo?"

"No . . . 'I have traveled the world for a long time.' But the world, kings or republics, has understood me."

And while humming the first notes of the great aria of *La Gioconda*, he indicated the rutilant rosette that ornamented his white jacket. Finally, as majestic as Louis XIV climbing into a coach, Monsieur di Sant'Angiolo took his place beside me.

"Drive on, Benedetto!" he cried. "Cast off, animal! Quickly! *Subito! Vite et vite!* We're late."

Three different languages in the same sentence? What a polyglot! To what diabolical country could he belong? That bistre complexion, those advanced lips and that excessively curly hair were certainly not the features of an Italian. A very handsome male, nevertheless!

Thus maltreated, Benedetto, the coachman, muttered an imprecation. "*Subito! Vite et vite . . . !*" And he set his horses in motion.

---

1 Presumably based on the Grand Hotel Cocumella, which is still advertised as the best hotel in Sorrento.

XIV
Monsieur di Sant'Angiolo

And slowly, at a processional speed, the caleche traversed the streets of Castellamare. At times, Benedetto glanced at the lover of vermouth slyly, his eyes seeming to say to him: "How one obeys your orders, eh?" *Un dispetto!* But Sant'Angiolo feigned indifference; he had lit a noxious virginia, and was expelling spirals of bitter smoke into the air, plaguing me with his tobacco.

In the Principe Umberto square numerous red, yellow and green posters were displayed, which only contained one word: CAMPOFIORI. Here and there, one also saw the illuminated portrait of the Diva. Clad in a very low-cut dress, her fleuroned crown on her head, the princesse was cynically exhibited to the eyes of passers-by: sailors from the port and workmen from the Arsenal. But everywhere, coarse gibes and untranslatable witticisms, mud and ordure, soiled the mage of the cantatrice; men stopped in order to shake their fists at her, women spat on the ground with imprecations; a seminarian in violet stockings made the sign of the cross.

My neighbor had adjusted his monocle and criticized: "A bad launch! Unintelligent advertisement! The impresario doesn't know his métier."

"Is it true?" I asked. "The Princesse is going to appear on stage again?"

"In a month. Artistic event! Immense, Monsieur! An entire revolution in mores!"

"What does the Campofiori family think about it?"

"The abomination of desolation! They're enraged. Think of it: five archbishops and three cardinals among the noble ancestors!"

"What sort of man was Prince Gaetan?"

"A man, that? No, a puppet. Short, puny, sickly, with albino hair, eyes the color of porcelain, the blood of a turnip. He lacks prestige."

Sant'Angiolo stuck out his superb chest, stretched his moustaches, and his triumphant gaze said clearly to me: "Compare!"

"Why did he kill himself?"

"Pooh! *Chi lo sa?* Doubtless an ironic glance from his wife, the flash of a scornful smile! *Il balen de suo sorriso* . . . oh, that smile, Monsieur! One morning, Gaetan was picked up, bloody and gasping, the imbecile, outside the door of the conjugal bedroom. He had cut his throat with a razor. Our princesse was sleeping her slumber of innocence: *Dormi pure, dormi contenta* . . . When she awoke, and the adventure was announced to her, she started smiling again."

"A dolorous story!"

"Terrible! Don't you think, illustrious master, that the director of San Carlo lacks artistic sensibility? He ought to have costumed our dear Diva quite differently."

"To represent her in a role from her repertoire?"

"More simply. Do you know the fresco in Pompeii, the Aphrodite Pandemos? No? Go and admire it, then. It resembles your future model astonishingly, in every detail—you can take my word for it. Oh, if the posters had reproduced that masterpiece with only two words: CAMPOFIORI! CAMPOFIORI! What a stupefying advertisement! But in Naples, there's no concern for the Beautiful."

And baritoning for a second time, he caressed the multicolored rosette of his decoration.

Benedetto was now striving to make up the lost time. Our carriage was flying at top speed, and, very agitated, Cecco was abusing the two chestnut horses: "Hup! Hup! Devil's mares! Hurry up! We're going to miss the padre!" The heat had become overwhelming. In the azure transparency of the sky, the sun of the heat-wave darted its burning rays upon the dusty road that went along the Riviera; the sea was dazzling; without even the whiteness of a cloud the Apennines profiled their ashy jagged outline against the fleeing indigo of the horizon . . .

"Hup! Hup! Idlers!"

And in the strident concert of cicadas, under the buzzing swarm of flies, of the sound of little bells shake by the harness, the rises and the descents, the caleche rolled, devouring space. The villages succeeded one another: Vico Equense, Montechiaro, Alinuri, Meta. All their windows were closed, the shops shut; from Posillipo to Punto Campanella, townspeople and citizens were abandoning themselves to the delights of the siesta . . .

But Sant'Angiolo was not asleep. He recounted to me his numerous theatrical conquests in Europe, Asia and Africa. In Smyrna, Levantine women with the eyes of gazelles had offered him a crown decorated with their bracelets; in Cairo, two wives of a pacha had fled their harem in order to come to sigh in his dressing-room. Better still, he had enthused Paris, redoubtable Paris!

"You have heard me, I suppose, at the Gaité-Lyrique, in the divine Rossini's *Figaro*: *Un barbière di qualità, di qualità . . .* What brio, eh? What stunning verve! I burned the boards! All the illustrious French critics came to congratulate me."

Angelo also revealed to me that he had been born in Salonika and was descended from the Byzantine Caesars. A Comnenus or a Paleologue? My man did not know exactly, but he affirmed that Alexis, Michel or Constantine, his ancestors, had employed Greek Fire to slay the Arab and the Ottoman. He preferred less bloody laurels; he was a "singer-tragedian." For several minutes that negroid heir of the Autokratos savored the memories of his triumphs, and then, abruptly:

"Do you know the name of a certain Monsieur Marcellus?"

"Marcel Lautrem, the author of *Leucosia*? He was one of my dearest friends."

"Celebrated, that Monsieur? An immortal of your Académie?"

I shook my head; no, my comrade had not donned the green coat.

"What! Not even in the Académie! Is he still alive, your un-lucky writer?"

"Alas, no. So Mademoiselle Diva has mentioned Marcellus to you?"

"Never! Well, well! They knew one another? However, I admire every day, in the palace of our princesse, the numerous gifts, homages rendered to her beauty, but none of them evoke the memory of this Monsieur Lautrem. I shall consult my catalogue."

"Make enquiries, Monsieur di Sant'Angiolo, and perhaps you will be amply informed . . . why are you talking to me about my friend?"

The San Carlo theater is going to revive *Leucosia*."

"What are you telling me? *Leucosia* is going to be performed again?"

"Yes, in six weeks. Madame de Campofiori desired, even demanded, that the play be performed."

"I can divine her reasons. Mademoiselle Diva owns all the author's rights."

"With me, if you please. I have translated, enlivened—or, to put it better, entirely rewritten—that formless rhapsody. Our heady Venus will sing the role of the Siren, and your servant that of Lazarus."

"You're debuting with her at San Carlo?"

"I hope so; Diva has asked for me. Her director can refuse nothing to a cantatrice, a star among stars. As a last resort, she will impose my engagement."

And with a cynical gesture, the clown with the beautiful moustaches, informed me that in their honor, Esther had proposed to finance it.

"Yes, I shall play Lazarus," the fop went on. "And yet, I don't understand that character at all. What does he want of us with his *oremus*? He's a monsieur of the good God, agreed, but a man, of flesh and bone! I want to change the ending. Why, when the Siren summons that speech-maker, does he not fall into the arms of the magicienne? Passion, Monsieur, always passion!"

"You have an inflammable heart, Monsieur di Sant'Angiolo?"

"A Vesuvius! Our artistic life is only made of passion. One encounters a divine *prima donna*; she pleases; she seems desirable; discreetly, one makes her understand the ardor of one's amour. Oh, no sonnet, no prosaic words; song accompanied by sighs . . . *il balen del suo sorriso* . . . and then . . ."

"Then the heir of the Byzantine Caesars is installed at the Palazzo Sirena."

"Joker! Something else bothers me: how was Lazarus dressed? In black, in gray, in white? The robe of a Dominican would suit me well enough. With my pale face, further embellished by a brown beard, I'd produce a powerful effect. Yes, but was this Lazarus accoutered as Savonarola? Personally, I want to respect historical verity. Can you furnish me with a few details on that subject?"

"Address yourself to the messieurs of *La Crusca*."

"They won't reply to me. Where the devil am I going to procure that information?"

He remained pensive momentarily, and then suddenly slapped his forehead. "Eureka! In a little while, if we encounter the monk, I'll pose my question to him."

"What monk? A priest expert in theatrical costumes?"

"An astonishing monk! The earth, Heaven and Hell no longer have any secrets for him. With a gesture he makes the orange-trees blossom, brings the tuna and the scorpion-fish into the mesh of nets, destroys caterpillars or weasels, distributes the dew, the rain, the wind and the sunlight at his will. Cattle, horses, chickens, hysterical women and convulsed children—this monsieur cures every sick creature."

"A thaumaturge! Your physicians and veterinarians must abominate him."

"They'd like to hang him, but how can they catch him? The fellow has the gift of ubiquity. Is he seen in Sorrento? It's because he's in La Campanella. Is he seen in his cell? Then he's walking on Capri. Our peasants claim that the body of the holy man is a human appearance, a divine emanation, and that he can duplicate himself."

"Why do the monks of his Order not impose silence on such reportage?"

"They've been dispersed, and the convent of La Campanella subjected to the formalities of sequestration. It's only inhabited by three infirm old men, of whom our man is the superior. And then, between us, such a maker of marvels is like a goose that lays golden eggs. Messieurs the cowl-wearers refrain carefully from demolishing such a lucrative legend."

"Them, I understand, but the police? They tolerate the practices of this charlatan?"

"The police are too prudent; perhaps they're afraid of great annoyance. This *frataccio*, who, moreover, cares for and cures gratuitously, acts as master in our rural areas. The country folk venerate him like a fetish; if a policeman laid a hand on such a sacrosanct person, we'd have a riot."

"A riot!"

"Exactly as in Sicily or your Bretagne. Yes, Monsieur, a fetish. One doesn't touch objects that are taboo. Hold on, you're about to hear the most devoted of his fanatics deliberating our Old Man of the Mountain . . . Cecco! Friend, is it true that the padre accomplished prodigies?"

"He expels demons," replied Francesco, in a convinced but menacing voice.

"What do you call demons, imbecile?"

"Don't play the pagan thus; you won't impose it on me! Demons resemble the one you know."

"Name her then, if you dare!"

"The woman of the Palazzo Sirena."

"She furnishes you with your bread, wretch."

"Her bread is too bitter for me; I no longer want to eat it."

Sant'Angiolo burst out laughing. "Ignorant! Lazzarone! Product of the Chiaia! I, Monsieur Blondel, don't believe in Hell any more than in Paradise. My father translated the books of

274

Schopenhauer into Turkish, and he transmitted his philosophical soul to me. I remember that on Mount Athos, debating with an Archimandrite . . ."

I did not hear the continuation of the palpitating narration; overwhelmed by fatigue, I had dozed off.

Abruptly, Cecco's voice woke me up.

"Halt! There he is! I have to talk to him!"

XV
The Padre

The vehicle had just stopped in the main square of Sant'Agnello. A silent town, it appeared very pretty to me, with its houses painted blue, pink or yellow, its orchards whose somber verdure allowed glimpses of the saffroned gold of lemons and oranges, and its elegant church preceded by a double stairway in the form of a *scala santa*.

Already, the festival of the Assumption had begun; several fairground merchants' stalls were exposing under their canvas awnings many objects of pleasant piety: chaplets with beads sculpted in cheese; Madonnas as varied as Italian women; San Gennaro, the nursing father of macaroni-eaters; Santa Lucia, the unparalleled virgin who put out her eyes in order not to be subjected to the soiling of a pagan marriage—all intermingled with less authentic saints: Garibaldi, Cavour, Mazzini, the royal gallant. Petards, rockets and sparklers were displayed there with the rosaries, for one cannot celebrate the powers of paradise without sending them the orison of a firework display.

Before the church of Sant'Agnello a Franciscan monk was standing, clad in an ashen maroon robe. Senile, already curbed by age, he must have been almost blind; his hand was leaning on the shoulder of a youth, his guide. Men in working clothes, bare-legged women and ragged children surrounded him and there was a concert of supplications: "Padre, my husband . . . my son . . . my father . . . my cousin . . . my fiancé is ill. Cure him. We'll offer you baskets full of quail for your convent then . . ."

Further away, a *daziere* remained seated, a customs officer in a braided white cap, and the miscreant was sniggering. Six o'clock had just chimed. The Angelus bell was ringing gently in the sonorous air under a durable blue sky; the spectacle was amusingly picturesque and resembled a painting by Léopold Robert.

My companion got down and headed toward the Franciscan, but Cecco got there ahead of him.

The thaumaturge interested me. In Rome, in the Trastevere, I had seen several of his peers at work, also accustomed to prodigies, who were able to cure malaria, make lottery numbers come up and bring an infidel mistress back to her lover. Any distributor of miracles merits a quick sketch, so I took my album and approached him.

Similar to some figure of Zurbaran, he was a monk of bizarre, grim, not to say disquieting aspect. His thinness was painful to behold, and the minor friar's habit dressed a skeleton. Perhaps the accentuated features of his face had once had their beauty, but the practices of asceticism, malady or the suffering of the soul had emaciated it hideously, hollowing it out, even dissecting it, and his jaundiced pallor gave him a cadaverous appearance. Although he was not yet an old man, the Franciscan appeared to be very ancient. Profound wrinkles furrowed his forehead, and fissured the corners of his mouth; the gray hair around his shaven cranium was sparse. In passing over that man, the torments of life had only left a human rag.

At the ringing of the bell he had straightened his tall frame, and, raising his eyes, recited the angelic salutation; the peasants knelt down.

"*Angelus Domini nuntiavit Mariae* . . ."

Meanwhile, Cecco had slipped near to the holy man. With both hands he seized the rope that secured the brown robe and placed his lips devotedly upon it.

"Padre, do you recognize me?"

"*Ecce ancilla Domini . . . Ave Maria gratia plena . . .*"

"I'm Francesco Balbi, Teresa's son."

"*Et nunc, et in hord mortis nostrae. Amen.*"

"*Amen,*" repeated the peasants, getting up.

His prayer finished, the monk made a sign to Cecco to come nearer, looked at him very closely, the said in an amicable tone: "Yes, I know you . . . Francesco Balbi, one of my young invalids . . . the child of Teresa, the excellent and pious woman I placed at the Tramontano. How is the mamma?"

"The mamma has quit the hotel; we're presently domestics at the Palazzo Sirena."

The Franciscan started, and then said harshly: "You've done wrong, a great wrong. Good Christians in the house of a reprobate!"

"At the Tramontano Teresa only earned twenty-five sous a week. The clients of the hotel, almost all English heretics, aren't generous and . . ."

"And she preferred to compromise her soul and that of her son! On the day of judgment, the very stones of the accursed house will accuse your mother."

"Oh, padre! We're going to leave the service of the reprobate as soon as possible."

"Good! You desire to speak to me?"

"Yes, but don't look at me with such a terrible expression; I'm afraid . . . this is it. Teresa implores you to cure Luigi, my little brother."

"I won't cross the threshold of La Sirena. Call a physician."

"Oh physicians! We're very poor and can't pay them; they threw me out. Even Signor Gargioule said to me: 'Since the *co-collato* cared for you, let him care for your brother.'"

"A physician! So that's what philosophism calls human solidarity! The ignominy of the merchants of the Temple! From what malady is Luigi suffering?"

"He's possessed by a demon."

The monk shuddered; a rictus of anger contracted his face.

"No, Francesco, no; Beelzebub does not reign again in our land; he will not be the master, even though his daughter Astaroth has already installed her court."

A quiver of hatred agitated the peasants. "*Stregona! Sputo, vomito del diavolo!*" they clamored. The widow of suicides, Diva, Princesse Campofiori, was certainly not popular under the sun of Sorrento.

"Luigi is the prey of the demon, venerable father," said Cecco. "For several days, at noon, he utters savage cries, rolls on the ground, writhing and thrashing like the possessed; his eyes bulge from his head and bloody drool runs from his mouth . . ."

"Worrying symptoms, I agree! Nevertheless, is it truly a possession? I don't know yet. Continue."

". . . And while vociferating, he proffers blasphemies. Dear maman has beautiful images in her room, the greatest saints of Paradise; my brother insults them, and the other day he tore them up, and then chewed them with his teeth. Yesterday, while he was contorted, the mamma threw holy water over him; he started to howl as if a hot iron had been plunged into his body. The mamma put her own scapular over his breast; then . . . oh, then . . ."

"I was there," a woman interjected. "He barked! Padre, have compassion on the bambino."

"I won't enter into La Sirena."

"But padre!" the woman exclaimed, "are all the devils in Hell going to take possession of our children, then? The demon is tormenting that ragazzo; it's your duty to expel him."

"My duty . . . ? Yes," replied the Franciscan, "that poor creature seems to me to be cruelly possessed. In fact, the malign spirit who is torturing Luigi is one of my old acquaintances: the demon of noon, the crawling dog who prowls around all children in order to devour their souls. It's redoubtable."

A cry of horror greeted that alarming explanation; the men made the sign of the cross, the mothers clutched their bambini tightly. As for me, I was stupefied. Was the monk joking? But no; his bleak and tragic face, his visionary eyes, and the tremor of his lips all said that he too believed in demons, and that he execrated them.

"Padre! Padre!" Cecco implored.

The monk appeared to consult himself; then, with the gesture of a man making a difficult resolution he said: "I won't enter La Sirena."

A few murmurs were heard, but he allowed an imperious gaze to wander over the supplicants who permitted themselves to criticize him, and they dispersed submissively.

"*Ebbene!*" muttered Teresa's son. "I'll take charge of strangling the spell-caster myself.

"No," riposted the monk, harshly. "God alone has the right to accomplish his Vengeance."

Then, replacing his hand on his guide's shoulder, he tried to set forth on his way; but Sant'Angiolo barred his passage,

Diva's protégé had stood to one side, next to me, while I sketched the blissful figure of a peasant woman. The story of the crawling dog had amused him, and while smoking his tenth virginia he philosophized: "Astaroth? Madame de Campofiori, I imagine. In a little while we'll laugh, when I salute the Princesse with that Biblical appellation . . . Astaroth!"

"Are you numerous at the moment at the Palazzo?"

"A dozen cheerful companions; the theaters and café-concerts of Naples have furnished their contingent of comrades. Every evening we sup, dance and make merry. Let's amuse ourselves, damn it! Life is so short, and . . . but our fellow is going away; let's catch up with him.

He ran to the monk, and planted himself before him in a cavalier fashion.

"Excuse me, venerable monsieur, I too desire to present my request to you."

The casual manner of such a statement doubtless displeased the "venerable monsieur," for he continued on his way. "The

Angelus has just sounded; it's getting late; I don't have time to listen to you, my friend."

My friend? What disdainful familiarity! The baritone's voice growled like a *basso profundo*: "I'm Angelo di Saint'Angiolo, the lyrical artiste. Perhaps that name is known to you."

"Quite unknown, Monsieur. The rumor of your theaters doesn't rise as far as my cell."

"Of course! You perch so high at La Campanella."

"Not so high, however, that the noise of shameful scandals cannot reach it"

"I don't understand. You're said to be knowledgeable, my estimable monsieur; perhaps you can help me to resolve a historical problem."

"Ask your director."

"He's more ignorant than a lobster-fisher."

"Address yourself to the great men of the Academy."

Two rebuffs! But Sant'Angiolo did not let go of his prey; he was walking backwards in front of the Franciscan; I followed him, amused by his disconcertion.

"Lazarus, dear Monsieur and . . . friend, did he not put on a monastic habit like you?"

"What Lazarus are you talking about?"

"The true the only, the inimitable Lazarus; the resuscitated, the amphityron of the philosopher Jesus."

The monk slowed down, and said, haughtily: "Spare me, if you please, the worn-out pleasantries of your petty rationalism."

"Understood! I'd like to know, nevertheless, what costume Lazarus wore when . . ."

"A shroud! The habit, Monsieur Actor, that must one day cover many stupidities and many human turpitudes."

"Bravo! Tit for tat! But the question is interesting, and I'll continue. Was Lazarus a Capuchin, a Carmelite or a Recollect when he encountered the siren Leucosia on Capri?"

At the word "Leucosia" the Franciscan stopped dead. He stretched his neck, trying to make out the features of the ignorant person who was pursuing him; then, very emotional, he said: "Who has told you that story, Monsieur?

"Having read it in old books, I took it as the subject of an opera."

"You are the author of *Leucosia?* You, Monsieur? You?"

"Me. Or, rather, I have rendered attractive a certain pasquinade, a formless and grotesque mess; from that dung-heap I have extracted a pearl."

"A dung-heap? A pearl! You have the genius of a Virgil, Monsieur . . . my compliments!"

"So you refuse to respond to me?"

"Dare I ask you, in my turn, in what theater and in what epoch your . . . masterpiece is to be performed?"

"Very imminently, in San Carlo."

"Ah! Who are your interpreters?"

"Myself and the celebrated Diva, my friend."

A sudden blush illuminated the pale face of the monk; his eyes darted a malevolent gaze, but immediately, putting his hand to his left arm, he grasped it violently. A few drops of blood ran along his fingers; he was concealing a bracelet of sharp nails under his robe, and was martyrizing himself. Then, moving the boor aside with an imperious gesture, he said: "Retire, Monsieur, and announce to your Siren that Lazarus is finally going to emerge from his tomb."

Half past six chimed; the old man drew away. But while marching he pressed his instrument of torture with his fingers, inflicting pain on himself frenziedly. "*Miserere mei, Domine,*" he said in a loud voice. "*Miserere! Miserere!*" And here and here, traces of blood speckled the whiteness of the road on which each of his footsteps tottered.

During the acrimonious colloquium I had observed the miracle-worker at length, and my curiosity had gradually turned to stupor . . .

Marcellus! Marcel Lautrem hiding for ten years of the dolors of his life in the convent of La Campanella! Was that possible?

Had ten years been sufficient to transform into an old man a man in the prime of life, to curb his stature like that, to incline him toward the tomb already?

And yet, it was him. Ought I to approach him in order to have myself recognized? No, not for the moment! The presence of Sant'Angiolo would have hindered me in my effusions. Later—tomorrow—I would accomplish a painful duty of amity; I would converse with Lautrem without importunate witnesses; he would tell me about the beatitudes of his ascetic life, and tell me how, by annihilating himself in God, he had been able to kill his miserable amour.

For a long time, evoking the image of what he had been, I followed that revenant from the dead with my gaze. He was leaning heavily on the shoulder of his guide, dragging himself along with difficulty, and his heavy sandals were kicking up the dust of the road.

XVI
La Campofiori

The Hotel de la Cocoumella, although rarely patronized by French tourists, is an inn famous throughout the Sorrento Riviera. Situated some distance from the city, adjacent to the gardens of the Palazzo Campofiori and overlooking from its terraces the scintillating azure of the Gulf of Naples, the former Jesuit convent left me a durable memory.

At first sight, its monastic aspect enchanted me, and later, the silence of its mysterious corridors, the picturesque quality of its patio, enveloped by trained arcades of vines, the meditative air of its refectory enabled me to find the old-fashioned and bizarre osteria exquisite. Yes, far from the turbulence of Paris, its reeking atmosphere, automobiles, their horns and their benzene, louts thirsty for absinthe, and cockneys perched on removal carts, I would be able, under a sky of light, in a fluid air, to understand idleness and enjoy a delightful vacation.

La Campofiori was waiting for me, flanked by Monsieur Sullivan, the proprietor of the hotel. Clad in white lawn, with her arms bare, but garlanded with roses and foliage, she resembled some shepherdess of the amiable Watteau or the precious Boucher. Esther Mosselman had not aged. Ten years had passed over her without even brushing her with a single wrinkle, and, surprised, I admired the persistence of that unalterable youth. Diva extended her hand to me.

"How kind it is of you to hasten to my first appeal. I would have liked to receive you under my roof, but we're rehearsing a new play, *Leucosia*, or rather transforming it . . ."

"Let's take care of the final act!" Sant'Angiolo interjected. "I believe I have the denouement."

"So, I was obliged to invite the general staff of my theater. I'm also lodging a few comrades: La Grossi, who plays tearful mothers at the Fondo; Rosina, the Bellini's ingénue, who represents virgins, and is a virgin herself, if she can be believed; the celebrated mime Costa; Rodolfo the tenor; this great fool Angelo; and five or six understudies, demoiselles without any talent, but agreeable to rub shoulders with. You won't be bored."

She turned to the baritone and, addressing him in the familiar manner of actors: "Salut, handsome Luna. Did the numbers that you dreamed emerge from the lottery draw?"

"Alas, no—not the slightest quine. Five hundred lire expended for nothing."

"You've squandered my five hundred francs on lottery tickets?"

"Well, yes! I was hopeful. My tailor, my boot-maker and my hairdresser are assassinating me with their bills. And then, my fortune-teller in the Via Vico Vasto had told me . . ."

"Good, good. Let's not whine, strong mind; I'll give you another advance."

"O divine Providence of the unfortunate! Siren so adored!"

He made as if to kiss her but she pushed him away. "No caresses! We're not in the wings; you'll compromise me."

Her large dark eyes, however, were gazing voluptuously at the moustached Antinous with the biceps of a fairground wrestler; each of her glances revealed that the Siren was no more insensible than he.

"He's my tenebrous beau," she said. "Luna, the Signor di Luna, the faint-hearted jealous lover of *Il Trovatore*: '*Il balen de suo sorriso* . . .' Sing a little, pretty puppet, irresistible Pierrot. Let's see whether your numerous vermouths have spoiled the velvet of your voice."

The "irresistible Pierrot" grimaced a chagrined smile, and then said brutally: "Why does the monk call you Astaroth?"

"What monk?" she said, shuddering.

"The fellow who cures coughs and expels demons."

"Oh, I know . . . the malevolent clown, the illuminate who vituperates and preaches against me . . . But *basta!*"

"*Basta?* You ought to beware of him; he's making threats."

"A madman. I'll write to my *patito*, the prefect of Naples, to have the vagabond interned in a lunatic asylum."

"We encountered him just now," I said, looking at La Campofiori. "He has an astonishing resemblance to a friend I had believed dead for many years."

"What is the name of your friend?"

"Marcellus . . . Marcel Lautrem."

Esther Mosselman's strange pale face was still smiling. "Lautrem? Marcellus? I don't know him."

"There! What did I tell you?" cried Sant'Angiolo, triumphantly. "That name doesn't figure on the list."

A rather long silence followed that shameless lie. Diva observed me, mockingly. Was she thinking about Lautrem?

"This," she resumed, tranquilly, "will be the program of your sojourn among us: little work and a great deal of pleasure; we're in the land of sweet idleness. My whole house belongs to you. So, come, command my personnel, dispose of my carriage, sack my flower-beds, pay court to Rosina, may your wishes be granted by that unparalleled virgin; I see nothing and don't want to know anything. Every day, your place will be set at my table, for I hope you'll deign to sit down among the comrades."

"And tomorrow, I'll commence your portrait."

"No, tomorrow, rest. Tonight we're going in a joyous band to Capri; my yacht is ready to sail. We'll sing barcaroles as we go; we'll see the nascent sun gilding the waves, and glorify Nature, Great Pan and Venus, daughter of the waves, by means of varied canticles . . ."

"You'd do better to stay in your bed," declared Sant'Angiolo.

"A truce on ludicrous observations! Tonight I shall go to the *Grotta Verde* to render a visit to Leucosia. Such is my idea and I don't like anyone to thwart my caprices. All our friends will make my escort. You too will accompany me, stubborn individual. Above all, be careful to bring your photographic apparatus; I want to figure as a siren on the posters at San Carlo. Will you come with us, Monsieur Blondel?"

"Gladly, dear Madame."

"Thank you. I'm counting on your exactitude; the rendezvous is at my house, at eleven o'clock precisely. Now, *bon appetit* and *au revoir*. Offer me your arm, heir of Comnenius."

And, chatting, laughing and singing, they both set forth for the Palazzo.

XVIII
British Respectability

"Would you care to come into my office?" Monsieur Sullivan said to me then. "I have to talk to you seriously."

Surprised by the solemn tone of the Englishman with the blond clergyman's side-whiskers, I followed him, and first had to inscribe my name in the register of guests.

"A tedious formality," he said, "but thanks to Mademoiselle Diva, the police have become troublesome."

"Don't retain me too long; I'm dying of hunger."

"Ah! *Bon appetit*, good health! Your dinner is ready. The Princesse had had her chef prepare you a menu in the best taste. A Belshazzar's feast, indeed: turtle soup and Welsh rarebit, port wine and Barolo. I recommend especially, a certain sherry from India, Capital! A nectar for the palate of noblemen."

He clicked his tongue, and then exhaled a sigh. "Oh, Monsieur, Mademoiselle Diva knows how to look after great men, while she maltreats the rest of us, the poor people. It's a pity."

"The signora, it seems to me, is not very popular among your country folk."

"They abominate her. When that carnival princess risks herself outside La Sirena, our peasants insult her; only yesterday they threw stones at her carriage."

"However, she seems to me to be amiable . . ."

"Amiable? A monster, a true demon of egotism, insolence and perversity. Gog and Magog are lodged in the body of that woman. She never deigns to address a word to the little people. They're splashed, knocked down and crushed. Last week, the carriage with the sky-blue livery collided with a little girl. Anyone but that Diva would have got down to see whether the poor thing was injured, but no: *Avanti! Avanti!* And the beautiful Madame went on her way. Hard, very hard! No help for the sick, not the slightest alms for those who are hungry; our sultana has even trained two mastiffs to devour beggars. Beware of those dogs, Monsieur; they wander in the park all night long, and are ferocious . . . Now I'll arrive at the object of our conversation."

As majestic as the speaker of the Commons sitting on the woolsack,[1] Monsieur Sullivan took a chair and, emphasizing each of his words, said: "Have you known the Princesse Campofiori very long?"

"I was speaking to her just now for the first time."

---

1 It is actually the Speaker of the House of Lords who sits on the woolsack.

"I suspected as much. So you don't know that a warrant has just been issued against her?"

"A legal warrant? She's going to be arrested?"

"A simple summons to the Vicaria of Naples . . . for the moment, at least."

"Of what crime is she accused?"

"Has anyone told you the story of Prince Gaetan?"

"Her husband? He killed himself.

"He was killed."

"Get away! The prince cut his throat with a razor."

"Pshaw! A razor! What about the arsenic that was found in his viscera? What do you make of that?"

"I was unaware of that troubling detail."

"The two turtle-doves, Gaetan and Mademoiselle Diva, made a reciprocal donation of their fortune in the marriage contract. Do you understand now?"

"Nothing proves that, idolizing his wife and in despair at her scorn, the prince didn't want to kill himself. In any case, why such a belated investigation?"

"The widow thought herself shielded from all suspicion, but an anonymous letter denounced her. The relatives, nephews and cousins, were up in arms; they lodged a complaint; Gaetan's body was exhumed and the autopsy revealed that powdered sugar is not always good to eat."

"No, Monsieur Sullivan! Calumnies and vengeances of people frustrated of their inheritance!"

"Oh, no one doubts that Mademoiselle Diva will emerge from the adventure exonerated."

"Of course, if she's innocent."

"Monsieur, when a pretty woman can sit down on her judge's knees, she is always innocent."

"Your Italian magistrates have very sensible hearts!"

"And yours, Monsieur Frenchman?"

The atrocity of such insinuations reminded me of my conversation with the austere Meurisier. Speaking of Davison, he had said: "He was assisted to die." So, two husbands two suicides, two accusations of murder. Disquieting Diva! Do you too, my beauty, know the recipe for succession powders?"[1]

"Thank you for your information, Monsieur. I'll profit from it."

"You'll doubtless judge me indiscreet, incorrect, even improper. I thought, nevertheless, that it was necessary to warn you. Armand Blondel, the French Gainsborough, honors me by lodging with me; I am, therefore, responsible for his repose. It's my duty, dear master, my duty as a loyal Englishman!"

XVIII
The Gardens of La Sirena

A jolly fellow indeed! His Britannic conscience satisfied, the loyal Sullivan conducted me to the apartment destined for me. The bedroom was comfortable, the drawing room spacious; I declared myself delighted.

"Splendid and respectable," he announced to me. "The Dean of Kidderminster lodged here with his wife. No mosquitoes. You'll dine on the terrace, I suppose?"

He opened the door of the drawing room and indicated a large platform that linked the two wings of the patio. A magnificent panorama was offered to my view: Vesuvius, Portici, Naples, Posillipo, and to the left, in an opaline distance, the isle of Capri.

---

1 "Succession powder" was the nickname given to the substances supposedly employed by the Marquise de Brinvilliers (1630-1676), who allegedly murdered her husband and two brothers at the behest of her lover. The evidence against her was slender, and the confession she made was extracted by torture, but she became legendary in France after her execution because further allegations were made after her death—with no evidence whatsoever—that she had been involved in other poisonings, prompting the notorious panic known as "the affair of the poisons," which involved several minor members of Louis XIV's court in accusations of poisoning and witchcraft; fanciful confessions extracted by torture added significant imagery to the legendry of the "black mass."

"What is the elegant house that I perceive in that park at the foot of the terrace?" I asked.

"La Sirena. You're overlooking its gardens."

In front of me, a few hundred meters away, stood a dainty villa of white marble, preceded by a rather high landing. The grass of a vast lawn extended before the façade, and two thick clumps of trees framed the verdant nudity of that bowling green. Already the dusk was filling their mysterious profundity with darkness, but the decreasing crowds of branches indicated that the park descended toward the sea. No sound could be heard in the palazzo; everything seemed quiet there, a voluptuous meditation, a silent hymn of joy.

"That's Messalina's brothel," muttered my host. "Soon, the bacchanalia. But don't go down: *cave canem!* Beware of the dogs!"

"What do you call her bacchanalia? You're literate, Monsieur Sullivan."

"Former pupil of Rugby school! All the polichinelles that Mademoiselle Diva feeds are pure rabble. They play cards, argue, chirp, dance and set off fireworks: *grand noce*, as you say in Paris. Haven't they now frightened the ladies and demoiselles, my honorable guests, with their indecency? They stroll in the gardens in theatrical costumes, rehearse amorous scenes there, kissing and embracing, playing Juliet and Romeo. The most odious of those clowns is a mime who studies his roles of specters or clowns by moonlight. So, three mothers of families quit me yesterday with their children; two misses and their fiancés—clergymen Monsieur!—have announced their imminent departure; all my clients are going to leave. No, such a scandal can't go on; I'll bring a lawsuit. Hetaira! A woman of no account, come from nothing, worth less than nothing and afraid of nothing, that Campofiori is the opprobrium and the ruination of our unfortunate country!"

My place was set at table and I was able to swallow, without further discourse, the delicacies that Diva had sent me. When my dinner was finished I stretched myself out in a rocking chair, lit a cigar and plunged into the dreamy intoxication of the Havana.

Dusk fell. In the distance, pale lights appeared on the Posilippo; the lighthouse of the Môle San Gennaro was already piercing the semi-darkness; Vesuvius was no more than in indeterminate form from which ruddy vapors were rising, and in the vast silence of the religious hour, the sea sang over the beach, caressing the rocks of the Sorrentine marina.

Almost dozing, I allowed my thought to wander: Esther Mosselman . . . Marcellus . . . Davison . . . Gaetan di Campofiori . . . Sant'Angiolo . . . How many others whose names I didn't know! Kisses first; then tears; then blood . . . ! Astaroth! Oh, good God, what does it matter to you, Blondel? Are you the husband of that courtesan, her brother, her cousin, the director of her conscience? Do you demand a certificate of innocence from your models? Do you ask anything of them except beauty? Go on, my friend Pangloss, everything is for the best in the best of all possible worlds. Let our sad humanity, then, speak ill, calumniate, defame, outrage and debase: you, my dear, cultivate your garden . . .

And time went by. Night, having fallen completely, became dewy, but warm, stifling and luminous, diamond-studded with stars; not a frisson of breeze stirred the foliage of the cedars or magnolias; heady fragrances were exhaled by the flower-beds; I fell asleep.

Suddenly, furious barking woke me up.

XIX
Nocturnal Effects

The Palazzo was animated. Brilliantly illuminated, while trails of light expanded from its ground floor; milky gleams were spread over the somber verdure of the lawn, but the profound clumps of trees were darker still.

People were singing over there; two actors were rehearsing their roles. The voice of the Diva reached me, vibrantly, through the open windows, pathetic, expertly nuanced and admirable. She was declaiming a recitative, and I recognized the chant: the incantation of Leucosia when she perceives Lazarus:

You whom the waves rock and the wind caresses. . . .

That superb piece that not been understood before; would it have more success tomorrow, on an Italian stage? Perhaps, but I recalled the scandal of Monte Carlo: Lautrem mocked; jokes, whistles, bursts of laughter, while Esther Mosselaman strutted over the debris of the symbolist drama . . . Unfortunate Marcellus!

O pale voyager, come to the enchantress!

Suddenly, the barking drew nearer; the mastiffs must have been giving chase to a marauder. But suddenly, again, the howls of rage changed into moans; the two beasts uttered the long and lugubrious canine sobs that dogs utter when they are afraid. What was happening in the Campofiori gardens? I went to lean on the terrace, but my head was blurred by too much "capital" sherry; Spanish things are full of treachery.

Wait! What was that!

A distant and fantastic vision, it was a man clad in black fabric, a robe or mantle, standing on the grass, listening. The dogs were observing him from a distance, crawling, not daring to attack, and their whining gave evidence of fear; they were "mourning the dead." He stood motionless, as if fixed to the ground, like a wooden statue, and his rigid arms were extended toward the windows from which the song of the Siren was escaping. One might have thought him one of those individuals that Fra Angelico loved to paint, of a monk in a state of supreme languor. Perceiving and absorbed in the harmonies of seraphic harps, rebec and viols: the ineffable concert of Paradise . . . the "insatiability" of mystics!

Meanwhile, Diva continued. She was sighing, at present, the words of seduction, the speech of lust that even maddens saints and causes their perdition.

The reckless Siren is all voluptuousness.

The man took a step, heading toward that appeal.

Soon, however, another voice rose up in the silence; Lazarus was giving the reply to Leucosia. Sant'Angiolo began to growl, to roar. Uncultivated and pretentious, his baritone strove to produce "effects", inventing pauses, lavishing cadences or flourishes.

The man, the bizarre phantom, stopped. He extended his fist as if to menace the imbecilic massacre of notes; his mimicry expressed a violent anger. And beneath the pallor poured out by the moon, his black silhouette standing out against the wan lawn, the individual with the movements of an automaton seemed a soul in pain, a dolorous specter that the tomb had not been able to retain . . .

The duet ended: "Glory to Christ the liberator!" The splendid soprano of the cantatrice celebrated in a brilliant finale the defeat of sin, the end of Satan, the liberation of the world, the victory of the Cross. People applauded. Then, there was a long and incomprehensible silence . . .

Immobile at the bottom of the perron, the man appeared to be waiting.

And for a second time, the piano resonated; it modulated the first chords that accompanied Schubert's *Adieu*, and the sobbing voice of Campofiori commenced:

> *Adieu until the dawn*
> *Of the day in which I have faith . . .*

Doubtless satisfied, obtaining what he desired, the man advanced again, his arms extended, the hands open. He appeared to want to seize, to enlace and hug the woman who was giving him that strange rendezvous.

> . . . *Of the day that will again*
> *Unite me with . . .*

Abruptly, Diva interrupted herself: two arpeggios . . . another motif . . . the allegro of a vulgar ditty . . . the plebeian burst of laughter of Neapolitan drunkenness. *Ha ha ha!* . . . the couplets of *Le Francese!* One might have imagined that Esther Mosselman had suddenly thought about Lautrem, and that she wanted to profane the memory . . .

"Ha ha ha!" repeated the comrades, in chorus

The man made a sort of gesture of despair; he had been extracted from his ecstasy . . . Finally, at a slow, spasmodic pace, a veritable machine moved by springs, he headed for the shadow of the trees, plunged into it, and disappeared. The dogs followed him, whining.

Yes, what was that? Had I been dreaming? Had the sherry for the usage of noblemen troubled by brain? Had Davison's manes or the shade of Gaetan been wandering by night in the gardens of La Sirena? That was all that was needed to put the last of my hotelier's guests to flight! Nevertheless, I quickly took account of what I had glimpsed. Studying some scenic effect, one of the actors, doubtless the mime Costa, had just prepared one of his roles. Evidently!

Why then, had the two mastiffs "mourned the dead"?

Eleven o'clock chimed; I remembered the rendezvous and had myself taken to the Palazzo. An excursion to the isle of Capri, in joyful society, was about the chase away the memory of the pseudo-phantom—or, rather, the fumes of the redoubtable sherry.

XIX
Prophecies

Utterly gracious, Diva took me to the drawing room where her guests were waiting for me. The piano was still open; a handwritten score was on the music-holder. I had not, therefore, been dreaming.

"Bravo, my dear Monsieur, what exactitude!" she said to me. "But I fear that we're departing too late; we'll never arrive at Capri before daybreak. Gennaro, my crewmaster, has made his calculations poorly. Such stupidity merits a lesson; he'll receive one. I would have liked so much to enable you to admire the Emerald Grotto by torchlight!"

She had taken off her costume of a Watteau shepherdess in order to dress as an oceanide; her tumbling hair was crowned with seashells, the coiffure of the Siren in the final act of *Leucosia*, and a kind of ball-wrap hid the near nudity of the costume. I took her hands and contemplated her for a long time, marveling again at that fatal beauty, that inalterable youthfulness. What fount of youth, what wonderful secret did she have in her possession in order to remain thus an Aphrodite ignorant of the outrage of the years? A smiling and mocking idol, as scantly grim as a Venus Meretrix, she allowed herself tranquilly to be contemplated, studied and detailed. Around us the good comrades formed a circle of walk-on parts, the messieurs smoking, the ladies powdering their faces, all of them jealous.

"First," she said, "I want to introduce you to our traveling companions. My friends, show your appreciation for the illustrious Blondel!"

Twenty hands applauded me rhythmically; hurrahs followed; the "bacchanalia" recommenced. Then I made the acquaintance of amusing figures: the mime Costa, the soul in pain who had just bewildered me; Rodolfo, the tenor; Grossi, the duenna; Rosina Vivente, the ingénue, and other stars and planets of lesser magnitude. I remarked, nevertheless, that nine of the artistes appearing at San Carlo were among the frolicsome characters of that Roman Comedy.

Rosina, the "virgin" of the Bellini, immediately took possession of me. She spoke French fluently, having once paraded her operetta innocence on many stages in my homeland, from Lille to Bordeaux and from Nantes to Toulouse. The ingénue addressed murderous winks to me, showing me the whiteness of her teeth or the smallness of her footwear, indiscreetly piling up the transparency of her skirts, sometimes even palpitating as at the end of the fourth act. But I observed the most sage restraint; we had not yet reached the psychological moment of a denouement.

"En route!" La Campofiori took me by the arm and we went down toward the shore. Sant'Angiolo dogged our footsteps. Clad in a silk-lined dinner jacket ornamented by his gaudy rosette, developing the magnificence of his broad chest, the handsome Luna was nonchalantly carrying a photographic apparatus. While walking, Diva turned her head to address a malicious glance at the beloved; in return, he arched his back, hummed, and sent back smiles, doubtless thinking about the tailor, the bootmaker and the capillary artist whose unpaid bills troubled the delights of his nights.

Near the shore a sort of two-master bilancella was rocking gently but daintily, elegant in form and painted white, ornamented with golden arabesques; it was the yacht that Gennaro was going to pilot. At the prow and from the yardarms, numerous Venetian lanterns hung, scarlet glass lanterns also decorated a launch attached by a tow-rope to our brigantine. Four mariners in comic-opera costumes, including Cecco, the brother of the possessed child, were waiting for us, lined up on the strand. They were furnished with baskets full of victuals, for a feast was to conclude the excursion.

La Campofiori had already set foot on the gangplank when a long body, an old man clad in a soutanelle, emerged from the shadow projected by the cliff. I recognized Mosselman. The ten years that had elapsed since our previous encounter had not spared him. Whitened and bent by age, ragged, grotesque and pitiful, he seemed to be the wretched image of Poverty.

The Caraïte came to stand in front of his niece, and said, in a suppliant voice:

"Esther, my Esther, don't go into the Siren's grotto! The prophet Amos has said: *My Judgment will be like the abyss of waters, my Anger like a savage sea.*"

La Campofiori stopped, and then spoke rudely to the inconvenient individual: "Enough, triple idiot, dirty drunkard. My name is not Esther and I forbid you to address me as *tu*. In any case, your Amos is talking nonsense. Look: his savage sea is as tranquil as a pond."

"Esther, my Esther, another prophet also said: *The gulf extends more profoundly under the slumber of the waters than beneath the tumult of the tides.*"

"Go back to your attic, maniac, or I'll set my dogs on you."

A transport of indignant fury agitated the miserable carcass of Uncle Mardochée. He straightened up and then, a prophet imploring his Iaveh: "Oh, that's too much! Esther, these are my adieux! May the arm of the One who chastises ingrate children fall upon your sins, accursed woman! I have suffered too much through you: let him avenge me!"

"*Amen!* I don't care!"

She launched herself on to the gangplank. Sant'Angiolo came to sit down beside that amiable niece, took her by the hand and deposited his lips upon it. The enraged Siren immediately calmed down. Diva seemed to have forgotten me; I therefore installed myself next to Rosine at the rear of the boat; the other passengers gathered around La Grossi; the mariners lifted the anchors, cast off the mooring ropes and hoisted the sails; we were sailing.

XX
Barques and Barcaroles

A nocturnal splendor: warm, perfumed and luminous; a blue velvet jewel-case ornamented by stars! The Milky Way extended into space its pale dust of stars in formation, and in the immensity of the firmament, myriads of worlds swarmed—worlds in which people must also be loving and dying, since they attract one another and they perish. A faint breeze scarcely rippled the phosphorescent undulation of the waves; our sails flapped along the masts; the bilancella was only advancing slowly, and our boatmen had taken up the oars. No, we would not arrive on Capri before the first light of day.

La Grossi, who was getting bored with her comrades, attacked a barcarole: *Addio, mia belli Napoli.* Tenors and baritones, sopranos and contraltos took it up quietly; our mariners formed a chorus, and I compared, not without chagrin, the accurate, warmed and well-pitched voices of those singers, sons of the sun, with the winy drone of our populace when making merry.

"What do you think of Campofiori," asked my neighbor, La Vivente.

"A remarkable artiste; another Falcon."

"Her canary notes please me well enough, but her playing, dear master, oh, her puppet play! When your Falcon is on stage, one would think her a mechanical doll with a serinette in her throat. No soul palpitates within her; that Diva truly has no soul."

She stuck her ferrety thinness against me, simpering. "Is it true that you're deigning to paint her portrait?"

"I'll commence tomorrow."

"Good luck! How will you dress our princesse? As a widow of Malabar?"

"Much more simply."

"*In naturalibus?* I can guess: the Pompeiian fresco. Diva resembles it, and takes vanity therefrom. Oh, that Venus, what a *lupa!* Her madonna!"

"I'll go to see the painting and think about it."

"Don't take the trouble, Costume your model as Madame Lafarge."[1]

That venomous allusion to the death of Prince Campofiori displeased me. "You also, Mademoiselle, believe stupid calumnies?"

"Poor Gaetan! Do you know that I knew him well?"

"A joyous fellow, I'm told, a great connoisseur of pretty faces."

"Flatterer! Yes, he paid court to me, and if I had wanted . . ." Rosina the irreducible virgin, turned toward the landscape that was fleeing behind us, and them with a gesture worthy of a leading role: "Oh, if I had been less severe, a marble palace, gardens of orange-trees! Hey, look over there, at that boat without sails that is following us."

"Some belated fisherman."

"I can't see any net, and the boatman has no companion. How hard he's rowing, that fellow! I suppose he's going to Massa. Hey there, friend! Are you going to bring back a lot of fritters?"

She waved her handkerchief, expecting a reply; the man addressed made no response.

We were advancing now. The rare lanterns, the smoky illumination of Massa-Lubrense, had disappeared; to our left. The escarpment of Punto Campanella loomed up; the isle of Capri drew nearer . . .

The tenor of the troupe intoned a second barcarole, but the rolling of the sea, which had become fleecy, had paralyzed all enthusiasm. Sant'Angiolo now had his arm around Diva's waist. She leaned her head on the obliging shoulder of the robust male, closed her eyes and appeared to fall asleep . . . *Il balen del suo sorrio*: the gallant posed a kiss on the smiling lips. She

1 Marie Lafarge (1815-1852) was controversially convicted of poisoning her husband with arsenic on the basis of forensic evidence considered dubious even at the time.

shuddered, and then her fingers caressed the powdered face of the uncouth Lovelace.

"Look at Juliet and Romeo, then," murmured the benevolent Rosine. "A princesse! She poses with us, more arrogantly than the Madame of the twenty-five quarters, and she swoons in public in the arms of a ruffian!"

"Amour, Mademoiselle Vivente."

"Where does she come from, what den of spinners? She's said to be Levantine, a former café-concert tramp. In any case, she's not Venetian. We daughters of the Giudecca know how to choose better. Personally, when I've found my ideal . . . But the wind's becoming frisky, my dear Monsieur; you're going to catch cold, and I have a responsibility. Permit me to attach to your shoulders a lace from my homeland."

She stood up in order to pick up her handbag, and immediately uttered a cry of fright.

"Monsieur, Monsieur! The boat is still there! It's still following us!"

Day was just breaking, but its first pallors did not permit the man who was giving chase to us to be distinguished clearly. Drowned in the vapors of the dawn, I could only perceive a boat; it was pitching and rolling, tossed by the play of the waves. The breeze had freshened; a south-westerly wind was blowing from the sea; the splashing brine sent us some spray, and the prow of the fantastic boat caused jets of foam to spring forth. The person manning it had to be a vigorous rower; he was gaining on us rapidly, and yet he did not move aside from our wake.

Rosine took out her opera-glasses, aimed them, and then let her arm drop, nonplussed.

"*Dio mio!* A monk! *The monk of Murano!*"

In my turn, I aimed the binoculars. Yes, it really was a monk. Curbed over the oars, struggling with an incredible strength against the undulation of the waves, he was not seeking to reconnoiter his route, following us, pursuing us, without deviating by a brass, and I only glimpsed a cowl pulled over his cranium. Bizarre! Very bizarre, in fact!

Sant'Angiolo raised his voice. He had chosen a languorous nocturne to inform us of the intoxication of joy that filled his heart, the barcarole from *The Tales of Hoffmann*:

O night of amour, O enchantress night . . .

Without quitting her slothful pose, Diva sighed that ballad, and—a soulless doll according to the envious Rosine—she was swooning with lust. But the ingénue of the Bellini was no longer occupied with her comrade; frightened, her eyes haggard, she was observing her monk of Murano.

"What is that Venetian superstition?" I asked her. "An absurd tale, no doubt."

La Vivente extended the index finger and the little finger of her right hand, to ward off some *gettatura*.

"It's not a tale! Yes, Monsieur the accursed *frataccio* exists, and roams the seas. In Venice he haunts our lagoons. Sometimes, at nightfall, that revenant accompanies at a distance a gondola in which lovers are embracing. Woe betide Paolo then, and woe betide Francesca! They have only to prepare for the great sleep of the Campo-santo. The isle of Murano, Monsieur, is situated near our cemetery."

Stupidities! That songbird of the Giudecca was more credulous than a little schoolgirl of the Oiseaux . . . . And the irresistible Luna made the notes of his barcarole vibrate; and the lover abandoned herself to the enlacement of the beloved; and the phantom boat followed them: "O night of amour, O enchantress night!"

The grayness of the morning twilight was now taking on rosy tints; first light was becoming dawn; Capri displayed the abrupt walls of its cliffs to us clearly, the whiteness of its villas and the somber foliage of its gardens. We had doubled the Punta Tragara and passed the Petite Marine, but everything was asleep on the isle of ancient lasciviousness and Tiberian orgies, and the coral-selling Graziellas were scarcely dreaming there of Sejanus or Germanicus.

"Look out!" shouted Gennaro, who was manning the tiller. "Here's the Grotta Verde. Lower the sails and man the oars! You, Cecco, your arms are made of cotton; a little more vigor, idler."

The helmsman interrupted his invective to look to the right.

"Good! The other's striving to get ahead of us. Hey, Padre! Padre! You're heading straight for a reef: beware of the Marcellino! He's avoided it, more by fear than cunning. To venture forth at such an hour in the middle of these reefs! Devil of a monk, monk of the Devil!"

He started to ply his rudder, swearing like a pagan: "Halt, *sangue di Cristo*! Back, back! Halt again! Oh, Cecco, my lad, I'll take the numbness out of your shoulder blades . . . Good! Now the anchors! Excellency, we've arrived."

XXI

In the *Grotta Verde*

Finally extracting herself from her amorous torpor, the "Excellency" Campofiori stood up, and abused the helmsman.

"You haven't obeyed my orders, then? Where are the boats I commanded?"

The crewmaster responded with a gesture of desolation; "Gone! We're more than an hour late; they haven't waited."

"Not waited? And that's your excuse? They're all idlers or stupid in your land!"

"We're worth more than you, witch!" muttered Cecco, standing near me. "I'll strangle you one day!"

Very annoyed by such a snag, our princesse addressed her guests:

"Excursion failed, my friends, by the fault of this idiot. I see myself obliged, therefore, to leave you all aboard. Gennaro, for having transmitted my instructions so poorly, you merit a punishment."

"A punishment? Eh, *Santa Madona*, it's not my fault! Madame, we're neither stupid nor idlers in my country."

"You're arguing? I'll dock you a week's wages."

"Oh, Princesse! I have so much need of a little money. My wife is soon going to give birth, and . . ."

"*Basta!* When one is poor, one doesn't have children. Have the launch that we're towing brought forward. You, Cecco, descend the *Aiguille*." She designated a minuscule nacelle that had been suspended from our side, a sort of Venetian *fisolera* that could scarcely hold two people.

"This is what we're going to do, then. Sant'Angiolo, with his photographic apparatus, will climb into the launch; you, Monsieur Blondel, will occupy a place of honor there, and our dear Rosine would wish me dead if I separated her from her new friend."

"I don't wish anyone dead, my beauty, but I'll obey you gladly," riposted the operetta ingénue, piqued and peevish.

"The thunderbolt, Monsieur Blondel! What a victory over a virgin heart! Gennaro, you'll guide their boat; as for me, I reserve the *Aiguille*. It alone can accost a head of rock that will serve me as a pedestal."

"Understood!" cried Sant'Angiolo. "A carpet of wrack under your feet, Leucosia! The Siren in her palace!"

"I prefer the pose of Astarte emerging from the waves."

"Always the Pompeiian fresco? An obsession, my dear. Do you care so much about this photograph?"

"The periodical *Artista* has asked me for it; it will be reproduced on postcards and I'll address a whole packet to the Campofiori family . . . now, Cecco, let's cast off.

She descended into the fisolera, which soon plunged under the opening in the cliff. We followed, but more slowly. Gennaro proffered a litany of insults against the "*lupa*"; Sant'Angiolo hummed his favorite ballad; Rosina remained silent, worried, and I admitted the filthy richness of the Neapolitan vocabulary.

The sun rose over the horizon; already the daylight was sliding through the narrow orifice of the grotto, but the extremity of the profound cavern still remained plunged in thick darkness. Gradually spreading, the light produced odd and indescribable effects. Everything illuminated by it was colored by an emerald tint: the vault and the side walls, the two boats, our garments and our faces. No breath of wind arrived from the sea; the water was dormant under our feet, green and stagnant; the air, saturated with warm mist, weighed heavily: the silence was overwhelming.

Diva was waiting for us in a vast chamber, the ceiling of which was curved in the form of a cupola. The echoes resonated there persistently and the slightest sounds were reverberated as if under the vaults of a cathedral. La Campofiori was standing upright, almost at water level, on a narrow rock that was carpeted with fucus, wrack and other marine algae; Siren or Astarte, the bewitching promiser of amour was posing gracefully.

Conforming to the indications of the photographer, Gennaro stopped us facing the cantatrice, at a distance of ten or twelve meters.

"Carina," said the indiscreet sigisbeo, then, "I'm at your orders. My plates are prepared; let's hurry."

Unfastening her wrap, the "carina" so impudently exploited offered herself to our gaze in her oceanide costume . . . What a disappointment! The apparition that I expected to be gracious was only unpleasant. Under the play of green-tinted light, Leucosia's pale face had taken on a cadaverous hue; her glaucous leotard seemed to be dressing a dead woman; or rather, one might have thought her a hieratic statue of jade standing in some Buddhist sanctuary, demonstrating to the agitated creatures of this world the despair of the three annihilations.

"What a horror!" murmured the pitiless Rosine. "The devil emerging from a font!"

Sant'Angiolo aimed his apparatus, disappeared under the photographer's veil and pronounced the sacramental: "Don't move."

Then: "It's finished, my beauty. Let's go and rejoin our companions."

But La Campofiori did not care about the comrades; she put on her mantle, and then addressed me.

"Let's pass on to another exercise now, Monsieur Blondel. I'm going to sing my recitative from *Leucosia*. You, who know how to compose a painting so well, observe my gestures and advise me."

"Gladly, Princesse."

"We're on stage; day is breaking; the Siren perceives Lazarus, calls to him, and desires to draw him into the abyss. Should I hold out my arms . . . ? No, that's not your opinion . . . a caryatid pose would be more effective . . . you're right. *Do, mi, so, do . . .* what sonority under this vault! I'll begin:

You whom the waves rock and the wind caresses . . .

She stopped, surprised. "What was that . . . ? Someone laughed!"

A snigger that the echo had repeated had just made itself heard. Soon, splashing under the oars, the dormant water was rippled; a boat emerged from the darkness of the shadow.

"The monk!" stammered Rosine, terrified. "One of us is going to die!"

Her Monk of Murano, the untiring rower who had followed our wake for such a long time, like a shark, had slipped into the Grotta Verde before us, but the confusion of the mooring maneuvers had caused me to lose sight of him. The cowl of his habit still covered half his face, but he was steering with an astonishing surety.

Slowly, he approached the cantatrice; his boat brushed the nereid's pedestal; the keel immediately grated against the reef, and the phantom boat remained motionless, wedged on the bottom, entangled by the wrack.

At that moment—very distant, very faint, scarcely perceptible—the sound of a bell reached us. Out there, in some convent on Capri, the office of Matins was being announced . . .

Immediately, the monk lifted his hood, and, amazed, I recognized Marcellus. He seemed to emerge from a profound slumber, and allowed his bewildered gaze to wander, believing himself tormented by a bad dream . . .

Finally, with a dolorous sigh: "What, my God, always and forever the same cross! Always my dream of sin, the rendezvous given by that woman! What do you demand of me today then, O Terrible One?"

I had understood: a monstrous case of somnambulism and autosuggestion! So, the bite of the wind, the pitching of the sea, the spray of the waves: none of that had been able to extract that man from his "second state"; but the distant ringing of a bell, at the hour when monks went to chant their first prayers, had sufficed to snatch him from his slumber. I was witnessing one of the terrifying phenomena of the doubling of the human personality and the complete abolition of the Self, the manifestations of which confound all metaphysics, all theology and all religion.

Initially frightened, La Campofiori was quickly reassured; she even addressed dubious pleasantries to the somnambulist.

"Accursed monk! He scared me . . . Bonjour, Reverend Father; you're disturbing our rehearsal. Park your boat, please. Would you like to listen to Leucosia, the siren who tempted Lazarus?"

But on hearing Diva's provocative voice, the Franciscan raised his head, and his lips pronounced a few words: "I will obey, vengeful God." He stood up, and then, arrogant, menacing and ironic:

"Leucosia, Lazarus has emerged from the tomb! Esther Mosselman, I am Marcel Lautrem."

XXII
"Vade Retro!"

For a long time, the pupil and fiancée of Marcellus looked at the man who had loved her so much. She saw the white and earthen face, the hollow cheeks, the toothless mouth, the extinct eyes, the graying hair, and the forehead furrowed by wrinkles; she saw her work of destruction, and an insulting burst of laughter was her response.

"Esther Mosselman," Lautrem went on, "I have failed gravely in my duty. Teresa's child is tormented by a demon; I ought to have run to deliver the son of that Christian woman, but I did not want to cross the threshold of your house."

"You were greatly mistaken, my friend. La Sirena would have offered your holy person a good supper, good shelter and perhaps the rest. I practice the broadest hospitality there. Call me Princesse, if you please."

"Esther Mosselman, God triumphs easily over our cowardly resistance. He has pushed me toward you, unconscious, in the night, over the waves, sealing my eyes with sleep, abolishing in me even the notion of my being, and here I am before your face."

"Permit me, Reverend Father, to have a cigarette; the sermon is threatening to be long, and I'll be less bored if I smoke."

She took a dainty silver-plated case from her mantle, lit the perfumed tobacco placidly, and then sat down on a block of stone that formed a projection.

"Esther Mosselman," Lautrem went on, impassively, "the turpitudes of your life and the impudent tranquility of your crimes scandalize an entire people whom God deigned to confide to my care. I ought to have expelled you a long time ago; the One who hates Evil will demand that I account for my weakness. Understand me, then. You are going to quit your La Sirena tomorrow, never to return to it."

"Indeed! An ingenious idea my dear. What do you offer me in exchange? A musician's attic near the empyrean in the Rue

Vavin? The catechism hall where the petty curate, my converter, perorates? But you don't even have such delights to offer me."

"You are going, Esther Mosselman"—the monk raised his voice—"to leave as soon as possible a country of which you are the filthy perdition."

"Oh, what do you take me for, insolent orator? Am I your penitent? Do you count me among the imbecile clientele of your confessional?"

"You are going to leave this land; I order it, I demand it."

"He orders . . . he demands. Look at this holy man who poses as a dictator!"

"You will obey . . . you will obey, or else . . ."

"Threats? Go on."

"Or else everything—palace, gardens, carriages, furniture. jewels, clothes—will burn, and the salary of your prostitutions, the profit of your poisonings, will rise as propitiatory smoke toward the throne of the terrible Being."

"Beautiful! You fabricate phrases very well; I know that. Come and find me, then, you and your peasants; I'll receive you."

"And the Court of Assizes; what will you do there, man of God?" Sant'Angiolo interjected.

The monk turned his head toward the actor; then, with an arrogant indifference: "When human justice is impotent, the man of God takes its place and chastises."

"Burning my dwelling, that's already very amiable," sniggered La Campofiori. "Something else, however, would complete your fête."

"Yes. God had Jezebel's body thrown to the dogs."

"Better and better! You would dare, Monsieur, to assassinate me?"

"An executor of Judgment is not an assassin; he is carrying out a sentence."

"And what is that sentence?"

"*My Anger will fall upon you, like a savage sea.* Renegade of the jealous God, your days are numbered."

Diva shivered; the illuminate had just repeated the words of the prophet Amos, Mosselman's imprecation. Nevertheless, she recovered very quickly.

"An amusing character," she said. "Excellent third role: the inquisitor in *Don Carlos*."[1]

An inquisitor, yes, certainly. Standing up, dominating with his tall stature the sinner he was threatening with expiatory death. Lautrem had made his speech in the style of Joseph de Maistre, without a gesture, his arms stick to his habit, in an imperious voice, in a tone that admitted no reply. In his grim tranquility, he seemed to believe blindly in his vision of an exterminating archangel, and everything announced that the fanatic would not recoil before arson, or even homicide.

Anxiety overtook me. What whim took Diva to provoke thus a man who possessed the power to have her massacred? From afar I engaged her to terminate the discussion and leave. But she responded to me that the "recognition," the fourth act of a "well-turned" play, had need of a piquant denouement, and that she proposed to bring it to one. An actress to her marrow, the prima donna saw herself on stage, playing for the gallery, desiring our applause.

"So," she resumed, "this padre, who has been roaming the countryside for three weeks inveighing against me, is named Marcel Lautrem. You are no longer, Monsieur, the sentimental fool, the faint-hearted lover that I found so ridiculous. My compliments! Here you are, transformed into Saint John the Baptist; you're preaching against Herodias. Oh, beware: Herodias might have the caprice to make herself loved."

"Reserve your tenderness for those who pay for it."

"How vulgar, my good father! To treat me so furiously, you must be very fearful of yourself?"

She threw away her cigarette, and the demoiselle of the Tunisian café-concerts reappeared in Princesse Diva Campofiori. "You've become very ugly, hideous, almost repulsive, my poor

---

1 The Grand Inquisitor is the fourth male role in Verdi's *Don Carlos* (1867).

Marcel; nevertheless, you please me today. A Savonarola for a lover, what luck! Come here, protagonist of morality; let's make peace; I'm opening my arms to you."

Lautrem extended his hands, as if to drive away some abominable vision.

"Ignoble and infamous woman! Another Astaroth!"

"Astaroth . . . Astarte . . . call me what you will, but I am Woman! Yes, Woman—do you hear, do you understand?—Woman, who knows her power and knows all the weakness of saints like you. Go on, I've divined you. The hatred that you have vowed against me is nothing but the frenzy of a disappointed passion. You love, and are subject to the torture of not being loved. In the convent to which you have fled, Woman . . . Esther, I imagine . . . pursues you relentlessly. Your soul, your heart and your flesh struggle under my possession; even at the feet of your God, you adore no other God but me. Have I analyzed you well? Dare to deny it. Astaroth, Monsieur cilice-wearer, is you."

And again she hurled the challenge of her insulting laughter.

"*You shall have no other God than me!*" accentuated the quivering voice of Marcellus "Woman, such are the words that on a similar day, twenty years ago, I heard under the icy hand of Astaroth. Who revealed my secret to you? Of what demon are you the confidante? Aha! You're no longer laughing. You finally understand that the laughter of Hell always ends in the gnashing of teeth."

"The man is mad! exclaimed La Campofiori, suddenly alarmed, getting to her feet. "Cecco, bring the *Aiguille*; let's go."

"Don't approach, Cecco," the Franciscan enjoined. "Say your prayer, my son, and ask Heaven to assist me. You, woman, on your knees!"

"Let's try to draw alongside," I said to Gennaro. "The monk no longer has his reason; the princesse may be in danger. Quickly, quickly, let's hurry."

"No, Monsieur, I won't budge. In our land, we're too stupid to understand, too idle to act. Furthermore, I too obey the commands of the padre."

He lay down in the skiff, and then started whistling an improvised ditty.

Wretch! I attempted to seize the oars, but he shoved me away, bruised by his fist and brutally wounded in the face. Sant'Angelo tried to come to my aid; a kick laid him down in the bottom of the launch. Then, unhooking his oars, the helmsman threw them away, out of our reach.

"There Monsieur Frenchman. Draw alongside now. *Addio, Diva* . . . you, the ruffian, remain tranquil. *Addio, materasso d'amore.*"

Soon, cast adrift, our boat moved away; a feeble current was drawing it toward the exit from the grotto.

"Don't abandon me!" begged La Campofiori. "I'm afraid! Angelo! Angelo!"

Alas, the valiant Luna could do nothing to help her. He did not know how to swim either, and *per Bacco*, that green-tinted water was very deep. Consternated, and tamed in any case by Gennaro's rude caress, he inclined his head over his knees, clenched his fists and, very dramatic, reminded me of Ugolino in the Tower of Hunger: *Ambo le mani di dolor morso* . . . A magnificent tragedian![1]

"Angelo! My Angelo!" cried the abandoned woman, desperately. "He's a madman . . . ! I'm in danger . . . Angelo! Coward . . . ! Oh, coward!"

Vain appeals, futile insults. The heir of Comnenius only responded to them with a superb gesture of desolation . . .

As for me, very alarmed, I called out to Marcellus, repeating my name, imploring him to come and join us. He did not hear, or did not want to hear. Rosina was hysterical, prey to a crisis of

---

1 The quotation, slightly adapted, is from Dante's *Inferno*, where the ill-fated Pisan nobleman Ugolino della Gherardesca appears as a character.

nerves. Cecco was muttering his paternosters. Gennaro was serenading his princesse. And, carried by the eddies, slowly—very slowly—our boat drew away.

A surprising transformation had just taken place in the Franciscan. The old man, almost blind, whom I had seen dragging himself along his path, decrepit, his spine curbed by suffering, had recovered a strange vigor of youth. Similar phenomena are not rare among neurotics, and alienist physicians have informed us what superhuman force sudden fits of dementia often develop. Lautrem had seized from his boat one of the heavy tridents that tuna fishermen use; he gripped it with both hands and fixed his bleak inquisitorial gaze upon the frightened Diva.

In the glaucous and uncertain light that illuminated us, the tall silhouette of that revenant of days past seemed to grow from one moment to the next, fantastic and formidable in his monastic robe. Esther bowed her head, and gradually collapsed on the couch of wrack; one might have thought her a sparrow paralyzed by terror under the flight of an osprey.

A few murmured words reached me confusedly: "*Venomous beast . . . ! Cunning serpent . . . ! Impurity of the Abyss . . . ! Breath of Hell . . . !*" Lazarus was exorcizing. In spite of such powerful formulae, however, Leucosia did not dissolve into vapors, and continued to call to us desperately.

"Esther!" demanded Lautrem, having become menacing. "Why do you slide every night into my cell, tormenting me relentlessly, obliging me to torture myself with blows of the whip? It's necessary that this torture ends! Are you Astaroth?"

"Help! Help!"

"Courtesan, poisoner, flesh of lust, spirit of perversity, the Accursed One inhabits your body. You are Astaroth."

"Help! Help!"

"No, you are not a woman; you have stolen human form! You are not a woman, demon! I finally recognize you. The waters of the Abyss have tinted your face green. You are not a woman, lemur with the aspect of a cadaver!"

"Help! Help!"

"Why have you drawn me here, into this cavern, your lair? Why your rendezvous? To tempt me again, to have yourself adored? Go on, confess: you are Astaroth."

Shaken by a frenzy of rage, he lifted his harpoon over the thief of human form: "Confess, confess and disappear!"

Terrified, Esther fell to her knees. "Don't kill me! Help! Help! Don't kill me! Pity! Pity! I confess."

But suddenly, standing up again, she threw off her ball-wrap and like the diabolical whores of Flemish temptations, appeared in a provocative obscenity; in order to save her life she was making a supreme effort.

"See! I'm beautiful! Look, look! Take me, then! I . . . I . . ." And, uttering her last burst of laughter, she cried: "I love you!"

The weapon immediately fell upon the temptress.

Stunned, bloodied, she tottered, and then collapsed in the fucus that covered the dormant water . . .

For a few seconds, sustained by the thick litter of seaweed, Leucosia appeared to float. Her hands clung on to the boat, but further thrusts broke her fingers . . .

A howl of distress . . . a blasphemy . . . and the Siren sank; Astaroth disappeared.

Then, responding to our clamors, the exorcist announced: "Justice is done! The Great Prostitute is vanquished."

The body of Princesse Campofiori was never recovered.

The tragic end of the celebrated *prima donna* was, for Italian newspapermen, a fortunate pretext for copy. Many portraits of the cantatrice were published; reporters fabricated many pompous panegyrics; poets wept in stanzas or sonnets, and a savant Academician consecrated a beautiful memoir to her. He demonstrated that Esther and Astaroth were the same word, which signified charm of the evening, nocturnal voluptuousness, heifer, ewe or wealth. Oh these Hebraists! Finally, as everything terminates down here with songs, a bad joker put the macabre adventure of the Grotta Verde into a ballad. *Caverna, inferna* and *sempiterna* rhymed therein as richly as in Dante, and that was the final funeral oration of Diva, Princesse Campofiori.

But the criminal trial of Lautrem offered a magnificent opportunity to philosophize. The Catholic newspapers took the Franciscan's side enthusiastically. Devoid of tenderness for the victim, they scourged the excesses of that new Messalina, vituperated against the infamous Esther Mosselman, twice renegade, deploring the weakness of the human justice that the courtesan had been able to seduce, and praising the meritorious action of Marcellus, veritable conscience. Is it licit to kill in order to accomplish a work of salvation, not to say moral propriety? Yes, certainly, and those messieurs cited the casuists: Navarre, Léander, Gomez, Hurtado, Diana, Doctor Angélique, *Aquinas ille!* Man acts, God leads him; the Almighty himself had directed a necessary execution.

On the other hand, free-thinking publicists spared Lautrem. They discoursed instead on somnambulism and "the second state," spoke about Lélut or Alfred Maury, invoking the authority of Lombroso, recognizing in the "assassin monk" a poor being retarded in evolution, ignorant of Progress, Solidarity and Altruism; an atrophied brain, still enmired in Medieval ignorance, remaining, alas a contemporary of Torquemada or Jacques Clément: an atavism of Mousterian ancestry, an anthropoid mentality. All religion produced cruelty, said those philosophers; Franciscan superstition inevitably became ferocious. Such was, in addition, at the assizes, the advice of the legal physician, a Darwinian militant, an enemy of Saint Janvier and a radical candidate.[1] No, an unconscious man could not be declared culpable.

Seized by doubt, the jury acquitted him.

---

1 "Saint Janvier" or San Gennaro, is the patron saint of Naples, where his relics are conserved in the cathedral.

Furthermore, that resounding case stirred up unspeakable annoyances for me. Summoned as a witness to the Vicaria of Naples, I made the acquaintance there of Dame Justice, and learned that, Italian, French or English, dressed in wool or silk, in back, red or ermine, that old Themis is not a person whose acquaintance is to be sought. Oh, my friends, refrain from any tête-à-tête with her!

❇

During the winter of 1909 I found myself in Naples again, at the Bertolini. The society there was agreeable, although somewhat spoiled by the noisy presence of French prostitutes, but their plastered faces scarcely attracted me.

In the course of my voyage I had encountered a respectable Englishwoman, Mrs. Hatchinson, who was accompanied by her daughters, Olivia and Margaret. About Olivia I have nothing to say. She was stern and harsh, reading the Bible too much, never quitting her high-necked dress and resembling one of those deaconesses who go to Shanghai to convert the wily Chinese. On the other hand, Margaret's flirtation had accomplished my conquest. Her eyes, the color of forget-me-nots; her hair, like ripe corn; her cheeks, rosier than a Northumberland lady-apple; her teeth, pearly although already lengthening; her keepsake face, her British grace and her discreet sighs when she looked at me all made my quadragenarian heart beat faster. I therefore completed at the Palace Hotel a romance of the most delicate amour.

"Dear Mama," Margaret had declared, "Monsieur Blondel pleases me greatly."

"Good gracious! Marry a Frenchman? You're not thinking of it, I hope?"

"Armand pleases me greatly . . . as much as my poor Papa pleased you. I shall marry him."

"Marry, darling, marry; Monsieur Blondel understands making money; he'd be worthy of being born English."

"Oh, Mama, you don't understand amour at all."

In spite of Britannic prejudice, however, we were engaged; Meg called me "my own"; I responded "my love." Judged worthy of having been born English, I absorbed *en famille* the decoction of Ceylon, boiled eggs, fried sole, bacon and Dundee marmalade. Every day, after luncheon, Margaret sat down at the piano to sing, with my intention, the most sentimental of her ballads: "Some day, some day!" Paradise was a guest at the Palace Hotel.

One morning, the prudent Mrs. Hatchinson confided her daughters to me. She was expecting the visit of a clergyman who distributed tracts to the lazzaroni, and she could not accompany us. Olivia put on her black sheath of a quakeress and coiffed herself in a Salvation Army hat; Margaret donned the most glamorous of her London-bought dresses and we set forth for Pompeii.

Scarcely had we entered the Via Marina than I rediscovered the Blondel of my adolescence, the pupil of the Villa Medici, passionate about antiquity. The bleak Pompeiian cemetery seemed more alive to me than a city swarming with life. Easily, I traversed in thought the space of eighteen elapsed centuries and, a Roman citizen, conversed with the Decurion Sallust under the grapes of his triclinium, and then condemned a gladiator fallen in the arena to have his throat cut. The enthusiasm of youthfulness, no doubt; on becomes so young again when one is happy!

But the Campanian necropolis left my two Englishwomen indifferent. Olivia ate sandwiches in the ruins of the forum, Margaret devoured plum cake; they were only able to find a "Shocking!" before the carbonized woman and her dolorous indecency.

From one quarter to another, our guide, a facetious Neapolitan, took us into a villa exhumed near the Porta Vesuvio.

"The house of the priestess of Venus," the joker announced. "The gay woman who inhabited it most have led the life of Madame Polichinelle. Look at the fauns and satyrs that decorate the atrium. One can't make those images for first communicants.

Let's pass on now into the sacellum, the chapel that . . . oh, but no! Not you, Signorina! Don't come in. All of our frescoes are not for the usage of demoiselles. Ancient rogues . . . ! You, Monsieur, come and see the lady that a Greek guttersnipe has dared to paint for the joy of our eyes: the sight of so many charms no longer costs anything."

In spite of Olivia's indignant mime, I followed the chatter-box, and went in.

The guide was right; it really was a sacellum, a clandestine chapel consecrated to the worship of some divinity once forbidden. A tripod for perfumes still occupied the middle of the cella, and displayed on the wall I saw a very curious fresco. To describe it is impossible. All the eroticism of antiquity was displayed in the posture of a woman who, standing on floating algae, seemed to be surging from a verdant sea, and in the gestures of obscene tritons surrounding her nudity, coveting her and imploring her. I examined the painting and I distinguished two words, almost effaced, deciphered them, and—O stupor!—read:

AST . . . LEUK . . .

"Astarte . . . Leucosia . . ."

"Bravo!" approved the cicerone. "A monsieur from the Museum would be less skillful; you're an archeologist! Yes: 'Dedicated to Astarte by Leucosia.' Our Leucosia is the young person whose flaking portrait figures at the door of the temple. Um! Was it a temple? Many temples of this sort are found in Chiaia. As for this Astarte, she must be the Venus *vulgivaga*, the Pandemos of the courtesans, prostitutes, as you say, I believe in Paris. Thus our scholars have decided, and they should know . . . What a pose, eh, my dear Monsieur! But also, what grace, what delicacy, what science of the beautiful! Admire."

I admired, even though preferring the studies of Titian or Rubens. Nevertheless, taking out my drawing-pad, I commenced a rapid sketch.

"Some claim," the orator continued, "that the face of Astarte is Israelite in type. It's supposed that a superb Jewess served as a model, and . . ."

"Esther . . . my Esther!" a voice suddenly interjected.

I started, and turned my head.

A sordid vagabond, a repulsive old man in rags, had just entered the villa, had plunged into a corner of the atrium, and appeared to be waiting for our departure. The uncertain gestures of the pauper announced a blind man. Like a hunting dog, however, he scented the Misses Hatchinson at a distance, uttered lubricious grunts, clicked his tongue and panted noisily: an idiot.

"*Eccolo!* Here's our madman," the Neapolitan said to me. "He comes every day to say many tender things to the fresco, with which he's besotted. Go away, Monsieur, you're distracting."

"Esther, my Diva!" sighed the ragged man. "Why do you refuse me the alms of your smile, you who said to me: 'I love you!' under the vault of the enchanted grotto, on the moving scatter of emeralds?'

"Dreadful! I'm afraid!" cried Margaret, who ran to place herself under my protection, followed by Olivia.

"Have no fear, my pretty ladies," declared our cicerone; "the poor fellow is more harmless than a sheep. He has passed through the assize court, but who among us, *per Giove*, has not sat or will sit in the iron cage?"

"That man lives in La Castellamare?" I asked, anguished.

"Yes and no. He's a former monk, once famous for his miracles . . . *Disgraziato!* More cracked today than a tureen in the Etruscan Museum. Charitable persons have placed him in an asylum near our city."

"He's allowed to wander at will?"

"An innocent, Monsieur! And so meek, so mild! Every day, at noon, he comes to render his little visit to Madame Astarte, to cajole her, to tell her a thousand silly things, to play the gallant, the *patito*. How can he direct himself with his almost-blind eyes? A mystery!"

"Or autosuggestion!" I said, fearfully. "You have all compassion for him, don't you?"

"What's the point of hindering a creature of the good God? Torquato Tasso[1]—that's what we call him, because he's a poet—doesn't beg; he sometimes accompanies a tourist, amuses him by his grimaces, and earns a few sous honorably. They make him sing songs in his fashion, declaim verses of his making, and he even dances like a ballerina on his wobbly legs. You'll see! Hey, Torquato Tasso. Hey, corybant! Perform that pyrrhic that the German professor talked about yesterday."

"No, please!" I cried. "Spare me the sight of such an ignominy."

The idiot had drawn nearer, however, and, falling to his knees, extending his arms toward the image of Aphrodite: "Esther, my Astarte! Oh, why can I not feel on my burning brow the cool, calming, ineffable sweetness of a single one of your kisses?"

"Indecent! I want to go," enjoined Miss Olivia, harshly. "This good-for-nothing is blocking the way; get rid of him!"

"At your orders, Signorina, but expelling him from here isn't easy . . . Get up, friend, get out . . . you're inconveniencing us."

"Esther, my Astaroth! Yes, I adored you more passionately than my God! Yes, I killed you, wretch, in order not to love you any longer. But no one can escape his destiny; I love you; I love you; I will always love you."

He repeated a few of the words that, mocking and wanting to stand up to the Franciscan, Diva Campofiori had pronounced in the Siren's grotto . . .

And, mute with astonishment, I recalled the mystical adventure that had happened to my school-friend: his vagabondage through the deserted streets of Pompeii, his entry into the accursed house, his hallucination; the kiss of entire, exclusive,

1 The famous poet Torquato Tasso (1544-1595) was committed to a madhouse in 1579 and remained there until 1586; his incarceration is featured in an oft-reprinted story by S. Henry Berthoud, "Le Fou," which exists in at least three different versions; the second, 1832 version, is translated as "The Madman."

indestructible possession that the Anadyomene had given him, and the menacing words of that Aphrodite, the mistress of our actions, the arbiter of our destinies, the final end of everything that lives suffers and dies down here: "You will know no other God than me."

Her words had been accomplished. The poet, the musician, Marcellus the ardent pursuer of the Ideal, even the monk of La Campanella who had once struggled against temptation, was no more; nothing remained of him but an erotomaniac. Like the Circe of Hellenic myth, Astaroth had transformed him into a beast, and that beast was still begging for amour.

Alas, who among us, in his flesh and in his heart, does not harbor an Astaroth?

The cicerone picked up a stone and threw it at the degenerate being, hitting him in the face, and the wretched human debris collapsed, howling.

A month later, I married the dainty and blushing Miss Hatchison. For two years the "honeymoon" has illuminated our household. Margaret makes her four meals a day, exhales, as Byron said, perfumes of bread and butter, meditates fashion magazines, plays bridge and, deeming herself happy, renders me very happy.

Sitting on the balcony of my elegant Renaissance town house, I saw her just now climbing into an automobile to go to a select five o'clock tea. In her pink and blonde youth she is truly a delectable little doll; but, although rather jealous, I don't experience any anxiety . . .

No, with her plumed hat, her hobble-skirt and her modest undergarments, my dear Margot bears no resemblance to a Pompeiian fresco.